-6/22

WAKERS

The Side Step Trilogy
BOOK ONE

WAKERS

ORSON SCOTT CARD

Margaret K. McElderry Books
NEW YORK   LONDON   TORONTO   SYDNEY   NEW DELHI

MARGARET K. McELDERRY BOOKS
An imprint of Simon & Schuster Children's Publishing Division
1230 Avenue of the Americas, New York, New York 10020
MARGARET K. McELDERRY BOOKS is a trademark
of Simon & Schuster, Inc.
For information about special discounts for bulk purchases, please contact
Simon & Schuster Special Sales at 1-866-506-1949 or
business@simonandschuster.com.
The Simon & Schuster Speakers Bureau can bring authors to your live
event. For more information or to book an event, contact the Simon
& Schuster Speakers Bureau at 1-866-248-3049 or visit our website at
www.simonspeakers.com.
Interior design by Jacquelynne Hudson
The text for this book was set in Janson Text.
Manufactured in the United States of America
First Edition
2 4 6 8 10 9 7 5 3 1
Library of Congress Cataloging-in-Publication Data
Names: Card, Orson Scott, author.
Title: Wakers / Orson Scott Card.
Description: First edition. | New York : Margaret K. McElderry Books,
[2022] | Series: Side step Trilogy ; 1 | Summary: Seventeen-year-old
Laz Hayerian wakes up on an abandoned Earth to discover that he and
his companion Ivy Downey are clones, and they must work together—
combining their talents to sense and step into and out of timestreams—to
save humanity from imminent extinction.
Identifiers: LCCN 2021023243 (print) | LCCN 2021023244 (ebook) |
ISBN 9781481496193 (hardcover) | ISBN 9781481496216 (ebook)
Subjects: CYAC: Space and time—Fiction. | Cloning—Fiction. | Science
fiction. | LCGFT: Novels. | Science fiction.
Classification: LCC PZ7.C1897 Wak 2022 (print) | LCC PZ7.C1897
(ebook) | DDC [Fic]—dc23
LC record available at https://lccn.loc.gov/2021023243
LC ebook record available at https://lccn.loc.gov/2021023244

TO DELPHA AND BRAD
BUILDING YOUR OWN TIMESTREAM
STEP BY STEP

1

BECAUSE HE WAS a teenager, and teenagers take pleasure in exploring wacky ideas, Laz Hayerian had wondered since the sixth grade whether we are the same person when we wake up that we were when we went to sleep. Specifically, he wondered if *he* was the same person, because sometimes his dreams persisted in memory as if they had been real events. Did dream memories change him the way real memories did?

This always led to the deeper question: Since Laz had memories that came, not from dreams, but from timestreams he had stepped out of, did his intertwined memories of other realities make him less sane? Or more experienced? Or both?

Since, as far as he knew, no one else in the world had the ability to side step from one timestream to another, there was no one he could ask, and no philosopher who had written about it.

As he woke up this morning—morning?—he felt very strange, and it wasn't the residual effect of some dream. He didn't even remember dreaming. It was his own past that felt like a disjointed dream, as if sometime in the night his whole life played out in his mind, but completely out of order, an incoherent scattering of scenes, facts, feelings, people, places.

When he opened his eyes, he was in nearly complete darkness.

Even on mornings at Dad's place, there was always plenty of light that seeped around the curtains.

All he could see was a tiny amount of green light coming from a few inches to his left.

He was lying on a plastic mattress that felt no more cushioned than the pad in the bottom of a portable crib. Yet he didn't feel any aches or sore spots, and when he flexed muscles up and down his body, nothing caused him pain.

So Laz did what he had always done since his earliest memories of childhood. He searched for the alternate paths through time that were always close enough for him to take hold and shift, changing the story of events in bold or barely perceptible ways. It didn't matter which, as long as it got him into a place where things made more sense.

For the first time in his life he could not find any of the alternate timestreams.

No, no, he was finding them, yes, thousands of them—as always. Only none of them went back even a moment earlier than the moment he woke up just now. And none of them showed him doing anything different, so there was no point in side stepping from one to another.

He was afraid. He had never reached out and found that all his pasts and all his futures were identical. It meant he had no choices. Whatever was going on right now, he was like other people—he was trapped.

He didn't like feeling trapped.

Why was he feeling trapped? He extended his hands away from his sides and they bumped into solid walls. He was in an actual container.

The green light came from some LED letters and numbers on

a panel at his left side, inside the box, but he didn't know what any of them meant. Someone else would explain them to him. If he was in some kind of—what? A medical treatment chamber? An anti-infection box while some damaged part of himself healed without gangrene? If somebody had operated on him, he had no idea where.

Laz reached up, straight out in front of his chest, and his hands almost instantly bumped into some kind of ceiling or lid or cap. It felt like plastic; it had a little bit of give to it. So he *was* in a sealed environment, though he didn't feel claustrophobic or even particularly warm. He was definitely a claustrophobe. The time his mother rented an RV and invited him to sleep on one of the bunk beds, he couldn't sleep that night at all. He didn't complain, though. His mother loved the RV. And Laz didn't want to ruin it for her.

He was only about eleven, maybe ten—before she remarried, so he knew that this RV experiment was meant to provide his mother with some kind of bonding opportunity. But when he asked her if he could please stay home instead of gallivanting along all summer, she seemed stricken. She also wanted to feel like a good mother. Now she felt like she had failed.

So Laz figured he had no choice but to side step into a timestream in which his mother had decided not to rent the RV after all. While Laz always remembered the alternate timestreams that he had lived through, even for a single hour, he knew that he had to make sure she never got back on this RV kick again. Now his mother had no idea she had ever rented an RV, and there was no timestream in which Laz told her how claustrophobic he was in an RV bunk bed. As long as she didn't get another RV, there was no need ever to have that conversation.

Here he was now, reaching out for timestreams that did not

provide him with any alternatives at all. Just waking up, feeling the thin plastic mattress, seeing his arm only vaguely in the green light, feeling the plastic lid arching over his bed—box? Container? Coffin?

Got to get things moving. He pushed on the lid. It gave a little, but now he pushed harder, then shifted his hands down near the edges of the lid. This time there was no give at all on the left side, but a lot more give on the right. He pushed harder with his right hand. The lid seemed to separate from the edge of the coffin/box/chamber and rise a few centimeters, then drift down when he stopped pushing.

Now he twisted his body and got both hands to the right-hand edge and pushed upward. An awkward pose, but it worked. The lid rose fairly easily and smoothly, and once it passed about twenty centimeters above the rim, the lid raised itself the rest of the way, and then seemed to slide down into the wall of the coffin.

He sat up. He couldn't see anything. The green light from the message panel did not illuminate anything outside his box.

Then, when he looked to the left, he saw a lot of blurry, twinkling green lights extending in a direct line away from his own instrument panel. And others, in other rows, above the head of his box and below the foot.

He looked back the other way and saw no lights, but he understood why. His own coffin only had a light on the left side. Therefore if there were boxes extending away on his right, all their green lights would be hidden behind the left wall of each chamber. He could be in the exact center, but only boxes to his left would reveal themselves to him.

Why hadn't somebody turned on the lights? Why didn't some kind of generalized lighting come on when his coffin lid opened?

At least some mechanical voice could have said, You are fully healed now, Lazarus Hayerian; your parents will arrive to pick you up and take you home within the hour.

Who designed this unfriendly system? Who decided to let somebody wake up with no greeting, no guide, no explanation?

Why couldn't he remember getting *in* this box? Or going in for some kind of treatment? Since he had always been able to avoid illness or accident by side stepping into a timestream where he hadn't caught the disease or hadn't made the choices that got him in the way of the accident, for him to be sick enough to need incarceration in a box like this one would have been memorable. He felt his abdomen, arms, shoulders; no sign of a healed injury or any kind of scar.

He remembered that he *did* have a kind of marker on his body. It was a weird toenail growth on his left little toe that had been there since he was four and would never go away. "Nonthreatening," said every doctor who looked at it, "so clip it if it gets big, there aren't any nerves in it, and wear socks." Laz reached with his right foot, rubbed it over the warty toe.

That growth was missing. Just a normal nail on the little toe.

What was really going on? Why would any hospital remove that warty growth on his toe? Accident or no accident, why would they include *that* in their treatment? Or did the healing box handle it automatically, because genetically it wasn't supposed to be there?

Laz started pressing every spot on the display panel but nothing gave him any feedback. There were no unlighted buttons or switches or levers, either. Whatever controls this healing cave had, they were on the outside of the box—which made sense, since a patient might accidently hit one of them in his sleep, and no medical professional would allow a patient to have a significant vote on his own treatment.

Maybe he had an illness or accident that attacked his brain and made him unconscious for a while. Then he wouldn't have memories of it.

His dreams had been an array of memories, playing out in almost random order. And it occurred to him that this box might not have been a healing chamber at all. Maybe his dreams came from recorded memories being played into his brain, his empty brain, because he wasn't actually the real Lazarus Hayerian. Maybe he was a copy.

He didn't know whether to be excited or dismayed. How far had cloning technologies advanced? Cloning nonverbal animals didn't allow for questionnaires about how well the clone remembered being the original animal, though they *had* experimented with memory recording and playback in sheep, pigs, dogs, and baboons—he had read about that stuff.

Did those experimental clones feel what he was feeling now, with memories forced on him, pushed to the front of his mind, but in no rational order?

While he was thinking, Laz did an ab crunch, and felt that his muscles were taut and strong. It was a feeling of strength beyond anything he'd ever felt before. He was a leisurely hiker, but summers of hiking everywhere left him with a decent core and great thighs and glutes and calves. But now his belly was as tight as a swimmer's. As a gymnast's. And sitting up from mid-crunch wasn't just easy, it was almost automatic. He was built to make this move; it required no particular exertion.

Still, it wasn't easy to get out of the box. The sides weren't more than fifteen centimeters high, but that was still an awkward lip to get his feet outside and over, and then raise himself up and slide his bare thighs and butt across the edge.

He was glad that however long he had spent in the box, his muscles hadn't atrophied. Once he was standing up on the cool hard floor, rubbing his buttocks and thighs to help get over the scraping they had just had, he realized that in some ways he was in better shape than ever. His arms and chest were well muscled and he had very little body fat—for the first time in his life, he actually had washboard abs.

But, feeling his thighs and calves, he realized that these could not be his own legs. *His* calves were ropy and wiry, his thighs well developed, his glutes tight from having spent all his teenage years taking long, long walks, many times over the mountains from the Valley down into Hollywood or Beverly Glen or to the houses of some of his friends in Brentwood or Highland Park, or even, once or twice, to Malibu or Topanga Canyon.

Southern California was full of long distances that required grown-ups to drive everywhere—but a kid like Laz, with no responsibilities and no fears, had all the time in the world to walk. Nobody ever accosted him or caused him grief, because any situation that had the potential to be dangerous or even just annoying caused Laz to side step into a timestream where the obstacle wasn't present.

He looked into his parallel timestreams and saw that in some of them, he had already discovered the packet of lightweight clothing on a shelf built into the head of his coffin. It fit loosely. It felt like paper. But it wasn't uncomfortable.

He could imagine his nonexistent guide explaining, We can't be sure if any of our clients are allergic to various fabrics, so we made our wakeup clothing out of hypoallergenic paper. If this causes you any discomfort, or if the fit is not just right, merely tell me and I'll bring you a replacement. We have cotton, rayon, silk, and hemp, though all of those are heavier and warmer than the paper.

There was no guide. But there *was* a paper costume, and it covered his body adequately. Unlike the normal hospital gown, which left your butt open to the air so you could get injected or bedpanned without formalities, these were genuinely modest.

Or at least no *less* modest than the pajamas his grandparents sent him every Christmas. Those always had two-snap flies, so that either you flashed other people every time you sat down, making the fly gape open above and below the middle snap, or you wore underwear, so that there was no particular reason for you to have the pajamas at all, since underwear was fine for sleeping in.

Dressed now, right down to the lightweight slippers on his feet, he rested his left hand on the lip of his own coffin and reached out with his right hand. The next coffin was close enough he didn't have to reach very far.

He leaned over that new coffin and found that it, too, had a green light, though the only numbers it showed were zeroes. He could see the other person's arm.

Only it wasn't an arm. It was a radius and ulna, with a humerus above the elbow. There was still some tissue there, stretched like parchment between the bones. Whoever was in that box, they weren't alive.

Laz suppressed ridiculous thoughts like the zombie apocalypse, which he thought would be even less likely to happen than the Christian rapture. He was still in the real world, where dead was dead.

Could the people here be prisoners? Was this a prison that kept its inmates in boxes where they could be sedated automatically? A prison where three consecutive fifty-year sentences could be served, even if you died thirty years into it. No wonder he woke up feeling groggy.

"Excuse me," he said aloud.

No, that's what he meant to say. What he said was more like a strangled whispery cough. He cleared his throat. Some phlegm came up and he didn't know what to do with it. Spit it onto the grimy floor? That felt too piggish—he was indoors, after all—and he certainly wasn't going to spit it into his bed. So he swallowed it. Which was difficult because his mouth and throat were really dry.

He hadn't been aware of thirst, but he certainly needed to get some water into his mouth and throat.

"Excuse me," he tried again. This time if someone had been there, they might have understood his words. "Drinking fountain, anyone?" he asked. "Bottled water? Don't care about the brand. Room temperature is fine."

No sound came back to him; there wasn't even an echo.

Either he was alone in a room full of healing boxes, or the observers could see him through heat-sensing lenses or infrared scopes and were watching to see what he would do.

Well, what *would* he do? Sleeping in that box hadn't hurt him at all—every joint was working smoothly, every muscle clearly had more power than he had ever felt. He thought he could run a marathon. He thought he could do a hundred chin-ups in a row. If the floor weren't filthy, he'd drop and do push-ups until he got tired of it, and the way he felt right now, that would be never. So whatever his silent observers had done, they hadn't tortured him, they hadn't weakened him.

Nobody was watching. He was alone in the room.

Unless Laz could find another timestream in which the other boxed-up human was *not* dead.

He couldn't. The timestreams were slightly different now. He dressed more quickly in some than in others. He had already found that his right-hand neighbor was dead in some, and he had not yet checked in others. But there was no reason to make a change, because none of the timestreams had any lights on, or any explanatory signs, and certainly no helpful attendants to make his waking up ceremonies more pleasant or understandable.

I'm a clone, Laz decided. Nothing else made sense.

Of course, being a clone didn't make sense, either. The process was still experimental and ridiculously expensive. Only the most important people in the world were having their DNA stored and new bodies grown. Not teenagers in SoCal whose sole contribution to humanity was walking every road, sidewalk, bike path, and trail from Oxnard to Koreatown. Who would be crazy enough to clone *him*?

His parents had a little money, but not like *that*. Plus, shouldn't he remember at least some kind of discussion about being cloned?

I can't figure out anything standing here. The fact that the lights in the coffins were on—even the ones that were zeroed out—suggested that this building had electric power, so that in the rooms where employees worked there were bound to be lights and explanations. Why not look for the light switch in here?

If he just started walking in any direction and kept going, he would eventually come to a wall, because this was an enclosed space and *something* was holding up the ceiling and keeping wind and weather out. Come to a wall and follow along until you come to a door. Open it if you can, walk through. Or at least search along the walls near the doors to find a light switch. That's where people put light switches, so they could turn them on as they entered the room.

The pulse display inside the healing cave showed his heart rate as forty-one. But now that he was outside the box and moving around, it must be reporting his last inside-the-box reading.

He put one hand on the long side of his healing cave, and the other hand on the side of the adjacent box. Then he started walking in the direction where his feet had been pointed inside the box. That was "down" and it was a direction, so why not?

Laz tried to count the boxes and he believed he was at fifteen when he thought, No, thirteen, and then he didn't know anymore. He stuck with fifteen.

At eighteen—or sixteen?—the boxes ended. At this point there was no light at all. The wall might be one meter or a hundred meters away. There might be a steep drop-off, though why there *would* be he couldn't guess.

If he got disoriented maybe he'd walk in circles in the dark and never find his way back. But if that happened, he could side step to a reality where he went in a different direction from his healing cave. It was sometimes wrenching to make such a shift, but apart from the concentration it required, it cost him nothing, so he never had to live long with the consequences of bad choices.

He had spent half of fifth grade thinking of ways that he could die without being able to side step in time. Like if somebody sprang from ambush and bashed him in the head with a meat tenderizer, immediately rendering him unconscious. They could stay there beating him until his brain was tartare on the sidewalk, and he would never be awake enough to side step.

Nobody wanted to kill him.

But if somebody did, there would be ways.

Back to his dilemma in the dark in the tomb room. What if *no* direction led anywhere useful? Would he then return to his healing cave? Take the clothes back off, fold them neatly, and get inside again? He couldn't pull down the lid because it had slid into some neverland without a trace. Should he choose a reality in which he never caused the lid to open? Then what, wait some long or even infinite time for somebody to notice he was awake?

Why *should* he go back? He was blind now, but he was blind back there, too, and he wouldn't learn anything by sitting around. If there were wardens or alien zookeepers watching him (he was flashing now on every movie and TV show he had ever seen) they should at least see him *try* to add more information to his meager supply.

He used gentle pressure from his fingers to push off simultaneously from both boxes under his hands, and tried to keep a steady direction as he moved out into nothingness. At first he felt gingerly with his toes before taking a step, but that was slow going, and if there was a precipice, he'd find out no matter how careful he was. Maybe there'd be a handrail. Dad worked in risk management for a school district—*he* would have made the schools put in handrails or guardrails on any floor that led to a drop-off or downward stairs.

How many steps? He hadn't counted. Eighteen boxes, but no idea how many steps he had taken after leaving them behind.

His foot kicked something. A wall. The slipper offered scant protection, so Laz was relieved that he had been walking so gingerly. He wouldn't have wanted to jam a toe.

It was a full-height wall, as high as he could reach. Should he go left or right? Left won, so it was his right hand trailing along the wall, feeling for any kind of gap or doorjamb.

It was a doorframe. The door was closed. He couldn't find a handle at any reasonable height.

There was no light switch or any kind of protuberance or indentation on the wall he had walked along. But on the far side of the door, there was a raised rectangle with two depressions in it, one over the other. A light switch?

He pressed the upper one.

The door opened.

There was a bright light in the corridor on the other side.

The corridor ran parallel to the wall Laz had just walked along. There were no written signs visible from where Laz was. He did not dare walk out into the corridor because the door might close behind him.

But now that some light was spilling into the big room, he could see that it was filled with row after row of healing caves—if that's what they were.

Would the door stay open?

Laz pressed the lower button. The door closed and everything was dark again.

He pressed the upper button. The door opened back up. Light.

Leaving the door open behind him, Laz walked to the nearest healing box. Now he could see that the lid was fully transparent. That had not been obvious before, because the whole room had been dark. Now, though, there was enough ambient light for him to see that this box was indeed occupied.

By a mummy. A desiccated human shape. This time he could see the whole corpse at once.

Laz cried out and stepped back toward the corridor.

Is that what I would have become, if I had never pushed on the lid and caused it to open?

He forced himself to go back and look into the box with the corpse inside.

The display panel was there, but everything said zero. Clearly this person had not had a heart rate worth recording for a long time.

Laz went to the next box, the next, the next. If these had once been healing caves, they had failed at their function. These occupants were beyond healing.

Most of them seemed to be small. Many were child-sized. Same size box as Laz's though, as if they were supposed to grow into them, like oversized hand-me-downs from older siblings—a concept which Laz, as an only child, had never experienced for himself.

Now as he looked out over the dim array of boxes, he knew that this was no hospital. It was more like a graveyard. All these boxes must contain dead bodies.

Why had his cave still functioned? Did these boxes all go dark because the clone inside was dead? Or did the occupants die because the boxes went dark?

Why am I alive? And why hasn't anyone come to meet me? To yell at me for getting out of my box without permission? It would be nice to get into a brisk argument with some idiotic adult who was castigating him for not obeying rules that Laz had never heard of.

Laz enjoyed arguments in which the opponent was locked into positions whose absurdity made it impossible for them to speak sensibly. Other kids would give up and walk away—or get mad and jab at him. But adults always had a completely unjustified certainty that if they just talked long enough at a younger person, they would prevail.

In this case, Laz would have liked the argument for a completely different reason: It would mean that there was another person present. It would mean he was not alone.

Laz walked back to the open door and stepped halfway through, one foot inside, one outside of the room. He saw controls for the door on the outside, too.

He would have to try the outside buttons. If they did not work and the door closed behind him, then he could decide whether to side step into a reality in which he had *not* chosen to step outside, or just live with the decision and continue exploring the building.

He pressed one set of buttons and the door closed and reopened. He pressed the other, and bright ceiling lamps flooded the interior of the huge room with light.

It turned out the corridor lights had not been bright at all—in fact, they were as dim as the EXIT lights in a theater. Laz realized that even the lights now illuminating the room were probably not all that bright—his eyes just weren't accustomed to having light at all.

His impressions of the big room had been correct. By chance he had gone the shortest way from his healing cave to the nearest wall; there had to be upwards of fifty rows in every direction. He could see that there were doors about every thirty meters along the walls, leading somewhere. It wasn't Laz's job to find out where, unless it turned out that *this* corridor led nowhere.

Laz turned off the light. He closed the door. Maybe there was another functioning healing cave inside another room, and maybe he would locate it and find a living human being.

Later. First he needed to find out where everybody was. Who was in control of this operation.

No. *First* he had to find a drink of water.

In the course of wandering around the corridors, he found two drinking fountains, but the chilling unit wasn't working in either one, and when he pressed the button, water didn't flow. It didn't even dribble out. The water seemed to have been cut off.

But I didn't dry out in my box, thought Laz. Moisture got to me somehow. My box kept me alive. *Something* in this place is still working.

The corridors formed a maze—or maybe it was a perfectly consistent pattern that he just didn't understand. There were doors in other walls, but they didn't respond to a button press.

Then it dawned on him that there was something else that *none* of the walls had.

Windows.

Maybe he was underground.

He went to the end of a wide corridor. It butted up against a wall.

To the left and right, though, there were buttons. No doors, no numbers, no labels, just buttons. He pressed one.

The whole floor, from the end wall to about six meters out, rose smoothly. A low wall appeared on the outside edge, enough to keep a rolling cart from falling off. The ceiling parted above him. He went past another floor, with dimly lighted corridors. This time when the ceiling above the elevator platform opened, there was a much brighter light. It was daylight, Laz knew, simply from the quality of the light. Nothing artificial. Sun through glass, that's what he was seeing.

The floor with his healing cave was two floors below daylight.

The elevator stopped—apparently this was as high as it went. The low barrier wall was gone. Laz stepped out into the sunlit corridor, which quickly led to a large open glass-walled reception area.

There was nobody at the reception desk. Nobody at the doors. Nobody on the furniture.

And not much furniture, either. It was as if all the good pieces had been removed, and only the ones with tatty upholstery were left. Like at an underfunded school.

There had once been electronic equipment at the reception station, but all that remained were sockets of various kinds.

This place screamed, Out of business.

Yet one of those healing caves two floors down had contained a living person. Did you all just forget me?

There were big letters on the glass wall. They were backward—they were sending their message out onto the street. But Laz easily read them, though he had to walk through the large open space for a while before he was sure he had seen all the letters.

From the outside, passersby would have read the word "Vivipartum." It sounded like a company name. Laz thought through his Latin roots and figured that it might mean something like "born alive." He had once had "parturition"—birth—as a vocabulary word, and "vivid" clearly was related to life.

And that was his confirmation of what this place was. Not a hospital at all. Not even a retirement home for dying people hoping to be kept alive till there was a cure.

He remembered the articles and essays and op-eds and diatribes and slogans from three or four years ago, when the technology for cloning and fast-growing human bodies had been developed. At that time, cloning was justified solely as a means of supplying organs and limbs for the genetic owner, in case things went badly and a transplant was needed. No more hoping for a liver donor or heart donor, no more matching blood types and using immunosuppressants. All transplant needs were met using organs and limbs that were genetically identical to the transplant recipient.

The clones will never be brought to consciousness, the proponents assured everyone. They will never have legal existence as people. They are not citizens. They are organ and limb banks, with individual proprietors whose DNA had been used to create them.

Meanwhile, religions were in a frenzy over the question of whether clones had souls, whether they were tainted by original sin, whether they were eligible for redemption. They were never alive and could not be resurrected; they were definitely alive and to kill one in order to harvest a vital organ was murder. So many people were sure that their view was the only one a decent person could have.

This was all mildly interesting to Laz as a kid. He remembered that the courts had allowed cloning and harvesting to continue, under the legal theory that clones never achieved consciousness or acted upon their own volition in any way, and were therefore nonpersons in the eyes of the law. Property.

The controversy didn't die down completely, so the big cloning corporations spun off the cloning operations into a lot of smaller companies with different names. They all pretended to be in another line of work, and most of them actually conducted other businesses.

In this Vivipartum building, all the rows of boxed clones were underground.

Maybe when the owners of the clones stopped making their payments, the life support was cut off and the clones all died. That made sense to Laz. These weren't people, so nobody cared if they died.

But somebody had kept up payments on Laz's body, so he lived.

And something else. The clones were never supposed to achieve sentience or volitional behavior. Yet here was Laz walking around, full of memories of a childhood that *this* body had never lived through. If he was in fact a clone.

He was a clone with a memory.

Had the technology moved forward, without anybody reporting on it? Could they take the memories out of the original owner's brain and then play them into the brain of the clone? Laz had never heard of such a technology, but then, after the huge brouhaha about cloning in the first place, the companies would keep such a development completely under wraps, because it would reopen the whole person/nonperson debate again, and who knew where the courts would land?

Laz had not been cloned to provide body parts for some older version of Laz. Laz had been given the *memories* of his life up to age seventeen. Laz was being prepared to be a *replacement*.

Ridiculous. Why replace somebody who wasn't dead? If his older original self had died, they could only revive him if they had recorded his memories while he was alive. Laz had no memory of that. If somebody judged a teenager like him to be important enough to record, Laz would not have forgotten it.

If his original self was alive, why would they be prepping Laz to replace him?

Maybe they now put memories into *all* the clones. Maybe so that they could do a brain transplant, if that was necessary. And it was just random chance that Laz's clone had survived when so many others downstairs had died.

Maybe I'm not a clone at all. Maybe I've read this whole situation wrong.

In the whole time he had been standing in the glass-walled reception area, not a single vehicle had passed by on the street outside.

Laz walked to the window, then to another spot in the glass wall, and he saw that the parking lot wasn't empty. There were a few cars in it, but they were parked any which way. Like nobody cared. And there were a couple of cars with people in them, but they weren't moving. Neither the cars nor the people.

There were crash bars on the doors—strictly according to fire code—but Laz was afraid again that once he went through the doors and let them close behind him, he wouldn't be able to get back in. Besides, he didn't know if the weather outside was sunny and hot or sunny and cold. He sure wasn't dressed for cold.

He pushed open the outside door. A blast of air came in. Cold. But not bitterly cold. Colder than Los Angeles. More like San Francisco standing near the water.

Holding one door open, he pulled on the handle of the other. Locked.

He looked for a way to unlock it. If nobody had noticed him so far, he wasn't going to count on being able to knock on the door and have somebody let him back in. He stepped back into the doorway and looked for a way to unlock the door mechanically. No such.

So he pulled one of the tatty sofas over to the door and awkwardly pushed it out between the two doors, to hold them both open. Surely this would bring some kind of security guy into the reception area.

It didn't.

Laz went outside and walked toward a car with a guy in it.

A dead guy. A guy who had been dead for a long time. A guy with a smashed-in head. Or a blasted head. There was no gun in the car, though, if he had killed himself.

The other car had a couple in it. Also dead. A long time dead. And a bottle that must have held pills. Suicide?

The other cars were all empty.

How long ago had they died? Why hadn't anybody cleaned up the mess? Why had three people chosen the same parking lot to kill themselves, one by gunshot and two by overdose? And who had removed the gunshot guy's pistol? Why had they left the empty pill bottle? Somebody had done *some* cleanup, yet they had left these corpses.

For me to find? thought Laz.

It's not about *you*, Laz could hear his mother saying. Don't be such a drama queen, Laz. The world doesn't revolve around you.

But what if nobody else was ever going to come out of that building to this parking lot? thought Laz.

The pill guy was wearing a jacket.

Could Laz wear a jacket whose owner had rotted away inside it?

A gust of wind told him, Yes, he could, because it was *cold* out here. He would try to replace it with something not so disgusting as soon as he could.

The car door opened when he pulled on the handle. Not locked. Laz tugged on the jacket. The body kind of fell apart inside it. Much of the body came out of the car with the jacket, but then fell out of it onto the asphalt. Laz felt a moment of nausea, a moment of horror, but he knew that the people in this car did not pose any danger to him, so he paused a moment to let his rational mind take control again.

Laz unzipped the jacket, shook it, beat it against the car to get all the body parts out of it. Then he pulled it on. It didn't smell. Well, it did, but not as bad as the inside of the car had smelled, and he could stand it. It blocked the wind. It was long enough to protect Laz's butt and privates as well as his stomach and chest and arms. It would keep him from dying of exposure wearing paper clothing out here.

Was that why they left these bodies? For him? So he'd realize there had been some kind of cataclysm, that civilization had ended and bodies were left where they died—and so that he could also salvage important articles of clothing from the corpses?

They could have left him a note and a nice warm set of clothes.

He reached back into the car and felt in the guy's pockets, trying not to stare down into the pelvic cavity surrounded by the waistline of the pants.

Nothing. No wallet, no car keys. No keys in the ignition, though he realized that this car would certainly have had a proximity key.

He went around to the other side because he saw the woman had a purse. He opened it. What would he do with a makeup compact? It had a mirror in the lid. He closed it, put it in his jacket pocket. There was also a small pocket knife. That might come in handy. But that was all. Surely women carried more than this in their purses.

Missing car keys. Missing wallet, missing money, missing almost everything. Somebody had taken from these bodies everything they didn't want Laz to have. He was allowed to have a small knife and a mirror. He could have a jacket. Nice of them.

He shuddered in the chilly breeze and gathered his thoughts. These things were not directed at *him*, at Lazarus Davit Hayerian, seventeen-year-old high school senior and smart mouth extraordinaire. Beware narcissism, you stupid heap.

No, this was *not* according to somebody's plan, or at least not a plan for *him*. Laz just happened to wake up right now and happened to be the person who found these bodies and these things.

But *somebody* took everything from the guy's pockets and most things from the purse. Somebody had taken the pistol from the guy who shot himself.

And in these cars, in the building, there hadn't been a scrap of paper with any writing on it. Not a book, not a pamphlet, not a newspaper, not a magazine on the tables in the reception area, not a wad of trash or packaging tumbleweeding down the street in the breeze.

There was nothing to show him the date. Nothing to show even the *year*. The weather told him it was during a cold season, but Laz didn't know enough about the sky to judge from the position of the sun whether it was the dead of winter or near one of the equinoxes. Nor could he guess where he was. The name Vivipartum didn't give him any clue to the latitude and longitude, and therefore whether this was as cold as it ever got around here, or if this was an unusually warm spell.

And still not a car had passed by on the street.

Why had everybody gone away and left him here to wake up alone?

He felt the impulse to get away, to simply *leave* and return to a better place. With people in it. With *his* people in it.

But before he could try to act on that impulse, and side step into a different set of conditions, he realized: He had learned before he was twelve years old that he could swap realities only by stepping into a version of himself that already existed in the different reality. That was a rule he had never been able to break. So whenever he side stepped, he got the whole set of memories of the version of Laz that already existed in that reality, plus his memories of the reality he had left behind.

If he was really a clone, though, then there *was* no version of *him* in any other reality. He and his original were not the same person, regardless of DNA or physical appearance or shared memories. He couldn't side step to get out of this situation, because this was the only reality in which *he*, Clone-Laz, had ever existed.

Then again, what if he was wrong?

He tried to side step, but couldn't find within his mind any other reality to move to, apart from realities since his waking, in which he was still inside the building, still in the dark, exploring a different wall, lying in the healing cave, walking along different corridors without realizing that there had to be elevators, or shivering in the wind *without* wearing the dead man's coat. Petty local differences. Nothing to move him out of this abandoned place. Nothing to put him in living human company.

He was stuck here.

No internet, no blogging. Since I may be the last human being on Earth, there's nobody to read the blog anyway. Of course, there might be five billion people in Asia, for all I know. But since I haven't found a working computer since I woke up, I can't post anything for them to read.

I'm going crazy not having anybody to talk to. I'm beginning to realize that I actually <u>did</u> need friends back in school. I just didn't notice the fact because I <u>had</u> friends.

So I'm inventing a new thing: the plog. Paper blog. I know, "blog" is itself a conflation of "biographical" and "log," but it's a word on its own now. Or it was back when I was alive. (Not sure yet if what I've got here is actually living.)

I got the idea of doing this when I broke into a *Staples* and found that the reams of paper that were wrapped in plastic had survived. So then I started trying pens. They were all dried out, even with their caps on. Paper-eating fungi, bacteria, and the moisture from this damp climate that seeps its way in wherever it can doomed the cardboard. The half-cardboard part of the packaging on the pens crumbled under my fingers. I remember you used to need heavy shears, a sturdy sharp knife, or lightning from heaven to get those packages open in the old days. Now they tear open like toilet paper. Like <u>damp</u> toilet paper.

So I tried mechanical pencils, because you don't have to sharpen them. But all the mechanisms are either frozen or completely ineffective. If the lead can't be advanced and then stay in place, you don't have a pencil, you have a stylus. And even when it did advance, it kept breaking. Really, crumbling. Becoming a smudge of graphite dust on the paper.

You know what I'm writing this with? A regular old-fashioned wooden pencil with an eraser on the end. The eraser is brittle and crumbles pretty easily, but for a while at least it worked, and it doesn't matter anyway because I'm not going to erase anything, I'm just putting down whatever comes into my head like I'm talking to you instead of writing to you, because I don't know if you, my future reader, will ever exist.

Here's the thing. Wooden pencils don't have any mechanical parts that will rust. Of course fungi and bacteria have been dining out on this pencil, but it still works anyway. And instead of a clunky mechanical sharpener, which I wouldn't want to lug around anyway, you know what works great? Those cheapo little plastic sharpeners with a razor blade in them to shave the pencil point at the correct angle. I carry a couple of those in my backpack now, along with a dozen pencils, and I have to remind myself that this ancient technology only came into existence in, like, the seventeen hundreds. Or the seventeenth century. Who cares when, but the Romans didn't have them, and the Babylonians and Egyptians and ancient Chinese didn't have them, and paper itself is only about a thousand years old or so, and that's all I remember from a couple of reports in school. Not mine, some other kids' reports, so this is proof I _was_ awake and I _did_ listen.

2

DURING WHAT REMAINED of this first afternoon awake, Laz had no leisure time for generalized exploration. His agenda had only a few items: warm clothes, water, food. There was no map, and no transportation other than his slippered feet. He toyed with the idea of going back to the Vivipartum parking lot and taking Poisoned Man's shoes—or maybe it was Gun Man's shoes that would fit him better. But no, slippers would do for now, and Laz had no time for doubling back.

In a town you don't know, without maps, with only traffic signs, how do you find a useful store? Since no cars were moving on the roads, Laz could not imagine that any stores were operational, or even if any of them would still have clothing that he could buy or borrow or beg or steal. But even if they were empty, they would have walls and probably roofs, and he would be warmer inside than out.

Once he got away from the direct neighborhood of Vivipartum, he found that so many ridiculously tall trees grew in this place that there was no meaningful view in any direction. If this town had any tall buildings, they would be hidden behind the trees. Even though there wasn't a leaf on most of them, they had so many twigs and branches that he couldn't see through them.

The wind was picking up, and as the day waned, the air was not getting warmer.

Nothing about any of the roads promised a built-up commercial area in any particular direction, but if the sun was trending to the west, then he would go south, because if it led nowhere he could side step to a reality in which he had chosen to go north or, at the first cross street, east or west.

He couldn't tell anything from the number of cars parked along the streets because there weren't any. No more dead people, either—not in cars and not on front lawns or porches. Had they left those corpses at Vivipartum so Laz could get a warm coat? Had there been a cataclysm or not?

He would get no answers on this walk. All that mattered was getting clothes. Especially shoes. The slippers were wearing out fast. He'd feel more optimistic if he had any idea where there might be a shopping center with a shoe store. Or a Walmart.

A nice wide street looked promising, but at first it led past nothing but a park and some school buildings, which had neither students nor parked cars. But he kept walking because ahead there was some kind of major intersection, with what looked to be an overpass. And then there was a sign that said FRIENDLY CENTER and an arrow. He walked to the left, up a short hill.

He ignored the hotel and restaurant on the left, though he thought he should remember the hotel because a smaller room would be easier to warm up with his body heat. At the brow of the hill he could see an outdoor shopping center where cars once parked right among the shops. And a couple of big stores announced themselves to be Macy's and Belk. Department stores usually had a men's department, and so if there was any merchandise at all, they might have clothing that would suit him.

He went all the way around both department stores in search

of an unlocked door. No such luck. But a nearby gas station had an open service bay with a few nice heavy steel implements. He chose a tire iron and a heavy object whose purpose he couldn't even guess at. Carrying them both was too awkward, he discovered after a couple of shopping-center blocks, so he set down the heavy object and carried the tire iron to a door of one of the stores—at ground level, he couldn't see any signs, but he didn't have any brand loyalty so it didn't matter which.

The tire iron couldn't get into a gap between the doors, so he finally stepped back and threw it at the glass doors. Nothing. Then at a big window. It didn't break, but it did make a lovely pattern of cracks and crazes. So Laz went back, got the heavier unidentified thing, and pitched it into the same window. The whole thing shattered and tumbled to the ground in a pile of glass kibbles rather than jagged shards. Safety glass. A very thoughtful design feature, planning for the safety and comfort of a future solitary burglar.

There were no lights in the store, and little outside light got through the doors and windows. But he could see that the store seemed to be well stocked, and with clothes appropriate for chilly weather. Once his eyes got used to the interior dimness, he found the men's department—in the darkest corner of the bottom floor, of course—and after rejecting the idea of a nice business suit, he found sweatpants, a sweatshirt, a T-shirt, an array of underwear, and a heavy jacket that hadn't been died and rotted in. He happily stripped off the dead man's coat and all the pathetic lightweight pajama stuff from Vivipartum, and wished, momentarily, for a shower. But Neanderthals didn't have showers either, he reminded himself, or soap, or deodorant. And Laz at least had warm clothes with a drawstring waist on the pants.

Shoes were easy. He rejected fancy athletic shoes in favor of simple walking shoes, light but rugged looking. And sweat socks that went way up his calves. Warm.

He thought of taking changes of clothing in the pockets of the jacket and then decided instead to find a backpack. It wasn't at the department store that he found one, but in a store with lots of camping gear. He chose a backpack that didn't require a frame, just something he could strap onto his shoulders to carry a change of clothes. Along with anything else he found, like food and water.

Water. They had a nice selection of canteens, plus packages of water purification tablets. Would they still work? Laz figured that he'd find out, knowing he could always step into a timestream in which he hadn't tried drinking water that he had "purified" with ineffective tablets.

He was clothed. He was shod. He had a water container. He had a small knife and a small mirror.

What he didn't have was a map or a clue. Where now?

How long had this town been empty? Was there any chance that grocery stores would have edible food?

Canned food. The soup aisle. The fruit juice aisle. He thought of Dole pineapple juice, which his mother used in the dressing for the fruit salad she made every Thanksgiving. She always let him drink the leftover juice. If it hadn't gone off, he could sure use some.

At the far end of the same shopping center, up on a hill, there was a huge grocery store named Harris Teeter, and this time he didn't have to try to break or pry his way in: One set of double doors stood open.

It meant that the produce section had been ransacked by animals long ago—years ago—and the frozen food section, full of faded packages depicting food, would be worthless. The butcher shop section had long since been gutted and this time the animals had eaten up every scrap.

But the aisles of canned and bottled goods looked promising.

Twist-off caps, that's what Laz needed right now. But first his gaze was drawn by a group of pineapple juice cans on the bottom shelf. Every one of them had been corroded near the bottom, and a stain of ancient spilled juice spread over the shelf and down on the floor. Laz's first thought was: What animal can gnaw through a metal can? But then he realized that the juice had eaten through the metal from the inside.

If pineapple juice was so acidic that it could eventually dissolve the metal can, didn't that mean that from the moment it was canned the process of destruction began? Didn't that mean that even the most freshly canned pineapple juice contained tiny bits of the dissolved metal? And I drank it, thought Laz. And it was delicious.

But it would not be delicious now. The juice remnant was just a stain—it wasn't even sticky, and certainly had no depth. Insects or larger creatures must have eaten it back when it was freshly spilled; there were the desiccated corpses of ants, or at least the *shadows* of the ants, embedded in the stains.

Laz reached for a bottle of V8 with a twist-off cap.

He hadn't had V8 since elementary school, and hadn't loved it then, but that might explain why it was still in its plastic bottles on the shelf. The stuff that was labeled as regular V8 was a dark brown, which was not encouraging. His purification tablets were for water, not decrepit vegetable juice. Some other kinds of V8, fusion this or fruit that, had twist-off plastic lids. They looked like they might still be something like the color they were meant to be, and so he opened one.

It passed the sniff test, meaning it didn't smell fermented or rotten or dead, and he sipped it. It didn't taste like any commercial beverage with a chance of success in the marketplace, but it also didn't make him gag or retch. He swallowed it. His stomach responded with a kind little thank-you gurgle, and he sipped a little more.

After about a minute—which wasn't long enough for a real safety test, Laz knew—he succumbed to thirst and guzzled the whole thing.

Then, his thirst satisfied, he stood there in the dim aisle and waited for some store manager to come screaming down onto the sales floor to demand that he *pay* for what he had just consumed.

No manager. Nor did his stomach rebel. He had half expected to vomit right there in the aisle, but no, his body seemed to be dealing with the liquid.

But now that he had drunk something, Laz needed to pee. A very quick passage into the blood and out through the kidneys, he thought, but then figured that maybe the liquid had merely made his body remember about urination. There was no catheter in the healing cave, so maybe he had been kept in a weird kind of stasis where his body fluids were kept in balance and he didn't need to pee. Maybe.

He decided against peeing right there inside the store, because even if he was the last person alive in this town, he didn't want to turn a future food resource into a urine-soaked latrine for the town's lone homeless person. He went back outside the store and peed into the gutter. This looked like a place where rain came often enough to clean out the gutters.

In the distance, far across the parking lot, he saw a couple of dogs trotting along, paying no attention to the urinating man by the Harris Teeter store.

Inside the store again, he looked for bottled water. He found the price tags on the fronts of the shelves, along with the expected brand names—Fiji, Aquafina, Dasani, Evian—but the water shelves had been completely cleared out. Wherever everybody went, they had apparently needed to take water with them. But not V8.

He found an aisle that sold flashlights. None of them worked. He pried open battery packages and put the batteries into a flashlight. He used the brand that claimed a ten-year shelf life. He had no idea how many years they had been there, but the flashlight gave a feeble light, so *some* juice must have remained.

He used the light to find the employee break room, where he looked for a church key opener for cans of beverage that didn't have a working pop-top cap. When he couldn't find one, he remembered that grocery stores sold some hardware, and on the kitchenware shelves he found a pristine church key plus a hand-cranked lid-removing can opener. Nothing that needed to be plugged in to operate.

He searched for some likely canned food and, even though he had a can opener, he chose some small tins of Vienna sausage and various kinds of potted meat products and Spam and dried beef in little glass jars, all of which could be opened without an opener.

The Vienna sausage cans opened right up with their pop-top arrangement, and when he poured off the greyish sludge, the sausages looked grey but intact. He knew they were supposed to be pink, but he bit into one and then sat on the floor deciding whether or not to swallow or spit it out.

He swallowed. Better to know than not to know.

He ended up eating the whole tin of sausages. That was enough experimentation with protein for now. A plastic jar of mandarin oranges looked vaguely orange in color and he ate those and drank off the sugary liquid and to his surprise, it all tasted pretty good, meaning that it tasted like nothing but at least it wasn't nauseating.

He thought of trying to get back to Vivipartum to sleep, but what would he do, crawl back into his box? Say good night to the resting dead? Vivipartum had nothing for him—no welcoming committee, no instructions, no explanations, nothing. Why go back there?

He knew why. To look for another survivor.

But that was for later. Right now he had to look out for his own survival.

He thought of the hotel he had passed, but it was over at the other side of the sprawling shopping center, and even though he had once been a long-distance hiker, that was with a different body; this one was strong but it wasn't used to hiking. So he went back to the break room, closed the door, made an awkward pillow out of his backpack and an inadequate blanket out of his jacket, switched off the dim flashlight, and went to sleep.

He figured that even though this place must have been filled with rats and whatever other wildlife was extant in this town back when the meat and produce were still edible, they would have learned long ago that there was nothing for *them* in this place. So if he was inspected by any small animals in his sleep, they were thoughtful enough not to wake him.

Laz woke up only once during the night. He had been dreaming, something about his dad honking the horn for him, impatient to get a move on, get out here to the car. When he woke up, worried that his dad might leave if he didn't get out there pronto, he realized where he was, knew that his dad couldn't possibly be there, and for a moment he tried to get back to sleep.

Then he felt around for the flashlight, turned it on, and found his way out to the open doors and onto the sidewalk fronting the vast parking lot. No cars. Certainly not any cars containing his dad or any other impatient human honking a horn. But there was the gutter that he had turned into a personal latrine, so he drained his bladder and tried to decide whether he felt nauseated from the old canned food and drink he had consumed. He didn't.

Laz went back in, found the break room, closed the door, crawled onto his bedlike arrangement, and went back to sleep. He forgave himself for the fact that he was kind of crying himself to sleep. After all, he had just woken up from a long nap in a kind of box that had turned out to be a coffin for most of the inmates of such boxes. He had no one to talk to and, when he thought about it, no particular reason to be alive. His survival was surely an accident, just like the placement of the dead people in the Vivipartum parking lot, because if it was somebody's deliberate plan, where the hell were they?

But even lonely self-pitying teenagers eventually sleep, and when he woke up again, opening the break room door revealed daylight streaming into the store. He had slept through the night.

There was a thin layer of snow on the parking lot outside. Or was it frost? He walked out into the parking lot. It was snow—though in the Los Angeles area he had never had any experience with either. His parents had taken him skiing a few times, but this wasn't skiing-type snow. This was more like slippery fall-on-your-butt-if-you-walk-carelessly snow. He watched his feet, walking carefully.

There were three dogs in the parking lot, much closer than the ones he had seen the night before. They were just standing there, looking at him. Could they possibly be familiar with humans? He tried to remember just how long dogs lived. If everybody had been gone for twenty years, it was probable that none of these dogs had seen a human before.

But they had seen mammals before—squirrels, certainly. Did he look like meat to them? They were all so skinny their ribs were showing. Hunger can make anything look like food. Including grey Vienna sausages.

Their stillness and silence were unnerving. He thought of talking to them, then decided against it.

He heard a sound behind him.

He turned very slowly and saw another dog between him and the store entrance. Surrounded. Smart dogs with a plan, apparently.

Laz wasn't even holding the flashlight, so if they decided to attack, he would have no defense.

From his hiking days, he knew that if you didn't want dogs around, you did *not* run away from them, because that triggered their chasing instinct. However, he was also reasonably sure that holding out his hand to be sniffed while saying, Good doggy, might not be any smarter.

He angled toward a part of the store entrance that was a little bit away from where the dog was. It stepped between him and the entrance.

My backpack is in there, thought Laz. It has a couple of tools in it.

It has a pry bar in it. That would make a nice resounding smack against the head of an attacking dog.

But getting to the pry bar would mean that either the dog had simply let him pass, which would mean he didn't need a weapon at all, or that he had outrun the dog and made it inside the closed break room door before the dog got to him, which seemed unlikely.

The dog in the doorway growled softly. A turn of his head revealed that the other dogs were much closer to him now. He was encircled.

He thought of continuing to walk toward the store entrance.

Then he decided that this was an excellent time to side step.

When he looked inside his mind for the threadlike timestreams, he didn't see images, not really. What he saw were threads leading to places different from *this* version of the present. It's not that he could step back into some earlier place in the timestream and then make different decisions—there was nothing time-travelly about his little trick. Instead he had to find a different *version* of the present moment in which he had already made different decisions that took him to a different situation, a different place but the same exact time.

Yet he couldn't always be sure of what he'd find.

He made a choice and stepped into it.

In this timestream, at the exact same moment, instead of being outside with the dogs, he was still in the break room. Had he slept longer? He consulted the memories he found in this version of himself, and yes, he had only just woken up, and had not even opened the break room door.

He pulled the pry bar out of the backpack, then shrugged the pack onto his shoulders. He made a few practice swings with the pry bar, and then carefully opened the door.

Well, hello. All four dogs—the same ones; he recognized their different mixed-up breeds—were sitting outside the door, waiting for him.

He closed the door again. Almost immediately, something thumped against the door, and the barking began.

All right, let's find another timestream.

In the next one he tried—again, at the exact moment in time when he had retreated back into the break room and the dogs had begun their sad little assault on the door—he was not in the break room. He was wearing the backpack, and he was in the dark stockroom in the back of the store, shining the flashlight around. Maybe the dogs were inside the store. Maybe they were out in the parking lot, waiting for him. Maybe they were in a different part of town. He had no intention of looking for them.

He hesitated before trying to stock up on more food, but finally decided that as long as the dogs weren't actually inside the store, he probably had time. He found the shelves he needed and added canned meat, canned pasta, canned fish, and plastic bottles of mandarin oranges to his backpack. It was way heavier now, but if the dogs—or something else—started chasing him, he'd drop the bag and hope to return to it later.

With the heavy backpack, he went into the stockroom and found a back door. When he tried the handle, it opened to the outside. Daylight, the expected skiff of snow—because it was rare for a timestream to have different weather—and no dogs.

But behind him, in the stockroom, he heard the padding of doggy feet.

He stepped out the door and pushed it closed behind him. It was slow going because the hydraulic hinge mechanism was sluggish, so before it was closed, a couple of noses were sticking out and there was a bit of growling. Laz looked around to make sure there weren't any canine co-conspirators lurking outside, but no, the little four-member pack seemed all to be on the inside. He finally got the door closed and latched. The dogs complained.

Laz took off walking along the asphalt behind the stores, wondering if the dogs would know enough to go out the front door and come around to find him in the back. So he picked up his pace. As long as the dogs couldn't see him, running was not forbidden. The snow made it dangerous—it wouldn't be good if the dogs found him lying on the ground with a sprained ankle—but he watched his path and planted his feet squarely. He didn't slip or skid.

And soon he was on a road headed back toward the lower part of the Friendly shopping center. Not so friendly this morning, he thought. Wouldn't it have been nice of the former inhabitants to take their dogs with them when they left?

But if it hadn't been dogs, it might have been something else. Not knowing where he was, for all he knew the woods nearby had bears and wolves, and he figured dogs were a much better choice of peril.

He needed a home base that didn't have a permanently open front door. On the other side of the street, over a high fence and then down a ways, there were houses. If he went to the end of this street and turned, maybe he'd connect up with a neighborhood. Either he'd find an inhabited house, in which case he could start finding out what was going on and maybe make phone calls to his parents, or he'd find a lot of empty houses, and he might be able to pry his way into one in such a way as to leave the door reclosable. A house would be nice. Houses were made by humans for humans, and he was a human, so . . . not a bad fit, maybe.

He was still moving quickly. Dogs had a great sense of smell. He certainly was giving off a scared human smell. Getting into a house soon would be nice.

There were several houses that had already been broken into. Any house with a dog door or a cat door had quickly become a shelter for raccoons or weasels or rats or possums or something that pooped everywhere and stank.

But there were also houses that had been sealed shut pretty well. He thought of prying a door away from the doorframe, but couldn't imagine how he would reclose it afterward. He settled on a window that seemed not to have any convenient fence or air conditioning unit for a raccoon or whatever to jump from. It was pretty easy persuading the window to open—apparently burglary became much easier when you weren't worried about alerting neighbors or waking the residents with the noise of prying at a window. He was about to toss his backpack into the room but then he realized: If I can't climb in after it, I've lost my backpack.

If I had a skinny little kid as an assistant, I could lower the kid inside, and then go around to the front door so the kid could let me in. Being the lone survivor from Vivipartum had its inconveniences.

Or am I the lone survivor?

It was a fascinating thought, because he had no reason to believe that *all* the boxes held mummies.

But now was not the time to go off on a wild-goose chase. Vivipartum could wait, at least until he had a reasonably secure nighttime shelter.

Even with the backpack on, Laz found it pretty easy to clamber in. The pack did not snag in the window frame. And there was a table right under the window, so he didn't have to fall inside and land on his head on the floor. He knocked a bunch of stuff off the table, but once inside, he recognized everything. Monitors, computer game consoles of several brands, controllers, and even a keyboard, as if one of the items was a real computer. It didn't matter—nothing switched on, there was no power in the house. And if somebody didn't like the mess he had made in the computer room, he'd have to ask their forgiveness later.

He went through the house and found a bed with a mattress. It had no bedbugs—what would they have been eating for the past umpteen years?—and even though it also had no sheets or blankets, it was going to be better than the floor of the break room in the Harris Teeter.

No food in the house. Not a book. Not an old magazine. Nothing to read. Nothing to eat. Toilets, but bone dry, so he didn't think he wanted to treat them like open pit latrines. Still, once he reclosed the window in the computer room, the wind wasn't getting inside, so this house might make a decent place to stay.

He went to the front door, unlocked it, opened it. Then he reclosed it and tried to see if it had locked automatically. It had. He found the little knobby thing that set the lock, turned it, and this time the door did not lock. He could leave the place and come back in through the front door. As if he lived here.

And why not? He was alive, and this was a decent place, until he found a better one. He could go back to Belk or Macy's or wherever and see if they still had blankets and sheets somewhere inside. Or maybe there was a Target or Walmart or something.

No pistol. No rifle. No ammunition. So he'd have to find a way to deal with dogs and other animal hazards using a poky or smacky weapon. Maybe a Walmart would have an archery set that still had some spring in the bow. It was a pretty sure bet none of them would have a nice javelin. But darts? Maybe darts. If there was a Walmart.

This was America. Of course there was a Walmart.

For now, all he had was a pry bar in his hand, a backpack on his back, and a conscious effort to keep track of his movements so he could find this house again.

By mid-afternoon, having located several small strip centers, a few useless restaurants, some gas stations, and a bicycle store that only had tires that crumbled when he tried to turn the wheels, he was starting to head back toward "his" house when once again he saw a shadow moving in the middle distance. He stopped cold and did not move at all. Finally he saw the motion again. It was a squirrel. As far as he knew, squirrels weren't dangerous to anybody, unless they had rabies. *Wouldn't it be pathetic if somebody spawned me as a very expensive clone and then I died from a squirrel bite? A whole lot of advanced technology wasted.*

There was electricity back at Vivipartum. Not a lot, but enough to keep his coffin—no, his healing box—running, giving off light from LEDs on the console. Keeping him alive. Electricity at Vivipartum might mean that it had its own generator—quite possible, once he thought about it—but it might also mean that the power grid was still working at some rudimentary level.

He walked behind some houses, found their power meter, and saw no motion at all. He did see labels saying DUKE POWER, which meant nothing to him. Pacific Gas and Electric would have been too much to hope for.

He used the pry bar to open the lids covering the water meter in a front yard, and there was a label saying GREENSBORO WATER AND SEWER, and warning that the city of Greensboro, North Carolina, was responsible for any leaks between the meter and the street, but the homeowner was responsible for leaks between the meter and the house.

It was the first informative writing Laz had seen. Now he knew what state he was in, and, having paid decent attention in geography class and looking at maps, Laz knew that North Carolina was on the east coast of the United States, and that even though he wasn't sure where the city of Greensboro actually was, it definitely wasn't in the mountains and it probably wasn't on the coast. For now, that was enough. It was not a far northern state that was likely to get a lot of Canadian weather. And come summer—yes, that was a good idea: Come, Summer!—he wouldn't be putting up with whatever hell Florida or Louisiana or Texas had to offer in the hot season.

How in the world had anybody decided to create his clone *here*, on the opposite side of the country from where he had lived his whole life?

But maybe that was the point.

Was the whole country evacuated, empty of people? Was it the whole world? Or was it just Greensboro, so that any clones that happened to wake up would be thrust onto their own resources? Was he being tested? Or had he been abandoned?

He got "home" well before dark, went inside, and ate another plastic jar of mandarin oranges, another little tin of Vienna sausages, a can of cold SpaghettiOs, and some more V8.

Then he discovered that all his bodily systems were, in fact, working, and he went outside and established a space to use as a latrine, then gathered up a supply of fallen leaves to use as toilet paper. It made lousy toilet paper, with tiny insects on the leaves that soon were on him, but it was better than nothing.

Back in the house he found that there were a few rolls of toilet paper in a cabinet under a bathroom sink. But when he tried to use toilet paper to do a final cleanup, it crumbled in his hands. Some things just didn't age well. So leaves it would be.

He imagined television commercials advertising "Oak leaves,

nature's finest hygienic cleanup device," or a public service announcement about watching out for poison ivy when wiping your bum. "Snakes like to hide in piles of leaves," said another imaginary PSA, "so keep a rake wherever you plan to have a poo, so you can rake through the leaves before you drop your drawers."

Such were Laz's not-very-amusing thoughts as he was going to sleep on a king-sized mattress in a master bedroom without a bit of clothing in the closets or bureau drawers to pile on top of himself as a blanket. But he was glad of what he had. Including fairly entertaining commercials and PSAs to fall asleep to.

Plog 1 (Well I suppose my original plog should be labeled as number one, but it was introductory. That was Plog Zero. This is Plog 1.)

Wandering around this ~~godforsaken~~ everybody-forsaken town, I'm confronted every day by all the things that don't work anymore. Stuff you just took for granted growing up in Hancock Park and then in the Glen.

So I've been thinking about which public utility I miss the most. Lots of candidates, and believe me, I've talked myself through a good solid case for all of them. But I know now which one is most important to me. The hardest to get along without.

Clean running water that comes right into your house at the turn of a tap. Complete with water pressure, and without any obvious floaters or sludge in it. I see drinking fountains and sinks with taps in lots of places and yeah I'm so dumb I keep trying them because what if one of them was still working?

But just because water comes out doesn't mean it's clean. It probably means it isn't because who would be maintaining the water treatment system, right? For all I know it's stale ancient sewage backing up in the system till it comes out the taps.

But if the miracle happened and a tap actually delivered, and drinking it didn't kill me, that would be better than getting the internet back. Better than hot buttered corn on the cob. You know I'm serious when I say that. Water!

Plog 2

My second favorite utility: electricity, because it makes possible things like lights, both indoors and at night; bug zappers; electric stoves, ovens, microwaves, toasters, blenders, <u>refrigerators</u>, freezers, space heaters, <u>air conditioning</u>, fans, computers. Ah, computers. Smart phones. Stupid phones. Phones.

3

WHEN LAZ WOKE up, cold and coverless on a bare mattress, he found that while his cloney self was well muscled and not at all soft or fat, all his walking was taking a toll on him. His hips were sore when he walked. There was a crick in his neck.

He knew enough to realize that these pains were not a reason to take it easy today—they were a reason to exercise every muscle in his body and push at least as hard as yesterday. His first long hike of the day took him to a wide street called Battleground, though he couldn't remember reading about a Battle of Greensboro in any history book in school. Both directions on Battleground looked built up with commercial buildings and long strip centers, so he turned left and walked on. He could have used a nice pedometer to track how far he had already walked, so he'd have a good idea of what it would take to walk back home. But since, no matter how far he walked, he would have to walk home anyway, did it matter? He would eventually learn to get better at tracking time by the sun, whether it came out from behind the clouds or not.

No dogs so far today, but more and more squirrels, and a few wooded patches where for all he knew some fierce predator might be making its rounds. Or an abandoned house cat. He had read a book whose premise was that all cats were savage predators, and house cats were simply murderous hunters who also had a subsidized living arrangement. Like college students.

Since Laz had never been a college student, he had no idea why that comparison leapt to mind. High school students were just as subsidized and, in their own ways, just as predatory. Not that any of them brought dead animals home to lay on their parents' doorsteps.

Cats are nocturnal hunters by preference, Laz remembered. But dogs are perfectly happy to hunt by day.

He tried to remember, as he walked along, what he knew about primitive humans' attempts to protect themselves from medium-sized predators like hyenas and wolves and jackals. The image came to mind of a bunch of women and naked children keeping a daylight fire alive, playing and tussling, but also practicing their skills. Not throwing javelins—Laz was never going to find a good throwing spear, or acquire the skill to launch a killing throw.

Throwing stones. That's what the boys and girls would have been doing—and the women, too, and the old men. Everybody who wasn't hunting had the job of guarding the perimeter of the camp and keeping jackals and wolves and hyenas from darting in and, while a few distracted the humans, snatching two or three unresisting babies and taking them back to their lairs for some undisturbed feasting.

If the human race was to survive, then while the strong, fast men were out hunting game big enough to feed the tribe, the left-behinds had to be capable of protecting the babies and toddlers.

Surely none of them could pick up a rock and throw a hundred-mile-per-hour fast pitch. Major League Baseball speeds wouldn't be possible for children.

How fast did ten-year-olds pitch in Little League? From what Laz remembered hearing, kids that young would throw their arms out if they tried to pitch that fast. So maybe they could only throw forty- or fifty-mile-an-hour stones at attacking hyenas. Would that do the job of stopping them?

When his world history teacher did a unit on prehistoric man, he read from an article about piles of tennis-ball-sized stones gathered around the entrances of caves used as habitats for early humans. The article talked about hunting with such stones, which could inflict damage from twenty meters off, and maybe injure prey enough that they could be killed with bigger stones from close quarters. There had even been a picture of some artist's imagined hunt with those rocks.

But now Laz realized, those stones were piled up near the cave entrance, not to bring down prey, but to beat off any attack by predators seeking human babies. And when there weren't any predators, the children would practice throwing those rocks at targets to improve their speed and accuracy.

That's something I can do, thought Laz.

He walked into a woodsy area near the road and searched for stones.

The soil here was so loamy that while he found lots of tiny stones about the size of overgrown gravel, there was nothing that would carry any weight.

Till he reached a stream. In winter—if this was winter—there wasn't a lot of water. Probably there'd be a lot more right after rain, but for now Laz was perfectly happy to pick up several good-sized stones somewhat smoothed by water and put them in the pockets of his jacket.

Then he went back across Battleground to a building that had a solid cinderblock wall, with no windows. Using one stone, he scratched an X on the wall at about the height of a dog's head. Then he stepped back twenty paces and threw the stone as hard as he could.

Yes, this was why he hadn't really enjoyed baseball as a kid. The first stone barely made it halfway toward the wall, and not at all in the direction of the target.

Were the stones too heavy? Or was he just too far away?

Laz walked closer, till he was about six paces away. If a hostile dog were that close, Laz had *better* be able to throw a rock and hit it.

He threw all seven of his stones, and six of them actually hit the wall, one of them within a few feet of the X. Then he picked them up and carried them back the same six paces and threw them all and retrieved them ten more times until his aching shoulder told him that there was a reason relief pitchers existed, because there was a limit to how many times you could throw in a game.

But then, just for the fun of it, Laz went back to the stream and picked up almost two dozen stones that were half the diameter and about an eighth of the weight of the stones he had picked up the first time.

Now when he threw them, they felt so lightweight that Laz was able to really zing them against the wall. They bounced off so far that some of them almost hit him. So he walked back, this time about fifteen paces, and threw a bunch more. With the smaller stones, he was more accurate and they flew faster and farther.

He didn't practice with this weight of stone as much as he had practiced with the heavier ones—no reason to make himself sore or injure himself in some permanent way. When he decided he was through, however, he filled his jacket pockets with about half of the smaller stones, and one of the bigger ones. Even at age seventeen—was he seventeen?—he didn't imagine he could pitch half so fast or aim half so well as a Little League pitcher. But he didn't have to. He just had to be able to discourage dogs from stalking him.

"I am not an idiot," he said out loud, in response to his own first impulse to go in search of his little pack of four dogs. Why pick a fight? If I never see them again, that's soon enough.

So he simply took the most direct route home, and when he didn't see the dogs, he thought, I'm fine with that. That's good enough for me. Not seeing them is what I *want*.

But he also knew he would carry the stones tomorrow.

Back when he used to walk all over Los Angeles County, Laz had always made it a point *not* to look like a jogger or a runner. He was just a pedestrian who happened to be wearing high-quality walking shoes. Not hiking boots. He wore long pants or, sometimes, sweats. He wasn't afraid to get his shoes or pants dirty, but he didn't want to have to worry about getting insects all over his legs or getting scratched by prickly plants if he cut across country now and then. He didn't worry about rain—it was southern California, for heaven's sake—but he did wear a hat of some kind because of the sun. And a light windbreaker, too, though he usually left it open. But he figured that he never looked like some clown out exercising. He looked like a teenager walking from point A to point B. That had to mean that he wasn't far from his destination, because what teenager that *wasn't* in athletic clothes would be exercising across the dozen miles from Westwood to Van Nuys by way of Beverly Glen? Traffic made it a dangerous walk—he never did it during peak traffic times—but the nearly twenty-five-mile round trip could use up a whole Saturday and at the end of it he was always pleasantly tired. He felt, not used up, but simply *used*.

He wanted to get back into that kind of shape, where a twenty-five-mile day was no big deal, unless he told Mom how far he had gone, and, worse yet, where. "Can't we join a gym?" she had demanded of her new husband.

"I'm not going to walk on a treadmill," said Laz. "Or use an elliptical."

"How about riding a bike?" asked Doofus—Laz's private name for his stepdad.

"So now instead of being hit by cars, I'll be going twenty-five miles an hour myself, so anything I hit will cause me to break bones or, you know, die. Good plan, Mr. Brown."

"You'd be wearing a helmet," said Doofus.

"No he wouldn't," said Mom. "Because he wants to end up paralyzed in a wheelchair for the rest of his life."

"I'm not walking for exercise," said Laz. "I'm not walking to 'stay fit.' I'm walking because that's how I like to get from point A to point B."

"Why can't you be like regular teenagers, and just ask to borrow the car?"

"Because," said Laz, "I want to enjoy every step along the way. You car drivers, you measure distances in terms of time—how many hours it takes to get from Sony to Universal at any given time of day."

"Because that's the measurement that matters," said Doofus.

"But I don't want my life to consist of staring at the exhaust-pumping ass of the car in front, and struggling to cross six lanes of traffic on the One-Oh-One so I don't get sucked into downtown when I'm really trying to get to Pasadena."

"Why in the world would you ever want to go to Pasadena?" asked Mom.

"Believe it or not, Mom," said Laz, "I doubt that I'll ever set out for Pasadena. But if I happen to end up there on one of my walks, I think that'll be cool."

"Do you at least carry your mobile, so you can call for a ride?" asked Doofus.

"Like one of you would drop everything to come pick me up in some remote part of the county," said Laz scornfully.

Doofus looked at him like he was insane. "I meant that you'd call Uber or a taxi or something."

"Don't worry. I'll just break a store window and wait for the cops to give me a ride home."

That was life in Mom's house. Dad never asked him what he did on Saturdays. Nor did he ever tell Laz what *he* was doing, either. Don't ask, don't tell.

So Laz didn't feel any pressing need to decide, before he left the house each day, what his destination would be. He remembered very well where his cache of rocks was out on Battleground; he assembled several other caches in other places. And he practiced all the time, throwing his rocks, then gathering them up, then throwing them again. He got so he could hit a hydrant with some force almost every time, from twenty paces out. He figured that for shying stones at dogs, that was good enough.

Not good enough that anybody would want him on their baseball team, of course. Twenty paces was nothing. Those guys had to throw from the outfield and have the ball go all the way to the infield, preferably right into some infielder's glove. Laz didn't even *want* to be that good.

One day he found himself in a vaguely familiar area, and in a minute he realized that he was close enough to see the Vivipartum building. Well, cool.

The front door still had a couch holding it open.

Well, of course? Who would have moved it?

For a moment Laz thought of throwing rocks at the windowy walls to see if the speed or the weight of the stones could shatter them. But then he thought, I don't know all the passageways inside. Have I already opened up those big coffin rooms to predators looking for meat? What if there's somebody else alive in one of those boxes? Should they wake up to a hungry raccoon prying open their box looking for somebody to eat the face off of?

And that made him think, Maybe this is a good time to look for somebody else alive in there. He had no other urgent appointments. And even if he did, his secretary would lie for him, the way Dad's did.

His backpack now contained a couple of dozen batteries for his LED flashlights so that he wouldn't be moving in the dark, even if the electricity inside went out. There also had to be stairs if the elevators stopped working. He wouldn't be trapped in Corpse Central.

So he clambered over the couch and went inside. There were animal droppings behind the reception desk, but all of the doors leading deeper into the building were closed. Many of them were locked, and all of them were latched in ways that raccoons probably couldn't open.

Laz decided to conduct a rational search. Top floor down. There would be daylight on the upper floors.

He saw a lot of desks. Clearly they had once been equipped with computers and phones, but there were no cables coming up from the floor or down from the ceiling. The file cabinets that had once marked out their rectangle shapes on the carpet were gone. Nothing written or printed on paper survived. Nothing electronic was even present, let alone working.

Did they take it all away because they needed it somewhere else? Or was it removed so that Laz couldn't find anything in the papers that might help him make sense of what was going on?

They apparently salvaged and carried away the things they cared about, thought Laz a little bitterly, but they left the garbage behind. All those heaps of dried-up protoplasm in their convenient little coffins. Too bad they forgot to unplug his.

No, Laz didn't think his survival was a mistake. He wasn't overlooked, he was *saved*. Like money in the bank.

Maybe somebody else still had an active account at Vivipartum. Maybe he was supposed to find them and wake them up and then he wouldn't be so oppressively lonely.

Laz knew that solitary confinement in prisons had been banned as cruel and unusual punishment, because people could not exist long in solitude. They start to go nuts.

I'm glad there's no chance of that happening to *me*, because I started out nuts, thank you very much.

Between searching the upper floors and brooding, he whiled away the afternoon before he got back to the ground floor. He knew now that if anything useful had survived, it would be on a lower floor. But the sky showed that it was time for him to head for home. He would have to come back and explore deeper into the building. On the way home, when it was still broad daylight, Laz saw the Pack of Four trotting along two blocks over. Going the opposite direction from him.

He fought down the temptation to go that direction and try out his stone-throwing on them. Because what if it wasn't good enough yet? And also, why should *he* attack *them*? If they were content to leave him alone, then leave it at that, right?

He didn't see them again that night. But remembering that he had seen them at Friendly Center that first morning, and then where he saw them that afternoon, he extrapolated what their foraging range might be. He really had no basis for his estimate—maybe he had run into them on the very edge of a range that usually kept them fifty miles away. But he had his pockets full of stones. And if he wasn't able to keep them off with his new speedy rocks, he'd side step into a reality where he wasn't so stupid as to seek out an encounter with feral dogs.

Then he had a thought that had come to mind many times over the years. What if there *was* no reality in which he had made the smarter, safer decision? What if he could only side step from one reality where the dogs shrugged off his pathetic stone-throwing and brought him down, to another reality where they also ended up eating his face?

Thanks to all those BBC and Nat Geo videos of predators eating their prey from the bowels up and the face on down, he had a clear idea of how a group of determined predators could bring down and devour larger prey. He remembered grainy nighttime footage of lions eating their way into the anus of an elephant that was still alive, still standing up. It was a terrifying image. Then again, what did he expect? Tigers that turned their victims into a nice meat pie before eating them with knife and fork?

Tomorrow he'd head back to Vivipartum and look for other survivors. That was the rational plan.

Except there was nothing rational about it. How long had he

been here? All the way from cold weather to hot, a few months at least. And in all that time, whenever he thought of returning to Vivipartum, he found something more urgent to do. He was *busy*.

But he wasn't all that busy. A couple of hours getting to a store, shoplifting whatever looked useful that he thought he could carry, and then wandering around for the rest of the day. Why was he holding back from returning to look in earnest for other survivors?

Because there might not be any, and then he would know he was really in this thing alone.

And because there might be somebody, but he had no idea how to get them out of the coffin safely.

Even if he got the other survivors out, then there would be other people and they would all think they knew better than Laz did what Laz should do. The story of his life: always a kid, and therefore every adult thought they had the right to tell him what to do.

I don't like being lonely, he thought, but I do like having my liberty.

The next morning, Laz loaded only a few cans from his stash, and instead of going straight to Vivipartum, he found himself headed into Pack of Four territory. He had five stones in his left hand and one in his right as he walked down the middle of every street, so nothing could spring at him out of hiding.

Apparently I'm stupid enough to pick a fight with four hungry dogs. I'm glad they aren't wolves. Or woolly mammoths.

It took a little bit of walking at random through downtown and residential blocks, but eventually, well before noon, there they were. Two a block away on the left, one a block away on the right, and one padding along directly behind Laz. The leader.

Laz stopped.

Leaderdog slowed down, but kept coming. Tongue lolling out. Maybe the tail was wagging, though it was held low enough that Laz couldn't see it well.

Laz scanned left and right, and sure enough, the other three dogs were now approaching. Are they telepaths? Or did they all see me and they knew what to do?

Laz reared back to throw.

Leaderdog didn't seem to care. Just kept coming.

This might work better if I were aiming at his side instead of his nose, thought Laz.

He threw.

The stone landed about three feet in front of Leaderdog and ricocheted up to his throat. Lucky, lucky, lucky shot.

Or did I side step to this timestream just to get that lucky shot?

No. I'd remember.

Leaderdog yelped and jumped back a few steps.

The other dogs also stopped and retreated a little.

The other dogs were broadside to Laz, and therefore much easier targets. But would it matter to Leaderdog if Laz hit one of his pals? No, because if Laz turned his attention to them, Leaderdog would have a chance to spring at him.

So Laz focused his attention on Leaderdog, reared back, and let fly.

The stone struck a glancing blow on Leaderdog's jaw. Leaderdog leapt to the side, yelping. This exposed some of his flank to Laz, and already he had another stone in his right hand, and without any elaborate pitching routine, he simply flung the rock at the side of Leaderdog's body.

Direct hit on his hind haunch. Who says practice is a waste of time?

This time Leaderdog ran away, limping quite noticeably, and giving whiny little yips to his team. They seemed reluctant to follow—after all, you don't remain the alpha dog if you run away—but when Laz pitched his largest rock at the nearest of the dogs and hit it solidly on the hip, the dog actually fell over. It got right back up, but it limped off even more panicked than Leaderdog. The other two didn't wait around for further demonstrations.

Laz waited till they were gone, then walked around and gathered up his spent ammunition. Why search for more river rocks when these had already proven their worth? Unlike hand grenades, rocks were pretty much reusable.

A good day's work, and it wasn't even noon yet.

He continued toward Vivipartum. Lots of time left in the day.

Weirdly, though, he couldn't stop thinking of how the two dogs he hit had run away, crying out in pain. Sure, they would have attacked him and eaten him without feeling a qualm, but they were dogs. Laz wasn't. Laz was supposed to be a good guy. What was he doing setting up dogs for injury and pain?

No, I'm training them, Laz told himself. I'm training them to leave human pedestrians alone. That's a good lesson for them to learn—for my safety.

Of course, these rocks are going to be meaningless if I run into a bear. Getting hit by a rock probably won't even annoy the bear. And if it does, it won't make the bear yell the bear equivalent of "owie" and run away.

Definitely need to see if I can find a working bow and arrows. I'd have to practice with *them* way more than I did with the stones.

Laz did not ride the elevator down. The stairs revealed more floors than the elevator went to, and eventually he found a door whose buttons were still working. The door slid open and inside was a serious array of computers stacked in trays. He had seen arrays like this in animation studios. He wasn't sure what these computers were for, but what mattered were three facts. First, all the upstairs computers had been removed, but these were still here. Second, there were blue, green, and amber LED displays in many places, proving that there was still electrical current running through this room. And third, on a single desk in the middle of the room, there was a computer monitor with a blinking cursor in the upper left corner of the screen.

So when he woke up and got out of his coffin, it hadn't caused everything to shut down. Maybe that meant there really was another living person somewhere in this place.

If Laz messed with the computer, he might trigger some self-defense system with unpredictable results.

Instead, he knew he had to go in search of a functioning healing cave. And the obvious place to start was the big coffin room where *he* had woken up.

He found it pretty quickly. At first he turned on the overhead lights, but then realized that he didn't want to have to look down into a thousand boxes that contained withered corpses that had died at various stages of development. So he turned the light back off, shut the door, and then stood there letting his eyes get used to the dark.

The first thing he noticed was the absence of green lights inside the coffins. They had all been on, displaying zeroes, when he first awoke. So he started to walk, slowly, among the coffins, touching them to make sure he kept going straight.

There it was. The green light from the only wide open, empty coffin in the place. The one Laz had come out of.

He only saw it when he was about four coffins away, and then only because he was on the correct side. He continued his slow patrol, and never saw another light.

Why were they all off now, except his? This might mean that the computer system had noticed that he was awake and his box was empty, so it switched off all the other lights. But why not his?

He was not going to be able to outguess the computer, and still less the programmers. But if somebody else was alive, he needed to know it.

It's worth looking, he reminded himself. I have to try.

He went to the coffin room one story above the one he had awoken in, and again darkened the space and patrolled slowly among the boxes. After a long time, discouraged, he thought of quitting, and turned back to face the other way. That was when he saw a tiny green light in a box he must have already passed. But now he could see what was on the other side of the interior.

Maybe it was another working coffin. Maybe somebody alive.

When he got there and shone his brighter light through the clear lid of the sleeping box, it wasn't a mummy. It was a girl. Sleeping, but she seemed to be alive. Laz wasn't sure what the instruments were saying, but they were saying *something*, unlike the zeroes that the instruments on Laz's own empty coffin now reported. For a moment he imagined her naked, as clearly as if it were a memory, but he instantly told himself to grow up. She was wearing the same kind of bland lightweight pajamas that Laz had been wearing. Laz couldn't guess her age—she could have been younger, she could have been older.

Alive. Apparently alive.

Laz studied the instruments, trying to figure out what condition she was in, trying to figure out how to tell the machinery to wake her up safely. He was pretty sure that prying up the lid with a crowbar would have deleterious effects. And even if he did get it open and she woke up and didn't die, what then? "Why did you wake me up?" "Well, see, I was alone for three months and I needed somebody to talk to." "So what's this wonderful thing you were dying to say?" "I don't know." "For this you woke me up?"

And if he woke her without first getting the coffin to play her memories back into her head, she might be a full-grown person without memories. Not just forgetting whatever happened to her in third grade, but forgetting human speech, walking, reading. What would he do then? Hand feed her for a few years?

I'm so glad I came back to Vivipartum. Now I know there's another living person in a healing box, and I'm still just as helpless, as ignorant, as solitary as before.

There was nothing to be gained by sitting around at Vivipartum all evening, feeling sorry and timid, deciding to access that one computer and then deciding not to access it ever. Everything he did might be wrong, and even if he could side step his way out of disastrous errors, it was quite possible that *every* choice would be bad, and he really needed the girl to wake up on her own when her healing box declared her ready.

But that wasn't what Laz had done for himself. He had reached up and pushed his own coffin lid out of the way. He had taken action. Why shouldn't he take action to release a potential companion?

He actually stood over the girl's healing box with the pry bar under the edge of the lid, deciding whether to use brute force to liberate the girl. Then he put the pry bar back into his backpack and walked to the door.

Someone else is alive in this town, someone who is not a dog or a squirrel, and I can't figure out what to do about that fact. Why had someone cloned her? Was she the clone of a supermodel? A hyper-rich pop singer? A famous athlete? Why would she give the time of day to Laz? He was as close to a nothing as you could be without becoming invisible.

How long had he stood there staring down through the lid at her faintly illuminated face? Long enough to memorize her features. Long enough to decide she was good-looking, even without makeup or any kind of facial expression. Even with stringy hair of no particular color except the faint green from the LED display.

His current home base was no longer going to work. He needed a point of supply and a safe sleeping place much closer to Vivipartum. Because now that he knew she existed, he didn't want to leave it to chance whether she woke up and found him. He wanted to be there, so they could start working out whatever relationship they were going to have.

He walked over the couch in the main entrance and back into the street. To the south was a poorer neighborhood that didn't support a major grocery store. He understood this town well enough to start walking northward.

Because he was thinking of other things now, the Pack of Four took him by surprise. But this time there was nothing menacing about them. The follower-dog that Laz had struck in the side was lying down on the ground, panting heavily. The two who hadn't been hit were standing vigil.

Leaderdog, though, *he* keyed in on Laz and watched, rotating his body to keep Laz in his line of sight. But he was also limping as he turned.

Apparently Laz's rocks had landed with more force than he expected. So two of the four dogs were not fit to forage, and that might spell the difference between eking out a living and dying of starvation.

Why should killing hungry dogs be part of his agenda in this place?

Laz stepped a few dozen paces away, squatted down, and opened the backpack. His larder wasn't huge. A can of tamales. A can of corn. No dog food, alas.

A couple of cans of tuna fish.

Laz used the lid-removing opener to expose the chunks of tuna inside one of the cans. When Laz had eaten from previous tuna cans, he hadn't been impressed by the flavor. But hey, it was tuna, it was cooked, and Laz himself had eaten a lot of tuna in his life. If he had anything that would appeal to a dog, it had to be this can of StarKist tuna.

Laz used the narrow handle of the can opener to dig down into the tuna and pry it out. He dumped it onto the sidewalk.

Leaderdog was alert to everything Laz was doing—but the dog made no effort to come closer. Injured as he was, Leaderdog probably preferred to stay out of Laz's throwing range.

Laz gathered up the tuna in his hands and walked slowly and obliquely toward the dogs.

Leaderdog gave a low warning growl.

Laz stopped approaching and knelt down with the offering of tuna fish. He held out his hands. Leaderdog came and sniffed.

"Hey, come on, I'm sorry," said Laz. "I know this stuff has lost a lot of its food value on the shelf for umpty-odd years, but it's the same stuff I eat, so I'm pretty sure it isn't poisonous."

He spoke low and soft, and Leaderdog kept coming closer.

Then its mouth was in Laz's hands, using tongue, lips, and teeth to pick up every scrap of tuna.

Then he ran over and spat out a lot of it, maybe all of it, right beside the dog with the more serious-looking injuries. Leaderdog stepped back a little, then nosed one of the healthy dogs toward it.

Soon they were all eating.

But Leaderdog didn't take his fair share. Instead, he ran over to where Laz had left his backpack and picked up the now-empty tuna can and trotted back with it. He pushed it onto Laz's lap, then into his hands. Laz wasn't quite sure he could interpret the gesture, but it sure seemed to him like Leaderdog was asking for more StarKist tuna.

"StarKist, huh?" asked Laz. "Can't have Chicken of the Sea, is that it?"

Laz got up and walked back to his backpack and found the other tuna can. He started cranking the opener.

Meanwhile, back with the rest of his little pack, Leaderdog had his nose inside the now-empty tuna can, as if he were licking up the last dregs of meat.

"So you now worship the god StarKist," said Laz. "The source of all goodness, the teat of all survivor dogs."

Laz brought over the second can of tuna—the last in his pack—and dumped the contents onto the grass and left the empty can for Leaderdog to clean out.

Leaderdog wasn't a name, it was a job description. "Your name is StarKist now," Laz said. "And I'm Laz. Let's see if we're friends tomorrow."

Leaving the dogs behind, Laz went on north. About a mile later,

Laz found a shopping center that contained another Harris Teeter. This time the front doors were not standing open.

Laz thought of using the universal passkey—a well-thrown cinderblock—and decided that what he needed was a place with doors. Maybe there was a way in that wouldn't involve breaking something irreparably.

It was a long walk around to the back, but he was lucky there— the back door was solidly closed, but the handle turned easily and Laz stepped inside. There were no growling animals, and no stench of decay. Laz started to reach for his flashlight to get through the dark stock room, but then he realized that there was a faint light. Not from an open window. It was from a partly open door.

Laz carefully made his way toward the light and soon discovered that it was a bathroom light over a mirror. An honest-to-god electric light. *On.*

Laz went inside. There was water in the toilet. He pressed the lever. The toilet flushed noisily, and then, miraculously, filled back up again.

It was such a joy, such a relief, that Laz would have used the toilet whether he needed it or not. But he needed it. And there was toilet paper, too—not the old kind, not a crumbling roll, but rather a pad of tear-away butt-wipe papers that felt more like paper towels than toilet paper.

A light. A flush toilet. Water in the sink for washing, maybe drinking. A blower on the wall that actually sensed the presence of his hands and noisily dried him off.

This is home now, thought Laz.

Laz grabbed some tarps from a pile in a corner and hauled them out into the store. Maybe it was only chance that kept a light and a flush toilet and running water in this store, but there was also the possibility that somebody visited this place from time to time, and the last thing Laz wanted was to have someone chance upon him when he was asleep. He had done a lot of thieving and vandalizing in this empty town, and if someone was going to hold him criminally responsible for it, he wanted to be awake to see it coming.

But he wasn't going to leave the store tonight. The lights did *not* work in the store itself, so it would be too dark for him to give the place a proper scavenging. That would be tomorrow, so tonight he was sleeping inside the store.

He laid out the tarps like a really stiff, uncomfortable bedroll, behind the customer service counter, where he wouldn't be visible from anywhere in the store itself. Then he walked to the front window and looked out over the gathering dark.

The Pack of Four were huddled near the east doors, where the wind from the west was mostly blocked.

I have more tuna fish, or at least the store shelf probably has more. What matters is that they *believe* I have more. They're not here to escape the wind—there are far more sheltered places where they can sleep. They're here for breakfast.

Not supper, lads, thought Laz. I'm not opening that door without a stone or a pry bar in my hand. I'm trying to make peace with you, but I don't trust you yet. Dogs may have evolved in a kind of symbiosis with humans, but you've been out of practice for too long. And I recently injured you, though apparently you're all still ambulatory, so, that's good. Are you here for food, friendship, or revenge? Or maybe all three, depending on what I do.

They must have known he entered via the back door; he couldn't have left his scent anywhere along the front of the building. The back of the store had much better spots for sheltering from the cold. Could the dogs be smart enough to look for a spot where he would have a better chance of seeing them?

Looking at them through the glass doors made him think of looking down at that girl through the clear lid of her healing box. She *was* pretty, in a no-makeup, lying-on-her-back kind of way. But was she also smart? Was it possible that the girl who happened to be alive in that box would turn out to be the one girl about Laz's age who would actually allow him to talk with her? He certainly hadn't met many of those in middle school or high school. Not that he had done an exhaustive survey—after a few rejections you stop trying, right?

Then he thought of something. She was wearing her pajama-like clothes in the box. But Laz had been starkers, and only put on the clothes after he got out. He tried to remember the dried-up corpses in the other boxes he saw. They hadn't been wearing any clothes, either, had they? Weirdly, he could remember them both ways—no clothing, just shriveled-up skin stretched across bone; and then also with loose pajamas covering groin, torso, and legs.

Having contradictory memories was always a sign that Laz had side stepped. But he didn't remember doing so.

That meant he had done it reflexively. And now he knew exactly when and why. When he first found the coffin with the living girl inside, she must have been as naked as Laz had been, as all the corpses were. He remembered now that as he scanned along her body with his dim flashlight, it felt weird. It was a violation. How could he hope to establish a decent relationship with this person if she knew he had looked at her naked body while she was sleeping? He looked away. He remembered looking away.

But he also remembered seeing her for the first time, wearing those pajamas so she wasn't naked at all. So when he first found her naked and looked away, he had apparently side stepped into a timestream in which someone in the distant past had decided to clothe all the clones in the boxes, so they weren't lying there naked. He hadn't gone back in time, of course—*he* hadn't caused the change. He had only stepped into a stream where modesty had trumped economy.

What didn't change was this: Laz still had a clear memory of the girl, naked in the healing box, looking pretty from head to toe. He didn't want to remember seeing her like that. He also didn't want to forget anything about her. He was a human male, she was a human female, and that fact was going to be a part of their relationship, however it developed.

When he went to sleep on his uncomfortable tarp, with another tarp covering him, and a few closed umbrellas as a pillow, he tried very hard to think only of elephants getting devoured alive by lions, in order to distract himself from the image that kept trying to get to the surface: naked girl. Why did that memory keep coming back? Why couldn't he pick and choose which memories he carried with him when he side stepped?

He was thinking of orcas catching seals, tossing them up, and swallowing them whole, when he finally drifted off to sleep.

Plog 3

When I woke up I knew my name, knew my parents, remembered all the places I had lived, knew how old I was, remembered the normal array of random stuff from school. Like Lake Maracaibo, which is absolutely <u>not</u> a lake, since it's really a bay of the

Caribbean *Sea*, into which the tides dump more seawater every day. I remembered <u>that</u>, and how annoyed I was to find that it was sometimes considered the largest lake in *South America*, when that title clearly belongs to Lake Titicaca.

I can remember absolutely ridiculous stuff like that. So sure, my memory got vacuumed up and then they hosed it back in and all kinds of things are there.

Let's take seventh and eighth grade. I had a lot of great times with *Stever*. Neither of us took classes seriously because it was all so easy that we didn't bother studying. Sometimes I opened a book while I sat there waiting for a test to start, and that quick glance would raise my grade from a C to some level of B. If you can do that by just looking at headings in the textbooks, what was the point of meaningless homework or even showing up in class?

So *Stever* and I cut school kind of a lot, and even when we were there, we were messing around, pranking people. Not bullying pranks, like the jocks did, where you pick on weak people or scared people or outsiders. We picked on the jocks. We figured that putting a really hot pepper solution into the jockstraps of athletes was a kind of justice, after the stuff they did to other kids.

And it required skills. Picking the Master Locks in the gym dressing room, which I was best at, and dousing the straps with *Stever's* pepper formula, then putting the jockstraps back in the right lockers and refastening the locks and... that was so <u>sweet</u>, because the next time they put on those jockstraps was for a <u>game</u> against East, another middle school across town, one that our school usually dominated, and our guys could hardly walk, and half the team ended up fleeing for the locker room before the game was over.

Showering and soaping didn't help at all, not at first, it just spread the stinging around. Until like the fifth or sixth soaping. And the shower water hitting them in the crotch—that was painful, too. How could they get the shower to rinse them at the bottom edge of where the jockstraps went? That place behind the scrotum was where the pepper solution joined with chafing of cloth against skin, really rubbing it in, and that was also where the water was <u>least</u> likely to strike.

It was hilarious. Or at least, I remember that it was hilarious when Stever and I were imagining it, planning it, even doing it. So funny. Gonna be <u>so</u> funny.

I clearly remember this. Me and Stever laughing our brains out. It happened.

But I also remember getting called into the principal's office and thinking, how could anybody know it was us? They can't have security cams in the locker rooms because, like, privacy. But it wasn't cams. It was the fact that Stever had to <u>see</u> what was happening, so as these athletes were writhing naked on the shower floor, struggling to get the shower spray to rinse behind their scrota, there was Stever, not just watching, not just laughing, but taking pictures with his phone.

At first I assumed Stever ratted me out, and I was so pissed. But probably not. Everybody knew that if Stever did anything, I would be with him. And vice versa. We were that inseparable.

Only I wasn't with him, or I would have stopped him from going into the locker room because how stupid was that?

But then I have memories of Stever not getting us in trouble by such a stupid move. I mean of course I don't remember it not happening—how can you remember that? But I remember going months farther into eighth grade, long after football season, and Stever thinking of putting a pipe bomb under Vice Principal Evans's car, and that was one prank too many for me, bombs are too much like terrorism, but Stever did it anyway and in spite of both me and Stever insisting that I had not helped with that bombing in any way, and reminding them that nobody got hurt— Evans came out to his car and the bomb had already gone off and his car caught on fire and the gas tank blew up, but nobody was hurt—I still remember the principal and the police telling both of us, and our parents, that Stever and I were both going to stand trial, and both of us were permanently expelled.

I clearly remember that day, that hour.

Only that could not possibly have happened if we had been caught doing the peppercrotch prank, which I also remembered.

And that's where it got weird. Because I have tons of memories of both seventh and eighth grade where I was living a completely different life. Studying. Straight A's. Awards and commendations. No friends at all, except a few other smart kids who would talk to me, but no friends who felt like part of my own soul. In other words, seventh and eighth grades without Stever.

Why give me memories of two whole grades where Steven Weaver was the center of my universe, and of the same two grades without him?

How could they have played back into my head two contradictory sets of memories—three, if you count the caught-with-the-peppercrotching and not-caught-with-the-peppercrotching versions of the with-Stever memories? Why do I remember all of them as equally real?

If they were able to see my memories and edit them, selecting the ones they wanted, then how could they make sense of these wildly different memories? During the years without Stever, I remember <u>missing</u> him even though he wasn't at that school during those years. Yet I remembered the timestreams in which he existed, even as I lived through a timestream where he did not. That's when I realized that I kept memories of abandoned timestreams.

Sometime in the summer after eighth grade, getting ready for high school, thinking about everything that happened and then didn't happen after all, I was finally able to sort through my memories well enough to realize that the reason things always seemed to work out well for me, throughout my whole childhood, was because I had this ability to side step from one timestream to another. I think I was aware of it when I used it to help me open combination locks on the jocks' lockers—I started randomly turning the dials and then side stepped into the first timestream I found in which the lock opened—but those were easy, trivial changes, like getting rid of Mom's fling with the RV.

I think the first time I did something major with it was after the peppercrotch prank. The consequences were so unpleasant that I wanted it not to have happened. At first I wanted Stever to have had brains enough not to go in with a phone to take pictures of the suffering jocks. But then I wanted it not to have happened, because we caused real pain, and it wasn't funny. To me, anyway. I thought: How are we better than them, when we take pleasure in other people's suffering just like they do?

And inside my head, not really knowing what I was doing, I saw a path that skipped the whole thing, where we never acquired the stuff, where I never broke into the lockers, where we were, in fact, not such wretched little tormentors. And then I stepped across some invisible boundary.

I remember talking to Stever later and mentioning the peppercrotch incident and he had no idea what I was talking about. So I understood that I could move myself from one timestream to another, and remember both—but Stever only remembered what had happened in <u>this</u> timestream, the one where we didn't poison the jockstraps.

I have a power, I realized. I can do a thing that other people can't do.

So when we were facing prosecution because of a car bomb that, let's face it, <u>could</u> have really hurt someone—like if a bunch of kids had been leaning against the car talking when the bomb went off—I already knew I could make it all go away. But because I remembered Peppercrotch, I knew that as long as Stever and I were together in middle school, we would do stupid dangerous stuff.

And besides, by then I also realized that I didn't want to go into high school as a C-plus student. Having seen the shame and worry in my parents' eyes when I was facing trial, I realized that I wanted them to be proud of me.

I realized that I was bad for Stever, and Stever was bad for me.

I didn't erase him. I didn't hurt him in any way. I just stepped into a timestream where his dad never got the job that took him into Southern California and put Stever into the same school as me. Stever was still fine—I'm sure he was just as happy, or maybe happier, without knowing me.

I did not go back in time and fix things. That was the hard thing for me to understand myself. There is no such thing as time travel. Once something has happened, it happened—in that timestream.

But every decision point makes a new stream. As long as I exist in another timestream, I can side step into it. I don't go back and change anything, I simply move into a timestream where it's already been changed.

So I found a timestream where the Weavers hadn't moved to Southern California and Stever and I never met. And it happened that without Stever, I actually was a straight-A student. That's just what I had already chosen to do for the years of middle school, and I remembered being that student. And getting teased by jocks and ignored by the idiot "cool" girls but having other friends. Videogame and Dungeons & Dragons friends. Friends who also did their homework and studied for tests so doing all that didn't make me uncool to them.

I was both versions of me. The prankster jerk and the ideal student. I had freely made all those choices in both timestreams. I didn't have to go back in time and tell myself to shape up. I never got out of shape, morally speaking, in a timestream without Stever.

No, that didn't make all the prank stuff his fault. I made at least half the horrible choices. We just egged each other on.

And that's when I realized how I opened locks. I didn't

actually know how to pick locks, and besides, all the lockers had combinations anyway, how do you "pick" a lock with no keyhole? No, even then I simply held the lock and spun the cylinder right two turns, left one turn, and right again until it popped open. Only inside my head, I found the timestream—the incredibly unlikely but nevertheless already-existent timestream—in which those random spins happened to land on the correct numbers and the lock popped open. Stever was blown away by that, since to him it looked like I opened it on the first try. He kept demanding that I tell him the secret and called me six kinds of asshole when I wouldn't—but I couldn't, because at that time I didn't really understand how I was doing it. Till then all my side stepping was a reflex, an unconscious process. I simply knew that everything would turn out fine, and in the back of my mind, I made sure of it.

Later I did know. By using timestreams, I pretty much got an infinite number of tries at the combination, but I only had to physically work the combination once.

That was how I began to realize what I could do. What I can do. I doubt I would have understood it without Stever—without the dire pressure that made me need to change timestreams. I still owe the lad big time, though I came to live in a reality in which he and I never met.

And now I don't live in any of those timestreams. When they cloned me, they dumped all those memories in my head, so I remember making those discoveries and side stepping all those times—and a lot since then. But that wasn't me, that was the original Lazarus whose brain they raided and then dumped into my brain. I did none of that stuff. So I can't jump into any timestream that contains <u>him</u>, the original. I can only side step into timestreams that contain me, Mr. Junior Cloneboy.

As superpowers go, this one sucks. What is it good for? So far in my life—and the original Laz's life—all I've ever done is save myself from facing the consequences of my own bad decisions.

But you know what? It doesn't matter that nobody else has that capability, that other people have to pay for their misdeeds, or live them down. It's grossly unfair that I can skip out on all my penalties and they can't—but that doesn't mean I'm going to stop doing it.

Give me credit, though. I've spent my life—or, rather, the Original Heap of Protoplasm named Laz spent his life since middle school—trying to avoid the bad choices that make side stepping necessary.

And it wasn't entirely selfish. When Dad got in that horrible accident where he tried to avoid a drunken pedestrian on Sunset and put his car into a hydrant, that was a disaster I could choose for us not to live with.

So the Original Heap of Laz remembered the accident, the death of the pedestrian, all the suffering Dad went through, all wired up in the hospital, unable to talk, unable to stop weeping because he killed the guy. Therefore Laz also remembered those terrible hours.

But he also remembered that Original Heap of Laz had side stepped in order to live in a reality in which Dad had not had the accident. He had worked late that night. Nobody dead, nobody injured. Dad didn't have to spend months in rehab to relearn little things like walking. Dad's life was better.

So yes, now and then my little talent has helped somebody besides me.

Or has it? Because here's the big question. The one that keeps chasing me down and has made me waste all this paper and so much pencil that I've had to sharpen it five times for this plog.

I'm in this timestream. Original Heap was in a better timestream. But just because I, or he, left a timestream didn't wipe it out. There was still a whole reality, a whole set of realities in which that drunk pedestrian died and Dad's car killed him, in which Dad was all bashed up. And I didn't erase those timestreams, because nothing can. They're as real now as the timestream I'm living in. I'm just not there to see them.

Only I _am_ there. A version of me is there. A version of Original Heap of Protoplasm was there. So what is this "I" I keep talking about? What is it that steps from one timestream to another? "I" was already in every timestream I've ever side stepped into, and another version of me was left behind in every timestream I escaped from. Who is the "I" that side steps and remembers?

And are the left-behind versions of me still me? Is there a version of me, of Original Heap of Laz, that stood trial for the car bomb? A version of me that was outed and ostracized as a conspirator in the great Peppercrotch Incident? A version of me that couldn't open any of the lockers in order to get to the jockstraps? A version of me that's home taking care of my dad

77

because he was never able to recover from his injuries?

How many iterations of me, clone and Original Heap, are there in the world? And why am "I" the lucky one who gets to avoid all the bad consequences, while all the other versions of me can never get away with anything?

So here I am, still with that side stepping talent. Apparently it was built into my DNA so that cloning me preserved that talent. Only I have clear memories of a past that is not actually mine, even though they feel like they're mine. But I can't side step into any of the paths generated by other choices back in that life because that life isn't mine, wasn't mine. My life began when I woke up in a box in Coffin Central, Greensboro, North Carolina.

I remember very clearly, at the end of freshman year of high school, that a bunch of stuff happened—good stuff, but not terribly important stuff—and I found myself wanting to call Stever. I found myself typing his name into my phone so I could text him, only his name didn't cause a number to come up. I remember deciding to go home and google his name and find out what happened to Steven Weaver.

I don't remember if I ever did. I don't even remember if that means I did it, and hated what I found, so I side stepped into a reality where I never looked him up. I can't trust my memories, not because the Vivipartum people meddled with them, but because I meddled with them.

I miss my brain's infrastructure. I miss my brain. Because this isn't my brain. This is a copy, and it's a copy that did not develop its structures in response to my needs and experiences. It was created as a tabula rasa, with a fractal structure at best, pure chaos at worst, and my memories were forced into it and had to make their own pathways as best they could.

Somehow these memories of Stever were included in the process.

That's what I want. I want Stever here with me. I don't want to be alone.

Man, that was long enough that I should count it as a double issue. Plogs 3 and 4.

4

WHEN LAZ WOKE up, he didn't linger in his stiff-tarpaulin bed. He was cold and various parts of him ached from the hard floor. He needed to move.

He headed to the stock room and found his way to the bathroom. Business done, he went out into the store and located toothbrushes and toothpaste. He found his brand of both and headed back to the john. He was disappointed to find that nothing came out of the toothpaste tube—the contents had apparently dried up, even with the cap on. Still, a toothbrush and water were better than no toothbrush at all. Maybe he could mix up a version of toothpaste out of baking soda and water. Or tooth powder? Wasn't there some kind of tooth-cleaning concoction that didn't come in a tube?

Only when he laid the toothbrush down on the back of the sink did Laz remember what actually mattered today. First, he had to see if the Pack of Four were still in front of the store, and see about befriending them with more tuna. Second, he had to think about what to do about not-naked-anymore girl. He wasn't alone in the world, and that was something. But he had no idea how to wake her without damaging her, or even *if* he should waken her. Why should *she* be inconvenienced or endangered because he was lonely?

The dogs were still out front by the door. Leaderdog himself raised his head and looked at Laz. "Hi, StarKist," said Laz. "No, I'm not coming through that door. But I'll get some more tuna for you."

Laz went along the shelves and picked up a couple of tuna cans, and also a couple of cans of Vienna sausage and potted meat product. And a can of Spam. The dogs were smaller than he was, but they were painfully skinny, and they probably needed about as many calories as he did.

He opened all the cans and placed them inside a grocery bag— not the plastic kind, they were all gone, as were the paper bags. But the fancy reusable clothlike bags were still there, waiting for somebody to buy them. So he used one of those.

He went out the back door, wearing his backpack because what if it was locked when he came back? What if he had to find somewhere else to go? He didn't want his backpack to be inside the store if he had to abandon this place.

Laz walked all the way around the store to the front. Because the cans of meat and fish were all open, he wasn't surprised that StarKist was there to greet him when he rounded the corner. He had smelled Laz coming.

But StarKist didn't go for the bag with canned meat. He simply fell in beside Laz, maybe a little in front. As if he were leading Laz to the other three dogs. "You're a good leader, StarKist," said Laz. "Looking out for your pack before eating yourself."

Laz set down the bag and then reached in to bring out each open can. Using the end of his can opener, he poked the Spam out of its can. It came in several crumbly chunks. The dogs nosed it, but didn't eat. He shook out the Vienna sausages and pried out the potted meat product. Still the dogs didn't eat.

Then, at last, the tuna. He spilled it on the pavement in front of the dogs. Immediately the three pack dogs started eating it. StarKist ignored the tuna while they ate.

"You think I'm going to bring you a special private supply of tuna later, StarKist?" Laz asked the dog.

StarKist looked at him, then back down at the Spam and Vienna sausages.

Laz picked up one of the Vienna sausages and took a small nibble from the side that hadn't been on the ground. Then he put the rest of the sausage back on the pavement.

Now StarKist was willing to give the sausages a try. He chewed it a couple of times—Laz well knew that it was soft as baby food—and then spat it out.

"Well, excuse me if the cuisine isn't up to your standards, Monsieur StarKist," said Laz.

But no, StarKist thought about it a minute and then picked up the half-chewed Vienna sausage and this time swallowed it right down. Then another. Then another.

Now the other dogs noticed what was happening, and each of them got a sausage or two. Nobody threw up. But they did go back to nosing the empty tuna cans. They had a definite preference.

As for the Spam, Laz didn't care whether they liked it or not. It was meat, it probably had at least *some* food value left, so if they wanted food, there it was.

Laz walked away.

The three pack dogs stayed with the food. StarKist came with Laz.

"If you think I'm taking you into the store, think again," said Laz. "I don't want dog poo in there, or dog pee either. So whether you wait here in front or there in back is no skin off my nose, but you won't be going in."

StarKist didn't get the message, and tried to force his way past Laz as soon as he started opening the back door. Laz had to grab StarKist at the shoulders and heave him backward a couple of yards, then slip through the door and draw it closed. Fortunately, unlike the back door of the first Harris Teeter, this one closed quickly, automatically, and the latch made a satisfying click.

This time, there was no sound of a dog throwing himself against the closed door. Okay, StarKist was able to learn. Maybe he'd accept that he wasn't welcome inside the house. Maybe he'd go back to waiting in front with the rest of the pack. But Laz was glad he hadn't tried to open the front door. It was a modern door, so it had to have a way to open with a push. But crash bars and such were not meant to allow the door to be re-closed. So if he had tried to take food out to the dogs through the front, they would certainly have made it inside the store before he could stop them. He didn't want to have to walk around in the dark hoping not to step in dog poo. He imagined himself slipping on the stuff and falling down and cracking his skull on the unyielding floor. So he'd be concussed *and* smell like poo at the same time. Might as well invite a skunk into the store too.

He shouldn't work himself up to some kind of anger about the dogs. They were managing their conversion from feral into semi-domesticated with some ease. StarKist was showing traits of tameness, without losing his command over the others. Laz figured that when he went out on further expeditions, as long as he took cans of tuna or sausages, or jars of chipped beef or whatever, he wouldn't have to worry if he ran into the Pack of Four—or if they followed him from the start. They weren't fully tame yet, but they also weren't seeking to trap him and bring him down like a biped deer.

Laz knew he should go back and see if he could learn anything from the active computer at Vivipartum. Like who the girl was, and why she was alive, and whether it was safe to waken her. Or maybe find out the schedule when the machines were already planning to wake her up. Assuming that the machines had decided when to let Laz wake up. But Laz had no confidence in his ability to run computer programs that he wasn't familiar with, and that probably had security protocols that he wouldn't be able to get past anyway. Maybe if he started messing with the computer, though, that might finally alert somebody in some remote location that he was alive and awake and running around Greensboro, North Carolina. If that mattered to them, then they might come and explain things to him.

Or arrest him. Because he had been living a life of continuous crime ever since he got out of the box. But with everybody gone from this town, except for a handful of corpses in the Vivipartum parking lot, who was he hurting? He only made use of what they left behind when they skedaddled.

He didn't go back to Vivipartum that day, or the next, or the next. The girl would keep. His loneliness now was more tolerable, what with StarKist and his crew no longer trying to kill him, and a flush toilet and clean water source, and with the knowledge that another living human actually existed. In his own mind, he was considerably more at peace.

Even if he did wake up now and then with his face covered with tears, because he had dreamed of something about his mother or his father, and cried himself awake. He felt vaguely foolish, because he hadn't thought he was that close to either of them. But even though they'd been divorced for most of his life, they were why he was alive at all, and there was no way he could think of this whole cloning situation without assuming that they were now considerably older than he remembered them. If they were still alive at all. Whatever had happened to all the people in Greensboro must have happened to them as well. And he wasn't really their son, he was just a copy of their son. Would they even consider him to be their kin now? Or was he property? Legally, clones were just property. He hadn't cared much before, because what were clones to him?

Why hadn't he ever done something about Mom's and Dad's divorce? Surely there was some timestream where they had stayed together.

And now that he thought about it, yes, he started thinking about undoing the divorce after the Stever debacle when he first understood what he could and couldn't do. He thought of moving to a timestream where the whole family was together. He remembered even searching for such a timestream.

And then he stopped himself. He was in high school by then, but side stepping the divorce was only available on an extremely rare path in the Stever timestream.

Since the divorce was clearly his parents' overwhelming choice, he decided it would be better to stay in the timestream in which he was a good student and a much more cooperative and honest son to his parents, and he and Stever weren't devoted to destroying each other's future.

Upon sober reflection, Laz realized that his parents were both reasonably happy, and he could see no sign that either of them missed the other. They were both decent to Laz. Whatever caused their divorce—which happened before Laz was even in kindergarten—must have made them want to not be together. What if choosing a united-family timestream meant a home life of fighting and mistrust and anger and yelling and weeping, like some of his friends' parents? Laz couldn't remember his parents being together, or whether it had been good or bad. But if he chose that sole together-timestream, what if it was worse than this one?

In the middle of reviewing all his memories of his parents and of the time he found a path that had kept them together, it dawned on him that *those* were memories implanted in this brain. *He* had never had any such choice. *He*, clone Laz, never had any parents at all. He had memories of parents, but they were Original Laz's memories. Original Heap's parents. And he no longer had access to any of the timestreams that OrigiLaz had known of back in middle school.

Then he tried to figure out if he kept waking up crying because he missed his parents. Or because he never had parents.

He filled his days with something other than wandering around. He had pretty much explored Greensboro—not every inch, but certainly every main road. There were lots of buildings that might be worth breaking into, but his home at the running-water Harris Teeter was serving him well and he had no urgent need to search out another domicile. Now it was a matter of trying to improve his quality of life. It might be nice if, when the girl woke up, he could show her that he had actually accomplished something other than becoming a pretty decent stone thrower.

He found a couple of bicycle shops and while all the regular tires couldn't hold air, even if they didn't crumble under his fingers, there *were* some airless tires, which he found he could mount on some bicycle wheels. And then there were Kevlar tires, which retained flexibility and durability much better than the regular fabric-and-rubber tires. He couldn't find any tubes that would stay inflated for long, but once he found a bicycle pump that hadn't dried out completely and so could still pump air, Laz got himself onto a bicycle and rode around town on it.

The Pack of Four really enjoyed running after his bike and barking at him, and once he was sure that when he stopped they weren't going to attack him, it became a kind of game, taking the dogs out for a run. The real problem was the quality of the roads. Nothing had been repaired, and even though there weren't any cars or trucks putting wear and tear on the asphalt, winter still happened, and rain and tree roots, so there were cracks and potholes and places where the ground heaved up under a stretch of road.

The bicycle would have increased his range, but when he took the bike out of the city, the rural roads were apparently much weaker in their construction standards, or more susceptible to damage from nearby tree roots, because the roads were much more broken up. Also, storms had felled many trees across the roads, and nobody had come out with chain saws to break them up and get them out of the way. Laz soon gave up on using a bicycle as a way to get out of town and find out if maybe Greensboro was the only fully abandoned city.

Mileage signs on the big highways suggested that other towns were fairly near, but he had no idea whether Mayodan or Reidsville or Asheboro or Burlington would be bigger or smaller than Greensboro. At least Greensboro was big enough to supply his needs for a while. At some point, if he needed to, he would probably try to walk to another town or city, just to see if he could find somebody alive.

Unless, of course, what he found were loons with working shotguns who didn't take to strangers. But then he'd side step to a timestream where he was cautious enough not to go wandering alone.

Not that the dogs let him do much of anything alone. Apparently the way to make friends with a dog was to injure him and a buddy with a thrown rock, and then open cans of meat and fish for them.

If he walked too far, the not-so-naked girl might wake up while he was gone and find the city empty. If she wandered away from Vivipartum, would he be able to find her?

He began to check on her every few days. And pretty soon it was every day. He told himself that it was because he liked to look at another living human being. Even if it meant walking past the corpses in the abandoned cars.

He began making chalk marks on the concrete under an overpass, where rain wouldn't wash them away. He had no idea of a date, so he simply started making hash marks—four verticals and then a line through them.

Then he decided that because he still thought in weeks, he would make six verticals and then a slash, so each grouping would be a week. He had no idea how many days had passed between waking up and starting to make his calendar, but it was at least three or four weeks after he found the girl when he even began making the marks.

He could imagine showing his calendar to her, and she'd say, "Well, what was the starting date," and he'd say, "Date? It was still cool at night, but beginning to be pretty warm, and the whole town was in bloom, so, you know, spring." And then what would she say? What would she think? Scorn would be appropriate. "How long did it take you to even *think* of keeping track of the days?" And he'd have to answer, "I only started marking the days to keep track of how often I checked in on you to see whether your healing cave had woken you up yet."

"And how often did you do that?"

"Every day that I wasn't exploring in some other direction. Most days."

"What mark on the calendar says, 'I visited the girl in the box today'?"

He'd have to say, "I didn't mark that, because I usually came to mark the days *before* I knew whether I'd see you that day or not."

"So in what sense did this calendar help you remember anything about visiting me?"

And Laz would shrug and say, "During every week, I could still remember what I had done the day before and in the days before that. So I had a pretty firm idea that I visited your coffin four or five times a week. Sometimes six times. Sometimes every day."

"Thanks for keeping me company."

"You were a dull conversationalist," Laz might admit. "But since I never brought you flowers or chocolates, I guess I didn't earn anything from you."

And she'd say, "The chocolates I understand, since they wouldn't be edible, but if you didn't bring flowers, why did I wake up and find various kinds of flower stems and dried-out blossoms all over the floor?"

And he'd get all bashful and say, "Well, I *did* bring you flowers from people's abandoned gardens. For a while. But you never seemed to like them, so I gave up."

"When was the last time you brought flowers?"

And he'd sheepishly say, "Yesterday."

Because in fact he often collected flowers on the way to visit her, just in case he found her awake, and he could say, "Here, these are for you," and she could say, "And what the hell am I supposed to do with these?" And he would have no answer at all, because he'd never have the courage to say, "Braid them into a crown and wear them on your head?" The only time he had seen girls do anything like that was in grade school.

He conducted a lot of imaginary conversations like that. So even asleep in her healing cave, she was providing him with decent company. A little challenging, sometimes, because she had *such* a mouth on her, and he was more than a little awkward and shy with her. She blew everything he said out of the water. She always knew when he was lying or faking or pretending to be cooler than he was. With any luck, the *real* girl would wake up and be much kinder to him than his imaginary version of her.

One time he and the dogs walked north on US 29, which was wide enough not to be blocked by any one fallen tree. It wasn't a commercially built-up road, so he couldn't go all that far, because he only had the supplies in his backpack and was unlikely to be able to replenish them. It had signs promising that someday it would be a freeway in the Interstate Highway System, but apparently that had never happened, not before everybody was evacuated, anyway. Laz just enjoyed the walk on a sunny morning in early summer, and the dogs frolicked along with him, and it was kind of like being alive.

He had a lot of things to think about and even worry about. For one thing, he was losing weight—and because he had come out of the box with relatively little body fat, the weight loss had to be muscle. He was eating plenty of canned meat, but he had no way of guessing how much food value remained in those old cans. Apparently not enough. He could eat till he was full, but he woke famished every morning, and he had less energy now than when he first woke up in Vivipartum. The only rational conclusion was that on a diet of old canned food, he was slowly starving to death. It couldn't be any more nourishing to the dogs. But what choice did he have?

Maybe when the trees and bushes started bearing, he could find nuts with all their protein value. Fruits would come into season, though he wasn't sure which trees were fruit-bearing. He had some idea that acorns weren't edible for humans, and he didn't know what other kinds of nuts might grow. He was beginning to find blueberries that were ripe enough to eat without getting diarrhea, though he had to compete with birds and squirrels to get any of the fruit at all. There were wild strawberries everywhere, but they were tiny and nearly flavorless, most of the time—though every now and then there were wild strawberries that were crazy sweet and tart. He learned that the good strawberries had fruit that hung downward, and the bland ones had fruit that stuck upright. Wow, I'm practically a naturalist, to notice that, he thought.

That was the kind of thing passing through his mind when he noticed that the dogs were barking pretty incessantly and it didn't sound frolicsome anymore. He looked for them. They weren't on the road so it took a while walking toward the sound before he saw them well off the road barking at something in the woods.

Then they suddenly took off running right toward Laz. And behind them lumbered a black bear with a couple of smaller bears right behind her.

Not that he could tell the sex of the bear at that distance, but from what documentaries had taught him about bears, this could only be a mother with half-grown cubs. The dogs had probably started barking at the cubs, and now Mama was coming to deal with the dogs.

In all likelihood, the dogs could outrun the bear. But Laz

couldn't. Thanks a lot, StarKist. I was really hoping to get killed by an angry mother bear.

But instead of running away, Laz side stepped into a timestream where he had *not* gone to find out what the dogs were barking at. Instead, he had timidly gone back toward Greensboro, away from the barking dogs. When the mother bear emerged from the woods in pursuit of the dogs, Laz was so far away he doubted the bear even noticed him, though she *could* have seen him.

By the time the dogs caught up with Laz, the bear was completely out of sight. Laz wondered if there were timestreams where the bear killed some of the dogs. Or killed Laz, while the dogs watched and then, when he was dead, joined in feeding on his corpse.

He decided that it was not worth trying to find out.

On the day of the bear, having realized that he might die without the girl ever reviving, he went to Vivipartum as soon as he got back to town. Only instead of going down to look at her in her coffin, he went to the computer room and sat down in front of the screen. There was a keyboard. There was a mouse. And when he moved the mouse, the screen changed.

At the top, it said, in blinking letters, "Date not found."

Well, of course. It would have been too nice of the people of Greensboro to leave him a working computer that kept track of the date and time.

A log-in screen popped up. It wanted a username. And the space was already filled in with seven dots. Was it possible that the username had auto-filled? He pressed enter. The screen returned with a request for a password. And again, the space was filled, this time with eight dots. Whoever worked at this terminal should be fired, he thought, for leaving his machine so vulnerable to any intruder.

He pressed enter. Apparently the password had been auto-filled, too, because he was in.

The screen showed about a dozen icons. Laz found three of them that weren't obviously games. One of those was a game, too. But the two non-game icons both brought up software that seemed to maintain lists of this and that.

He couldn't find a list of the names of the inmates of the coffins, but he did find a list of names of the owners.

He only recognized one of the names, but he hadn't expected to recognize more than that. The owner of one box turned out to be Narek Tigran Hojrian.

Laz's dad.

The status of that box was hard to interpret. But by comparing it with the status of a few other boxes, he found that the ones with corpses inside were "lapsed." There were others that were "vacant," so maybe not all the boxes had corpses. Laz's own box—or rather, the box his father owned—was listed as "complete."

He scanned the lists looking for any that didn't say lapsed or vacant. None of them said "complete" except his own.

Finally, far down the list—and there was nothing like alphabetical order involved—he found an entry for a box that was "pending."

The owner was someone named Arya Daenerys Lopez. Laz had no idea what language the first two names were in, but he recognized Lopez as Hispanic. He tried to think whether the girl looked Latina or Spanish or—

And then, because the only picture of her that came into his mind involved his memory of her without pajamas, he stopped trying to decide. He just kept scanning the list. And even though there were hundreds of entries, by the end, the only two that weren't lapsed or vacant were Laz's box, "complete," and the box owned by Lopez, marked "pending."

He wondered if the girl in the box was named Arya Daenerys Lopez, or if that was her parent. The box might have been owned by the original of the girl, in which case she would wake up thinking her name was the same as the name of the owner. But maybe it was a parent, just like the owner of Laz's coffin, in which case he still had no idea of the girl's name.

Laz scanned through all the other lists offered by the program and came to the conclusion that this program was only informational—he couldn't see a way to make any alterations. If there was a command that said, Wake up the pending girl, he didn't find it.

So he switched to the other non-game program. This one was full of gibberish. Commands that meant nothing to him. And no lists at all.

He opened both programs at once and figured out how to tile them on the screen. Now he found a code number associated with his own coffin and entered it into various fields in the other program, to see what happened. After all, he wasn't *in* his box, so if he accidentally issued a wrong command, it wouldn't hurt anybody.

Mostly when he entered his box code, nothing happened or the program came back with "Not a valid entry." But in a couple of the fields, entering the code brought up a menu. One item on the menu was "report." He clicked on it, and immediately there came a small report, which said, "Complete. Perfect health. Self-actuated exit."

That didn't seem to have damaged anything. So . . . safe enough? He entered the code from the Lopez coffin and clicked report.

The result was a much longer report, headed by "Pending." It included, not a summary like "perfect health," but a lot of very specific numbers, some of which he recognized or could guess at—pulse, blood iron and oxygen levels, hormone levels or glandular activity, various scans—and others that were completely inscrutable to him.

He didn't know whether he needed to know more about anatomy or about computers in order to understand them. But the report said that she was alive. And if he knew what "pending" meant, he might have some idea whether she was ready to be wakened or not.

He also had no idea whether *he* was ready to waken her.

But "pending" suggested that the program was waiting for some kind of change—perhaps a command from the computer console, perhaps some aspect of her condition in the box, or maybe a command from a faraway computer controlled by somebody else.

It was getting late. Laz had no watch, but his level of sleepiness told him that it was time to get back on the street so he could reach his Harris Teeter before dark.

The dogs were waiting in the main lobby of Vivipartum. They didn't exactly leap for joy when they saw him, but they got up and padded along after him. He walked onto the couch and through the doors; they leapt on and off after him. They headed north without waiting to see where he would go. So they knew the way home, and assumed that he was going there. That was good.

He wondered if he should have turned off the computer, but he decided not. It had already been on when he arrived, so it woke up with nothing but the moving of a mouse. It probably would blank out after a certain period of inactivity, so it was okay he hadn't turned it off. Probably.

He got back home to the Harris Teeter with the toilet, shut the back door with no dogs getting through—they really didn't make a serious try anymore, though they still offered to come in with him.

He lay down on top of the tarps—the weather was warm enough that he didn't need to cover himself. He slept in the clothes he was wearing now, shorts and a T-shirt, in case he needed to get up in the night.

As he drifted off to sleep, he wondered if at some remote location, somebody had noticed that the computer at Vivipartum had been accessed. Maybe in a while somebody would reach out to him. Maybe when he got back to the computer—tomorrow? In a week?—he'd get an instant message from somebody on the network, saying something friendly like, "Hi, Laz," or "Who the hell is using this computer!" He would answer politely either way.

He didn't dream about the bear getting him. Maybe he would have, but he woke up in the middle of the night, perhaps before bear dreams were scheduled to begin.

Laz lay there for a few moments, trying to think what had woken him. It wasn't his bladder. It wasn't some animal licking his face or biting his toes.

He heard the distant slamming of a door.

Ah, that would explain it.

Laz sat up, pulled on his shoes as quietly as he could, then picked up his backpack, in case he had to make his escape without further warning. He did not pick up a weapon, because he had no idea how to fight with anybody who was likely to show up at this store.

There was another person in this city. Heck, the good news was that there was somebody alive in the *world*.

Unless it was the girl. Lopez, or whoever she was. Could she have woken up on her own? But how would she know to come here?

Laz thought of going to the back of the store and confronting whoever was there. But after so many months of solitude, he felt weirdly shy about meeting whoever was in the building. It was probably somebody who used this place as a way station—a restroom, at least—and he undoubtedly expected the place to be unoccupied.

Laz quietly walked out from behind the customer service counter and padded noiselessly—or so he thought—toward the front entrances. It was still nighttime outside, but there was about a half moon, so some light filtered into the store.

"Don't bother trying to leave," said a man's voice from the back of the store. "I know you're here, and I'm not going to hurt you or, really, do anything at all. So there's no reason to try to get away."

The man's voice sounded calm and unthreatening.

Laz said nothing.

"Or you can go, if you want. I've already made my report about you, so please don't bother trying to kill me, if you're desperate to keep your presence here a secret. The secret's out."

Laz walked back into the main part of the store. "Where are you?" he asked.

"Entrance to the stock room," said the man. And then the lights came on.

Laz was blinded, and stood there blinking and feeling foolish. "I tried all the switches," he said.

"You have to turn on the master switch first," said the man. "When that's on, you can turn on a few other things. Not everything. The refrigerators and freezers have been dismantled and raided for parts long ago."

By now Laz could see fairly well. The guy was leaning on the dairy case beside the stockroom door.

"So there are working refrigerators somewhere else?" Laz asked.

"In the New Place, of course," said the man. "As you well know."

"Actually," said Laz, "I have no idea what you mean by New Place. Is this the Old Place?"

"This is the old Earth," said the man. "Only they're both Earth. But come on, what game are you playing? You snuck through the Portal somehow, because there's nobody authorized to be in Greensboro or, really, anywhere between the Portal and California. So, you know, good for you. It's hard to get through the Portal without triggering a massive manhunt. But now they know you're here, so law enforcement will undoubtedly arrive soon to take you back."

"How can I go *back* to a place where I've never been?" asked Laz. "And what is this Portal?"

The man laughed. "Okay, play it however you want. If you stay here, they'll give you a nice helicopter ride back to the Portal and then figure out where you're from and find out how you snuck through. You look young, so if you're a minor, they'll turn you over to your parents, unless they were in on this with you. If your parents are looters, it'll go hard with them, but if you're still legally a child, you'll just get a slap on the wrist."

"If you aren't law enforcement," said Laz, "who *are* you?"

"Truck driver for Harris Teeter," said the man. "There are still some things that only grow well in California, so we're keeping a bunch of farmers there until the last possible minute, which probably isn't for a few years yet. Or months, they don't report things like that to me. I drive a refrigerated truck to bring produce back to the Portal so we can supply the New Place. I have way stations all across the country, and when a road gets impassable, I call out a crew to clear it or patch it."

So somebody *was* doing road maintenance. Just not on the roads where Laz had cycled or hiked.

The guy seemed pleasant enough, and Laz had to find out whatever he could. "Let's pretend," said Laz, "for the sake of argument, that I didn't pass through the Portal. Let's pretend that I woke up in a clone factory here in Greensboro, and I have no idea why this city is empty or why anybody would hunt down someone who came through a Portal."

The man laughed. "Oh, you're a clever one. But there's nothing working here, nothing electronic, except a few fixtures in this store. Greensboro is part of the dead zone—can't even connect with a cell tower. It's all satellite through this area. So no, I don't buy the story of a clone farm."

"That's why I said we should *pretend* that I don't know anything, as if I *were* from a clone factory or farm or whatever. Maybe even one called Vivipartum."

"That's the name of the biggest chain of clone shops," said the man, "but they were shut down years ago, when clones here in the Old Place were declared to be a waste of resources."

"I know. Almost all the others were dead and dried up in their coffins."

"Speaking hypothetically, I'm sure," said the man. "Since we're just pretending impossible things now, right?"

"What's this New Place versus Old Place thing?" asked Laz.

"About forty years ago, astronomers detected a wandering planet about the size of Jupiter and Saturn combined. It was probably flung from some faraway solar system when its star went nova or something. Anyway, it's just a stone-cold ball of ice careening along, influenced by the gravity of a lot of different stars. It took about three years of tracking it before its likely trajectory could be calculated. But this is all high school stuff, so you already know it."

"Pretending. Hypothetically. I know absolutely nothing, so this is news to me. Does this planet have a name?"

"In every language, they called it something different. In English, the Brits and Canadians called it Zeus. The Aussies and Kiwis called it Gallipoli. In America, the name that caught on was Shiva."

"Because Hinduism is so important to Americans," said Laz.

"Because Shiva is the Destroyer," said the Harris Teeter man.

"So the planet is going to collide with Earth?"

The man laughed. "Not likely. Earth doesn't have enough gravity to attract a planet that size. No, it's not going to collide with anything. But it's going to pass close enough, to the south of our solar system, that all the big planets will change their orbits just a little."

"We don't live on the big planets," said Laz.

"But their gravity affects us. So when Jupiter slows down a little and moves closer to the Sun, and so do Saturn and the other big guys, the inner planets all go crazy. Mercury and Venus will go into the Sun within a few months. Earth will take longer, but after six months we'll be too hot here for anything to be alive. End of the world."

"Well, good-bye, then," said Laz.

"Except!" said the man.

"A race of aliens came along and offered to take us to a safe planet light-years away?" asked Laz.

"No. Instead, scientists figured out a way to open a Portal between this doomed version of Earth and a different version where Shiva isn't coming."

Laz recognized this as sounding a little like his own ability to side step. But to take the whole world along? That would be crazy powerful.

"About a dozen Portals were opened, some on every populated continent, leading to different places on the newer, safer Earth," Harris Teeter Man said. "Everybody's been quite civilized about it. Like, Indians and Pakistanis are using the same Portal, and Israelis and Arabs, and nobody's killed anybody. Like that."

"Hard to believe," said Laz. "I'll take your word for it."

"You should. I taught high school history for ten years. I know what I'm talking about because I lived through it. I know you're actually interested because two or three times in my teaching career, I had a student who actually cared, who wanted to learn, so I know that look on your face."

"But now you drive a truck."

"I drove a truck when we were first loading all of civilization through the Portal," said Harris Teeter Man. "Everybody had to help with that. So when they needed a truck driver again, to bring produce with certain microbes in it from the soil of California, I volunteered. Nobody should do the same job for more than ten years. You start to think that's who you are."

"So the New Place is utopia. Or . . . is it heaven?" asked Laz.

"It's peaceful, compared to the Old Place," said Harris Teeter Man. "The New Place is well settled, with productive agriculture and industry. A new world economy there. They did everything as cleanly as possible. Trying to get it right on a planet that never had any land animals bigger than insects until we got there."

"Come on," said Laz.

"It couldn't be just like old Earth. Finding a place with Shiva not bent on a course of destruction meant a timestream in which things were a little different from the Big Bang on outward."

Laz was thinking: And if it's that different, I could never have found the place, because I wouldn't already have been there. I can side step only to places where I can find myself.

"Evolution started differently," said Harris Teeter Man, "and later, as near as anybody can tell. No vertebrates yet, not even in the ocean. And yes, all our animals and useful insects and microbes and, of course, our plants are wreaking havoc with the old ecosystem, but we needed a place where *we* could live, not a museum of alien flora and fauna. We've exported every kind of fish and amphibian and reptile and mammal and bird, and the New Place is already swarming with recognizable life. Including billions of humans. It took a long time to get everybody through the Portals—and a lot of people didn't want to come because they had to leave most of their possessions behind. But now they can buy new stuff manufactured there. And we didn't leave anybody a choice about whether to come."

Somebody must have invented a side-stepping machine that was way more powerful than Laz's pathetic little inborn talent.

"Well," said Laz, "when they were shutting down all the clone farms, they overlooked me. I'm a little hurt by that, but presumably the original version of me still exists so nobody wants the new copy to show up. Still, if *this* world is going to burn up, I think I'd rather go to the New Place. If any of this is true."

"It's all true. You know it's true, kid. But this is all wearing thin. I've had my piss and my drink of water, and I'm going to catch a nap in the cab of my truck. You can stay asleep here—the choppers probably won't come till daylight to pick you up. I'm not any kind of law enforcement, so I won't try to detain you or track you or anything because that's their job. They have the tools for it."

Laz smiled. "Thank you for telling me all this. There's not a scrap of printed paper in this town—no newspapers, no history books, no magazines, and of course no computers so I could look anything up. There was no way for me to know anything about this."

The man smiled and shook his head. "You're persistent, that's for sure." Then he turned away and went back into the stock room.

"Wait!" called Laz.

The man reappeared in the doorway.

"I haven't had any fresh food for months. I'm kind of starving to death on the contents of the cans on the shelves—they apparently don't have many nutrients left. You have fresh food in your truck?"

"You've been living on the cans here?" Harris Teeter Man asked. "Well, you're right, they're in pretty sad shape, not much food value."

"It's all I could find." Laz was hoping he'd take the hint and offer him some fresh produce from his truck.

"Bag yourself a deer," said Harris Teeter Man. "Trap some raccoons. Plenty of fresh meat that way. But take my word for it, opossum is way too oily and stringy. You have to be desperate before you go for rat-tailed marsupials."

"I'll kill me a coon with a pea blown through a soda straw," said Laz. "Or maybe I can throw a rock hard enough to bring down a deer."

"Oh, that's right. They took all the guns. Tough on an illegal like you."

"How am I illegal?" asked Laz. "I was *manufactured* here."

"It's illegal to be here without a license like mine and all the farmers in California. We're all guaranteed a pickup before the Portal becomes impassable. But illegals like you aren't promised anything."

"Not nice," said Laz.

"Sneaking through the Portal illegally isn't nice either," said Harris Teeter Man.

"And waking up in a clone box at Vivipartum is obviously not a good thing either," said Laz.

"Whatever," said the man. "Sleep tight, kid."

"Like *that's* going to be possible now," said Laz.

"Your call. By the way, you got a name?"

"My friends call me Laz," said Laz. "And so do total strangers."

"Your name is Laz, and you claim you don't know anything." The man chortled as he went back into the stock room.

What does my name have to do with anything? Laz wanted to ask him. But he was gone.

Apparently nobody was going to believe that he was created in this town. He was going to be treated like an interloper. An illegal immigrant to the Old Place.

He had to decide whether to sit there and wait for law enforcement to take him to a civilized world with billions of people in it who were *not* all trying to kill each other. Which seemed like a good idea. Or whether he should hide from them until he could find out more about himself and Vivipartum and the girl. Which sounded crazy. Except that if they refused to listen to him or take him seriously, what would happen to *her*? She would eventually wake up, as he had, and then what? If he was gone, she'd be as lost and alone as he had been. And maybe she'd never meet Harris Teeter Man and get an account of what was going on. Maybe she wouldn't get any help before she starved to death eating canned food with fading nutrients. Maybe StarKist and his buddies would kill her and eat her. Maybe she'd run afoul of a bear.

I don't owe her anything, thought Laz. I certainly have no reason to die for her. I'll tell the law enforcement people about her. I have a name for the owner of her healing cave, so they can check, right? They'll check, they'll find out I'm not lying, and she'll be saved.

Only she's a clone. She has no legal existence, no rights. Would they even spend the money and time to check on her at Vivipartum? Letting her burn up with the Old Place would be fine with a lot of people. Clones just complicated things.

He couldn't just let them take him away until he knew that she'd be all right. Besides, when they realized he really *was* a clone, and not an escapee from the New Place, what would they do with *him*? Push him back through the Portal so he, too, could fall into the Sun, the ultimate garbage disposal unit?

Laz walked back to the front of the store, ascertained that the dogs were all at the east door, and walked briskly to the west door. He followed the instruction to "In Emergency PUSH Door." It opened with difficulty because nobody was lubricating anything here at the front of the store. But he still managed to close it tightly again, and felt a catch get set so that it wouldn't just fall open. Apparently he finished up just in time, because when he turned around, there was the Pack of Four, watching him expectantly, like children saying, "Are we there yet?"

Laz had no idea where "there" was.

But he knew there was a truck behind the store that had fresh produce from California. There might not be anything the dogs would like, but Laz didn't like how much weight he had already lost.

If the guy hasn't gone to sleep yet, I'll ask if he can spare me some.

If Harris Teeter Man *is* asleep, I'll see whether I can get the truck open without waking him.

Laz came around the corner of the building and there was the truck. He had been expecting something with wheels, but no, it only had struts to stand on. He realized that it must ride on a cushion of air, so it was never actually in contact with the road while it traveled.

Self-aiming solar panels covered the roof of the trailer. Did the thing really run on solar-generated electricity, or did it use some kind of fuel?

Laz couldn't see Harris Teeter Man anywhere.

Laz walked quietly around to the back of the truck.

Harris Teeter Man was standing there. "I heard you ask about the food I was carrying," he said to Laz. "I know you want it. I know you need it. But when I said to bring down a deer, I meant it. The animal's fat will contain all the vitamins and minerals you need. There are also herbs growing around here that will supply vitamins and minerals."

"Somebody took all the books away from the library," said Laz. "And my laptop can't find any Wi-Fi to connect to. No internet."

Harris Teeter Man nodded. "I'm beginning to think you may very well be telling some version of the truth. Maybe they didn't completely shut down all the clone farms. Maybe you are exactly what you say you are."

"That's my opinion, anyway," said Laz.

"Here's a fact. There's a complete inventory of this truck, weighed down to the gram. If I don't have my complete load when I arrive, minus the ordinary losses from the passage of time, it's not just a black mark on my record, it's a crime. A serious crime."

"So," said Laz, "not quite a utopia after all."

"We're feeding billions of people in the New Place, and agriculture is just starting up. Very little of what I'm carrying is intended to be eaten, it's meant to be grown in the ground in the New Place, it's meant to have its holobiome harvested and the soils and animal skin and guts invested with microbes that the New Place lacks."

"While I starve to death," said Laz.

"I hope you don't. In fact, I know you won't, because the authorities are already on their way to rescue you."

"And by 'rescue' I think you mean 'haul me off to jail'?"

"Not my purview, son. I didn't put you here, I just found you. And, hey, thanks for taking care of the restroom. Neat and clean. Back in the New Place, there are a lot of people who have no idea how to treat a public restroom."

"Next time you come through here, maybe I'll be sitting on the commode, dead as a doornail. I promise that I don't mind if you just shove me out of the way. I only ask that you refrain from peeing on my corpse."

"You won't be here," said Harris Teeter Man.

"A single apple?" asked Laz.

"There's a truck from Washington that carries apples."

"Avocados?"

"Laz, is that what you call yourself?" asked Harris Teeter Man.

"It's what my dad and mom called me, so it seemed reasonable for me to continue the tradition."

"Laz, I've got nothing against you. I like you. But if you come any closer to this truck, the defense mechanisms will automatically kick in. I can't stop them. You and the dogs will probably die, either immediately or within a few hours."

"Wow. Things are getting pretty unfriendly. I think I'll head back down Elm Street."

"What an excellent plan," said Harris Teeter Man. "I wish you well."

Laz waved his hand airily. "Been nice attending your class."

Laz got to Elm Street and turned left. Back toward Vivipartum. Then he led the dogs off the street and into people's yards and along the backs of buildings.

"Perhaps you're wondering why I called this meeting," Laz said to the Pack of Four.

Nobody responded.

"We're going to go somewhere," said Laz, "and hide from helicopters and thermal sensing devices. Try to be as hot as possible, kids, because I want them to sense mostly you, and see me as a fifth dog in the pack. And maybe if we're inside a building somewhere, the thermal imaging won't even pick us up. What do you think?"

Everything Harris Teeter Man had said was so weird that it wouldn't even be all that surprising if StarKist had answered him, saying, "Sounds fine to me, boss."

There were choppers with searchlights over in the direction of the Harris Teeter store by the time they got to Vivipartum. So the cops hadn't waited till daylight.

Laz went over the couch into Vivipartum. Once he and the dogs were inside, he pulled the couch back into the foyer, allowing the doors to fall shut behind it. He had enough supplies to last him and the dogs for a couple of days. They could poop wherever they wanted. He was going to be several levels down, trying to figure out what "pending" meant and how to get the Lopez girl out of her coffin and into the land of the living before the world burned up. Thermal imaging surely couldn't locate him two or three basement levels down. And if they flew along the street, they wouldn't see a couch holding the door open. He didn't think he'd need any more concealment than that. They wouldn't work too hard to find a petty lawbreaker whose biggest crime was apparently sneaking past security at an interplanetary Portal.

My third favorite utility: Sewage systems that carry away both pee and poo, out of sight, gone, done away, no permanent stench, no attracting flies, the world's best vanishing act. And along with it, clean water-soluble toilet paper that doesn't carry as many biting insects, fungi, and bacteria as fallen leaves do.

5

IF A HELICOPTER had landed near Vivipartum, if scary-looking men had jumped out and made any kind of approach, friendly or hostile, Laz would have side stepped to a timestream where they didn't do that, or to a stream where he wasn't inside the building, or a stream where he had never been found by Harris Teeter Man.

But they didn't approach the building. And soon the chopper noises were far away and getting fainter. He cheerfully said aloud, "Looks like you scared them off, StarKist. Good watchdog."

StarKist took this praise as if it had been well deserved by some extraordinary and invisible action of his own. Who says dogs aren't like people?

Laz wasn't going to get cocky. He wasn't leaving this building again tonight.

He opened cans of tuna and sausages and a couple of kinds of pasta. "Sorry to make you lick this off the floor, but it's better than the concrete outside," he said to the Pack of Four. They were lapping it all up as Laz headed down to the computer station.

Maybe he should have checked the girl's coffin first, to see if she was either dead or out of the box. But he figured the computer would tell him.

It did. She was still pending.

He began to read all the commands on all the menus, trying to see if he could make sense of any of them. There wasn't a waken command or a kill command, so the two things he knew *could* happen weren't apparently within his power to *cause* to happen.

He went back to the program that seemed to be all about reports, found the Lopez coffin's record, and read every number on every report associated with it. He compared them with the readouts from the dead people, which still contained data, and he began to try to figure out which numbers were all about the difference between alive and dead, and which ones were carrying different information.

The data in these reports had meant something to someone, or the programs and the coffins wouldn't have been designed to collect it and display it.

His breakthrough came when he realized that two of the reports were not about what was going on with the body in the coffin, but were rather about whether the coffin itself was functioning properly. He found that only three coffins reported themselves as nonfunctional, and those three were all unoccupied and unowned. But the Lopez coffin was listed as functional. Every part of it was functional.

And every functional part was testable, from this remote location.

He didn't play with anything that looked like life support. But he did find a routine for testing the closure of the healing cave.

He initiated the test sequence. The report came back instantly— too quickly for the lid to have opened and closed again. All functional.

Then he tried a couple of commands on the same menu and the report was not so quick. When it came, it said, "open."

And back on the first big list, the Lopez healing cave no longer said "pending." It said "delivering."

Like birth.

Surely this was what the report must have said about Laz's coffin when he lay there trying to figure out where he was.

She'll be doing that right now.

Or gasping for air, or screaming because her memory dump wasn't complete, or lying there dead staring at the ceiling.

But just in case my fiddling didn't kill her . . .

He practically flew down the stairs to the big coffin room where he had found her. He flipped on the lights. Now it was obvious which box was hers—it was the only one with an open lid.

She sat up in the box, using her arm to shelter her eyes from the bright light.

"Sorry," said Laz, still at a distance, about five rows away. "We've only got two choices, too dark and too bright. Bright's better."

She nodded vaguely, but didn't try to look at him. Well, that's fine—that would delay the moment when he would see her be disappointed that it was only him there to meet her.

"They didn't send anybody to meet *me*," he said.

"Somebody sent you here?"

"No," said Laz. "I sent myself, because it was confusing to *me* when I first woke up in the dark and nobody came."

"So you're here to explain everything to me?" she asked.

"I can only explain what I actually understand myself."

"Do you understand your own name?" she said.

Laz didn't get the question.

"Tell me your name," she said, now with a tone like someone explaining something to a very stupid child.

"Laz," he said.

"Is that short for something?" she asked.

"Lazarus Davit Hayerian," he said. "But Armenian names usually confuse people."

"That's just stupid," she said. "Everybody knows the name Lazarus Davit Hayerian. But sure, I'll call you Laz."

"Can I call you something besides Coffin Girl, or maybe Only Surviving Woman?"

She now had her eyes fully open and she looked at his face, as if trying to read something there. "Did you open my healing cave?" she asked.

"I may have set off the sequence, from the computer room."

"Did you *mean* to set it off?" she asked.

"Do you have a name?" asked Laz. "Before you ream me out for doing something wrong, I'd at least like to know who's mad at me."

"I'm not mad," she said.

"You sound totally pissed."

"I always sound like that," she said.

"Why?" he asked.

"Because I'm always pissed off. And sometimes *totally* so."

"And yet nameless," said Laz.

"If I tell you my name, you'll be able to cast a spell on me."

Laz paused, wordless. Could she possibly be that disconnected from reality?

"I'm Ivy," she said. "At some point, I'd be glad to give you a lesson in a thing called 'joking.'"

"So we're both blessed with three-letter names," said Laz. "Assuming you spell Ivy like the plant."

"Except Ivy really is my first name, complete. Whereas Laz is just a nickname."

"Why would anybody know the name Lazarus Davit Hayerian?"

She grinned, then looked around. "This is a clone farm, isn't it," she said.

"It was. But the only two living clones are awake now, so we're harvested and ready for market. The others are dead, so I think this place is now a sepulcher. A mausoleum."

"Only two of us?"

"This world is ending, so all the clone farms were shut down. Except for a couple of coffins here, and probably a few in other places. Or not. They don't make reports for my edification."

She hoisted herself up onto the lip of the coffin and then dropped to the floor. She was already wearing the slippers.

"We can head straight for a department store, Ivy, so you can get better clothing. Better shoes especially. When I woke up it was still winter, I think. No leaves on the trees, and a wind that could suck the breath right out of your mouth."

"I take it that it's warmer now?" she asked.

"I can't give you numbers, Ivy, because I haven't found a working thermometer."

"Or a calendar?"

"Nothing."

"Can't even look at your phone?" asked Ivy.

He shook his head and looked somewhere other than at her.

"My full name," she said, "is Ivy Maisie Downey."

"Lots of 'ee' sounds at the end of every name," said Laz.

"When I find my mother, I'll be sure to tell her that a brilliant critic has condemned her choice of names for me."

"All three names end in 'ee' sounds," said Laz. "Not a criticism, not a condemnation, just a fact."

"A fact I've been aware of since I first started acquiring language."

Either she already hates me, thought Laz, or she's a complete jerk.

"Sorry for noticing it out loud. Still too early in our friendship for me to know what's going to tick you off."

"So why are we still standing down here?" asked Ivy.

"I don't want to rush you," said Laz.

"Or are you just remembering how I look naked?" she asked.

He froze.

"Oh, yes, I see. You looked away and hopped to another reality immediately, didn't you. So you think that makes it all right."

How could she possibly know that he had seen her naked? That was in another timestream. She shouldn't have any idea of that.

"I've always been able to see timestreams," she said. "I read about your scientific work in timestream theory a couple of years ago. If it's actually you, since I had the impression you were, like, forty years old."

"I only have memories up to age seventeen," said Laz. "You've heard of me?"

"A clone farm, right. So I guess I've heard of your original."

"*I* haven't," said Laz.

"You're quite possibly the most famous scientist in the world," she said.

"Not likely. I'm not particularly good at science."

"You will be by age forty," Ivy answered.

"So I've been awake for months, struggling to stay alive, completely alone, and finally I manage to get the other clone in the building to wake up, and you already know *everything*?"

"What's everything?"

Laz recounted everything he could remember from Harris Teeter Man's explanation.

"So you must have—I mean, your original must have opened the Portal to the New Place," said Ivy. "The new version of Earth. And no, I didn't know that a Portal had actually been found. Or opened."

"I can't possibly be the one who did it," said Laz. "Because I can only side step into timestreams where I already exist. A limitation that I assume also confined the activities of my original."

"Hmmm," she said. "Not possible, you say. So they're all delusional, and the New Place is going to die right on schedule, along with all the other 'places.'"

"Why are you being sarcastic with me?" asked Laz. "I should have stayed in the computer room. I should have gone out onto the street and let you find me whenever you happened to find me."

"All I care about," Ivy said, "is, when's lunch?"

"Lunch will be deteriorating, low-nutrition canned food that has been sitting on grocery store shelves for many years," said Laz. "Or you can wander the streets looking for something edible in people's long-abandoned yards. There are lots of wild strawberries, but most of them are bland. The squirrels have long since harvested all the nuts from last fall. The orchards have blossomed, but the fruit is still hard little knobs of green. We're too far north for any of them to be citrus. There are faded and fallen-down signs that promise apple orchards and some peaches, too, but I have no idea of how plentiful the harvest is going to be."

"Thank you for your report, Lazarus Davit Hayerian," she said.

"Do you approve of my advance work, preparing for the arrival of Ivy Maisie Downey?"

"No," she said. "But I'm sure it was the best you could do under the circumstance of being ignorant of anything that matters."

Laz was getting pretty fed up with her superior tone. "Next time," he said, "*you* wake up first with no information to guide you, and prepare for *me* to wake up."

"If that ever happens," she answered, "I would leave you naked as a jaybird, because being nude when the other person is dressed leaves one at such a disadvantage."

"Is there anything I've done so far that meets with your approval?"

"As I said, I'm sure you did your best," said Ivy.

"You know, I was kind of hopeful about what would happen when you woke up," said Laz. "I didn't want to wake you before the machines played your memories into your brain, or before all your internal organs were working. So I held off until there was an external threat. Still, I had thought that it would be nice to have someone to talk to."

"You just didn't think I'd answer," said Ivy.

"I knew you'd answer. I used to imagine dialogues between us, and in all of them, you were snotty and insulting."

"So . . . I'm living up to expectations," she said.

"Not at all," said Laz. "Because in my imaginary dialogues, you were always smart and sometimes right. The conversations were worth having. Not just a bunch of whining about how badly the servants have done up the country house in preparation for your arrival."

Ivy said, "So let's accept our mutual disappointment, and see what the world holds for us."

"Not until tomorrow morning," said Laz.

"I'm not spending the night with you," said Ivy.

"Do what you want. Though I think you'll be glad if I introduce you to the Pack of Four, so StarKist can decide whether you're prey or not."

"What are you talking about?"

"Dogs," said Laz. "I assumed you knew. You know everything else."

"I don't know anything but what you tell me, and what I find out from your side steps in the past few months."

Laz walked to the door and, without checking to see how far she was from it, he turned off the overhead lights. Now the only light was whatever spilled in from the corridor.

"Please leave the door open till I've passed through it," said Ivy.

"Press the buttons beside the door on the left," said Laz. "The upper button opens the door, the lower one closes it."

Ivy did it. The door opened again as soon as it closed. "Is that the extent of your electronics training?" she asked.

"Except for one working computer on another floor, doors and elevators in this building are the only functioning electronics," said Laz.

"So . . . you really have trained me in everything."

"I can show you what I learned from the computer, but since you and I were the only living people in the coffins, I don't know what the point of that would be."

"I would like a drink of water," said Ivy.

"So would I," said Laz. "But my water needs are met from the sludgy liquids inside the cans of meat and vegetables and fruits that I'm living on."

"Are you going to share any of that with me?"

"I assumed I wasn't cool enough to sit at your lunch table," said Laz.

"You're not," said Ivy. "But for now, you'll have to do. Especially because you have food and I don't."

They rode the elevator up to the ground floor and soon found where the Pack of Four had eaten everything from the open cans. StarKist was dragging the backpack around the floor, probably expecting a can of something to spring out of the bag and open itself. "StarKist," said Laz sharply.

StarKist trotted up to him, and when he stopped, he cocked his head in an annoyingly cute way.

"Aw," said Ivy. "He likes you."

"He knows I can open cans, and he can't," said Laz. "StarKist, bring me my backpack."

StarKist didn't know this command, so he did nothing.

Laz pointed at the backpack five meters away. "Bring me my backpack."

StarKist turned and looked in the direction Laz was pointing. It was not possible that StarKist didn't see the backpack. He just didn't know what he was supposed to do with it.

"Have you tried 'fetch'?" asked Ivy.

"He was born after all the humans left here, so he's never heard the word 'fetch' before."

"I bet 'bring me my backpack' is just as unfamiliar," said Ivy.

Laz pointed at the backpack again. "Ivy Maisie Downey, please fetch the backpack."

She looked outraged.

"So *you* don't understand English either," he said. He strode to the backpack, squatted, and started pulling out cans. Including a plastic jar of mandarin oranges.

She walked over to him. "That was a joke, then, right? You didn't really think you could command me to fetch stuff."

"I didn't command," said Laz. "I said 'please.'"

"Oh, right. You didn't say 'please' to the dog, so asking *me* to 'please' fetch did not reduce me to the level of a pet at *all*."

"StarKist isn't a pet," said Laz. "He's a predator and leader of a pack of four feral dogs, whom I persuaded not to eat me by providing substitute sources of food, and also by injuring two of them by throwing rocks."

Ivy pointedly looked him up and down. "You don't look like much of a rock thrower."

Laz reached into the bag and pulled out a handful of stones—four of them.

Immediately all four dogs shied back and then ran toward the door, which was no longer held open by the couch. But they jumped up on the couch that *had* been holding it open.

"I see," said Ivy. "They remember the stones."

"Why would they?" asked Laz. "I'm not much of a rock thrower."

"I apologize, I wasn't trying to insult you, it just surprised me that you would know how to throw rocks hard enough to intimidate four feral dogs."

"I practiced," said Laz. "Even before you were here to tell me I should."

"Wow," she said. "I'm used to pissing people off, but you really take *everything* personally."

"Well, yeah, I do, because I happen to be, in fact, a person," said Laz.

"Sorry. When I'm nervous I get snippy with people."

"Oh, well then my feelings can't possibly be hurt because *now* I know you're nervous."

"I'm not nervous, I'm scared. I just woke up in a clone farm in a place where I've never been, and my only companion is a boy who looks to be about fifteen—"

"Seventeen," said Laz.

"Like it matters," said Ivy.

"You don't sound scared," said Laz.

"That's the point of going on attack," said Ivy. "So people don't know I'm scared."

"But I don't *care* if you're scared," said Laz. "All I know is that when I ask you to help even a little to get the food and water that your body is going to need a lot of fairly soon, you take umbrage because you're apparently too lofty to deign to pick up a backpack full of food and carry it to the person who gathered it and carried it here for you. I can do *kilometers* of hiking and carrying for your supper, and you can't do five meters."

"You shouldn't have used the word 'fetch,'" said Ivy.

"It was your word," said Laz. "You suggested it."

"This is getting nowhere."

Laz held out the jar of mandarin oranges and a plastic fork. "It works better if you spear mandarin oranges and eat them till the level of liquid is a lot lower. Then when you tip it up to drink off the rest of the liquid, it won't splash all over your face and down your shirt."

"You call it liquid," said Ivy.

"It looks like sludge, but it was once the sugary juice that the oranges were packed in, and it still tastes sweet, and it didn't make my stomach revolt."

"How many jars like this have you already eaten?" she asked.

"A lot," said Laz. "No ill effects. But also, not much food value."

She cocked her head like StarKist, waiting for more explanation.

"You see how skinny I am," said Laz. "When I woke up maybe six months ago, I was like you—perfectly toned muscle, the right balance of bone and flesh and fat."

"How sweet of you to notice my body mass index," said Ivy.

"I remember how it felt, and that's how you look," said Laz. "But eating old canned goods for half a year, I've lost some weight. And most of what I lost was muscle tone. The muscles I'm using—for walking and carrying—they're still okay, but other muscles are atrophying because my body is eating itself to make up for the nutrients that I'm missing in my diet."

"So you haven't been finding fresh food?" asked Ivy. "No, I didn't mean that to sound contemptuous, really."

"The produce departments of the grocery stores have not been restocked. In winter and early spring, there weren't many vegetables and fruits around town."

"So why don't you have scurvy?" asked Ivy.

"Maybe there are enough vitamins in these nutritionally fortified cans of fish and sausages and Chef Boyardee."

"But you do know where there are edible greens."

"Lots of green here. This town's name is Greensboro. I'm sure that with all your expertise in salads, you'll be able to point out which greens I should pick."

"I can pick them," she said.

"Unless I ask you to," said Laz.

"I thought you were mocking me by saying 'fetch,'" she said. "Can't you just let that go?"

"I always let things go," said Laz, "when I believe people are sorry that they acted like a ridiculous prima donna."

"I'm sorry I didn't fetch your backpack on command," said Ivy.

"Yes, I'm completely convinced by *that* sarcastic apology," said Laz.

"You're not my father," said Ivy.

"I know that," said Laz.

"So don't get snotty with me like an impatient father," said Ivy.

Laz just shook his head. "Because you're the expert on how people should talk to each other when they first meet."

She tipped the mandarin orange jar up to drink from it, and the liquid sloshed all over her face and into her hair and down her shirt.

"I'm so sorry," said Laz. "If only I had thought to warn you that might happen."

"So where do you wash clothes around here?" asked Ivy.

"When we leave this building tomorrow, assuming the helicopters are gone, we'll head for Macy's and Belk and you can pick out new clothes. These pajamas are just temps. We'll pick up some blankets and stuff to sleep on."

"Separate bedrooms, laddie," said Ivy.

"Just shut up," said Laz.

"Together twenty minutes and you already want your sole human companion to shut up," she said.

Laz said nothing. Because no matter what he said, it would just make her more obnoxious. Like it or not, she was the only companion he had, and she knew more than he did about the world, including some idea of who his original had been, so he had to stay with her. Until he learned all he could. Then he could take her to the bear.

No, she'd be able to see when he side stepped away from the bear. Hard to lay a trap when she already knew everything.

The bear probably wasn't anywhere near Greensboro now.

Or it was waiting just around the corner outside.

The sound of a chopper approaching.

"If you don't mind," said Laz, "I'd like them not to look into these huge windows and see us inside."

She nodded and he led her through a door and out of sight. The dogs made no effort to follow. They were finishing off the can of tuna he had just opened for Ivy. He'd get another for her later. Even if she despised him and he was constantly annoyed with her, it was his responsibility to feed her until she got a backpack and can opener of her own.

And her own pack of half-tamed dogs, which she would undoubtedly train much better than he had trained StarKist and the boys.

"Don't they have, like, heat-sensing equipment?" asked Ivy.

"If they do," said Laz, "I'll side step to a timestream where we had already happened to go down into the basement. Though I'm not sure whether even that would stop them from sensing our location."

"So they really are looking for us?" asked Ivy.

"The helicopters came after Harris Teeter Man told me he had notified the authorities that I had somehow gotten through a Portal that I didn't know existed. I assume that they're still looking for me. An illegal immigrant."

"So . . . not you in particular. By name."

"I told him my name was Laz and he laughed at me."

"I don't see why," said Ivy. "It was a really popular name when I was a kid."

"I think he thought it proved that I knew more than I had let on."

Ivy shrugged. "So these guys came and patrolled, but they

didn't find you inside the building through thermal imaging."

"Or they *did* find me, and didn't choose to interfere with what I was doing."

"Which was what?"

"Waking you up," said Laz.

"So in this paranoid fantasy of yours," said Ivy, "somebody put us into this clone orchard so that when they woke you up, after a while you'd figure out how to wake *me* up."

"Which could have been accomplished by leaving me a list of instructions. Week twenty-five, figure out how to activate waking sequence in Ivy Downey's healing cave."

She sat down on the floor in the corridor.

"Oh, is this nap time?" asked Laz.

"Either they spotted us or they didn't," she said. "No need to keep walking. In fact, isn't it better to stay near the places where they might enter the building, so you know right away if you have to side step?"

"Thanks for planning out how you'll assign me to use an ability that I have and you don't."

"Apparently the ability *I* have that *you* don't is the power of rational thought," said Ivy.

"Well, Mr. Holmes, I'm eager to hear the result of your superior ratiocination," said Laz.

Ivy got a tiny hint of a smile. "You're the only person in the world who can actually side step, plus you're the foremost scientific authority on the nascent science of timestreams. And I happen to be the only person who can see timestreams that I'm not in. And by 'see' of course I mean only 'sense' because visuals are almost never part of it."

"You think they hope that we'll work together somehow," said Laz.

"No," said Ivy. "I think that the Portals that link the New Place with old Earth are proof that our originals *did* work together, because how else would you be able to side step into a world so radically different that the wandering planet—Shiva, right?—wouldn't exist?"

"That's a lot of far-fetched guessing," said Laz. "Who's the one with weird conspiracy theories now?"

"Now I see your point," said Ivy. "Only two clones were alive in the whole orchard. One was you, the other was me. Coincidence or somebody's plan?"

"I bet you have trouble with the theory of evolution," said Laz.

"They cloned you and me, and didn't discard us during the great migration to the New Place, because they thought they might still have some use for us. For *us*, not just for you. They wanted us together. They wanted us dependent on each other for survival."

"But here's the flaw in their plan," said Laz, "assuming there *was* a plan."

"Yes? The flaw?"

"If they had ever met your original, and your original was anything like you, they'd be seriously worried that I might side step away from you."

"Except that you're curious to know if our abilities really can work together."

"Or, if I couldn't get away by shifting timestreams, then I might use my handy new rock-throwing ability to drive you away, injure you, or, you know, kill you."

126

"You're not really that angry," she said.

"I'm very angry," said Laz. "The fact that you're alive and unbruised says that I'm really not that angry *yet*."

"You're not the kind of guy who hits people," said Ivy.

Laz was relieved to know she thought so. "I didn't even like hurting the dogs, and they posed a real threat."

"Whereas I'm just annoying," said Ivy.

Laz shrugged.

They kept their silence for a long moment, till Ivy spoke again. "You're forgetting one very important thing they did to make sure you *wouldn't* side step away from me no matter how annoying I got."

Laz waited for her to explain.

She didn't.

And then he knew what she meant. "They put everybody in their coffins stark naked, so they'd know that I would find *you* that way."

"And you're a teenage boy, so—"

"Give me credit. I side stepped and you woke up with clothes on," Laz reminded her.

"And you can't get the image of naked me out of your head. So you aren't going to side step away and abandon me."

"If I ever thought you were at all attractive," said Laz, "you've obliterated such ideas."

"And yet you're still here."

"Because I've already got systems for surviving," said Laz. "And, being a compassionate human being, I'm not going to leave you, not until you can fend for yourself."

No answer.

Then: "Why don't you sit down, Laz, so we can talk to each other at eye level?" she asked.

"You're the one who chose the lower eye level by sitting down."

"You're significantly taller than me," said Ivy. "So standing up, we're *not* at eye level."

Laz sat down beside her, but not too close.

"My theory is far-fetched," said Ivy, "but so is everything that's happened so far. So are the abilities we have. So let's perform a simple test. Let me find a timestream and *you* cause us both to side step to it."

"I travel alone, thanks."

"You don't know whether you do or not," said Ivy. "Because you've never tried it."

"And how are you going to put a timestream into my mind?"

As if in answer, a timestream popped up in Laz's mind. It looked just like what he sensed when he was looking for a timestream to step into, except it was only the one timestream, not a whole shifting array of them.

He could tell that versions of him and Ivy were in that timestream; he couldn't immediately sense a difference between that stream and this one.

So he reached out and leaned toward her; she also held out her hand. He took her hand, held it perhaps more tightly than he needed to, and side stepped.

"See?" she said. "Not hard at all."

"Nothing changed," said Laz.

Then the sound of four sets of paws came down the corridor.

"Oh," said Laz. "In *this* timestream, we brought the dogs with us."

"In this timestream you didn't show me the stones, so the dogs didn't flee from you right before the helicopters approached, so when we dodged out of sight into the corridors, the dogs came with us," said Ivy. "You mean you really didn't see that before you side stepped?"

"That's exactly what I meant," said Laz.

"So you really did trust me," said Ivy.

"I thought you were leading me to a place that wasn't significantly different from where we already were."

"In other words, you trusted me not to have laid a trap for you."

"Yes," said Laz. "But the very fact that you thought of setting a trap for me as a possible thing—*that* makes me not trust you."

StarKist came up and lay down with his head on Laz's thigh.

"True love," said Ivy.

Laz thought that was the last straw. He side stepped to a timestream where he was nowhere near Ivy.

Till she turned a corner in a different corridor and came up to him. "Laz," she said, "any nearby timestream is going to have both of us in it. And I can always sense what you're doing with timestreams. You can't really get away from me, if I don't want to be gotten away from."

"So you *can* side step yourself," said Laz.

"No," she said. "You notice I deliberately left out the epithets 'dimwit,' 'bonehead,' and 'idiot.'"

"Thanks for that kindness," said Laz.

"I was already in this timestream. But since you did the side stepping, *you're* the one who swapped places with the version of you that was already here. Me, I was just me, here. I could sense you made the step, so I came looking for you to tell you that I knew what you had done."

"You proved I can never get away from you, thus giving me an incentive to turn myself in to the helicopter guys."

"But now you're already thinking of me naked and deciding not to leave."

"As you said, I'm never going to see that glorious sight again," said Laz.

"I know it wasn't glorious. It was merely interesting to someone with serious testosterone poisoning. And even though you know there's *no* hope of your getting it on with me—isn't that what your generation called it?—hope springs eternal in the hormones."

"Where do you get off acting so superior?" asked Laz, really angry now.

"I'm not *acting* superior," said Ivy. "I'm just not concealing it from you."

"I'm the one who side steps," said Laz.

"And I'm the one you can't get away from," said Ivy. "Come on, let's take another little trip. Let's find another place to be, right now."

"With or without the dogs?" asked Laz.

"That'll be good research. Let's see if we can bring them with us."

Ivy sat down. Laz slid across the corridor to be right beside her, their thighs touching as they sat cross-legged on the floor. Then they each cuddled or held or somehow touched two dogs.

When Laz side stepped, they were all there inside the house that had been Laz's first home base. "I guess this is where I would have taken you if we hadn't been hiding in Vivipartum."

"Not your family's house, I take it," said Ivy.

"I'm from California, remember?"

"Is this my bedroom?"

"It has my sweat all over the mattress from living here for months until I found the Harris Teeter with a working flush toilet."

"So this doesn't have one," said Ivy.

"You can select a latrine area in the front yard, since I'm already using the back."

"You want me to poo in the front yard?"

"The neighbors aren't prone to watching other people's yards," said Laz. "Not a nosy neighborhood."

"I guess privacy is only an issue between you and me," said Ivy.

"Until the choppers come back."

"Maybe we need to work on side stepping together without being close enough to be in physical contact," said Ivy.

"I know I don't want to go back to the Harris Teeter with running water, not with the border patrol knowing I was living there for a while."

"I'll take another bedroom in this house, for now," said Ivy. "I assume you already chose the best bed."

"I don't know," said Laz. "It's the only one I ever slept on, so I can't compare."

Ivy sighed and left the room.

The dogs sat in a row, their heads alert as they watched her go. But they stayed with Laz.

"Are you loyal or just lazy?" Laz asked the Pack of Four.

We're completely loyal, he imagined them saying. You can trust us enough to let us sleep right beside you, where if we get hungry enough we can eat you from the face down or the anus up.

Just the way you can trust Ivy Maisie Downey.

Fourth favorite ~~utility~~ infrastructure: the street department. Fixing potholes, sure. But also to keep <u>trees</u> from growing in the middle of the street. And clearing away fallen trees. And stripping old pavement and replacing it with new. Maintaining street signs. Especially signs that tell how far from here to somewhere else.

6

LAZ RODE A bike till he got tired of hoisting it over fallen trees. Then he continued to follow the signs until he got to the airport.

There were a few terminals and some planes at various gates, some with the jetway still attached. He looked and saw that the airplane doors were open, so that if he wanted to, he could get onto an airplane and sit in first class, the way Dad used to except when traveling with Laz. "Am I not worth first class?" he asked one time. "Your butt isn't big enough to need first class," Dad told him. "Yours is," Laz answered.

"But with you beside me in the middle seat," said Dad, "my butt and belly only intrude into *your* space, and you're barely using two-thirds of it, so nobody is discommoded."

I'm discommoded now, Dad, Laz said silently. Only one working commode in the whole city, and now I don't dare get to it.

Hadn't these planes been needed to transport people to the Portal? Why would any of them come back here? Did they simply run out of airports to stack them in?

Were there airports now in the New Place? With a different geological history, did the New Place even have fossil fuels? Maybe they built dirigibles there—after all, the supply of helium in the New Place wouldn't have been depleted by centuries of children's party balloons.

If by some combination of our talents Ivy and I—Original Ivy and Original Laz—created the Portal, why do they still need us? Why were our clones kept viable? Why were we wakened now?

It seemed that however it was done, the world was now saved, and *this* old Earth could be allowed to fall into the Sun whenever that happened to occur.

But they did keep us alive. We did wake up. The border patrol didn't catch us, even if they knew exactly where we were. We have something of value yet to do.

It was stupid of them not to provide Laz with any written information or any living guide when he woke up. What would it have hurt to let him have some information? Or lunch, for that matter. With a Harris Teeter truck bringing produce from California to the Portal, why couldn't they have set up a nice deli for him on each visit?

They were trying to teach him a lesson, that's why. They wanted him to find out what he could for himself, figure things out, stay alive somehow.

Instead, I'm slowly starving to death, and now I have the constant annoyance of a female person who thinks I can do no right.

Laz got into the airport terminal by climbing up the outside stair of a jetway and coming through the door into the passenger ramp. Then he wandered all over and remembered airplanes and rental cars and a lot of company names that used to be common knowledge.

All deserted. All with phones that didn't work, computers that couldn't boot up. Airlines that couldn't take reservations or check baggage. Baggage claim belts that would never slide along again, while passengers snagged their luggage as it passed.

Whatever they want me to do, thought Laz, they think I need Ivy to do it. And they arranged it so that instead of my being at least twenty years older than her, we're about the same age. So what wasn't working out with our originals? Was it the fact that I was too much older and treated her like a child? Or did I, as an adult, lose patience with her utterly imbecilic propensity to resist everything and ridicule me?

I was the older one. The one who should have been mature enough to keep our goal in mind. Was it my failure that made it so they needed a copy of me? Or did I just get cancer and die?

If that's the case, why would they need a new Ivy instead of continuing to work with her original?

And to accomplish what? With Portals already open and working, did they need us to shut them? Surely they worked out a way to do that, so that when the Old Place veered out of orbit, it wouldn't leave the Portal open to outer space, so all the atmosphere would get sucked away. Besides, I have no idea how to turn what I do, or what Ivy and I do together, into a Portal that other people can use.

Maybe she knows. It's obvious she knows more than I do, and more than she's willing to tell me.

Whatever the human race needs, it needs me *and* Ivy to do it. What other conclusion can I possibly reach?

And if that's the case, I need to make friends with Ivy. I need to ignore her provocations and try to understand how her mind works. I need to stop thinking like a lonely high schooler who resents every pretty girl who ignores me, and start thinking like a hero with one superpower that works best when I combine forces with another superhero.

Except neither of us is a hero and neither of us is really all that super.

Laz slept the night at the airport. Since airports really were fairly secure and there was nothing to eat; there was no rodent population and definitely no larger predators. The place was warm, but the high ceilings kept it from being unbearable down near the floor. The benches were designed to make sleeping impossible or at least horribly uncomfortable, but the floor was all right, and there were some neck pillows in a gift shop that still had their filling and spring, so in some ways it was better than the house he had lived in and way better than the floor behind the service counter at Harris Teeter.

Laz woke up in the morning feeling rather good. He held on to the pillow, and then realized it would be polite to get a second one for her. The dogs could fend for themselves.

He couldn't side step back to Ivy, because he would have to occupy a version of himself that had no neck pillows. So he walked and bicycled back to the house.

An open door into his original bedroom showed her asleep on the bed that *had* been his. He chose another bedroom, tossed his pillow onto his bed, and then walked into her room. She was still lying on the bed, but apparently had already woken up. "Hoping to find me naked again?" she asked sleepily.

He set the pillow on the floor beside the bed and left the room without saying a word.

Ivy followed him back into the bedroom where he would be sleeping tonight. "Got these at the airport?" she asked, holding up her pillow.

"There they were," said Laz.

"And you thought of bringing one for me," she said.

"Rude not to, don't you think?" said Laz.

"Are we friends now?" asked Ivy.

He wanted to say a curt no, and leave it at that. Instead he said, "Ivy, I don't think we're going to accomplish anything useful on our own. We need to be able to communicate clearly and fully, and I think we even need to trust each other. I need to know that when I follow a timestream you put in my head, it's not going to land me inside a rock. And you need to know that I'm not going to go off and leave you."

Ivy opened her mouth several times during Laz's speech, but ended up saying nothing at all. Now, when he was finished, she said, "That's pretty much what I was thinking while you were gone."

"How did you know that I was gone? And hadn't just stepped into another stream?"

"If you had done that, a version of you would still have been here, being you: shy, resentful, kind, generous, suspicious, and angry."

"I hope there's more to me than that list."

"Probably. I expect I'll find out. But that's a good enough list for me to realize I'd been treating you like a jerk when you don't actually deserve it."

Laz didn't say anything, because everything that came to mind was snippy and sarcastic and counterproductive.

"My apology gets no answer?" she said.

"It deserves a more kind and generous answer than I'm able to think of yet," said Laz.

"Well, that's honest enough," said Ivy. "I had to practice that one while you were gone. Talking to myself, of course, or to the dogs. They're *my* dogs now, in case you were wondering."

Laz walked out into the living room. No dogs. He opened the front door. They were gathered in the soft grass of what was probably once a lush front lawn. They all got up when Laz appeared.

Ivy was right behind him. "We explored without you yesterday," she said. "It involved getting me more clothes and stuffing our backpacks with canned food. What do you think the Pack of Four deserve, tuna or Spam or canned pancakes?"

"Please tell me that there's no such thing as canned pancakes."

"I hoped you'd think that was funny."

"I did," said Laz. "I do."

Ivy held up two can openers and handed one to Laz. "Want to do this sitting on the front porch where they can see us do it?" asked Ivy. "So they know that we're both food bringers now?"

Laz sat beside her on the porch, opening cans. He was more deft at it, having had six months more practice. "I suppose this means that when we do get to the Portal, we'll have to bring the dogs with us."

"It seems unkind to leave them here to be charred to ash by the sun," said Ivy.

"What do you think the bosses back in the New Place want us for?"

"I gave that considerable thought while you were away," said Ivy. "And here's what I think. One of us is dead—one of our originals, I mean. *Or* both of us are dead. Or gone away. Something. And they've discovered that there's something wrong with the New Place, and they need more Portals so they can move again."

"And then there'll be something wrong with the New New Place," said Laz. "Only they'll be fresh out of clonatoriums so if they use *us* up, they'll be out of luck."

"Or they just decided," said Ivy, "that the New Place is too small for the billions of people from Earth. Maybe they want several closely adjacent New Places, with Portals between them for trade and exchange students, one for Hindus and one for Pakistanis, one for Brazilians and one for—who does Brazil not get along with?"

"Never heard of any great hatred of Brazilians by anyone," said Laz.

"But maybe one world for all the Portuguese speakers—Angola, Mozambique, Guinea-Bissau, São Tomé and Principe, Cape Verde, Madeira, East Timor, and of course Portugal and Brazil. "

"One for all English speakers? Spanish speakers?" asked Laz.

"Do you think that all the speakers of Polynesian languages could live in peace on one whole planet?" asked Ivy.

"There's bound to be an infinite number of timestreams, so if every language and dialect and culture and religion wants a place of their own . . ."

"But they'd need us," said Ivy.

"No," said Laz. "They would only need me. I can side step into any timestream where I already exist. The fact that they kept *you* alive and allowed me to revive you—"

"They need the kind of new world," said Ivy, "that can only be reached by the two of us working together."

"So I'm thinking," said Laz, "that the most important thing we can do, aside from feeding the dogs so they don't kill us in our sleep, is learn how to work together to do whatever trick it was that enabled us to create a Portal between versions of Earth that *don't* already include any versions of us."

"Won't it be fun to figure out how to do something," said Ivy, "that the morons who stored us up and shoved us together already know about, so if they weren't stupid, they'd just tell us and save an amazing amount of time."

"I wonder if we can find a timestream where that is, in fact, what they already did—came to us and gave us an idea of what they want us to do."

"Let me see if I can find such a timestream," said Ivy. "One where the people in power are smart."

Laz laughed. "Meanwhile, I'll see if StarKist wants to learn how to fetch."

She gave him a wincing expression. "Is that a word we want to use very much?"

"Is there any word we're afraid to use between each other?" asked Laz.

"You don't like it when I say 'naked,'" said Ivy.

"And yet you say it," said Laz. "And I'll get used to it. As you'll get used to fetch. No poison words that can't be said. Okay?"

"First big question," said Ivy, "is how we're able to create a Portal that other people can use to pass between worlds."

"But Ivy," said Laz. "If you find a timestream where they're telling us all about what our originals used to do, then we won't have to figure it out."

"Maybe they're hoping we'll think of a better way if we don't know the way we did it before," said Ivy.

"Maybe they can stick that little plan where the sun don't shine," said Laz. "Let's find the place where they care enough to help us with this amazing task they need us to accomplish, by telling us how we did it before."

"And in the meantime," said Ivy, "thanks again for the pillow."

When Ivy told him, a few hours later, that she was giving up on finding a timestream where the government was sensible, Laz didn't know if she found it boring to keep searching, or if there really wasn't a timestream where the powers that be decided to help. Or if she was lying to hide some kind of secret that would benefit her and harm him.

So when it came to trust—that was still beyond him.

But it was essential for him to *pretend* to trust her. And to let her call the shots for a while. See where her heart was.

"We can carry stuff with us," said Ivy. "Because we arrive with, like, clothes on. And our backpacks."

"And the Pack of Four."

"Maybe they do their own side stepping," said Ivy.

"We'll see them do their own can opening first," said Laz.

"Don't underestimate dogs," said Ivy.

"You were making a point about taking things with us," said Laz.

"What if we held the two ends of a long rope, and I stay behind while you side step. Then the rope would extend from you to me— you in one timestream, me in the other."

"Or we'd each be holding the end of a rope cut in half by time."

"I know a way we can find out," said Ivy.

"I don't carry a lot of rope around with me," said Laz.

"But *I* carry *string*," said Ivy. "I found a ball of string in a hardware store, and I thought it might be useful."

"So I hold one end of a string and you hold the other and then I side step somewhere, and you don't come with me, but we're holding the string."

"No," said Ivy. "Think about it. If you side step to a place where you already are, then the Laz that already exists there, *he* won't be holding a string."

Laz absorbed that. Maybe she was right. "So the Ariadne-and-Theseus method doesn't work."

"Hold on," said Ivy. "What I'm thinking is that the problem isn't the string, it's you."

"Hey, thanks for the vote of confidence."

"You side step from wherever you are to another place where you already are. I either come along or don't, but you can't carry anything with you."

"No," said Laz. "I show up wearing clothes, whatever's in my pockets."

"You were *already* wearing those clothes. Side stepping there doesn't change the clothes you were already wearing in the target location. It doesn't put anything in your pockets. It just shifts some memories over and *adds* them to what the Laz of the new timestream remembers."

"I guess you're right. I'm not actually moving. I'm pretty much doing nothing."

"Because you can only *find* timestreams you're already in."

Laz finally got what she was saying. "But if *you* choose a timestream that I'm *not* in, what happens then?"

"Then I think your physical body leaves the timestream you're in and physically moves to the new timestream. It really displaces you. It's genuine travel."

"So if I'm holding my end of a string when you pick a location I'm not already in . . ."

"Then the string we're holding marks a passageway. Somebody following along that string might be able to walk from one timestream to the other."

"A Portal," said Laz.

"I can find timestreams I'm not in and you're not in," said Ivy. "I just can't *go* to them. But you *can* go to them, once I show you where they are."

Laz laughed softly. StarKist cocked his head, then trotted up to him. Laz pried out some Vienna sausages and StarKist ate them out of his hand.

"I think you should hold your end of the same string I'm holding on to," said Ivy, "and you should also hold strings tied around the necks of the Pack of Four."

"To see if the dogs can be pulled by the strings into my new timestream," said Laz.

"Seems plausible to me," said Ivy. "If it works, then we know a way for you to take more than one person through at a time."

"I think we should also tie a string to a tree," said Laz. "To see if I can leave one end fixed to an unmoving object."

Ivy laughed now. "Seems to me that either we're going to have a spectacular success or an explosion like a thermonuclear bomb."

"I know which one I'm hoping for," said Laz.

"Come on," said Ivy. "We know it'll work."

"And we know this how?" asked Laz.

"Because the Portals exist," said Ivy, "and nobody but us could have made them."

"Nobody but our originals," said Laz.

"Us, generation one point oh," said Ivy.

"Just one question, which I think is pretty important," said Laz. "If I'm going to side step into a place where I am not already located, how will you know if the place is even habitable? I don't want to side step into a methane bubble, or the hard cold of outer space, or the bottom of a lake."

Ivy got a little hint of a smile.

"If you say, 'Don't tempt me,'" said Laz, "I'm not doing it."

"I didn't say it, and it's only a joke. Everybody loses if I can't send you to a place with breathable air," said Ivy.

"Because you can only send me to Earth, and you can only send me to this exact moment in time, so what we're picking is the whole geological, climatological, ecological, evolutionary history up to then. Mountain ranges may have grown in different configurations. Volcanos will have popped up in different places. Pangaea might have split in different places and made unfamiliar continents."

"Relax, Laz," said Ivy. "I'm not going to send you anywhere like that."

"How can you be sure?"

"Because I'll know where I'm sending you. I know the address. I get a kind of preview."

"But you don't get a breath of the atmosphere, do you?" asked Laz.

"If you don't like the smell of the place, then side step back."

"Can I?" asked Laz. "I will have disappeared from the timestream I left from, so I can't just go back, because I'm not there."

"Follow the string," said Ivy.

"If I can't breathe the atmosphere, how many steps will I stay alive to take?"

"Laz," said Ivy, "I'll send you to a place with humans, okay? Just not *you*."

"Someplace where I already died?"

"Someplace where you were never cloned," said Ivy.

Laz held out a hand. "Tie a string around my wrist and I'll tie the other end around a tree."

"Just hold the string," said Ivy.

"What if I trip and drop my end of the string?" asked Laz. "Tie it on my wrist, please."

The dogs allowed Ivy to tie strings around their necks—not tightly, but not so loosely the strings would fall off. She played out about five meters of string for each link.

"Is the string long enough?" asked Laz.

"We'll find out, won't we," said Ivy cheerfully.

"I don't want the dogs to be, like, cut in half because the new Portal isn't long enough."

"Look," she said. "I've tied the other end of this one to my ankle. You're all strung up, like a cat's cradle with dogs and a tree and me attached. Do you want me to feed you your new timestream now?"

"Don't you have to search for one?"

"I spend my entire life finding timestreams. They're always there. I've selected a good one. There are humans in North America, but not a lot of them—you can breathe the atmosphere, and you won't be attacked immediately."

"Will I be able to practice playing the piano?" asked Laz.

Ivy rolled her eyes. "I'm going to send it to you now."

Laz waited. Nothing happened.

"Not sending it after all?" asked Laz.

Ivy didn't answer, because Ivy wasn't there. Nobody was anywhere. There were trees and there was some grass and there were clouds in the sky and rolling hills and not a single building of any kind.

And six strings leading away from Lazarus's left wrist into a fuzzy place about two meters away. Just a spot in the air that was fuzzy.

Laz pulled on one of the dog strings.

It wasn't StarKist, but one of the Pack of Four came through and then turned around and tried to run back, only he didn't get into the fuzzy patch, so he just ran around there in that new place.

Laz found the tree string and started winding it up and walking toward the fuzzy area. Then he stopped abruptly and walked to a nearby sapling and tied his Ivy-string to the tree. So there'd be something a string was fastened to that wasn't a dog.

Laz followed the tree string back toward the fuzzy place in the air. As he reached it, the fuzzy got bigger. Big enough for him to step into it. The passage had no duration. He wasn't in the original timestream, and sometime in midstep, he *was* in the original timestream.

"You don't have my string," said Ivy.

"I tied your string to a tree," said Laz. "So you can go through."

"We're missing a dog," said Ivy.

Laz held up his wrist. One string didn't lead to the three dogs in the original timestream. It led to a fuzzy place in the air.

"So you can still bring back the missing dog," said Ivy.

"Unless he got loose from the string," said Laz.

"Which he can probably do whenever he wants," said Ivy.

"So follow your string to the tree on the other side and then make sure our puppy friend makes it back home again."

"But my string will only be connected on the far side," said Ivy.

"Tie another string to a tree here and have two strings," suggested Laz.

"I won't have a lot of mobility that way, tethered at both ends," said Ivy.

"For Pete's sake," said Laz. "You just sent me to a place where I didn't exist. What happened *here*, did I just disappear?"

"Yes," said Ivy. "It was really creepy and scary and I don't want to do it myself." Yet even as she said this, she was tying a new length of string to one of the front porch posts of the house, and then tying the other end to her wrist.

"Let me do that," said Laz. "You can't make as good a knot one-handed."

She watched his knot tying. "You were a Boy Scout?" she asked.

"If I learned knots in Boy Scouts, I'd be talking about a rabbit coming out of his hole and running around a bunch of stuff and going back into his hole."

"So how do you picture it?" asked Ivy.

"My old way of knot tying was to make twisty motions with the two ends of the string and then side step to whatever timestream had a good knot. But then I decided a couple of years ago to learn the actual knots instead of side stepping my way to success."

"That's almost puritan of you," said Ivy.

"Sometimes it's better to know how to do it for real, instead of faking it and side stepping."

Ivy made sure both her strings were still intact, and then started moving toward the fuzzy place in the air. Laz watched until she stepped into it and blinked out of existence. A minute later, the dog flew out of the fuzzy place and landed squealing and complaining on a patch of grass. Ivy must have picked him up and tossed him.

Laz took hold of the flying dog's string and followed his own string through the fuzzy place, pretty much dragging a really confused dog behind him. There was Ivy, standing around, looking at the scenery. "I wish I knew my trees better," said Ivy. "I don't know if these are the same species we have or not."

"Why wouldn't they be? You said humans evolved here, so the path of evolution should be pretty similar."

"Did I say they were human? I didn't do a DNA check. People—they looked like people to me. But human? That's a pretty broad claim."

"So this wouldn't be a viable place for a new human settlement."

"I don't know why I know this except maybe I read it in an article—by you. Or heard it in a speech—by you."

"What?"

"The rules. No side stepping into a timestream where our technology, our sheer existence would co-opt some other human culture or human species."

"Yeah, that's a good rule," said Laz.

"But there's an even bigger problem with this timestream."

"Namely?" asked Laz.

"We don't know if Shiva is still coming. I don't know how to figure out if we've gotten to a timestream where the wandering planet doesn't show up after all. And yet that's got to be the criterion for the New Place. Maybe our originals tied strings to a bunch of astronomers with backpacks full of telescopic equipment and they did a bunch of sightings and said, 'Okay, Shiva's still coming, let's try again,' or they said, 'This is a non-Shiva timestream, so let's pitch some tents and start running huge cables to connect the timestreams and frame a full-fledged Portal."

"You think we really did this? To open the Portals?" asked Laz.

"Something like this," said Ivy. "But you know what? I don't like being here, when all that's tying me back to the original Earth is a string."

"You chose the string," said Laz.

"It doesn't matter who chose it," said Ivy, rolling her eyes like a teenager with stupid parents. "It's just a string and it scares me. Rats bite through strings all the time. Squirrels and chipmunks, too. That yard was literally crawling with rodents."

"So let's go back," said Laz. "I'll carry the dog, he's kind of freaking out."

And in a few steps, they were back in the timestream they had started in. The interdimensional dog took about a half hour to calm down. Laz had no idea what his jaunt into another timestream had felt like to the dog. They could sense things that people couldn't, like upcoming earthquakes and stuff. So maybe he could tell he was changing timestreams. Maybe it scared him. Or maybe there were weird smells in the other place. Maybe the predators and the prey smelled like things he wasn't used to.

"Looks like side stepping doesn't thrill our canine explorer," said Ivy.

"Or maybe it was getting thrown back through the fuzzy place the first time that made him loony," said Laz.

"We did a good day's work," said Ivy.

"You did," said Laz. "What you can do is amazing."

"Not like that boring side-step thing you do," said Ivy.

"So we make a pretty good team," said Laz.

"What went wrong, then?" asked Ivy. "Why did they need to wake up our clones? Where are Original Laz and Original Ivy?"

"Maybe they just want to train us to keep up the work," said Laz.

"Don't forget the possibility that one of us is dead," said Ivy.

"*We* aren't dead," said Laz. "So why do I care what may or may not have happened to my original?"

"It's about your future possibility of promotion," said Ivy.

"Clones don't get promoted into real humans, Ivy," said Laz.

"We do if we're going to do anything to help them."

"Pretty defiant," said Laz. "We doom the human race because they wouldn't let us join in any reindeer games?"

"If we aren't human, then what does the survival of humanity have to do with us?" asked Ivy.

"There's still too much we don't know," said Laz. "But we can always side step to a wild version of North America, without needing to find a timestream we already existed in. We can find a timestream where Shiva doesn't come."

"You're not my Adam," said Ivy. "And I'm not your Eve." After a moment, she added, with a grimace, "Yet."

"If they force us to find our own way around Shiva, because they won't let us be a real boy and a real girl, then we have plenty of time to decide whether we're just on holiday at a low-service resort, or whether we're planning to reestablish the human race," said Laz.

"Come on," said Ivy. "You know that we'll relent, in the end."

Laz grinned. "Yeah. I just didn't know if *you* knew it."

"Whatever we decide when we actually meet the humans-in-charge, for now we just learned some cool things we can do. Strings attached. Good for us," said Ivy.

They did an air high five and an air fist bump, because Ivy really hated high-fiving and Laz hated fist-bumping, but hey, they were Americans, right? They knew how to celebrate.

Fifth favorite infrastructure:
Internal combustion cars and motorcycles, with the gas stations and garages that fuel and fix them. What a miracle—engines that can make the drive train spin billions of times, as long as you keep it lubed. Oil that comes up out of the sand or the shale

and flows out of a hose within a few blocks of home.

Of course it was good to have the changeover to electric—it meant that cars could be fueled by solar, hydro, wind, or coal—power sources that are far from portable. But that ties you to the grid. You can't carry a can of electricity along a road to get your car started again. Even though we needed gas stations and that's a lot of infrastructure, there wasn't a gasoline grid. Each gas station had its own underground tanks.

And you still needed electricity to make the pumps work. There's probably gasoline in the tanks of every station around town, and I can't get to any of it. If I could find a vehicle that hasn't frozen up from years of non-use. And—hello, electricity!—the battery would certainly be dead, and even if it could be recharged, I have no way to do that.

But the internal combustion engine was the best non-animal-powered means of transportation, because you could fill up and then go <u>wherever</u>. Alone.

Sixth favorite infrastructure:
Libraries that have actual physical books so you can read them even when the power is out—especially when it's out for twenty years.

This includes encyclopedias on paper so that people stranded alone on planet Earth can look stuff up instead of sitting in the dark, saying, Alexa, how can I turn murky water into something I can drink? Hey Siri, how can I tame a feral dog? Okay Google, how do you cook sparrows once you've knocked them over the head with a board?

Infrastructure:

In the absence of telephones, how about a decent postal service? Hard to maintain it when there's only a couple of people and nobody else to write to, though. Still, what if there <u>was</u> somebody else in the world? The postal service would have to know their address so they could deliver mail, right?

So I can address a letter to Person who is not Laz or Ivy, and is also not this postal carrier, wherever you are, though I hope you're close enough we might actually meet.

But where can I buy a stamp? Do "forever" stamps still work?

7

Another favorite infrastructure: emergency medical services.

That's what EMS stands for, right? EMT = emergency medical... technician?

I miss you guys. I miss living carelessly because if stuff goes really wrong, there you'll be, helping us recover and survive. There you'll be with antibiotics that still work, kind of. There you'll be with paddles to say, "Clear!" and then restart the heart and keep life going. Splints and bandages, oxygen masks and clamps to shut down arteries pumping in open wounds.

I have never, never had to call upon your services in my charmed life. But I lived with a lot more freedom and hope because I knew in the back of my mind that you were always there. What's the cash value of that?

Health insurance isn't about health—it's about money. So is fire insurance, life insurance, car insurance. You don't insure anything, you just get a promise of money to make you feel better or to replace the thing you lost, except when it's irreplaceable. The only real health insurance is medical professionals who know what to do and have the tools to do it. And the money stuff is just to make sure those lifesavers get paid. They can never be paid their real value, but they can be paid enough to induce them to train and do well at their jobs.

Maybe not having you EMTs around is the worst thing about being alone in the world.

What a self-deluding clown you are, Lazarus. You don't need medical professionals to feel safe. You can always choose a timestream where nothing bad happened to you after all.

If you ever write in my plog again, Ivy, I'll choose a timestream where you fall from a cliff and die a slow and agonizing death of dehydration, exposure, and butt-tunneling animals.

Laz stared at the plog. Just when you think your partner in this insane enterprise is somebody you can trust, she gets into your stuff when you're having a poo in the back yard and has the gall to write in your book, making fun of it and of you.

Laz was so furious when he saw it that he gathered up everything he owned—which wasn't much, but it included some winter clothing and his pencils and his plog—and side stepped into a timestream where he hadn't yet woken Ivy and she was still in the box.

It was a timestream in which he had eventually killed two of the Pack of Four, using ever-heavier stones. It hadn't occurred to him to feed them, in this timestream. So here he didn't have StarKist or the other dogs. But to compensate for that, he also didn't have Ivy.

Why should Laz keep showing remorse for seeing her naked at the moment when he discovered that she existed? I looked away, didn't I? I side stepped to a timestream where everybody had clothes on, didn't I? I didn't do anything wrong.

In *this* timestream, she was still stark naked in the box; in this timestream, he had also woken up naked himself, and found his pajamas neatly folded outside his coffin.

But he was doing something wrong now, as he made his way into the huge clone orchard inside Vivipartum where he knew she would be lying in her healing cave. His initial plan was to violate her privacy as she had violated his, by standing there and looking at her naked body as long as he wanted.

When it came to it, though, after he turned on the overhead lights he didn't walk over to where she would be lying in her coffin. Because it was still wrong. Just because she wrote in his plog didn't give him the right . . .

She didn't have the right to write in his plog, either, but what did *she* care about *his* privacy? She didn't have to, because she knew as well as he did that she was the powerful one. She was the one with vision. He was just the mechanic.

She was the pilot, that was it, and he was just the guy who fueled up the plane and made sure the parts all worked. And even though every passenger on a plane entrusted their lives to the mechanics every bit as much as to the pilot, the mechanics were just . . . manual laborers, after all. The pilot was the glorious one. The one who got to do whatever he wanted, even if it hurt other people deeply.

Laz sat down and leaned against the wall near the door. He closed his eyes and thought about napping. But that wasn't going to happen. He didn't like being in this timestream where he had committed canicide and where he had planned to avenge himself on Ivy by gazing on her naked body in the box it came in. Pristine condition, ready to make top dollar on eBay. It made him sick with embarrassment to find out that he was that kind of guy. Even if in fact he *wasn't* that kind of guy, he had gone this far, hadn't he?

He heard a sound.

He recognized it. Though it was farther away, and fainter, it was the sound of the lid of a coffin sliding open.

Laz stood up and walked quietly out of the room.

He thought of turning off the lights, but she should have the lights on, it would make everything easier.

He thought of closing the door, but she should see an open door so she'd come out the right way.

He didn't take the elevator up to the ground floor. Instead he used the stairs, so the elevator was still on her floor. If she realized what it was, she could use it.

Then he went up to the lobby—whose door was *not* held open by a couch—and lay down on that couch and dozed off.

He woke up with the sound of someone opening and closing drawers and cupboard doors. It was Ivy, dressed in her pajamas, her hair still long and unshaped from lying in the box, checking to see if there was anything in the compartments under the reception counter. Laz already knew there was nothing there. He also wasn't sure he wanted to engage in any kind of conversation with *this* Ivy. This Ivy was newly hatched and hadn't yet been annoying and mean, hadn't yet agreed that they needed to trust each other and then read his private writings and actually written in them. This Ivy was still innocent. At this point, most of her memories came from someone else's head—someone who was genetically identical to her, but still was *not* her. He couldn't speak to her as if he already knew her, because she didn't know *him*.

Or did she? He didn't know what memories had been pumped into her brain. Nor did he know how much she could learn from her ability to search into timestreams. Would she immediately know that he had been in the coffin room and turned the lights on? Almost certainly. Would she know that he had been with her in another timestream, and side stepped to this one in a huff?

Why should she think he valued his privacy, considering that with her around, any notion of privacy was purely imaginary? She knew too much all the time, while he knew *nothing*. He had the power, she had the knowledge, and it was impossible to function that way.

It was possible she hadn't actually noticed him here on the couch. So he swung his legs off, rose to his feet, and quietly moved away.

"I hope I didn't wake you up," she said.

"No, you were loudly opening and closing drawers and doors in order to help me sleep," said Laz.

She stood looking at him, expressionless. "All right," she finally said, "that's fair. I was trying to wake you up. But I wanted to do it kind of naturally and accidentally, instead of coming up and prodding you and saying, 'Wakey wakey, sleepy time's over.'"

"Good choice," said Laz.

"I know who you are," she said. "It makes sense that they'd have a clone of you here, too. But isn't there anybody in charge?"

"It's you and me, kid," said Laz.

Again she studied him. "It really is just us here in this city, isn't it."

He realized that she must have scanned the timestreams and figured out that they were the only ones there in all of them. "I don't want to stay in this timestream," he said. "In this timestream, my dog is dead, and I killed him."

She studied him more. "So you loved the dog," she said.

"Not in *this* timestream. He killed and ate a squirrel I had trained to come out on the patio of the house where I was squatting. I had *tamed* that squirrel, so it felt safe around me, and he leapt out and killed it. I had rocks, he was only a meter away from me, I threw as hard as I could—"

"And you hit him in the head and he dropped dead at your feet," said Ivy. "That's a really sad story."

"It's in another timestream where he and I made friends. In this one, I just scared him enough to keep him away from me. I never fed him. And there was that tame squirrel."

"So how does this work?" she said. "You side step to another timestream, and you leave me behind here?"

"I leave *me* behind here, too. I don't know what part of me it is that makes me *me*, but my side stepping is really just going from one timestream's version of me to another's. So I imagine that you and I will go on having charming adventures here, probably coming to hate each other, even though the Traveler part of me will be somewhere else."

She nodded wisely. "So you've got this all figured out."

"I've got nothing figured out," said Laz. "For instance, when I leave—when this Traveler leaves—will the version of Lazarus that I leave behind here also be able to side step? Does *every* version of me have that power? If so, why aren't every version of you and every version of me opening up Portals to other timestreams?"

She looked taken aback. "Do you think I understand what in hell you're talking about?"

"The version of you that I know best has been side stepping with me for a couple of months now. You supply the destination, you put the timestream into my mind, I hold your hand and pull you with me into it."

"Okay, okay," she said. "What about me? Do I step into the body

I already had in that new timestream, just like you do? Or do you physically bring me in, even if it means there'll be two copies of me in the new timestream, and none at all in the old one?"

"I'm not sure how we'd experiment with that to find out. I mean, if you come with me, there you are. If I side step into the old place, are you also still there? And if you aren't, does that mean I took you with me to the new place, or just that I can't find you in the old one?"

She laughed. "There's a version of our past where we've already talked about this and done a lot of stuff, right?"

"You know already," said Laz. "You always already know everything."

"People hate that," said Ivy. "But until I heard about *you* and your side-stepping thing, I thought that knowing about everybody's past, all the choices they made, the things that *could* have happened if they had chosen differently—I thought that's all that my talent *was*. I didn't know that I could put a timestream into your mind and you could take us both there."

So Laz filled her in on the Portals and the New Place and Shiva that was coming to destroy them. "But come on," said Laz. "You already knew all that."

"I did not," she said. "But I can see that you've lived a long time with another version of me, and you told her all this, and she told you everything that she could see, and you don't like her."

Laz shrugged. "She won't let me," he said.

"Why not?" she asked.

"I don't know," said Laz. "Just when I think we've worked out a truce, and we talk about trusting each other, she reads my private journal and writes in it."

"Well, that's a lousy thing to do," she said. But he could see that she was also trying to keep from smiling.

"Yeah," he said, "that's the sort of thing you find amusing."

"Yes," she answered. "Come on, so do you."

He winced. "I used to play a prank or two. It went too far. It got out of hand."

"So don't you think that when some other version of me is particularly mean and hostile and untrustworthy, maybe it's *her* way of keeping us apart?"

Laz put his hands in front of his face. "You just woke up. You don't have a right to psychoanalyze me yet, not until I've provided you with canned food that has lost most of its flavor and food value."

"I'm not psychoanalyzing *you*," she said. "I'm analyzing *me*."

"You're quite the specimen," said Laz.

"You think I'm pretty," she said.

He shrugged. "Doesn't matter."

"Why doesn't it matter?" she asked.

"We're supposed to be working together, not creating some kind of relationship."

"Who says?" she asked. "I don't see a lot of people coming into these timestreams and giving us instructions and rules."

"No," said Laz. "No, we're on our own."

"So we're making the rules."

"No we're not," said Laz, "because we can't agree on anything. I just know that you don't like me and you constantly make me feel awkward and wrong."

She sat down on the couch, but backward, her knees against the back of the couch. Her thigh right up against his thigh. She put her hands on his shoulders, then slid them around behind his neck. She drew herself close and kissed him.

He tried to draw back. This isn't right, he was thinking. This will wreck everything.

Except that she was a good kisser and he really liked it.

"You've never been kissed before," she said. Their lips were still so close together that he could taste her breath coming into his nose and mouth when she talked. Then she kissed him again. He thought maybe he did a better job of kissing her back, now that he wasn't trying to get away.

"Not a lot," he said. "Never."

"Why not?" she asked.

"Nobody offered," said Laz. "And the ones I tried to get to know better made it clear that no part of my body was ever going to touch any part of *their* body."

"That's mean," she said.

"They didn't say it outright."

"Oh, you mean that you performed romantic triage and removed yourself before you could even find out what might have happened?"

"I always knew what was going to happen."

She rolled her eyes.

"Look, Ivy," he said, "you're you, so you should remember that I'm me. I tried to start conversations, I offered to help with homework, I asked a couple of girls out."

"And when you started feeling awkward, you bailed. You side stepped."

"It was easier to get through every day at school if there weren't any girls who knew that they had flamed me out of existence for daring to think I was worthy of using up oxygen in their presence. I was just another heap of protoplasm whom they had *never* humiliated by scorning my feeble, awkward attempts to—"

"You big baby," she said. Then she kissed him again.

"You've got to stop doing that," he said.

"Why?" she asked.

"It's a bad idea. You never did that before."

"Well, *this* time I haven't had a chance to get to know how despicable and repulsive you are."

Laz almost side stepped, that hurt so badly. But instead he slid away from her on the couch.

"You didn't side step," she said.

"Oh, trust me, I'm going to."

"So why didn't you?" she asked. "Don't make up some stupid rationalization. You didn't side step because you really liked me kissing you and you don't want to leave the timestream in which this happened."

"In the other timestream," said Laz, "the one I came here from, you and I have worked out how to go into timestreams where neither of us exists. We know how to leave a string connecting one of these unrelated timestreams to the other. We still don't know half enough about how it all works, but that Ivy knows how to do it and . . ."

"You think I can't learn it all?" she said. "Just cause I got a late start?"

"It's just not right," he said. "She did all that work, and now I'm going to cut her out of it?"

"Not *she*," said Ivy. "Me. It's me."

"No it isn't," said Laz.

"So let's say you go back to her. And to your dogs, who are still alive and eating out of your hand. You think she won't *know* that you and I sat here making out for a few minutes?"

"Of course she'll know," said Laz. "And she'll ridicule me for getting into it like a puppy dog, and she'll make fun of me for wanting to kiss her."

"*I* won't," said Ivy. "Because the whole kissing thing was my idea. My way of getting a good close working relationship with the scientific genius of the age."

Laz closed his eyes.

"Oh, you don't like being famous?" she asked.

"*I'm* not famous. My original was. Is. I've done nothing to earn it."

"It's so hard to be a clone, isn't it," she said, in a teasing, mock sympathetic way.

"Yes," said Laz. "And it's hard to be a seventeen-year-old kid who suddenly wakes up in a coffin in the dark with not another soul in the city—a city that he's never been to before in his life. That's hard."

"Thanks for leaving the lights on for me."

"I almost didn't," said Laz.

"Because you were still angry at that bitch Ivy who treated you so badly back in the Land of Dogs."

She said it so pertly, with just the right blend of coquettishness and ridicule, that he had to laugh. "I was really mad," he said.

"If you take me back to the Land of Dogs," said Ivy, "what do you think will happen? Will that rude unkissable Ivy still be there? Or will my coming make her disappear? Or will I do what you do, and simply *become* her, including all her memories, plus these memories?"

"I have no idea," said Laz.

"You've never tried the experiment?"

"I always bring her with me," said Laz. "Well, almost always. And when I don't, then I don't make contact with any version of her in the other timestream."

"Until now," said Ivy.

"Is that what we were doing?" asked Laz. "Making contact?"

She laughed. Not a mean laugh, not a snide laugh, not a you're-the-joke laugh. It was a happy laugh, a we're-in-this-together laugh. It was a laugh that promised he could kiss her again, and maybe something more, maybe become a friend, a real friend. Her boyfriend.

And then she'd say something or do something to take it all away, to make him ashamed that he had let himself admit how much he liked her, how much he'd like to find out if he loved her, and if she could possibly love him. She'd lead him on to commit to something and then taunt him for it. Make him ashamed in front of the only other person in the world. The person who would matter most to him even if there *were* other people.

"You don't trust me," said Ivy.

"I've been burned every time I tried to make friends with you," said Laz.

"And you think I haven't?"

"You never tried to make friends with me," said Laz. "Not in any way that I could recognize."

"You can't say never," said Ivy, "because I just kissed your brains out and you know it."

"The other Ivy. The other versions. I admit, this was nice. You're nice. I'm just not sure how I can believe it. Why should I try?"

"Maybe your coming here on the very day that the healing cave woke me up, maybe that means we get a fresh start. You woke the other Ivy ahead of schedule. Maybe the machinery hadn't installed my niceness unit yet. I wasn't ripe."

Laz laughed. "Okay, maybe that's it."

"I'm ripe now," she said. She held out her arms.

He wanted to slide back to her on the couch, he wanted to go back to the kissing, he wanted to . . .

He stood up and walked away, walked over by the curving stairway that led up to the next floor.

"Walking away like an ordinary man, not side stepping like the wizard of the timestreams," said Ivy.

"Apparently so," said Laz. "Wizard of the timestreams? Is that what somebody called me?"

"It's what everybody called you. Maybe not to your face. In those days, I was nowhere near your face. I never thought I'd meet you."

"You didn't. That guy, him you never met."

"True. He was already old. I mean, compared to me. But you're not. It's like I got a backstage pass and instead of hanging out with the big celebrity guy, I get to meet this kind of shy, completely decent guy who is seventeen years old and isn't full of himself or surrounded by groupies or constantly so busy he wouldn't have time to meet a girl like me and let her do this."

She had walked up to him by now, and her arms were around him. She slid her hands into his back pockets. She kissed him, and he cooperated because even on tiptoes she wasn't quite tall enough unless he bent to her. And he bent, and put his arms around her, and . . .

Side stepped.

He was on the porch of the house, opening cans of food for the dogs.

Ivy came out the front door almost immediately. She stood behind him for a while. Reading my timestreams, he thought. She's seeing everything because why would I want to have any privacy?

"So you met the real me," said Ivy.

"No," said Laz. "Just another fake. In this town, it's all clones and clowns."

"Did you like the way I kissed you?"

"Yes," said Laz. Because there was no point in lying, even though he knew the truth gave her power over him. Trying to deny the truth would give her even more power.

"I found out that I could do that," she said, "because I saw it in the timestreams. I knew I was reasonably pretty, but it didn't matter. Because there are always girls who know the great secret of teenage romance."

"And what is that?"

"What my hornier self did on your little jaunt into the Land of No Dogs."

"Just walk up to a guy and start to kiss him?"

"It's amazing how often it works. Not always. Some guys don't like to be touched. Some don't like girls. Some think they're too good for me and they don't want to be *seen* kissing me. But yeah, I could pick a guy, chat with him for a second, get him laughing, and then kiss him. I'm a natural, it didn't take any time at all to be good at it. Or at least good enough for shy, lonely, awkward guys to feel really good."

"You actually did that."

"I saw the timestreams where I did it," said Ivy. "And I knew how it would work out."

"Of course you did," said Laz.

"He'd end up caring about me a lot more than I cared about him. Needing me more than I needed him. So I would break up with him and then he'd feel hurt and cheated and betrayed. Because I hurt him and I cheated him and I betrayed him. It made sense."

"So you didn't walk up and kiss them after all."

"Every now and then," she said, "I'd walk up to a good guy who deserved to have some woman love him. And I'd put my fingers on his lips, and I'd say, 'There's a woman who's going to kiss those lips of yours and love you, and you're going to love her back. No, it isn't me. But you deserve to know that it's possible for you, that it's going to happen. You need to think of yourself as the kind of guy that a smart and pretty woman is going to want to kiss.' And then I'd walk away."

"Leaving him as a heap of ashes still looking like a living person but completely dead inside."

"Don't be an idiot," said Ivy. "It made their day. Their week. Their year. It changed the way they walked. The way they talked to people, especially girls, especially strangers. They had more confidence. More hope."

"Let me guess. That happened because unless you could see that happy outcome in the timestreams in which you did that, you wouldn't do it. You only did it when it was guaranteed to succeed."

"That was my rule. Doesn't mean there weren't also timestreams in which it backfired. But I figured, as long as most of the timestreams led to good places, it was worth doing."

"Except to me," said Laz. "Somehow letting me know that you thought of me as being worthy to love, *that* wouldn't work out well."

"I did," she said. "You just got back from getting my slobbery kisses all over you."

"Just on my mouth," said Laz. "Try to be accurate. And that wasn't you."

"It was Ivy Maisie Downey," she said. "And that's me."

"No," he said. "*This* Ivy reads my journal, my inmost hopes and fears, and writes a mocking comment in it. That's a little different from kissing my face off. Don't you agree?"

She nodded and sat down on the porch beside him, picked up a can of Spam and opened it. She pried out the meat product and let it drop onto the ancient rubber welcome mat at the bottom of the porch stairs.

"I take that as a yes," said Laz.

"She really did get cooked in the healing cave a little longer than me," said Ivy. "So even though our genes are identical, maybe she's better at this business of being a human."

"You're plenty human," said Laz.

"So I see the timestreams in which I lean over and kiss you, just like she did, but in every one of those timestreams you pull away and things get *really* weird between us."

"They're already weird. They've always been weird," said Laz.

"She kissed you and you liked it, because you knew that *she* had never teased you or ridiculed you. You thought that maybe she meant it. The kisses."

"Sure," said Laz. "Probably. I don't know. I was so mad at *you* that maybe this was like, I don't know, making out with your sister?"

"You weren't getting revenge," said Ivy.

"You don't know what's in my heart."

"Neither do you," she said. "But you went to Vivipartum and

you found a version of me that wasn't wearing those pajamas. You were going to get even with me for violating your privacy by violating *mine*."

Laz said nothing. She couldn't see into his mind.

"Here's what I know about you," said Ivy. "I know all the timestreams that were gathered there when you opened the door and turned on the lights in that clone orchard. But there was *no* timestream in which you walked over and looked at my naked body in the coffin. Your fury and desire for revenge got you into that place, but nothing could make you actually shame me by staring at my naked body."

Laz shook his head.

"Admit it, Laz. You're a decent guy."

He shook his head even harder. "I don't know about decent. I don't know about moral principles. I just knew that if I did that, you'd know it, and you could never . . ."

"Never what?"

"You've seen the timestreams, you've already heard everything that I might say."

"You didn't violate my privacy," said Ivy, "because you care about me. You care more about my happiness than about your anger."

Again, Laz didn't say anything.

"And you think that if we actually got some romantic thing going, we couldn't work together. We couldn't save the world because we'd only think about love."

"And now the damage is done," said Laz. "Because I *have* kissed Ivy Maisie Downey. Not the one I was actually in love with. But the one who wanted to kiss me, so . . . it was all I was ever going to get."

That was when he realized that the secret had spilled out of him before he knew it himself. The one I was actually in love with. He was in love with her—with the Dogland version of her. And he had just told her.

Not that she showed any sign of having heard. "And you liked it," she said.

"I keep wondering what would have happened if I had brought *her* with me," said Laz.

Ivy shook her head. "I'm already here. You didn't bring *her*, not physically, but you came back to me, and I saw the timestreams, and the ones I was in, I could take them in like memories. I absolutely remember kissing you. I remember wondering why you didn't try to take it further."

"You were fresh out of the box," said Laz. "I don't take advantage of a woman just because she's so looney as to kiss me."

"And there we are," said Ivy. "You hate the way I talk and act, my flippancy and my unconcern for your feelings, but it's only because I'm socially awkward and even though I can see all kinds of bad consequences I still can't help but be who I am. You don't know how many times I *didn't* say something that would have been far worse. Unforgivable."

"I'm not sure that I'm glad to know you thought of things that were too horrible for even *you* to say," said Laz.

"I know you love me," said Ivy. "I already knew. You were in love with me, or at least the idea of me, when I was still in the box. And that scares the Chef Boyardee out of me."

"At this moment," said Laz, "you've made me feel way more naked and ashamed than you could ever have felt if I had looked at you naked in the coffin."

"Quite possibly," said Ivy. "But you've got nothing to be ashamed of."

"I'm ashamed that you know my heart when you . . ."

"Laz," said Ivy, "I don't *have* a heart."

"Bull," said Laz.

"I always see down every road," said Ivy. "So instead of hopes and dreams, I have information. I can select from a menu. I'm socially awkward but I choose to say the wrong thing even when I don't have to, even when I don't just blurt it out, and you know why? Because what if somebody loved me? What would I do about that?"

"And now you know," said Laz.

"Yes," she said. "I make his life hellish so he wants to get away from me and even kills his beloved dogs to do it."

"And then you kiss me and make me feel—"

"Horny," she said.

"Loved," he finished.

She shrugged. "There," she said. "I've done it again."

"Yeah," he said. "You have." He reached down and stroked StarKist's fur, and scratched under the chin of the dog he called Hip, because he had thrown a stone and hit him in the hip and injured him, back when he first tamed the Pack of Four. These were the ones he had killed when they massacred his tame squirrel, in that other timestream. The one where Ivy woke up and kissed him.

Laz got up and went inside the house. It was dark inside; there were light switches but he knew that they'd do nothing. He couldn't say, "Alexa, play *Scheherazade* by Rimsky-Korsakov," the way Dad did. Dad loved that piece. And Laz—no, the Original Heap of Laz— would sit by him in the living room and watch Dad's hands move subtly as if he were conducting the orchestra. And now and then Dad would murmur, "Too slow, too melodramatic, keep it lively, you're telling a story."

One time Laz had asked him, "If he conducts it wrong, why do you always listen to *this* recording? Hasn't somebody recorded a version that's right?"

"Yes," he said. "A couple of recordings that are glorious and even though they're quite different, the conductors' and the musicians' choices were all completely defensible."

"So why don't you listen to those?" said Laz.

"I do, sometimes," said Dad. "But they're so good, they're so right, they don't *need* me. How will they ever get better if somebody doesn't tell them what they're doing wrong?"

"You know that's insane, Dad," said Laz.

"That's why I only do it in front of you," said Dad.

Laz lay on his bed, his head nestled in the curved airplane pillow.

She read my plog and she ridiculed it. I'm trying to be a grown-up, but she's as lost and scared as I am. She's trying to figure out right things to do, just like me.

And she's right, I loved her from the start, and if I love her I can't punish her in retaliation for when she hurt me.

I *hate* it that I love her. Because like she said, she hasn't got a heart. She isn't ever going to love me back. She'll bestow kisses as a favor, like scattering coins from the king's carriage as he rides through town. But she won't love me, she won't let herself need me.

But she *does* need me. Not for love, but for our work. We have a job to do, that's what we were cloned for, and someday they're going to come and tell us what they want us to do. And on that day she'll need me with her, and I'll need her with me, and we'll find the place, the timestream, that will do what they need. And when we accomplish it, we'll love each other the way good colleagues do. We'll rely on each other and we'll come through for each other.

Or if we don't, it won't be because I didn't try.

The door to his room opened. Of course it was Ivy—who else would it be? He didn't need to open his eyes to look at her. So he lay there and listened.

"Laz," she said. Her voice was very soft. "I really do care about you. I want you to be happy. I'll kiss you again, I'll . . . sleep with you if you want. Right now."

Laz shook his head. "Ivy, you know perfectly well that you would not have come to my room and said that, if you had seen any timestreams in which I said yes and we went ahead and did it."

She took a couple of steps and plopped down on the bed beside him. "Try me," she said.

"And you can say that," said Laz, "because you knew there were no timestreams in which I would touch you here on this bed."

She made a huffish sound and put her hands behind her head. "You're a selfish son-of-a-bitch, you know."

"I know," he said.

"You won't let me make you happy," she said, "and then you feel persecuted because I don't make you happy."

"If such a thing as you proposed were ever to happen, it would happen because I believed you actually meant it," said Laz.

"You and your rules," said Ivy. She swung her legs off the bed and walked out of his bedroom, slamming the door behind her.

He looked for timestreams in which he said, Wait, wait, please come back. They existed. There were even timestreams where he

opened his eyes when she came into the room and saw by her desha-
bille that she really meant what she was offering. But it was already
too late. Because if he side stepped into one of those timestreams,
he would only *remember* making love to her. It would already be in
the past. It would be even worse than merely imagining it, because
he'd know that it happened but he hadn't been man enough to be
genuinely present for it. He was too busy trying to be a responsible
grown-up and a decent human for him to reach out and take a gift
that was offered to him, just because he knew that the giver didn't
really want him to take it.

Tomorrow we'll go back to stringing ourselves together and
tying ourselves to trees and the dogs and then going to other worlds
where there are no humans, to see what we find there, and to learn
how to turn strings into Portals. At some point, our overlords will
decide we've figured out enough by ourselves, and they'll come and
tell us what we're alive to accomplish.

When she wrote in his plog, it wasn't after he wrote about his
desire to be a grown-up. It was the entry right before it. About emergency medical technicians. It was a nothing plog. He shouldn't have
been so hurt.

But the plog entry right after it, it was already there when she
read it. If she read the EMT bit, she had to have read the next bit,
about how do you know when you're growing up. And after she read
it, she wrote her snide little post *between* the two plog entries. It
looked like it was just an answer to the EMT post, but he knew that
it was really her answer to his self-examination. It still hurt that she
had written what she wrote.

He pulled his plog out of his backpack and read again the entry
that it really hurt him for her to read and ridicule.

How do you know when you're growing up? How do you know when you've actually achieved grown-up status? It can't be just a matter of "when you're responsible for somebody else," because even though kids are bad at that, so are a lot of adults.

I've taken on StarKist, who was getting along without me, and if I dropped dead or stepped into a timestream where he didn't already exist and I didn't bring him along (would I even do that?) he'd undoubtedly go back to doing just fine without me.

And never has Ivy shown any sign of recognizing that she might ever need me for any reason, except to step into a stream where, as she points out repeatedly, she already exists, or at least a copy of her does. So am I responsible for her? She makes sure I know that she already knew <u>everything</u> I tell her. She always responds with impatience. Yes, yes, of course, as if everybody knew that so why did I think it was worth saying? Only I <u>know</u> she didn't already know all of it.

Maybe she thinks that being grown-up means already knowing everything, so to give that impression, she has to make me feel stupid for thinking it might be worth telling her something.

But what <u>is</u> being grown-up? I think not getting mad at her for her superior attitude is probably a grown-up way to behave. But should I not even notice or care how condescendingly she always treats me? To be a real grown-up, do I accept the subservience she thinks is my proper place? When I feel like walking off and leaving her, and then I don't do it because, you know, what if she needs me, is staying with her a grown-up decision? Or is it just pathetic?

She makes fun of me or at least rolls her eyes when I refer to myself as a man. But I don't think she'd like it if I called her a "girl" all the time. I try to think of myself as a man so I won't do kid stuff. Like deliberately repeating, over and over, something she asked me to stop doing. No, a good <u>man</u> doesn't behave like a brat. So I try not to. When I catch myself in time.

I have to give her credit for one thing, though. She's seen me writing this stuff, but she's never asked me about it, she's never pilfered it or teased me about it, and above all, she's never read it.

As far as I know, I should say. Maybe she's read it and she's hiding the fact from me. Maybe she thinks that reading this will be a good way to get to know the "real me," whatever that means.

That would mean she was deceiving me all the time, pretending that she's not even interested in reading my plogs when in fact she reads them all. Probably speed-reads them when I'm in the back yard laying a loaf.

If you <u>are</u> reading this, Ivy, and you make fun of me for trying to figure out just how much shit I should put up with from you in my effort to be a grown-up, then please understand that you are wrecking any hope of friendship and cooperation because how can I trust you if you deceive me day after day?

Please remember that while I don't have your amazing power to see all timestreams all the time, I am keenly aware of some easy-to-reach timestreams in which I did not wake you up at all, did not greet you when the machinery woke you up. Streams in which we have not yet met, and you're still figuring out how to get food out of a grocery store.

Back when you lived in a box, you never gave me any grief.

Having reread this plog, Laz realized that he practically challenged her to reveal that she had been reading the plogs. If she only had a few seconds, then what she wrote between the plogs was probably all she had time for while he was having a poo.

Maybe she was trying to create some kind of honesty between them. The little shit.

Laz picked up his pencil and began a new plog entry.

Another favorite infrastructure:

Airplanes with schedules and regulations and air traffic controllers.

Or failing that, one perpetually fueled airplane that has a really good instruction manual and airbags that deploy under the plane when it crashes so you can live through bad landings.

Sure, it never existed before, but as long as we're recreating an idealized infrastructure, why not improve on what we had?

How about really huge rubber-band-driven airplanes? The airplanes couldn't be huge, just the rubber bands.

Wind it up and fly from LAX to Hawaii. Or at least John Wayne Airport. Or Burbank.

8

How do you know when you know enough to make good decisions? Is there ever such a time? Maybe when you think you <u>do</u> know enough, that's when you're most likely to make really disastrous decisions.

Because whenever you think you truly know something, you turn out to be wrong, and the more certain you feel, the wronger you probably are.

Of course, by "you" I mean "me."

Later on that evening, Laz found himself wondering if Ivy was actually sleeping, or if she was lying awake brooding about things the way he was. Probably not brooding about the *same* things, like remembering how she kissed him and how it felt, and how it felt to have his arms around her, his hands on her back, knowing she was wearing nothing under that ridiculous flimsy pajama top. And thinking how it was a really good thing that she had chosen much more substantial clothing in several layers in *this* timestream.

Pretty sure she wasn't thinking about that stuff.

But there were other things he brooded about. What were their overlords waiting for? Hadn't the experiment paid off? Ivy and Laz had discovered a way to go to other worlds together, worlds where no humans existed. But they couldn't find a world in which Shiva wasn't coming, because Shiva was undetectable to the human eye. Even if it were reflecting sunlight and were quite visible in the night sky, he wouldn't know what he was seeing, because he had no idea what the sky was supposed to look like.

So if they really needed Laz and Ivy to accomplish some mighty task—or even to open new Portals to slightly different versions of the New Place, so that they could give a whole world to each language group, instead of having to coexist with each other and have all the old wars spark up again—then why didn't they get on with it?

Maybe the guys that Harris Teeter Man called in to look for him, maybe they were his one chance to integrate himself into the life of the New Place. Maybe by evading them he had signed his own death warrant because he'd be swallowed up by the Sun.

Maybe there *was* no purpose for waking them up. Maybe they had no idea about what the machinery at Vivipartum did. An alarm clock went off, saying Wake-up Time for Laz, and the machine woke him up. Maybe the people who set that alarm died without telling anybody, or simply forgot that they had set it. People forget things, especially when the alarm wasn't ringing in *their* bedroom.

Maybe there *was* no purpose for Ivy and Laz to be awake, except whatever purpose they made for themselves.

If anybody meant for Laz to be awake, why did people come to capture him when Harris Teeter Man found him? "We got an unauthorized kid calling himself Laz running around loose in the Old Place and he claims not to know anything about the New Place." When that report comes in, why send helicopters? Why not just say, "We know, leave him alone"?

Or maybe they said, "We know. Go pick him up, it's time." But it *hadn't* been time, because Ivy was still asleep.

Laz got up from his bed and saw that it was late afternoon because even though his window faced east, he could see that the whole yard, the whole street, was in shadow. They probably had about an hour till full dark. He must have slept twenty hours. No wonder he felt bleary and sweaty and uncomfortable.

He opened the door and padded into the family room on bare feet. His thought was to sit down on the couch and stare at the TV screen, because that's what you did in the evening when you were bored and none of your personal screens had any juice.

Trouble was, Ivy was already in there doing the same thing. Staring at the black screen. She didn't turn her head when he came in; he saw her eyes flick toward him and then back to the screen.

"Guess you're seeing a better show than I'm seeing."

"You're looking at me," said Ivy blandly, "so, yeah."

"You've got a point," said Laz.

"You know, I wasn't lonely in here," said Ivy.

"But I was bored with my own thoughts. I overslept, I think. I didn't come in here looking for you, I came in here because it was someplace to walk while there was still light coming into the house."

"Yet here I am, not wishing for company."

"Yet here you are, receiving unwanted company and still trying to be civil."

"No I'm not."

"By your standards, you're downright welcoming," said Laz.

Now she did look at him, with a cool and calculating eye. "Is this your idea of flirting?"

"I have no idea of flirting," said Laz. "I've read the word in books, but I've never done it successfully, or seen it done, least of all to me."

Ivy continued looking at him. "You know why I was always borderline angry with you?"

"Borderline?" asked Laz.

"You know why I *showed* way more anger than I felt?" said Ivy, apparently rephrasing.

"I do not," said Laz.

"Because I don't see myself as being even marginally attractive to men or, for that matter, women. I'm a person who skates through life because even though I can't side step like you, I know what recently happened and what soon might happen in all the available timestreams, so I have a general idea of how things will turn out if I do things this way or that."

"And so you chose which timestreams you wanted to avoid, and treated me in such a way as to avoid them," said Laz.

"That's it," said Ivy.

"So what hideous thing were you trying to avoid?"

"It's a sci-fi cliché," said Ivy. "At the end of the story, the only male and the only female survivor of the crashed spaceship turn to each other and the man says, 'Well, Eve, I guess we're going to be here for a long time,' and the woman says, 'That's right, Adam. Let's call this place Earth.'"

Laz had to laugh. "Mind if I sit down on the same couch with you?"

"It'll save me from having to crane my neck upward to converse with you," said Ivy.

Laz sat down at the opposite end of the couch, then rotated his body so that his right leg was on the couch while his left leg stayed on the floor. So that he was facing her.

"After my behavior yesterday—both of me," said Ivy, "I'm trying to guess what you think when you look at me. Am I huggy-kissy girl? Am I smart-mouth ass-face girl? Am I what-did-I-do-to-deserve-all-this-crap girl? Or did I underestimate you and am I, in fact, still naked girl?"

"Can we please leave naked girl out of the conversation, now and forever?" asked Laz.

"That bad, huh?" asked Ivy.

"What I was thinking about," said Laz, "was our relationship. Sure, at first I thought about it because we crossed several firm boundary lines yesterday and I didn't know whether I thought that was wonderful or terrible and so I *stopped* thinking about that and instead thought about whether nobody knows or cares that we're awake, or everybody knows and cares desperately about what we can figure out about our amazing superpowers, and if it's the latter, how can we possibly communicate with them and get on with the job? And if it's the former, at what point should I say, 'Well, Ivy, the world's going to burn to a cinder sometime in the next few years, so whaddya say, you wanna get it on?'"

Her first facial expression seemed poised to say something acerbic, but then she smiled. "Given the ridiculous offer I made a little while ago, I think maybe we already reached that point."

"If only we knew what they still needed from us," said Laz. "Our originals got them a Portal to another world. They've migrated billions of people to it, which is pretty remarkable— *we* didn't do that, it's a triumph of organization and good government."

"Unless they were machine-gunning anybody who refused to go," said Ivy.

"I've read a lot of history," said Laz, "and sometimes that's what passes for good enough government. Maybe the rest of the country, or the rest of the world, maybe it isn't as efficiently empty as Greensboro, North Carolina, but it seems to me as if they've probably done all they can to get people off this future ash heap."

"It'll only be an ash heap for a little while," said Ivy. "Then it falls into the Sun and becomes nuclear fuel."

"I wish I understood how things really worked. How can the Earth be destroyed in some timestreams, but still be out here orbiting the Sun from a safe distance in others?"

"And that world we visited," said Ivy. "How do human beings *not* evolve?"

"Maybe all the other animals caught sight of the timestreams *with* humans and voted us out of existence," said Laz.

Ivy gave a bitter little chuckle.

"Ivy," said Laz. "Unless we know how to tell whether we're in a Shiva-is-coming or a Shiva-is-*not*-coming timestream, nothing we do is going to matter at all. And there's nothing that can happen here on Earth or even in the solar system that can affect the movement of Shiva in any way."

"So maybe there *is* no good timestream?" asked Ivy.

"They think they found one," said Laz. "That's why they went to all the trouble of moving everybody there."

"Except us," said Ivy. "And a bunch of farmers in California."

"And the Harris Teeter Man," added Laz.

Ivy grinned. "And the Pack of Four."

"Ivy," said Laz. "Can we be friends now? Not just when the mood strikes us, but all the time? Even when one of us is pissed off at the other?"

"I'm willing, if I know what 'friends' means."

"It means that we care about treating each other with respect, and listening to each other, and making decisions together," said Laz.

"But we keep all our clothes on?" asked Ivy.

"We keep our hands to ourselves," said Laz. "And our mouths."

She genuinely looked a little stricken at that. Or maybe it only offended her that *he* was the one to say it.

"That's not a comment on the quality of the hands and mouths not being kept to ourselves yesterday," said Laz.

"I just hate to think I forced myself upon you," said Ivy.

"Every part of me except my brain approved," said Laz. And then he blushed, because he didn't particularly want her thinking about the various parts of him.

"Laz," said Ivy, "how are we going to make them move us to the next stage?"

"If we knew where the Portal was, we could go there," said Laz.

"We could go back to the Harris Teeter where you met the guy," said Ivy, "and wait for the next driver to stop and take a leak in that restroom."

"If someone ever comes," said Laz.

"Where there's a working toilet, they will come," said Ivy.

"Or we could try planting something. Or find where some over-grown garden still has volunteer vegetables coming up, and then weed them and wait," said Laz. "Start trying to figure out a way to stay alive and not starve to death on the dying cans of food we've been scavenging."

"In other words, give up."

"I'm not sure planting or tending crops counts as 'giving up,'" said Laz.

"It does," said Ivy, "if our goal is to find out how we might be of use to the human race."

"How about this," said Laz. "Instead of going back to Harris Teeter right now, let's go back to Vivipartum and see if there's any way to communicate with our overlords from there."

It was weird how returning to Vivipartum felt to Laz more and more like coming home. Even the dogs seemed to be comfortable going back there. After all, the huge lobby of Vivipartum was the only indoor space where they actually got fed. Dry, out of the wind, *and* eating— sure, that was enough to make it the Garden of Eden for dogs.

Leaving the dogs in the lobby with a few piles of dis-canned food, Laz took Ivy down the stairs to the computer room. Nothing was changed—the computer desk was as Laz had left it. He pulled over another wheeled chair for Ivy, but by then she had already stationed herself in what he thought of as *his* chair, right in front of the keyboard. He almost protested, and then remembered that he was not the boss here, nobody was. So there was no reason *he* shouldn't sit in the second chair.

She had the screen awake—easy to do, since all she had to do was move the mouse. He pointed out the two programs he had used, the different lists and menus. He essentially walked her through all his discoveries. "And you woke me up . . . how?" she said.

"I don't think I woke you up at all," said Laz. "I think the computer just reached a preprogrammed time to open your lid. Or it got a remote order from some other computer, maybe in the New Place."

"I woke up when you were there," said Ivy. "You spent a lot of time *not* there, but the lid happens to open when you're sitting at this computer?"

"I went to meet you before you climbed out," said Laz.

"Not afraid that seeing . . . my apparition would turn you to stone?"

He appreciated her *not* saying "naked girl" again. And he did not respond with a joke. "You're no gorgon," said Laz. He brushed his hand through some locks of her hair. "No snakes."

She found her listing. "So my mother's written down as the owner of my healing cave."

"Arya Daenerys Lopez," said Laz. "Not Downey."

"I'm sure it's just a legal-name thing," said Ivy. "Mom said that where she was born, women kept their own last name when they married and just added their husband's name to it. But we were in America, where the Latin American way was just weird. So I was registered at school and on my birth certificate with my dad's last name, but Mom kept signing her name as Arya Daenerys Lopez."

"Nice to have that teeny-weeny mystery resolved," said Laz.

"I'm sitting here thinking, How could my mother do this to me," said Ivy. "But then, she *didn't* do it to her actual daughter. She did it to a nameless clump of dividing cells that turned into me, a clone, property. It was like buying her daughter a purse, or maybe even a puppy. Her daughter paid *no* cost. All the confusion and loneliness were paid by this . . ."

"Heap of protoplasm," Laz offered.

"Yeah," said Ivy. "That isn't outdated slang in this case. It's the simple truth."

"We have to remember that even though *we* have memories of our families, *they* have no memories of us," said Laz. "So even if they're alive in the New Place, they won't know us."

She was looking now at Laz's entry. "And what's with your owner's name here. Narek Tigran Hojrian. I learned about you in school with the last name Hayerian."

Laz shrugged. "Dad and Mom decided that Americans would never figure out how to pronounce Hojrian. The J is just too confusing. So they anglicized the name a little more, and we became the Hayerians. Only Dad kept the old Armenian name while the rest of us became true blue Yankees."

"And your stepfather didn't demand that you take *his* name?" asked Ivy.

"My mom didn't even take his name," said Laz. "And as for me, he couldn't adopt me even if he wanted to, because my father was alive and when Dad asked me if I wanted him to terminate his parental rights so Doofus *could* adopt me, I told him where he could stick that idea."

"What an ambiguous moment. You tell your dad to shove the idea of severing parental rights up his ass, which is normally crude and offensive, but in fact it's a ringing affirmation of your desire to keep him as your father."

"I'm sure it made him happy-mad. Mad-happy?"

"Happy-mad," said Ivy. "Ambivalence is a good thing to cultivate in your parents. That way they're never quite sure where they stand."

"I think it's better if parents can trust their kids, and vice versa," said Laz.

"And it sounds like you did. And do."

Laz chuckled. "Till they stuck me in this hellhole to wake up all alone."

"Now, now. You're not really their kid, so—"

"It isn't a hellhole, either. I was more comfortable in that damn coffin than I have ever been trying to sleep anywhere else in this town."

"You think the machines would take us back?" asked Ivy.

"I don't really want to try," said Laz. "What if they let us back in, close the lids, then realize we're not supposed to be there and stop functioning? No life support, no air exchange, and we end up like all those other inhabitants of coffins here."

"Such an excellent, nightmarish idea," said Ivy.

"What's with your mother's names? They don't sound Spanish."

"Her mother named her for a beloved character from a book she grew up on. Or a TV show. I'm not sure I ever actually knew."

"As good a reason to name a kid as any other."

"And my middle name is from the actress who played another favorite character from the same show. Can't have been the book—there aren't any actresses in books."

"Why is it your mom's name and not your dad's?"

"Why shouldn't it be my mom's name?" asked Ivy.

"I was prying. I wondered if your parents were still married."

"They're very Catholic. Nobody divorces inside the very serious Catholic Church," said Ivy.

"They weren't happy together?" asked Laz.

"How would I know?" said Ivy.

"Come on," said Laz. "Kids know."

"'Happy' is such a strong word," said Ivy. "Dad never came home drunk. His whole paycheck came into the house and was not spent on a bunch of outside women or his drinking buddies. Where I grew up, that made him a model husband and father."

"I think it's taken that way in most places," said Laz.

"Dad was an Anglo, and he never learned Spanish," said Ivy.

"Ah. So your mom had to learn English."

"Yes, she did. Only she didn't do it."

"Are you serious?" asked Laz.

"She had shopkeeper English," said Ivy. "And Dad had pick-up-girls Spanish. That's how they met."

"And it never got better?" asked Laz.

"When they got mad, I learned how to swear fluently in three different languages."

"Three?" asked Laz.

"My mother's dad was Brazilian."

"Oh, come on."

"You asked about my family. It's not that uncommon in Latin America. For you Anglos, the Rio Grande and the Florida Strait are a huge barrier. But for us, between any two Latin American countries, the borders matter, sure, especially during football games, but the cultural barrier just isn't that big. Chileans don't speak the same Spanish as Venezuelans, and nobody speaks the Spanish of Cuba, but my grandparents didn't think a Brazilian marrying a Costa Rican girl was a big deal."

"And everybody stayed married even though nobody could talk to anybody else."

"Everybody talked to everybody!" said Ivy, laughing. "Loudly. Waving their hands and their arms. Explaining dirty jokes to each other, with us kids translating the Spanish for my dad and my grandfather saying the perfectly good Spanish sentence, 'Aprenda Castellano.'"

"Learn Castilian," Laz guessed.

"There are lots of different versions of Spanish even in Spain," said Ivy. "But to Brazilians, Spanish *is* Castilian. Only my grandfather was actually saying it in Portuguese. It just happens to be exactly the same except for the vowels. And the Brazilian accent."

"So you *are* the melting pot of America," said Laz.

"Said the Armenian boy," said Ivy.

"No, I'm *just* American now."

"A luxury available to boys who look so Anglo."

"You look American to me," said Laz. "Everybody does."

Ivy seemed to think about that for a moment. "How do we signal them from here?" asked Ivy.

"Change something," said Laz.

"Like what?"

"Maybe the way they knew to wake you up was that I was calling up lists and making choices on the menu. That told them—if they have remote access—that told them I was awake and I had found the computer room and activated the computer which they had obviously left running so I could find it."

"So why didn't they come right *then* and pick us up?" asked Ivy.

"You've got the time order wrong," said Laz. "I came back to Vivipartum *because* they had helicopters out looking for me. I thought: If they arrest me and nobody listens to me, that girl is going to wake up with nobody to help her get through her first few days."

Ivy said nothing. Then she dabbed at an eye.

"Oh, come on," said Laz.

"You came back for me," she said.

"I know how scared and confused I was. I figured if I could immediately introduce you to the canned sludge that constitutes the cuisine of American grocery stores at this stage in our nation's history, and if you met the Pack of Four, you wouldn't feel alone. And I knew where the department stores with a lot of clothes were."

"You were, in fact, a lifesaver," said Ivy. "Because you *were* there,

I don't know what it would have felt like to wake up alone. Don't know if I'd've been a basket case or perfectly resourceful."

"You would have commanded the roads to smooth out and lead you where you wanted to go."

"I didn't have to strip any clothing off of corpses."

"It was summer," said Laz.

"So now I've issued five commands, causing the lists to re-sort and re-format and all. Do you think that's enough to get their notice?"

"If there's anyone looking, sure," said Laz. "Why not?"

"So now we go to the beach and spend the afternoon working on our tans?"

"Except for the beach part, sure." And despite all his efforts at controlling his thoughts, he pictured Ivy lying naked on the sand asking him to apply suntan lotion everywhere. SPF 30? Or SPF 6? How dark would she want to be?

"You're right," she said. "No tanning. The tourists are always underfoot on the beach, anyway."

Laz almost said, Your skin is already a perfect color. Why would you want to mess with it? But that would be way too personal and too complimentary. It would suggest that he thought he had a *right* to an opinion about how brown she should get in the sun. And in fact he imagined that she might look even more gorgeous if she was browner, because right now, having just woken up in the box a few weeks ago, she wasn't all that brown. And she had an Anglo father, anyway.

Get your mind off her skin, off her body, off her beauty, Laz told himself savagely.

"So our work here is done," said Ivy.

"Bring up that ownership list again," said Laz.

"Okay," she said, doing it. "Why?"

"See if you can get an edit menu on your entry."

She could and did.

"Okay," said Laz. "Remove your mother's name and put in yours."

She grinned and chuckled as she did it. But when she chose save it reverted right back to her mother's name.

"I thought it was worth a shot," said Laz.

"Oh, definitely," said Ivy. "If somebody's monitoring this computer, then they saw an attempt to put *my* name in the ownership slot. Nobody knows my name, at least not in this computer. So . . . maybe somebody will get a *very* clear message."

They went back and found that the dogs had eaten everything. They had also apparently pooped in a few places, then walked through it, and then left footprints everywhere. "Why would they do that?" asked Laz.

"Because they're dogs," said Ivy. "They're not ashamed of their poo. It's like writing their names on a wall."

"They're not sleeping on *my* bed tonight," said Laz.

"They don't come indoors at *all*," said Ivy.

"Just sayin'," said Laz.

When they got home, stopping at a couple of grocery stores along the way in order to restock their larder, they found that a bear was messing around in the back yard.

"Let him do whatever he wants back there," said Ivy. "It's your toilet anyway."

"We can't leave the dogs out here with him around," said Laz.

"They know how to run fast," said Ivy.

"We've tamed them," said Laz. "That attaches them to this house, to us, and they might *not* run as soon or as fast as they should."

"Remember that at least a couple of them have completely poopy feet," said Ivy.

"A lot of that poop was worn off their feet during the trek back home," said Laz.

"While we stand here having this scintillating discussion, the bear could be rambling around to the front yard," said Ivy.

Laz opened the front door. "Do you think bears can operate doorknobs?"

"I think that if a bear wants to get into the house," said Ivy, "none of these doors and windows are likely to stop him." She followed him into the house, then stood aside as Laz held the door open for the Pack of Four.

It took a minute for them to believe the invitation. Then all the dogs *but* StarKist trotted in. From the smell as they passed, Laz knew exactly which dog had poopy feet.

Then Laz turned to StarKist. "You can stay out here if you want," said Laz, "but there's a bear nearby and even if you don't smell him, I bet he smells you."

Behind him, Ivy said in a slightly impatient tone, "He's waiting for an invitation, Laz. You're the alpha and he doesn't want to displease you."

"Please come in, O honored and respected StarKist, who didst not step in poo today, and therefore art all the more welcome."

StarKist declined his head, then rose to his feet and walked in, with a far more stately attitude than his comrades.

Laz closed the door behind him, and locked it.

"That's a good lock," said Ivy. "I'm so glad you locked it. That's the special anti-bear lock from Home Depot, isn't it?"

"Yes it is," said Laz, deciding not to take offense at her mockery and instead pretend that he had a sense of humor. "We need to cross a river sometime without a bridge, so the dogs have to swim for it. Wash off some of their filth."

"Let's side step to a timestream where nobody knows about Shiva and therefore there's still running water everywhere. Hoses and showers—hot showers—and towels and even deodorant and . . ."

"There's deodorant in all the drugstores," said Laz.

"I'm not bothering with it until you do," said Ivy.

"All I've seen for men is antiperspirant," said Laz. "My skin was designed to perspire in order to regulate my body temperature. I'm not putting on any chemicals designed to interfere with the natural function of my pores. Especially not when they're sadly out of date."

"Antiperspirants give you a rash?" asked Ivy.

"Red ugly itching rash," said Laz.

"If it isn't red and ugly and itching," said Ivy, "why bother getting a rash at all?"

They sat in the kitchen, watching the bear cavort in the back yard. He even climbed a hickory tree. They wondered if there was a beehive up there, but he didn't come down with either bee stings *or* honey. He was just lazing around. Not looking terribly hungry. Maybe he already harvested and snacked on all the squirrels and chipmunks in the area.

"I hope he doesn't decide to hibernate in the crawl space under the house," said Ivy.

"I think it's still too early for that," said Laz. "I mean, it isn't all that cold yet, not even at night. The leaves haven't even begun to turn."

"So you think bears don't choose their winter den until it's already so cold they need it?" asked Ivy.

"Why should bears be smarter than humans?" asked Laz.

"Because they are," said Ivy. "Have *you* picked out your den for winter?"

"No," said Laz. "I don't plan to hibernate."

"Good plan," said Ivy. "Because you sure haven't packed on enough fat to keep you through winter. As in, not an ounce of fat on your body."

Her turn to get personal, he thought. "This is the diet the world was waiting for," Laz said. "Stuff yourself like a pig every day, but use food so free of nutrients, even the bad ingredients, that you lose weight as if you were on an extended fast."

"If they send somebody to pick us up," said Ivy, "they better bring food, or I might team up with the bear and eat them."

This plog, as opposed to earlier and later ones:

All right, I've lost count and I think I left the rest of my plogs back at the house because I no longer care if she reads them. Actually I do care but I can't police her so I've decided not to worry about it. Except what I'm writing right now definitely constitutes worrying so who am I kidding?

The light is no longer on in the Harris Teeter. Did the bulb burn out, or is the electricity off? The toilet still flushes and then refills, the faucet still puts out cold water that seems drinkable enough, so maybe they aren't experimenting on us, or maybe they are. There aren't any light bulbs in the store so we can't try changing the bulb. Unscrew the bulb that might be burnt out, and then stick my tongue into the socket to see if it's live? An effective test, but what would I do with that information, if I lived?

Maybe bring a light bulb or two from the house to see if they'll work? I'm not sticking my tongue in the socket that was a joke and also supremely stupid. Though continuing to hang around with Ivy in this post-kissing phase of our relationship is not altogether different from the socket test—it can only cause me either disappointment or pain. Or brain damage. That's already happening.

What do they want from us? Smoke signals?

Ivy thinks we should leave town and see if there are people in Burlington or Winston or Reidsville or whatever other towns we come across. Did they empty out just this city or is the whole country really empty? If it's important to them to keep us isolated, then walking to another town might force their hand. If there really isn't anybody there, at least we'd be scavenging in a new place.

And the Pack of Four clearly need a nice long walk, because they've already run away from all the local bears and raccoons, being spineless and feebleminded canines, and they're stinking up our house even though we keep them in the living room and family room and never let them in the bedrooms. They aren't housebroken, and we decided moving out is easier than cleaning up, so who's the pigs, the Pack of Four or us?

It's really a matter of deciding which route will be smoother or safer or maybe even shorter. We still don't have a map, so anything we do is guesswork. We do have a pretty good idea that the town to the south of us, Asheboro, has or had the state zoo. It might be interesting to see what happened to the animals.

Then again, it might be fatal to see what happened to the animals. If they had, for instance, lions, we might be lucky that they didn't come ranging north to Greensboro already. I don't think my stone-throwing would impress any hunting lionesses. Nor would my ability to open a tuna fish can.

9

THE ATTEMPT TO walk to Burlington didn't get far. The overpasses were all intact, and despite the BRIDGE FREEZES BEFORE ROAD signs, the weather wasn't cold enough at night for that to be a problem. The problem was the number of cans they were trying to carry with them. They ended up opening half of them, leaving the dogs to eat their brains out, and walking back to Greensboro to find some kind of cart.

They found a bike trailer meant to carry children in the same bike store that had the solid tubeless tires, and after a while it was rolling smoothly enough. They rigged up a makeshift grip and each of them was able to pull it one-handed, even when it was fully loaded with about ten times the canned goods they had been able to carry in their overloaded backpacks.

Also, the Pack of Four hadn't followed them back into the city. Either they got eaten by something bigger than them—Laz's thoughts went back to the hunting lionesses—or they didn't care where Laz and Ivy went. Either way was fine—it's not as if they had bought the dogs as pets or paid for them to be wormed. But Laz realized that he missed StarKist. What ever happened to loyalty? After all the secrets Laz had spoken to StarKist, now the dog was probably going to go blabbing to everybody.

This time they got a lot further, past several freeway

interchanges. It turned out that getting the bike trailer up the slopes on the freeway was hard work—it took both of them gripping the handle with one hand, and when it was steepest, or the pavement was somewhat broken up, they both had to grip the handle with both hands and walk backward, or, on the steepest hill, Ivy pushed it from behind while Laz pulled backward.

StarKist rejoined them at an interchange labeled ELON UNIVERSITY, and if Laz had been alone and there hadn't been the whole business of the cart, he might have checked to see if there were any books left in the university library. But since there weren't any living people visible yet, no lights at night, nothing, he figured it would be a waste of time taking a side trip.

"Can't you just side step to a timestream where we *did* take a side trip?" asked Ivy.

"We're deciding right now," said Laz, "which means we couldn't have taken a side trip yet. So my side step would be to right here. This isn't time travel, please remember. I can't step into the future, that wouldn't be a side step, it would be a giant leap forward and that's not my talent."

"Got it," said Ivy. "I probably knew that, I was just wishing."

"Here's what I think we've learned," said Laz. "They don't care if we go to the next town. Elon looks like it's a big enough place that if there were people here, we'd see them."

"They might be hiding," said Ivy.

"They might be watching us from invisible balloons overhead, too," said Laz. "The point is, whoever woke us up—if anyone did—they don't care where we go or they'd already have intercepted us."

"Or we go over that next overpass and on the other side there are like twenty cop cars with blue lights flashing plus a bunch of cops and guys in FBI vests pointing shotguns and automatic weapons at us and telling us to lie on the ground. And if we don't obey fast enough, one of them shoots StarKist."

"Why are you bringing StarKist into your weird scenario?" asked Laz.

"I watched a lot of cop shows as a kid," said Ivy.

"That's such a crazy idea that now I want to get over that hill to see if they're there."

"We'd see the blue lights flashing on the trees beside the road," said Ivy.

"If we give up and go back to Greensboro, where there are more grocery stores to ransack for canned goods, will we pull this trailer the whole way?"

"We'll eat some of the contents, so it'll be lighter," said Ivy.

"But we still don't want to waste all this food if in fact nobody's going to come looking for us ever."

"Come on," said Ivy, "if we've really been forgotten and Shiva is still coming, then when the Earth's orbit is disturbed and we head on into the Sun, for our last dinner we can finally have *hot* food out of some of these cans."

"Always the optimist, aren't you, Ivy."

"The glass is half full," she said. "Of whatever happens to be in the glass."

"So do we go on to Burlington or turn back now?" asked Laz.

"How about we lock the car so nobody steals our food, and walk on to Burlington, see what's there, and when it's nothing, we come back and reclaim our abandoned vehicle and then we don't have to pull it so far."

"Very funny," said Laz. "Only I don't have a license so I couldn't have driven."

There was nothing in Burlington except a town considerably smaller than Greensboro, and nothing that made them wish to remain there, though if they were in Greensboro long enough that it ran out of canned food then this was certainly a place they knew they could get to.

They also got some clothes out of the outlet stores near the freeway on the far side of town. They slung them over their shoulders, and even though it was a long hot walk back to the bike trailer, they didn't drop any of them, because they might want them this winter.

Nobody had stolen their canned goods or interfered with the bicycle trailer. They hauled the trailer back toward Greensboro.

It got dark. They slept under an overpass in case it rained, they said, until Laz was more honest. "There's not a cloud. I just don't want to sleep where there's nothing between me and the woods. In case some animal smells us and decides we're prey."

"Thank you for voicing my own personal fears. I never liked camping out. Central Park in Manhattan was too wild for me."

"You've been there?" asked Laz.

"Once as a kid. Family trip."

"And you didn't like Central Park."

"I thought my parents were planning to abandon me there," said Ivy.

"Right," said Laz.

"Don't disparage my childhood fears. The story of Hansel and Gretel really got to me. I knew the gingerbread cottage and the mad baking witch were stupid, but parents wishing they could get rid of their kids, *that* sounded like a true story to me."

Laz chuckled. "Maybe that's what's happening to us here."

"Well, they gave us these freeways so we could find our way back without breadcrumbs."

"What they didn't give us," said Laz, "was a map to the Portal."

"You've got a point. Very Hansely and Gretely."

They slept somewhat raggedly—Laz woke up to step away and pee about as often as his father did each night. If Ivy had any trouble sleeping, Laz wasn't aware of it. But they were both stiff and sore when they got up. Ivy did a few stretches. Laz just walked around to loosen himself up. Through their whole ritual of waking, neither of them said a thing.

There was no reason to talk. They were simply retracing their steps back to Greensboro. Then there came a situation where Laz felt the need to caution her.

"This was the steepest slope coming, so I'm afraid it might get away from us going down," said Laz.

So this time they turned the trailer around and held back on it so it didn't get away from them. It got away from them anyway, but it didn't go far, and it didn't even tip over and tumble the cans. So all in all, the trip back to Greensboro was uneventful.

When they opened the door of the house, it smelled so bad that Laz went in to retrieve the airplane pillows and his plog and a couple of items Ivy asked for. Then they left the front door open and they went back to the Harris Teeter with the flush toilet. A space into which the dogs had never been admitted and, they now decided, never would be.

"We could try to train them," said Ivy.

"I think they're too old to housebreak them. Besides, when you housebreak a dog, you have to walk him every morning and every night," said Laz. "My dad says he was a slave to the bladder of my mom's dog. That may be one reason for the divorce—she had to walk her own damn dog after that."

"Quoting your dad?"

"He wasn't a complainer or an explainer," said Laz. "But I knew he didn't mind not having to get up at an exact time in the morning in order to avoid urine on the carpets."

"Remember back when a pet pooping or peeing indoors was the worst thing that could possibly happen?" said Ivy.

"It was never the worst thing that *could* happen," said Laz. "Children get sick and die, parents get divorced, school shooters, runaways going to the big city and—"

"The worst thing that happened a lot," said Ivy. "There are always hideous things you can't plan on. Like a vagabond planet coming close enough to the solar system to end all human life."

"Maybe they want us to side step into a universe where the countries with space programs had already worked on some serious spaceships that could carry a significant number of humans out of our solar system in search of a Goldilocks planet somewhere farther away from Shiva's path."

Ivy was silent for a while. "Laz, that's such a brilliant idea that I bet we already thought of it—I mean, our originals did."

"The Portals allowed every nation to evacuate all their people," said Laz, "and the spaceship idea would be miraculous if it even saved a thousand. That thousand might save the human race."

"So let's scope that out," said Ivy. "We've got plenty of time, presumably, so let's try a few timestreams."

"How will we know if they have a space program?"

"We side step into a version of Greensboro with a working library and lots of people and, you know, Google."

"But we won't *be* in any timestream like that, because nobody would have revived us," said Laz. "Or, I guess, vived us, because you can't *re*-vive a clone who's never actually been alive."

"Have you forgotten, Laz? We can get to a version of Earth that *doesn't* include us."

"A couple of things about that, Ivy," said Laz. "If all the people are still in Greensboro, then it means they either don't know about Shiva or they gave up. Something's going to be seriously wrong."

"We won't stay long," said Ivy. "Just long enough to—"

"We could try ten thousand of them and not find one with a generation ship," said Laz. "If you could find yourself, or even me, in that timestream, then sure, you could check the threads to see if we get on a spaceship—"

"I can't see that far ahead," said Ivy. "And who says they'd let us go on their thousand-passenger ship?"

"Another excellent point," said Laz. "Plus I'm afraid that if we got to a populated future, I'd just end up in jail because I only know how to survive by robbing grocery stores."

"And camping out in strangers' houses," said Ivy.

"And the Pack of Four will surely be picked up by animal control and put down."

"And," said Ivy, "if we had a lot of other people around, you wouldn't love me anymore."

"I don't love you now," said Laz. He was relieved when she rolled her eyes instead of taking him seriously. Of course he loved her. He had said so. And he had meant it. Still meant it.

Whatever "love" meant.

"But you talk to me and you do projects with me, and you're

always sleeping in the next room or on the other side of the customer service counter."

"Maybe," said Laz, "we should sleep in a mattress store, and then walk to Harris Teeter to use the toilet."

"Not a bad plan, though that seems like a kind of long walk on a full bladder."

Laz didn't remind her that bladders could be emptied anywhere, as they had proven on their jaunt to Burlington.

They found a mattress outlet store, broke in by prying a back door open, left some food for the dogs outside, flipped over a couple of mattresses so they could sleep on the non-dusty side, cuddled up on their airplane pillows, and slept like babies.

They woke up with lights flashing in the room and men in some kind of uniform or ninja outfit looking everywhere in the store, under mattresses and behind signs and displays.

This is exactly what Laz had feared when he ran away from the New Place searchers back when Harris Teeter Man called them in. He had no idea what they needed him for, but he was reasonably sure these guys weren't going to ask him politely for anything.

He had been free too long for him to tolerate someone controlling him.

"Is this what you had in mind?" Laz called to Ivy.

She shook her head.

Laz got up and walked toward Ivy, holding out his hand. One of the men pointed a weapon at him. "No," the man said.

"She's scared. She needs me to hold her hand." Laz knew Ivy would make him pay for *that* remark. But she would do it later, after they got away from this kidnapping team.

The man did not move his weapon. "Our specific instruction is *not* to allow you any physical contact with each other."

Apparently they believed that Laz and Ivy had to be touching each other to side step. Maybe going to a world that didn't already have them, that might be true—they hadn't dared to try it without some connection, it was always with strings binding them together.

But side stepping to timestreams that were only right next door, for weeks they hadn't had to be in physical contact to take such steps. They already had a tight enough mental or emotional or psychic bond—they had no idea how to label it. But they could side step locally on the same ticket, without touching. It took only a little more concentration from both of them.

Laz felt Ivy push a destination timestream into his mind and he side stepped.

They found themselves in the same mattress store, just waking up, but with no dark-suited guys and no lights. "I bet they're still coming," said Ivy. "They just haven't got here yet."

"Think we can get away?" asked Laz.

"If not I'll find a timestream where we did," said Ivy.

"Do we leave the dogs behind?" asked Laz.

The Pack of Four bounded around to the back door as Ivy and Laz emerged.

"I guess they're coming," said Laz.

"Hi, kids," said Ivy. "Were you off hunting?"

No sound of choppers or vehicles, so maybe in this timestream the guys in uniforms weren't coming tonight after all.

"Why are we running away?" asked Ivy, as they walked past an Italian restaurant in a strip mall. "I thought we *wanted* them to show some interest in us."

Laz was gratified that, not understanding his purpose, she had accepted his decision and given them a good destination. "I didn't want the kind of interest," said Laz, "that has them forbidding us to touch each other."

"You already forbade me to do that anyway," said Ivy.

"That was *our* decision," said Laz.

"That's not how I remember it," said Ivy. "But I'm glad you knew how much I needed you to hold my hand while scary things were happening."

"I don't want to be abducted and carried off," said Laz. "Who knows what kind of drugs they would try to inject us with? Besides, how stupid *are* they? How did they think they could take us prisoner? They put is in handcuffs, and we're off to another timestream to get tools to take them off."

"You know the first thing they'd do is separate us," said Ivy. "In which case, *you're* safe enough. But what about me? I'll see all kinds of better timestreams, but I won't be able to step into them."

That's exactly what Laz was most afraid of, being without Ivy and unable to help her; but he was glad she was the one who said it.

"Now that we know they're afraid of us getting together, we sleep on the same bed every night," said Ivy. "And yes, I mean the same bed *as each other* so we're already touching when they come to wake us up."

"Um, you also remember that we didn't actually disappear from that timestream," said Laz. "They still arrested a version of us and they're doing to them whatever they planned to do."

"But it's not *us* us," said Ivy.

"Maybe *that* Laz is also able to side step. Why wouldn't he be able to?"

Ivy shook her head. "Thinking that way takes us into crazy town," she said. "Because the split second after you side stepped, the Laz you left behind *also* side stepped, and the one *he* left behind side stepped, and so on. An infinite chain of you side stepping."

"And the last one would *still* be caught by them," said Laz.

"Then they'll accomplish whatever they accomplish in that timestream. Maybe under torture we figure out how to comply with all their insane demands or something. Maybe we save the world again. But *we*, we're still free, for a while longer."

Laz had no idea where they were going. This road was fairly commercialized, but there were tree-shaded residential areas within a block on either side. Though Ivy showed no interest in crossing the street.

His mind was racing, but he felt like he was in neutral, his engine revving but not making a bit of progress and not really in control of what he thought about. That image of a whole series of Lazzes side stepping away from the ninjas intrigued him. If every copy of him in every timestream could side step, why hadn't any of them side stepped into his own timestream? It might mean suddenly getting a whole raft of memories that he hadn't had a moment before—but would the side stepper take over, or were they really the same person, so Laz himself—whatever that meant—would be in charge?

He had no memory of being side stepped into. And when *he* was the side stepper, he picked up all the memories of the Laz he just merged with—but he got no sense of another mind being present, or even of any resistance. Whatever the target Laz had been doing or planning, the body now belonged to side stepper Laz.

Maybe the will of the target Laz disappeared once he arrived and took over. Or maybe, when he abandoned a timestream, the whole thing faded away in a year or two. Maybe it was his presence that allowed a causal stream to continue to exist.

What do you think you are? he asked himself. The center of the universe?

And if he was, did that mean that he was the center of Ivy's universe, too? That thought finally got him out of his solipsistic reverie and into the present moment. "So I'm supposed to sleep on the same bed with you, in physical contact with you," said Laz. "That's the plan?"

"Any objections?" asked Ivy.

"I'm already going insane because of your proximity, lady who once kissed me passionately for about fifteen minutes."

"Yet I'm still mortally offended because I offered myself to you and you declined. So we'll work it out. We can both pout ourselves to sleep each night."

"I wonder what they're planning for us in *this* timestream?" said Laz.

"I wonder what triggered their interest in us in the timestream we just left," said Ivy.

They were walking in front of a huge brick warehouse building when some armed men stepped out in front of them. Laz immediately looked back to confirm that there were some behind them.

Laz remembered no timestream ever in which he had become trained in martial arts. So he only waited for Ivy to send him a destination.

Ivy, however, spoke to the guy who seemed to be in charge. "Look, you know that we could not possibly be armed," said Ivy. "So what are all the guns for? You afraid we've trained some bears to attack anybody who lays hands on us?"

A signal from the guy who seemed to be in command. The guns were lowered, then slung over their shoulders. "You do have dogs," he said mildly.

"Are you going to boss us around and tell us a bunch of stupid rules you've decided on without consulting us first?" asked Ivy. "Because if you're planning to do that, we're out of here, and you know you can't stop us."

"We can threaten to shoot the dogs," said the guy in charge.

"But you like dogs," said Laz, though he had no way of knowing whether the guy did or not. "And you have no reason to do that. If you tell us what you want us to do, chances are pretty good we'll want to do it. If we can do it as free human beings rather than as captives or prisoners."

"Well said, Laz," said Ivy.

"*You're* the champion negotiator here," said Laz.

"Deal," said the guy in charge. "Though of course you know that there's no way you can enforce this agreement."

"But we can always get out of it," said Ivy.

"Whatever you want from us," said Laz, "you'll only get it by asking nicely."

"We would be very grateful," said the guy in charge, "if you would get into our helicopter and go with us."

"Where is the helicopter going?" asked Ivy.

"To the Portal," said the guy in charge.

"And where is the Portal?" asked Laz.

"At the end of the helicopter ride," said the guy in charge. "I don't have a map to show you."

"You can say what city it's near to," said Ivy. "We've heard of a lot of cities and we have a pretty good idea of geography."

"American high school students?" said the guy in charge. "Not likely."

"Try us."

"It's near Florence, Kentucky," said the guy in charge.

"You deliberately picked an obscure town," said Laz.

"I bet it's right next to the Cincinnati Airport," said Ivy. "I flew through there and I remember it was in northern Kentucky."

The guy in charge grinned. "Nailed it," he said.

Ivy stood at the helicopter door. "How did this get here without us hearing it?"

"We landed hours ago," said the guy in charge.

"Get in," said another guy.

"I don't know if I'll get sick in a helicopter," said Ivy. "I get motion sickness."

"No problem," said the guy in charge. "We have vomit bags."

But Ivy still didn't get in.

Then StarKist and the Pack of Four came bounding up. Ivy couldn't get them to jump up into the chopper. The guy in charge kept shaking his head. "We don't have seat belts for them," he said.

"If they jump out, they jump out," said Ivy. "We don't *own* them, I'm just inviting them along."

"They don't seem interested," said the guy in charge.

Laz leaned out the door and beckoned StarKist in. When StarKist made the jump, the others followed. Then Ivy climbed in.

"Four dogs?" said the pilot.

"These are all the dogs in the world that we like," said Laz.

"We've been feeding them," said Ivy.

"The same stuff *you've* been eating?" asked the guy in charge.

"We're all still alive," said Laz.

"Will these dogs behave?" asked the guy in charge.

"Of course they will," said Laz.

"It might be uncooperative, hostile, or dangerous behavior, but they'll behave *some* way," said Ivy.

"StarKist usually does what I say," said Laz.

"Why?" asked the guy in charge.

"I hit him very hard with a rock," said Laz. "And then I fed him the same nutrient-poor diet I was eating. I also shared the same crap food with Ivy, but I never hit her with a rock, so she's way less cooperative."

Ivy glared at him and then smiled, which defeated the effect of the glare.

The doors closed. The chopper got loud as the rotors sped up. They were airborne. Ivy didn't throw up, but the dogs did, and they successfully avoided doing their puking into the airsick bags.

10

Maybe being a grown-up comes when you are finally entrusted with a job so important, and so far beyond your competence, that you know you'll fail, and yet you do it anyway.

There was no talking in the helicopter—or at least no private conversation, since only a shout could be heard above the noise. Even when the dogs vomited, nobody said anything about it because what was there to say? Look, the dogs threw up. All four of them. How consistent!

Once a door opened, the dogs were first on the ground. As was their custom, they didn't wait around for permission, they just took off to explore.

"I'm sorry there's such a nasty cleanup job," said Laz to the pilot.

"I won't have to do it," said the pilot. "No skin off my nose." Then he was back in the air, going wherever busy chopper pilots have to go. Maybe to the nearest helicopter detailing service.

While they were standing around waiting for ground transportation, Laz said softly to Ivy, "Now we know Harris Teeter Man was lying."

"About what?" asked Ivy.

"There's no way that a truck going from California to a Portal near Cincinnati would ever come anywhere near North Carolina."

"We don't know which roads are out," said Ivy.

"There are lots of better ways to get from California to Kentucky that don't involve going completely over the Appalachians to Greensboro and then back over them to Florence, Kentucky."

"So they've been manipulating us from the start," said Ivy. "Harris Teeter Man was sent to tell you about Shiva and the Portals—and nothing more."

"And he didn't give us any fresh produce because they wanted me to be seriously malnourished," said Laz.

"I could use a sandwich about now," said Ivy. "Especially if it involves bread. I'm bread-starving."

"I'm ready for some cheese," said Laz. "I grew up on goat cheese, feta, bufala mozzarella, Reggiano parmesan, and sharp cheddar."

"I don't know what any of that means because I don't think I've had any of them," said Ivy.

"A woman of the world like you?" asked Laz.

"I wonder what the Portal will look like," said Ivy. "How they keep it open without us there to tend it."

"Maybe that's what we're here for," said Laz.

"Maybe somebody will tell us."

At this point, Guy-in-Charge, who had sidled over to eavesdrop, spoke up. "That time is very soon now. Once we're on the other side of the Portal."

That's when Laz realized that there was a lot of vehicle traffic going in the same direction, and none coming back. "Are you evacuating this border checkpoint?" asked Laz.

"New calculations," said Guy-in-Charge. "We thought we still had a decade before Earth started getting shifted on its orbit by Shiva, but in the Old Place—here—there are signs that it's about to start pretty much any time. That's why we were sent with urgent instructions to gather you and bring you in."

"What about the farmers in California?" asked Ivy. "The Harris Teeter Man told Laz there were farmers there."

"All gathered up months ago," said Guy-in-Charge.

A uniformed woman came up. "Why did you bring dogs on the chopper?" she asked.

Guy-in-Charge answered, "They made it a condition of coming themselves."

The uniformed woman looked at Ivy suspiciously. "There are plenty of dogs in the New Place already," she said.

"But these dogs are used to my smell," said Laz. "Isn't there enough for them to eat in the New Place? Is the quota of dogs full up?"

The uniformed woman looked annoyed. "Of course not."

"Then please get off our case," said Ivy. "These dogs aren't staying here to burn."

Uniformed Woman wasn't done yet. "I understand you were doing a bit of squirrel watching, too. Bring any of them?"

"Let the squirrels burn," said Ivy. "They don't live that long anyway."

Uniformed Woman recoiled at Ivy's apparent heartlessness.

"Oh, does the woman who wanted us to leave our dogs to die find me *callous* about the furry little squirrels?" Ivy laughed. "Go away, we've got work to do."

It occurred to Laz that Ivy was not interested in making a good impression on anyone. She apparently sensed that they had the upper hand, and was making the most of it. Even if it meant alienating people unnecessarily.

Laz took her by the arm and led her to the other side of Guy-in-Charge. To him, Laz softly said, "We *do* have work to do, right? You didn't revive us and then pull us out in order to put us back in high school, did you?"

"In the car," said Guy-in-Charge.

"Then let's get in the car," said Ivy.

"Not yet," said Guy-in-Charge. "It'd be nice if you arrived in the New Place wearing clothes from there, instead of these Old Place duds."

"So we start with a shopping spree?" said Ivy. "Latest fall fashions from Walmart?"

"Walmart doesn't do retail in the New Place," said Guy-in-Charge, "and no, we picked out some clothes for you. We need you to change now."

Ivy started to pull off her top.

"Hey, wait!" said Guy-in-Charge. "I meant for you to change over here. A couple of separate offices you can use."

"You've been spying on us so long, I didn't think we had any modesty left to preserve," said Ivy.

Laz rather enjoyed how she was goading them. She really *can* be much brattier than she has been to me, he thought. In fact, in the past few months, by her standards, I think she has become downright nice.

"You do have modesty left," said Guy-in-Charge. "There were only a couple of guys actually monitoring the surveillance."

"Were you one of them?" asked Laz.

"Yes," said Guy-in-Charge.

"Who was the other one?" asked Ivy.

"Tom. He peeped at you once too often and went blind," said Laz.

Ivy grinned at him. "So now I'm living the Godiva legend."

"Some visions change your life forever," said Laz.

Guy-in-Charge showed them to the two small offices, where clothing for each of them was hanging on hooks, with underwear and socks folded on a desk. Laz closed his door and started changing. The clothing had all been sized for the body he emerged from the coffin with—it had been almost a year of malnutrition. He wasn't POW thin, or he wouldn't have been able to take all those long walks pulling a bike trailer loaded with cans. But he had to fold up the briefs and put them back on the desk because the elastic couldn't hold them up, his hips were so skinny.

The socks were fine, the pants stayed up with a belt, and the shirt was loose but comfortable. He couldn't identify any of the fabrics. They didn't bring any shoes, so he put his own back on.

When Laz was satisfied that he was wearing the new clothes as well as he could, he opened the door and came out.

"You've lost weight," said Guy-in-Charge.

"I'm going to complain to all the food manufacturers," said Laz, "because the nutrients didn't survive well enough after a decade or two on the shelf."

"We have better food in the New Place," said Guy-in-Charge.

"Enough to feed however many billions you've got there?"

"We're working on it," said Guy-in-Charge.

"How many starved to death so far?" asked Laz.

Guy-in-Charge looked at him coldly. "Not one," he said. "But we really had to scramble for the first few years. And there are some nutrients that don't occur naturally in any of the native vegetation. So we're still working on the right crops to provide a balanced diet."

Ivy emerged from her cubicle. "Um, is the neckline supposed to be like this?" she asked.

Laz thought the neckline looked just fine. Maybe a little low. A hint of breasts. But still . . . just fine. As long as she didn't bend over.

"You've lost some weight, too," said Guy-in-Charge. "Sorry about that."

Ivy held the neckline closed by pinching it with her fingers.

"I'm not comfortable with this neckline," said Ivy.

Guy-in-Charge just stood there.

"So go get her something smaller," said Laz.

"Something that fits," Ivy added.

"A lot of girls your age wear necklines more open than that," said the officer that he had just beckoned to. "It's right in style."

"I don't care about style," said Ivy. "But I do like to be reasonably covered."

"You know, we *arrived* in clothes that fit just fine," said Laz.

"If you show up wearing Old Place clothes, everybody who sees you will notice," said the guy in charge. "They'll know where the clothes came from. It'll make you stand out."

Laz turned to Ivy. "They don't care about style, either," he said. "They just don't want people to notice two young people who look an awful lot like Ivy Downey and Lazarus Hayerian, who obviously just arrived from the Old Place."

"Because they'll think," said Ivy, "that there's apparently a need for new Portals, which suggests that this New Place isn't safe after all."

Laz was opening his mouth to ask the obvious question—is Shiva coming to the New Place, too?—when Guy-in-Charge held up his hand. "Not out here," he said. "We don't want people to make wild guesses and panic."

Laz had wondered why there were so few people here at this border station. Less staff meant fewer eyes and fewer leaks.

The clothes guy came back with about five different tops for Ivy to try. She asked, "What are the fabrics? I can't wear wool and I don't like polyester or microfibers."

"Everything's natural plant fibers. All you're getting here is cotton or linen."

Ivy took the tops back into her changing room.

"No wool?" asked Laz.

"We're not ready to turn sheep loose in the New Place. We learned that much from Australian history," said Guy-in-Charge.

In about a minute Ivy came back out wearing a top whose neckline wasn't wide open along her shoulders.

"You tried all those tops in that amount of time?" asked Laz.

"I tried one," said Ivy, "and it fit. As I said, I don't care about style."

A big car pulled up in front of the glass doors. "That's our ride," said Guy-in-Charge.

"I don't recognize the model," said Laz.

"All cars are electric now," said Guy-in-Charge, "and there's only one car company in the American section."

"American?" asked Ivy.

"Referring to North and South America. Why duplicate manufacturing capacity when we don't need a lot of cars?"

"So the 'American Section' is English speaking," said Ivy.

"Spanish, Portuguese, English," said Guy-in-Charge. "Dutch and French speakers were given the option of crossing over with the Dutch and French through the European Portal, or staying with us and accepting their status as minority languages."

"Lots of different accents, I bet," said Laz.

"For now," said Guy-in-Charge. "No, nobody's going to squelch them, it's just that without artificial controls, languages tend to blend together through proximity, and split apart through separation. In five hundred years, none of the original languages are likely to be recognizable, and Dutch and French will be a regional accent of the common tongue. I'm a linguist in real life, when I'm not assigned border duty."

"And surveillance of teenagers alone in an abandoned town," said Ivy.

Guy-in-Charge didn't even look abashed.

By now they were in the car, which had no driver. When their lap restraints were all fastened, the car started to move. Guy-in-Charge swiveled his chair around to face them, so he was riding backward.

"Do you have a name?" asked Ivy.

"I've just been thinking of him as Guy-in-Charge," said Laz.

"Reinaldo Ferreira," said Guy-in-Charge. His pronunciation had a couple of guttural consonants and some strange diphthongs. "Brazilian name. Means 'Ron Smith.'"

"And do you go by Ron Smith now?" asked Ivy.

"It's way better than listening to Anglos trying to pronounce Reinaldo Ferreira."

"Same choice my family made," said Laz. "Americans didn't do well with Hojrian."

"People who speak only one language rarely do well with names from another," said Ron Smith.

"This car ride is supposed to give us answers," said Ivy. "We're waiting. For instance, why are you trying to make us blend in so nobody notices us?"

"As far as most people know, the New Place is a permanent refuge. The final home of humanity."

"Not in the sense of graveyard," said Laz.

"Back last winter," said Ron Smith, "Shiva was found in the sky there, too."

"Well, crap," said Laz.

"Not on the same trajectory. It'll be much farther away. Its effects will be much smaller. We won't actually fall into the Sun. But Jupiter's orbit will still be disturbed, which will disturb the orbits of the rocky planets. They're still doing the math on whether Mercury will plunge into the Sun or orbit a little farther away. Venus will rise above the plane of the ecliptic at one end of its orbit, below it on the other. Mars comes a little closer to the Sun. I don't understand the math, because I thought everything would have been pulled toward Shiva, but as I said, I'm a linguist."

"And Earth?"

"No quick trip to the Sun. But most plant life will be burnt up except near the poles. Only a small part of the Earth will be habitable."

"Not enough for billions of people," said Ivy.

"Not enough for more than about five million people at each pole. And even in the New Place, there isn't an arctic continent, it's just some big islands that can sustain life. Antarctica will fare better."

"Ocean life?" asked Ivy.

"It'll do fairly well," said Ron Smith. "So there are two plans for coping with this, and nobody knows which is the better choice. But both plans require, you know, you."

"How long do we have?" asked Laz.

"What are the plans?" asked Ivy.

"We think we have at least three years, maybe eight, before Shiva disturbs the New Place orbits enough to start affecting climate," said Ron Smith. "And the first plan is, the two of you open Portals to local timestreams that already include you—variant worlds that are topographically and biologically identical to what we already have. That means including all the Old Place plants and animals we've introduced and preserved. Farms and fields and all. So we don't have to redo the last decade and a half of work."

"I can see why that would be preferable," said Laz. "Especially since it took you a decade to get everybody from the Old Place through the Portals. You won't have that long next time."

"So in each *New* New Place," said Ron Smith, "we prepare to move all agriculture and habitation north and south, near the poles. Then we open enough of those timestreams that there's room for everybody to survive. This is the preferred plan," said Ron Smith. "People call it elegant."

"Interesting," said Laz.

"You see the problem, right?" Ivy asked Laz.

It took Laz a moment, but then he realized. "*I* see it," said Laz, "but Ron Smith here doesn't seem to understand the rules."

"Explain it to me, then," said Ron Smith.

"All by myself, the only kind of side step I could do was to places where I already existed. It's like a memory transfer. My body stays here, and presumably keeps on functioning perfectly normally. If something terrible was about to happen, which is why I side step, there's actually a copy of me still here, and I assume that the terrible thing happens to that version of me."

"That would be the local side step you're talking about," said Ivy. "We could open hundreds of Portals between those timestreams."

"But people would find it really confusing and probably terrifying," said Laz, "because everybody would already be there in all the timestreams. We'd be opening Portals between timestreams that have all of the population you're trying to save already there. So you'd be trying to move a billion people to a place that already has a billion people."

"The *same* billion people," said Ivy. "There'd be a copy of everybody. There'd be another Ron Smith in every timestream."

"You can't gain any more space in the viable regions near the pole," said Laz, "because every timestream will be looking for somewhere to put *their* excess people before the famines begin."

"No way around that?" asked Ron Smith.

"Give us ten years or so to work on it, maybe we'll find a way," said Laz. "Did the original versions of us, who created *this* Portal, did they have a different rule set? Because it's crazy not to let us find out how *they* did things."

"You're already doing it better," said Ron Smith.

"In your opinion," said Ivy. "Since we actually *do* it, we're the only competent judges of how much we have to learn from them. How much they can help us."

"The reason we need you," said Ron Smith, "is that they screwed up royally. They can no longer help us."

"All the more reason to make sure we know what they did so we don't repeat their mistakes," said Laz.

"I think you've already made all the necessary changes," said Ron Smith.

"In what way?" demanded Ivy. "I hate it when people think they're qualified to make important decisions *for* me."

"I understand that," said Ron Smith. "But here's how you're going to avoid their mistake."

"Listening," said Laz.

"I'm just deciding how to explain this," said Ron Smith.

"You already planned exactly what you were going to say. Probably memorized the speech before you came for us," said Ivy.

"Not quite, because we didn't know how you'd react to the pickup," said Ron Smith.

"We reacted very badly to the *first* pickup attempt," said Ivy.

"We only made the one," said Ron Smith.

"We side stepped to get to the timestream where it was you who picked us up," said Laz. "In the other one, our sleeping place was invaded by heavily armed men who apparently thought we could only side step if we were, like, holding hands. So they gave us orders and threatened us and we side stepped."

"Without touching," said Ron Smith.

"We'd show you, but it would be undetectable to you," said Laz.

"And you brought the dogs along?" asked Ron Smith.

"They were already there. Like we said. When we do a local side step to a timestream that already includes us, we carry our memory of the previous timestream into the new one, where they combine. Meanwhile, we *assume* that the old version of us remains in place and nobody knows that we—our memory collectors, our central selves—have gone anywhere."

"All right," said Ron Smith. "I know who it was who tried to collect you in that other timestream. He's a heap of coercive authority in every timestream, and I had to do some quick prevention to keep him from taking point on the pickup in this timestream. Makes me glad I fought and won."

"Us too, so far," said Laz.

"So Plan One, the favorite, is meaningless," said Ivy. "You'd still face the same problems so it solves nothing."

Ron Smith nodded. "Plan Two sounds tricky and maybe it's also doomed to failure. It depends on you guys even more, and we're pushing a firm deadline."

"Just tell us the plan, instead of critiquing it in advance," said Ivy.

"I assume you want us to use the method with twine and ropes," said Laz, "the one where Ivy finds a timestream with no humans or other sentient life in it, but still a friendly atmosphere and no massive predators. Preferably with a moon. Even better if it has vegetation. But it doesn't already have me, and it doesn't already have her, so when I side step, my body actually *leaves* the timestream we start from, and I physically appear in the target timestream."

"The goal is for you to find a Newer Place," said Ron Smith, "a *Safe* Place. Of course Earth has to be near enough to identical in size and shape and location that you can actually open Portals. But it has to be so different that Shiva isn't coming at all."

Laz reached over and took Ivy's hand. "I think that the roots of that change have to be in the Big Bang."

"Pretty much," said Ivy. "It's a mechanical universe, when it comes to heavenly bodies, and everything springs out of the first nanosecond of the Bang."

"But you can't access any timestreams that don't have Earth at all, and that don't have it right where it should be," said Ron Smith. "So it's not really an *infinite* set of possible worlds."

"No, it's worse than that," said Laz. "Because there is every likelihood that there *is* no timestream that has Earth in the right place, and that *doesn't* have Shiva."

"Plus," said Ivy, "*we* don't know how to detect whether Shiva is coming or not."

"Right," said Ron Smith. "Which is why we have a few dozen teams of terrific astronomical techs. Every time you open a Portal to a habitable world, they rush in, carry equipment through, and *they* search for Shiva."

"Failing to find it isn't the same as finding that it isn't there," said Laz.

"I took courses in the scientific method in college," said Ron Smith. "We know that. But if it's undetectable, maybe it's on a less threatening course. We keep checking while everybody's moving everything to the Safe Place, so if Shiva shows up we can rethink our plans."

"I think what you're counting on," said Laz, "is that we'll find multiple Safe Places, which contain *no* humans, and your techs will find that several of them have no Shiva coming."

Ivy was nodding. "So instead of trying to move the entire Earth population to a single world," she said, "through a few Portals like this one, we open Portals from here to, say, six different Safe Places. So you only have to move one-sixth as many people and their stuff through each Portal. And each Safe Place only has to provide for a sixth as many people during the startup phase."

"I assume you haven't told any of the other groups about this?" asked Laz.

"They all have astronomers, too," said Ron Smith. "It was the Indians who saw that Shiva was still coming in this timestream, just a little farther out. They knew that we had the side steppers who made the original Portals, and they wanted to know if they—your originals—were still alive and could find new, safer timestreams. So once you find at least one Safe Place, of course we'll open Portals."

"You didn't tell them that Original Laz was dead," said Ivy.

Laz recognized that Ivy was probing to find out *if* Laz was dead in the New Place.

"They would have found that discouraging," said Ron Smith. "Some of them might have tried to establish themselves at the poles and exclude everybody else."

The fact that Ron Smith ignored the implicit question was ambiguous. Did that mean that Original Laz was really dead, or that Ron Smith had no intention of discussing that topic?

"I'll bet," said Laz, "that you also have plans for doing exactly that."

"If anybody makes a move like that," said Ron Smith, "we'll take protective measures to be sure that some of our people also survive. We have no plans to block out everyone else."

Ivy laughed. "That only means that your higher-ups haven't told *you* about those plans."

"Since in your sub-infinite wisdom," said Laz to Ron Smith, "you chose to keep us ignorant of our purpose and are still keeping us away from any records of what our originals did, we've had to figure everything out for ourselves."

"We didn't want you shackled by what your originals did."

"No shackles," said Ivy, holding up her wrists. "Can you at least tell us whether we've come up to their quality and reliability?"

"In your experimentation," said Ron Smith, "you opened four Portals using your twine method. We have techs hardening those Portals—heavy chains by now, and the beginnings of the floor, roof, and walls. The astrotechs will tell us soon if there's any chance that any of these is a Safe Place. If it is—"

"As soon as we find one plausible Safe Place," said Ivy, "then we'll also find several adjacent timestreams, ones that have me and Laz in them, and whatever techs are there, but nobody else. If we lay down new Portals from each of those back to here, you can start migrating people across to all those timestreams, because none of them will already have a billion people."

"But since we don't know if Shiva will still turn up in that one Safe Place and all its adjacent ones," said Laz, "we'll keep looking for other, unrelated Safe Places. The more the safer, right?"

"I see you already thought this through," said Ron Smith.

"We're thinking it through right now," said Laz. "Right before your eyes. The Amazing Side Stepper Twins."

"I need to know what we're working with here," said Ivy. "I get what you need us to do, but when we open Portals to places that can sustain life, how long will it take the astrotechs to see whether Shiva is coming in that timestream?"

"If Shiva's still coming on a trajectory similar to the ones we know," said Ron Smith, "we'll know it within a few days. If that happens, they ditch that place and set up their equipment in the newest place you two have opened."

"And if they always detect Shiva in every possible world," said Laz, "or the biologists determine that humans *can't* live there after all, and so we have no Safe Place, or we find it so late that there isn't time to move everybody there, then what?"

"Then either human life ends on Earth, or only a small remnant survives near the poles, plus however many manage to get across into the Safe Place."

"And how do you decide which people get to have the poles?" asked Laz.

"Peacefully, I hope," said Ron Smith.

"In other words, through bloody genocidal war," said Laz.

"Don't worry, Laz," said Ivy. "Because we'll be the big heroes who failed, they'll undoubtedly kill us first."

"Seems likely," said Laz.

"Cheer up," said Ron Smith. "Maybe most of the candidates for the Safe Place will be Shiva-free."

"If it isn't Shiva it'll be something," said Laz. "An asteroid strike. A solar flare. Another rogue planet from a completely different direction."

"There's always something that might cause an extinction-level event," said Ron Smith. "But probably not within the next ten years. Or the next thousand. Or ten thousand. If we can find a Safe Place that can keep civilization going at a high technological level for now, then it's some later generation's problem to save the world when the new threat comes up."

"Like housework, saving the world is a job that's never done," said Ivy.

"You've never done housework in your life," said Laz.

"Nobody has," said Ivy. "We have machines now. But *their* work is never done."

"The long range plan," said Ron Smith, "is to figure out how to colonize other solar systems, so humanity can ride out an extinction on one planet by being fully established on others."

"We're enlisted," said Laz. "We will *try* to find a Safe Place, though we have no way of knowing what a Safe Place will look like to us."

Ron Smith pursed his lips for a moment.

"Annoyed?" asked Ivy.

"Frustrated," said Ron Smith. "I thought that you could see up and down the timestreams before you chose one."

"You're speaking to me," said Ivy.

"You're the one who sees," said Ron Smith.

"Maybe my original was way more talented than me," said Ivy. "I see a few days, sometimes a few weeks in both directions. I see farther back than forward. But not more than weeks, and never even close to a year."

Ron Smith covered his face. "We didn't understand that limitation."

"Maybe my original didn't have such a limitation," said Ivy. "Is she dead? Is that why you can't use her?" There was nothing subtle about *that* probing question.

Ron Smith kept his grief-stricken face covered a moment longer. Then he raised his head and looked out the car window. "We're about to pass through the Portal. I thought you should see it, to see what's been made of something that your originals *and* you have created using ropes and such."

They passed into a tunnel so wide you could have played regulation football inside it, including the highest kicks with the longest hang time.

"You take airplanes through?"

"We've never tried," said Ron Smith. "Except taxiing on the ground. Because if it doesn't work, we lose a plane and a pilot, at the very least."

"Never lost anybody on the ground, though," said Laz.

"You'll see," said Ron Smith.

As they crossed the threshold into the wide, high-roofed Portal, Laz felt a wrenching twist inside him that seemed to go on and on, as if an anaconda had him and was crushing him tighter every time he exhaled.

Still, Laz had enough control of himself, enough presence of mind, to see that the surface of the roof and walls and floor of the Portal were made of panels that could slide across each other like the steps of an escalator, or the overlapping plates of the luggage carousels at airports.

"The distance between worlds is constantly shifting," said Ron Smith. "Also the angles. Our timestream techs are sure that when Shiva makes the Old Place move out of position, the structure of the Portal will blow apart from the stress. That's how the engineers designed it—to blow apart, to cease to exist, when it gets too stressed and deformed."

They came out the other side of the Portal, and the twisting feeling ended. The anaconda let go. Laz gasped for breath, and so did Ivy. "Does anybody get used to this?" asked Ivy.

"No," said Ron Smith. "But we do it anyway. Even knowing that the whole thing might go kerblooey at any time."

"Come on, not really," said Laz.

"Nobody knows," said Ron Smith. "But the differences between the worlds are putting way more strain on the Portal than we expected by this time. Which may mean that Shiva is more massive than our estimates. If that's the case, we think we're going to lose the Old Place at any moment."

"Or ten weeks from now?" asked Ivy.

"Don't know," said Ron Smith. "We've never had a Portal and a wandering planet intruding into our solar system at the same time. Not a lot of history to draw on."

"It was pretty gutsy of you to come get us," said Laz.

"A team of volunteers," said Ron Smith. "And most of them didn't know who you were or why you mattered. They were told, Dangerous assignment, might be stranded in the Old Place when the devil planet comes, but if we can get these two ridiculous kids they might be able to make our families and futures more secure."

"Ridiculous kids?" asked Ivy.

"Did you see how you were dressed?" asked Ron Smith. "Did you hear how you talked?"

"You never answered my question," said Ivy. "You said we already made the necessary changes to avoid what went wrong with our originals. To avoid their big mistake."

"You two fell in love," said Ron Smith.

"*I* did," said Laz. "Pretty sure Ivy hasn't. Not yet anyway."

Ivy rolled her eyes. It would have made Laz feel a lot better if she had squeezed his hand.

"Close enough for government work," said Ron Smith.

"But how does that solve anything?" asked Ivy.

"The problem that killed Laz's original was that Original Laz and Original Ivy actively hated each other. And as best we understand it, at a key moment, Original Ivy 'let go' of Original Laz and he's lost out there. Can't come back. Doesn't know the way, can't find it without Ivy, and she can't side step to go get him."

"'Let go'?" demanded Ivy. "What does that even mean? She dropped her end of the twine? That's why we tie them to trees!"

"You don't know that he's actually dead," said Laz.

"Original Ivy didn't do it on purpose," said Ivy. "Come on."

"Nobody holds either of *you* responsible, so don't take it personally. We set you up to emerge at roughly the right age for each other, though we couldn't do anything about the fact that your memories were of different childhoods in different decades. We were hoping that normal human processes would kick in, with the two of you having no other humans around."

"You hoped that my fully resistible attractiveness would kick in," said Laz.

"An arranged marriage," said Ivy.

"Not a marriage," said Laz. "They must be disappointed we didn't actually mate."

"Even if they put you out to stud," said Ivy, "it was arranged." She sounded disgusted.

"Don't punish *me* for it," said Laz.

"What are you talking about? It's Ron Smith and his group that I'm pissed off at," said Ivy.

"But whatever feelings you have for me," said Laz, "you're going to resist them because you think we're being coerced, and so you'll tamp them down and I bet you *will* start to resent me for still being here. And still in love with you, because I *wasn't* coerced."

She started to react with scorn for that idea, but stopped herself. "Sounds about right," she admitted.

"They put us close to each other," said Laz, "but we still could have hated each other. We were well on the way to that, weren't we? And then we both decided to make it work."

Ivy cocked her head in thought. "Yes," she said.

"Can't we just keep doing that? Make it work, no matter how we've been manipulated? Because we're the only tool they've got that can side step between timestreams, and if what Ron Smith here says is true, we have a lot of work to do to save the human race."

"Yes," said Ivy.

"So can we still be friends?" asked Laz.

"Friends?" asked Ivy.

"I still feel how I already felt," said Laz. "I'm not asking you to feel that way toward me. I just want you to find me . . . tolerable. Even useful."

She touched his forearm with her hand. "You know I feel much more than that."

"Don't get all kissy in front of me," said Ron Smith.

"We don't care what you see," said Ivy. "You've already seen more than you should have."

"Sorry about that," said Ron Smith.

"You can always turn your chair back around," said Laz. "Face front, and whatever we do will be behind your back."

"Not that we're going to get all kissy," said Ivy. "We have a pact that we're going to remain clearheaded at all times."

Ron's chair rotated to face front. "The most important government and scientific structures," said Ron Smith, "are near the Portal. Just a few miles to where we're going."

"We haven't passed any significant buildings since we passed through," said Laz.

"You've passed several hundred buildings. They aren't underground, not completely, but soil is ramped up to give most of them a living biological layer of insulation, and since all vehicles are on air cushions, roads are simply smoothed ground with grass on it. The human footprint here is invisible, speaking atmospherically, chemically, biologically."

"Oh, sad," said Ivy.

"Sad?" asked Ron Smith.

"Oh, it's noble that you're trying to avoid the mistakes of the past," said Ivy.

"But Ivy and I have talked about utopias," said Laz. "Whenever there's a major upheaval, some people try to make it an opportunity to start a utopia. Everybody has a good idea of what they want to avoid about the *old* civilization, but people are really bad at anticipating what's going to go wrong with the new utopian one."

"Communism was a bust after the Russian Revolution, for instance," said Ivy. "Agriculture and commerce were collapsing. Only the black market worked. So Lenin came up with the Great Leap Forward or the New Economic Policy—we couldn't remember which one was Mao and which one was Lenin—but it was really a variation on the free market, because no matter what you do, nothing works as well at feeding the maximum number of people as the free market."

"Within careful limits," said Laz.

"Again, we're just making stuff up to explain whatever history we could remember between us," said Ivy.

"But we decided that the most terrible time in any utopia is between the beginning of its collapse—which is usually within about a half hour of its founding—and its abandonment," said Laz. "That's when heads roll at the guillotine. That's when the firing squads are busiest. It's also when people starve."

Ron Smith nodded. "Well, for kids with only high school and an imperfect knowledge of history—"

"Is there such a thing as a *perfect* knowledge of history?" asked Ivy.

"I think you're pretty insightful. So far, no firing squads, no hangings, no mob rule. And our earth-friendly architecture works fine where the water table is low enough that we can go deep and stay dry. Other places, our buildings stick up higher, but no skyscraper canyons anywhere in our zone. That may come later—we can't decide for all time—but we spend vastly less on heating and air conditioning, our energy requirements for climate and transportation are minuscule. But all the original coal and oil are still in the ground, all the iron is unmined, helium, copper, nickel and rare earth metals—a virgin world, running out of nothing. So on that score, we're doing okay."

"And politically?"

"Honestly," said Ron Smith, "we really hope that you won't try to learn anything about the political systems that are evolving and all the arguments that are under way on every conceivable subject. It'll only distract you. All you need to know is, so far, no killings, no firearms in private hands. You need to keep your minds on opening new Portals in new places until you find a Safe Place."

"Fair enough," said Ivy. "If the world ends because we fail, I won't care about all the social experiments you're doing on yourselves. And if we succeed, there's plenty of time to see how you manage a *second* huge migration from the New Place to the Safe Place."

"That's what most of the smart people are going to be working on," said Ron Smith.

"And by 'smart people,'" said Laz, "I assume you include people who *think* they're smart but only make things harder for all the actual smart people."

"My main concern," said Ron Smith, "is trying to stay in the one group and out of the other."

"Good plan," said Ivy. "How are you doing at it?"

"I got you two here," said Ron Smith. "By telling you the truth and letting you choose for yourselves."

"You've selected your information pretty carefully," said Laz.

"And you've made sure not to show me everything about your responses," said Ron Smith. "You're willing to show me the good quality of your relationship, and I believe it, I don't think you're pretending. But there's a lot of stuff you aren't telling me about how you work. I accept that."

"Which is your way," said Ivy, "of telling *us* that you have held back a lot of important information that in your judgment it's better for us not to know."

"Of course," said Ron Smith. "Like political squabbles."

"We'll make this work," said Laz, "because *we* want to and *you* want us to."

Ron Smith smiled as the car plunged underground on a ramp that hadn't been visible until they were driving just above it. Now they were in a brightly illuminated parking garage with comfortably familiar concrete pillars and floors and ceilings.

"Hey, honey," said Laz to Ivy. "We're home."

11

Ivy Begins a Plog of Her Own

Now that we're in a place with actual notebooks of lined paper and pens that flow with ink, I'm going to follow the example of my noted colleague and begin my own plog, which, like his, is not for public consumption. However, unlike him I know that whether I call it a diary or journal or blog or plog, someone will read it. Even if Laz never looks at it, I am quite sure that none of the kind people who are assisting us in our world-saving enterprise will shrink from reading anything and everything we write, just as I'm sure you have ways of monitoring all our conversations. After all, the world hangs in the balance, or so you say; we have no way of verifying it.

Whoever it is I'm writing to—and if only to myself, hi, self—I am in a quandary. If the world is going to end in four years or whatever, then at the present rate we're not going to be able to find anywhere to go, and even if we do, it will probably be so late in the game that there's no time to get any significant part of the population through the Portal into the Safe Place.

At present, we have tried three new Portals. Two of them already had human populations, even though I believed they did not. We did not stay long enough to ask if they knew about Shiva, because if they did, the last thing we wanted was to have them try to join us, since we are already just as doomed as we need to be, without more bodies.

And if they didn't know about Shiva, they would find out soon enough. Anyway, the point where they diverged from our known human history was recent enough that they look like us, they build like us, they're us.

So out of three tries, two were bad choices to begin with. I say this in all candor, since I'm the chooser. If the third one had been workable, then all would be forgiven, but the astronomy techs found that Shiva was inbound on the same course as in the New Place. So a timestream worthy to be called the Safe Place is no nearer discovery, and it has been three weeks since we went to work.

Here's the problem. I think everybody misunderstands what I "see" when I explore timestreams that I'm not in. Visually, I get nothing. It's not as if there's anything to see. I reach out and "know" some things about the recent past of a timestream and the upcoming probabilities. I become aware of certain elements that I think of as minimal. Is there vegetation that photosynthesizes? In other words, is the world green? Then it will probably have an atmosphere we can breathe, because photosynthesis poops out oxygen.

Obviously, though, I can't detect whether my failure to observe humans in that timestream means there aren't any, or only that they aren't involved in the space-time thread that I've glommed onto. Is that metaphysical enough for you? Talking to Laz—because he's the only other person we know of who "sees" timestreams—we have come to the tentative conclusion that timestreams aren't "reality" in any observable way.

What they are is strings of causality, like free-floating domino set-ups in which, if the first twenty dominoes fall, we can reasonably expect that the immediate future will include the fall of the rest of the dominoes in the line.

But causality isn't observable or measurable. Neither mechanical nor Aristotelian cause actually "exist." We can't function in our lives without believing in causality, so we can anticipate the results of our decisions, our actions, our words. But there is no instrument that can detect or measure causality. Laz and I, being sane, believe that the streams of causality we detect are real, if only because when I push one of them into Laz's "mind" (the quotation marks aren't to cast doubt on the existence of his mind, but rather to show that we know that "mind" is also a metaphysical construct which is neither detectable nor measurable, but which we have no choice but to believe in), he can side step into the exact timestream I shoved at him.

What I'm coming to is this: I don't know how to break it to our friends/handlers/wardens/guards that the job they need us to do is kind of impossible. I know, our originals did it—but they botched it, didn't they? The New Place was not, in fact, the necessary Safe Place. As far as I know, they simply chose the first timestream they came to that didn't have brontosaurs stomping around and turning mammals to jelly under their feet, and also didn't have a human population. And that was good enough because nobody detected Shiva coming until way later.

My doubts come because I don't know how many humanless timestreams we have to find before we can find one in which Shiva will not wipe out all life on Earth—if there is such a timestream. Because there may not be. But I can't see far enough down the road before I pass a timestream to Laz. Since there are no people, I can't foresee whether they'll be wiped out by Shiva. And I can't see animals at all, not individually. Humans have minds and make conscious choices—they cause timestreams to vary. Most animals seem to live in a much more mechanistic causal universe. They don't cause timestream variations near as often or as clearly as humans do. Butterflies can flap their wings without changing the weather. So in a nonhuman timestream, I can't follow anything or anybody far enough into the future to detect Shiva's destructive arrival—or the lack thereof.

I just read over this and it embarrassed me how pseudo-philosophical it sounds. Laz and I are just clones of high school kids who had talents that made us unusual. My guess is that <u>after</u> the Original Laz got famous as a scientist, Original Ivy, a kid, contacted him with her claim that she could detect timestreams. He, as an adult decades older than O-Ivy or Ivy-O, helped her learn how to pass timestreams to him, and together they did some great things. Ain't we cool. Only it wasn't us.

We don't have infinite time to keep following up on Laz's and my blind stabs into the fabric of causality. Relying on random chance works in space movies, but not with anything the human race really needs.

Here's what I believe, and the ultimatum I'm going to ask Laz to join me in issuing, if we don't have something like success pretty soon. And since I'm sure you boss-guys are reading this, you'll know it before Laz does. Somewhere in the New Place, my original is still alive. It's only Laz's original that you said was lost. So Original Ivy is around, but you won't let us talk to her.

Whatever you're afraid she'll tell us, how can it make anything worse than making random stabs until we run out of time? We have to open Portals and get off this planet, this timestream, before Earth moves out of synchronous orbit and we can't make a workable Portal. So what if talking to Ivy-O makes us loopy or confused or angry or whatever you're worried about? If she can tell us <u>anything</u> about <u>her</u> experience with timestreams that might help us make better choices, we need to have it. We need it <u>now</u>.

Meanwhile, Laz, if <u>you're</u> reading this, then shame on you, but at least now you'll understand how irresistible it was for me to know you were writing stuff that mattered to you and shutting me out of it. You're the most important person in the world—not just to me, to everyone.

I didn't know that, when I read your plogs and (shudder!) dared to write in them. But I knew you were the most important person in _my_ world at the time, being the only other human, _and_ being better at this timestream thing than I was, since you could actually go from stream to stream. Plus you knew how to get food and clothes and how to fix a bike.

You pretend not to be angry at me anymore, partly because our snogging episodes distracted you from hating me, but I can feel a seething resentment under the surface, or at least I think I can, and I want you to stop resenting me. I want you to believe that I'm truly your friend and partner in this. I don't believe you're actually in love with me, or if you are, I'm quite sure it's already in the process of passing.

Meanwhile, I need you to be my friend in this and help me persuade them or force them to let us meet Original Ivy, or Ivy-O. (Your vanished protoself would be OrigiLaz, which is actually a cool name.) (We have to call them _something_ to distinguish them from us, and I'm not changing _my_ name.)

End of Ivy's not-likely-to-be-private plog, episode 1.

Since they no longer slept in adjoining bedrooms, it took Laz a while to locate Ivy. He tried her room first, and there he found a journal with a plain black cover. He flipped it open enough to know she was writing in it, and saw her heading was "Ivy Begins a Plog of Her Own."

At that point, he closed the journal and took it with him as he went in search of her.

She was sitting on the back porch of their dormitory, if you could call it a porch and if you could figure out which entrance was the front or the back. He brandished the book as he sat down beside her.

"So you read it?" asked Ivy.

Laz chuckled. "How stupid do you think I am?"

"How can stupidity be enumerated?" asked Ivy.

"You left it out for me to find," said Laz. "You titled it so I would feel justified in reading it as retaliation. Except that it would also make me a hypocrite."

"So you opened it and read it."

"I read the title, I closed the cover, and I came to ask." Laz was enjoying this mock argument, though it was also kind of real. "Did you merely intend me to *find* it, and thus test my ability to live up to the standard of privacy I charged you with violating? Or do you actually want me to read it, because conversation wouldn't have been adequate to communicate what you had to say?"

Ivy smirked. Or smiled—but Laz was provoked enough now that any smile could only look like a smirk to him. He understood that, but it didn't change his further annoyance at her because of the smirking.

"I'm smiling because the one thing I didn't think you'd do was come to me with that diary."

"Plog," corrected Laz.

"I thought you'd either read it and then pretend you hadn't, or you'd *not* read it and pretend you hadn't found it. Instead you read the first line of it and came right to me. You're kind of a confrontational guy, did you know that about yourself?"

"Yes," said Laz.

"I'm sure our keepers have already read it," said Ivy, "and I'm fine with you reading it too."

"Not good enough," said Laz. "I'm not 'fine' with you being 'fine with it.' Did you intend me to read it?"

"I was ambiguous."

"I don't know an ambiguous way to read it and not-read it at the same time," said Laz. "So here it is." He handed her the book and when she refused to take it, he dropped it on the porch beside her. Then he sat down a couple of meters away and looked out over the landscape, which was lovely.

"How did this turn into a real fight?" she asked.

"If you want me to know what it says, read it to me," said Laz.

"That's just stupid. You can read it much faster for yourself."

"Speed isn't the issue," said Laz. "Consent is the issue. Clarity is the issue. If you read it to me, then you can never claim that I read your plog without your consent."

"It matters that much to you?"

"*Trust* matters to me," said Laz. "And part of trust is that your inability to resist teasing me will make this a constant irritant, unless you read it aloud to me and put any accusation of my having snuck in and read it secretly out of any future conversation."

"Baloney," said Ivy. "You want to be able to continue being the *only* poor victim whose privacy was violated, so you can hold it over my head."

"And if that's true—which is quite possibly at least one of my motives—is there any sense in which that is unjust? You laid a trap for me, I didn't step in it. Now read me the plog so I can see what it is you want me and our bosses to know."

"They would cringe at the word 'bosses,'" said Ivy.

"I know," said Laz. "But 'captors' or 'guards' would carry even worse connotations."

"And since they probably have very sensitive dish microphones trained on us right now, the cringing has already begun," said Ivy.

"I believe you're likely to be right," said Laz.

Ivy opened the journal and began reading from the first page.

"So you're picking a fight with them," said Laz, when she finished.

"I kind of thought I was picking it with you," said Ivy.

"Not really," said Laz. "I'm trying to be less easily provoked."

"Me too, you know." She kissed her finger and touched it to his lips.

"What do you think you'll learn from Ivy-O?" asked Laz.

"If I knew, I wouldn't need to meet her," said Ivy.

"What will you ask her?"

"I'd ask, 'How did you and OrigiLaz work together?' Then she'd try to explain, and I'd compare it with the way *we* work."

"We already know how we work," said Laz.

"But *they* found the New Place. How did she search for it and how did she know what it was when she found the timestream?"

Laz thought about it, nodded. "Makes sense," he said.

"So why won't they let—"

Laz held up a hand to stop her from going into that complaint again. "We can worry about their motives later," he said. "Right now, we know they still don't want us to meet her."

"Well, maybe they'll change their minds."

"You wrote this yesterday, right?" asked Laz. "So they read it before you got up in the morning, and they haven't come to us with Ivy-O's address or phone number or email. So their answer was no."

"Then I'm still stuck trying to do this on my own," said Ivy.

"I'm sure you meant *we're* stuck doing it on *our* own," said Laz.

"Yeah, like that."

"But Ivy, remember who we are. Somewhere, in all the decisions our keepers are making on our behalf, there's got to be a timestream where they said *yes* to your reasonable request."

Ivy grinned. "We've each been doing the things we do for years, but together is still so new that I forget sometimes just what you're capable of."

Laz sat on the porch looking at the scenery, looking at trees that weren't shaped quite right, at grass that wasn't quite the expected color. Green, but a kind of slightly bluish green. Soft as fescue. The kind of grass that begs you to take your shoes off.

So Laz took his shoes off and set his feet in the cool grass and it felt wonderful.

"I think I've found her," said Ivy.

"Are we both in that timestream?" asked Laz.

"We are, and we're together right this moment, approaching the place where we were told she lives."

She pushed the timestream into Laz's mind, and he side stepped, and there they were.

"Should we have brought flowers?" asked Laz.

"Like I should bring flowers to my own Original," said Ivy.

"There's no guarantee that she'll like you," said Laz. "Nobody else does."

"She will," said Ivy. "And *you* like me."

"I love you, though someone told me it was fading quickly."

While they talked, Laz was thinking back through memories that had accumulated in this going-to-meet-Ivy-O timestream before Laz side stepped here. Pretty much alike, except that after reading Ivy's plog, Ron Smith came to see them and they rode in a car, again driverless. Laz had a very clear memory of Ron Smith insisting on coming to the door with them, and Ivy saying, "Just spy on us like usual. Let us talk to my Original without obvious witnesses."

At the door, Laz hung back. Ivy should be the first person, the only person that Ivy-O would see at the door.

The door opened. Ivy-O stood there, maybe thirty years old, maybe thirty-five, but surely not forty.

"Just so you know," said Ivy-O, looking at Ivy, "I'm forty years old, and I don't like seeing you looking like that."

Ivy merely stood there, saying nothing.

Ivy-O looked around, saw Laz. "I never knew Laz could be so young," she said to him.

"Everybody starts out that way," said Laz.

"Ah, you already had your gift for saying the obvious."

Laz said nothing. If he could put up with Ivy's rudeness, he could tolerate the same rudeness from the older edition that he was meeting now for the first time.

"And you were able to stop your keepers from coming along with you?"

"I'm sure they're back at the car and six other locations, listening in with electronics," said Ivy.

"I assume my whole house is wired with spy gear," said Ivy-O. "If it isn't, then they're just lazy. Come on in."

They came in through the open door, which Ivy-O closed behind them. "Sit," she said.

There were a comfortable-looking sofa and several padded chairs. Ivy sat in a chair. Laz sat on the sofa.

Ivy-O said, "Are we doing social amenities? A glass of water, a cup of tea?"

"Don't we hate tea?" asked Ivy.

"Of course," said Ivy-O. "It's solely for guests."

"They're in this world for what, a decade, and they're already growing a commercial non-food product like tea?" asked Laz.

"We have two years' production from Java in warehouses here. We dragged along from the Old Place anything we didn't expect to be able to produce right away in the New Place."

"Everything seems to have been handled perfectly," said Ivy. "We admire the achievement. Do you know why they woke us up?"

"Do you?" asked Ivy-O.

"They tell us Shiva's still coming too close," said Ivy.

"You doubt them?" asked Ivy-O.

"Do they always tell the truth?" asked Ivy.

"To me they do," answered Ivy-O. "You're younger and more naive, but with your ability to check up on probabilities, Ivy, I bet they hew pretty close to what they believe is true."

"I can see causal threads, too," said Laz.

"Don't get jealous," said Ivy-O dismissively. "It shouldn't matter to you whether she's better at things than you are."

"It doesn't," said Laz. "It bothers me that you think she's the only one you're talking to here."

Ivy-O smiled at Ivy. Laz knew that they were only just barely managing not to say aloud, "Oh, men."

"Did you really strand OrigiLaz in some godforsaken timestream?" asked Ivy.

"OrigiLaz?" asked Ivy-O.

"We call you Ivy-O," said Laz. "To keep distinctions clear."

"How clever and rather sweet-sounding," said Ivy-O. "Don't believe all they tell you."

248

"You say they always tell you the truth," said Ivy.

"That doesn't mean they *know* the truth," said Ivy-O. "Not-lying is not the same thing as telling the truth."

"So what do you think they're telling us that we shouldn't believe?" asked Laz.

"It makes me very uncomfortable to have you here," said Ivy-O. "Why don't you wait outside so I can talk to my younger self without distractions?"

"Maybe there's a timestream where I do that," said Laz. "This isn't it."

Ivy said, "Laz, can't you help this go smoothly?"

"Cutting me out isn't about smoothness," said Laz. "No matter what she tells you, I need to hear it because I'm the one who has to do all the side stepping."

"I didn't abandon him," said Ivy-O.

"What, then?" said Laz. "You're here, he's not."

Ivy-O shrugged. "The man can side step. I can't control that."

"The keepers seem to think it was your job to keep him tethered to a known timestream," said Ivy.

"That's what Laz and I thought, too, at first," said Ivy-O.

"Did you also think you had to be touching each other to side step together?" asked Ivy.

Ivy-O paused. "You *don't*?"

"On local jaunts, no," said Ivy. "We don't know about steps into timestreams where we don't already exist."

Ivy-O leaned back in her chair, letting her hips slide forward a little, so her legs extended far forward. A lazy teenager posture. "Interesting," said Ivy-O. "I wonder if that's because you were revived at about the same age. Greater rapport because you're both young."

"I fell in love with her," said Laz. "Not sure that's relevant, though."

Ivy-O rolled her eyes. "And you think my Laz and I *didn't*?"

That left Laz completely nonplussed. "He's what, twenty years older than you?"

"Almost thirty," said Ivy-O. "He never married. Waiting for me, I think. Quite romantic."

"Or when he fell for you," said Laz, "he side stepped into a timestream where he had never married."

"He had no married timestreams," said Ivy-O.

"And he didn't marry *you*, either," said Ivy.

"No," she said. "And no, we didn't have a sexual relationship, you prurient boy." She directed that one at Laz, of course, and he blushed.

"So you were in love, but platonically," said Ivy.

"I prefer to think we loved socratically," said Ivy-O. "Always too full of questions to settle into a healthy relationship."

"Ma'am," said Laz. "We have very little time in which to locate a usable timestream. You found one, you and OrigiLaz. We need to find a better one and in far less time."

Ivy-O looked puzzled. "So do it," she said. "What do you need from me?"

"We've tried three so far," said Ivy. "Two had humans in them, in places remote from where we joined the timestream. Only one was human-free."

"Pesky little rascals, aren't they," said Ivy-O. "Like termites, always hiding until it's too late to eradicate them and save the building."

"Shiva's going to take care of the eradicating," said Ivy. "We want to save enough to reconstitute the human race on a version of Earth that doesn't have Shiva approaching."

"Good luck," said Ivy-O.

"You're not going to help us?" asked Laz.

Ivy-O smirked.

"What do you want from us?" asked Laz. "We've got no way to bargain with you, we just need your help."

Ivy leaned forward with her question. "Ivy-O, my older and wiser self, how did you know the New Place would be adequate?"

Ivy-O closed her eyes. "You really don't know how?"

"We wouldn't be here if we did," said Ivy.

"What are you looking for, anyway," said Ivy-O. "A place with chlorophyll. A place with green growing zones between the arctic and antarctic. Oxygen, carbon dioxide in a healthy mix. No humans. You won't even be able to detect versions of Earth that are not in the same orbit. But here's the trick, kids. If you really had to be positionally accurate, the Earth would have to be in the same orbit and in exactly the right position in that orbit. At X degrees around the orbital ellipse. Have you ever had to wait for that to align properly?"

Laz looked at Ivy. "Well, not for local side steps," said Laz.

"So no matter where Earth is in its orbit, on the timestream you're aiming at, you can step to a location on Earth. A leap in space. A huge one."

Laz had never thought of this.

"Not fair to either of you," said Ivy-O, "so don't be embarrassed. Your original, Laz, had decades of working with other scientists to calculate the mechanics of side stepping. His hypothesis was that it was affected by gravity. I don't think that explains it, but it was enough for him to proceed with confidence. He figured, wherever Earth is in the orbit, its gravity will keep all the causal chains in the right place. Voilà. Safety."

"Voi?" echoed Ivy, a bit mockingly. "La?"

"It's French for 'looky-here,'" said Ivy-O.

"I speak French," said Ivy.

"So do I," said Ivy-O, "and I speak it better."

"Yes, you're both sharp-witted and masters of using scorn as a cudgel," said Laz. "Let's say OrigiLaz was right, and we'll always end up on Earth in the right place, regardless of where Earth is in its orbit. So what?"

"It was his theory—no, hypothesis—"

"His *guess*," said Ivy.

"His guess," said Ivy-O, "that if our skills were affected by gravity, held in place by it, then gravity was part of our ability to sense timestreams. Therefore, without knowing it, we were sensing gravity, and that meant that if I just studied the timestreams carefully enough, I could detect which ones had Shiva's gravity in them and which ones did not."

Laz thought about it. "I don't know what gravity would feel like."

"Neither did I," said Ivy-O, "and neither did my Laz."

"So how is that part of your answer to our question?" asked Ivy.

"When you don't have a skill, you practice until you have it."

"That doesn't work with everything," said Laz. "How can you practice a skill you haven't acquired?"

"With minute focus on tiny things," said Ivy-O. "By twitching muscles you didn't know existed. By working on it like a basketball player practicing free throws."

"We don't have time," said Ivy.

"Too busy sawing to sharpen the saw?" asked Ivy-O. "Well, I can hardly expect the clones to be smarter than the originals."

"You're saying you didn't learn to do it, either?" asked Ivy.

"I'm saying we didn't learn to do it *in time*," said Ivy-O. "I can do it now. Not fully reliably. But it's not impossible at all. My Laz had been gone for six months when I got the hang of it."

"We don't have six months," Ivy began.

"You don't have six months to wait on blind, unskilled stabs in the dark," said Ivy-O. "Better to take six months learning how to do it in only a few tries."

"Are you sure it will take six months?" asked Laz.

"You're much more brilliant than us poor originals," said Ivy-O, "I'm sure you'll do it right away."

"We have the advantage of knowing that it's possible," said Laz. "And if you can show Ivy the difference in the timestreams with and without Shiva's gravity—"

"Maybe I can speed you up a bit," said Ivy-O.

"What Laz is hinting at," said Ivy, "is that he wants to partner with *you* rather than me, since you already have the skill."

Laz started to protest, but Ivy looked at him scornfully. "Give it a rest, Laz."

"It never crossed my mind," said Laz.

"Then why did I see timestreams open up that had the two of you partnered together?" asked Ivy.

"Because it crossed *my* mind," said Ivy-O. "But I have a very wise idea. Why don't we see if young Laz here can work with *me*, while you work on trying to wake up your gravity sense yourself. For all I know, you'll do it better than me. For all I know, young Laz and I will keep failing until you're ready to step in and save the day."

"For all we know," said Ivy, "you'll strand my Laz out somewhere in the realms of uncharted causality, just as you did with *your* Laz."

Ivy-O's face grew red with shame. No, thought Laz. With rage.

"I didn't strand Laz anywhere. I never let go of my end of the string. He got out there and side stepped away. I couldn't see where. I *still* don't know where. But it was entirely his doing. The string went slack. I pulled on it and it came back snipped. Not broken, sliced."

"And you couldn't follow him?" asked Laz.

"If he had tied it to a tree. A rock, anything. Then of course I could have followed. But he didn't tie it to anything. He didn't even *un*tie it from himself. He deliberately cut it with that little knife he always carried."

Laz knew that OrigiLaz had never been in Greensboro, so it couldn't be the same knife he took from the dead woman's purse in the Vivipartum parking lot. But it was nice to know that grown-up famous-scientist Laz also chose to carry a little knife.

"Didn't you say all this to your keepers?" asked Ivy.

"No," she said. "If they're listening in, this is the first they've heard of my side of the story."

"Why?" demanded Ivy.

"Because Laz told me, he said, 'Ivy, there's something I want to try.' And I said, 'How stupid and dangerous is it?' And he said, 'If it works, then it was perfectly safe.' And I say, 'And if it doesn't work?'"

Nothing.

"Come on," said Laz. "What did he say?"

"He said, 'Then find a timestream where you talked me out of it,'" said Ivy-O.

"But you can't side step," said Ivy.

"That wasn't a secret," said Ivy-O.

"The secret," said Ivy, "was that you were trying to learn to side step."

"It was easier to learn to detect gravity sources," said Ivy-O.

"How much easier?" asked Ivy.

"I actually learned to detect gravity sources," said Ivy-O. "But I haven't yet learned to side step."

"Still working on it?" said Laz.

"It's like constantly exercising a muscle you aren't sure that you have," said Ivy-O.

"Sounds very Zen," said Ivy.

"It *is* very Zen," said Ivy-O.

"Tell me what we just decided," Laz asked Ivy. "Is Ivy-O going to try to find timestreams that are habitable but don't have Shiva? Or is she going to concentrate on teaching you how to detect gravity in timestreams and then you and I will do that?"

"I don't know," said Ivy. "Can you trust her?"

"I don't know," said Laz. "Do you believe she really can detect gravity?" He turned to Ivy-O. "Do *you* believe you can do it?"

"I know I can," said Ivy-O. "I just don't know how *well* I can do it."

"Then I think we need to make a test," said Laz. "The three of us, together, so Ivy can see what Our Lady Original is doing when she does it. And maybe our first try together will get us to a good place. A Safe Place."

"Or the twentieth try," said Ivy-O. "Each try doesn't take all that long."

"I'm game," said Ivy. "Saving humanity is slightly more important to me than my grim determination to be the timestreamer who accomplishes it."

12

Saving the world is a lonely business, especially when you aren't sure if:

    A. The world actually needs saving.
    B. Your talents and skills are sufficient to save it if it does.
    C. You can bear the shame if you fail.

    I made the mistake of saying that to Laz and he just put a hand on my shoulder and said, "If we fail, at least there'll be nobody around to complain about it." Trust him to make a really dark joke out of it.

    But here's the way that it wasn't a mistake to tell him. He didn't tell anybody else. I didn't have anybody else reassuring me or pre-comforting me or anything. When I told Laz, that's as far as it went.

    I can tell things to that boy. That's a kind of trust. Did Ivy-O have that kind of trust in OrigiLaz?

Laz was supposed to go back to Ivy-O's place the next morning. Ron Smith promised him a car would come for him at nine a.m. But at eight thirty, Laz knocked on Ivy's door.

She came to the door dressed in what were probably her pajamas—sweatpants and a T-shirt. Barefoot. Hair bunned up in back, which told him that she wasn't a back-sleeper. "What are you doing here?" she asked.

"I wondered if you wanted to take a walk," said Laz.

"I haven't even peed yet," said Ivy.

"I'll just wait out here and picture something else. Anything else. While you take care of that."

"Why would I want to take a walk with you?"

"Because this is still a place where the sun comes up in the morning, and all day it either rains or it doesn't."

"Normal weather," said Ivy.

"I have no idea what climate zone we're in on this version of Earth, or even if the continents line up anything like the Earth we know. But no matter where we are, this is good weather. And you and I used to walk everywhere together."

"Well, I don't miss *you*," said Ivy.

"Didn't say I missed you either," said Laz.

"Why else you here, then?"

"Because even though you're so damn sure I'm already falling out of love with you, Ivy, I haven't yet caught an inkling of that. You think my so-called love is all about you ambush-snogging me that day at Vivipartum, but I know it isn't, because I was already in love with you."

"Nice try, Casanova," said Ivy.

"What I fell in love with was the woman, the girl, the female primate that I was walking with all over Greensboro."

"Yeah, okay, let's take a walk," said Ivy. "Wait here outside my room, I'll be out as soon as I change."

"Change what?" asked Laz.

"Clothes."

"What you're wearing already counts as clothes," said Laz. "And my plan is to walk only on the amazing barefoot grass around this building, so I'm taking my shoes *off*."

"I lied," she said. "Already peed, already brushed my teeth, and if we're doing barefoot, I've already got no shoes on." She leaned into him, snaked her arms up onto his shoulders, pulled herself up, and kissed him.

It felt better than even that first time at Vivipartum, because he had a better idea of his part in the play, and instead of being shocked that it was happening at all, he was calmer and better able to enjoy it. Though he was a little bit shocked, too, because hadn't they agreed not to do that again?

When the kiss ended, as all good things must, eventually, he said, "Didn't we say we weren't doing that anymore?"

"We sure were wrong, if anybody said anything so stupid," said Ivy.

It occurred to Laz that Ivy might be feeling jealous of his going off with Ivy-O to do their timestream search without her. Because even though they were genetically identical and shared memories of the exact same childhood, Ivy and Ivy-O were definitely *not* the same person.

"You do understand," said Laz, "that I can tell the difference between you and Ivy-O."

"You can't tell the difference between pajamas and walking clothes," said Ivy.

"And I do remember which one I love. The brand-new one, without any wrinkles on her face, who never betrayed me or any version of me."

"I haven't had time to betray you yet," said Ivy, "and she says *he* was the idiot who left *her*."

"Yes," said Laz. "And someday you'll have exactly the same wrinkles that the other copy has now. But when that happens, I'll love every wrinkle on your face."

"You're talking way too sweet for a high school boy. You've been reading up."

"Of course I've been reading," said Laz. "There are *books* again."

"We're not in English class anymore, so I doubt you were reading classics."

"I'm not going to learn about love in *Moby-Dick*," said Laz.

"I hope you're not comparing me to a whale," she said.

"I'm also not comparing myself to a harpoon. A smart teacher once told me, any guy who isn't reading chick lit has no hope of understanding women."

"You thinking you're going to understand me someday?" asked Ivy.

"Hoping. So I might have a better chance of making you happy," said Laz.

"What have you read so far?" she asked.

"I decided to start with Jane Austen and work my way forward through time."

"Never read any Austen," said Ivy.

"All the better," said Laz. "You won't know where my best lines come from."

By now they were outside and his shoes and socks were off and they were walking barefoot on the softest lawn anybody ever grew. "Gotta say," said Ivy, "it would be a good thing if we could save this grass."

"Assignment decided on," said Laz. "It's not just about avoiding Shiva this time. It's also about finding good lawns."

"I really do hope you and Ivy-O succeed," said Ivy.

"I know you do," said Laz.

"I also want you to fail. Not in any big destructive way. I just want to learn what I need to learn and then work with you again and still have some purpose in it."

"That also makes sense," said Laz.

"So go out there with Ivy-O today and do some really mediocre work," said Ivy. "And try to figure out a way to hate her, even though she is so very much like the woman you think you're in love with."

"Not anywhere near as much like her as you are," said Laz.

That's why Laz was wearing no shoes and was lying in the grass all tangled up with Ivy when Ron Smith walked up, not stealthily, so that they had time to untangle and sit up before he reached them.

"Glad to see you took the opportunity for some morning exercise today," Ron Smith said blandly.

"Calisthenics are more enjoyable in a very small group," said Laz.

"You're the ones who made me give you access to—what do you call her?—Ivy-O. So let's not make her wait past the appointed time."

Ivy stood up, brushing grass off her clothing. "I'm going to go get dressed for my day's work of trying to discover gravity."

"Newton's already been there," said Laz.

"If he was so smart," said Ivy, "why didn't *he* discover Shiva. Or Galileo, for that matter. Or any of the guys who discovered planets and asteroids."

"They knew there was no point in discovering Shiva until we existed," said Laz.

"You mean our originals," said Ivy.

Ron Smith interrupted. "No, you two are the ones we were waiting for. Your originals did pretty well, as a start. But it was you we needed all along."

Laz and Ivy stood there holding hands. "Your flattery is working pretty well at this moment," said Ivy.

"Not flattery. We needed you two to be getting along instead of fighting all the time like your originals did. He kept making her feel stupid because he had all kinds of elevated vocabulary and theory—most of which was wrong, of course, but he still had a need to make her feel stupid."

"I feel like such a jerk," said Laz. "And yet I don't remember doing it."

"Because you didn't," said Ron. "And since Ivy-O had the same need to constantly put your original down, Laz, it came out about even. The two of *you* are connected, and not just by twine. My money is on its being you two, and nobody else, who figure this out and get us some Portals to a Safe Place."

"I appreciate the vote of confidence," said Laz.

"All you have to do," said Ron Smith, "is figure out a way to work with Ivy-O *without* getting stranded somewhere in the timestreams, unable to come home."

"Ivy-O isn't going to strand him," said Ivy.

"You say that because you think she's you," said Ron Smith. "And maybe you even believe her story. But there are a lot of us who think that the string was cut on *her* side of the divide."

Laz heard this, felt a tremor of dread—which he knew was exactly what Ron Smith wanted him to feel. But he also knew something that Ron Smith couldn't possibly know. When he was on those three worlds that he and Ivy found when they were side stepping to places where Laz didn't already exist, he knew that there was no moment when he did not know exactly where Ivy was, and no moment when he didn't have a clear view of multiple timestreams that included him and Ivy, so he could always go back to one of *those* in a pinch.

If *he* could do that, then OrigiLaz could surely do it. Ivy-O's story rang true. It was OrigiLaz who took off unsupervised. Ivy-O didn't betray him at all.

Laz bent down and kissed Ivy again, but she pulled back after a moment and said, "Please, Laz, not in front of the help."

Laz thought this was very funny and grinned at her and said, "Seeya this afternoon."

"God willing," said Ivy.

"God already promised to end the world this time in fire," said Laz. "I'm not sure he's on our side at all."

"I think that was Robert Frost," said Ivy.

Then Laz gave one last little wave and led Ron Smith back to where he had taken off his shoes and socks.

Ivy-O had not dressed up for the occasion. She met him at the door in jeans and a loose-fitting top. Like she was going to work in the garden. Maybe that's how she dressed every day.

"Glad to see Ron Smith didn't talk you out of trusting me," said Ivy-O.

"He barely tried," said Laz. "He believes in leaving things up to us."

"To *you*," said Ivy-O. "He didn't leave me as many options."

"Well, here we are now," said Laz, "and I want to see if I can sense gravity when you point it out to me."

"I don't have a laser pointer that works between timestreams," said Ivy-O.

While they talked, Laz was surveying her. Body language, facial expressions, mannerisms. A toss of the head to get hair out of her face. The way her fingers kept touching her eyebrows, her cheeks, her chin. Just little touches and brushes, but these were mannerisms Ivy didn't have. Physical traits that came from habits formed during childhood, adolescence, adulthood. They weren't inborn, they were acquired. Ivy hadn't acquired them. Ivy-O really was not another version of Ivy. So it was no surprise that Laz felt no attraction to her. She was older than Laz, of course, but the real barrier was that Laz really did belong to Ivy, in ways he didn't understand himself. He was not available for even speculation about women who were so definitely not Ivy.

Good heavens, if I marry Ivy, I am apparently going to be a faithful husband.

Since his parents had never told him how or why their marriage ended, he had speculated endlessly throughout childhood about whether one was unfaithful to the other. Or whether they always fought, back before Laz was old enough to remember. He had tried to ask Mom once, and she didn't speak to him for the rest of the day—didn't answer him, didn't rebuke him, just stopped talking to him and answered nothing that he said. So he never even tried to talk to Dad about it. Doofus once tried to bring up the subject, but Laz walked away from *him*. He wasn't interested in whatever story Mom's second husband might try to sell him.

Love ends. That's what Laz had known almost from the cradle—though they didn't officially divorce until he was four.

What he hadn't understood, until Ivy, was how overwhelming love was while it lasted. Now, at this moment, he couldn't conceive of how it might end.

But it might. Ivy-O said she loved *her* Laz, but apparently one of them abandoned the other.

"What are you thinking?" asked Ivy-O. "The way you're studying me and not listening to anything I'm saying. Trying to see how much your Ivy and I are alike? Or different?"

"I was thinking about my own parents," said Laz, truthfully

enough. "I was wondering how love ends. I was wondering when you know that it's over."

Ivy-O stood there in her own living room, looking at him, perhaps pondering how to answer the question.

No. How to deflect it. "You do remember," said Ivy-O, "that we have work to do."

"And if we have a personal relationship it might go more smoothly," said Laz.

"By asking me a question you should have asked your mother?" asked Ivy-O.

"I did," said Laz. "She wouldn't answer."

"You do understand that that *was* an answer, yes?" asked Ivy-O.

"And you're going to shut me down, too?" asked Laz.

"I'm not interested in your sad repining about your miserable childhood," said Ivy-O.

"It wasn't miserable," said Laz.

"It was the same childhood *my* Laz had, remember? Your mother didn't speak to you the rest of the day, after you asked, am I remembering right?"

Laz nodded.

"My Laz and I went through it all, eventually," said Ivy-O. "We had years together. But he was far more mature than you. He had had time to reflect, to get some perspective. It's quite disappointing to realize that when he was young, he was so shallow."

"I haven't said enough for you to know that I'm shallow," said Laz.

"You didn't have to say anything at all for me to know that," said Ivy-O.

"Well, we're off to a fine start," said Laz.

"There are things that you can count on me to do," said Ivy-O. "Psychotherapy isn't one of them."

"Nor is causing me to need psychotherapy, I would have thought," said Laz.

"Simplest way to start," she said, "is for you to hold my hand and side step somewhere."

"Ivy and I don't have to be touching," said Laz.

"My Laz and I did," said Ivy-O.

"Did you ever try?"

"Without touching?" asked Ivy-O. "Since touching worked, why would we try any other way?"

Still not touching her, Laz side stepped into a near timestream, one in which Ivy-O was sitting on a chair.

She looked up at him and raised her eyebrows. "So you could bring my memories with you into this version of reality," she said.

"Without touching," said Laz.

"Did you ever go to worlds that didn't contain a version of you, without touching your Ivy?" she asked.

"Since strings worked," said Laz, "why would we try any other way?"

She pursed her lips. "So you have a nasty streak," she said.

He laughed aloud. "If OrigiLaz had a knife, why did he only use it on the string?"

"It wasn't long enough to get past my ribs into my heart."

"Did you love him or did you hate him?" asked Laz.

"I loved him," said Ivy-O. "I think he showed how he felt about me by cutting the string."

"He could have simply dropped it," said Laz. "Why cut it?"

"Symbolism," said Ivy-O.

"No," said Laz. "I think there was more to it than that. I think he wanted to leave the remnant of the string tied to his wrist. I think he *needed* to be attached to the string, even after it was cut."

"Since you have no idea what you're talking about—"

"Look," said Laz, "somehow I have to trust you. Somehow we have to be able to work together. And I *do* have some idea of what I'm talking about, because unlike you and your Laz, OrigiLaz and I have shared memories. Up to about age seventeen. And his telling you some of them isn't the same thing as actually remembering them. For instance, did he ever tell you about Stever?"

Ivy-O said nothing. Just looked up at him from her chair.

"Stever was really important to him once. They did everything together. Like a second self. But when the price of their somewhat toxic friendship got too high, he side stepped into a timestream where Stever never moved to California. Never went to school with OrigiLaz. They never met."

Something happened inside Ivy-O's eyes. Laz couldn't read it because he'd never seen such an expression in Ivy's face.

"He cut himself off from a friend," said Ivy-O. "Is that supposed to be a repetition of what OrigiLaz did when he cut himself off from me?"

"Is it?" asked Laz. "You say you loved him. Maybe he loved you, too. But when the cost of a friendship is too high, too destructive, he steps out of the timestream where it existed. Isn't that what happened with you?"

She fell silent again.

"He couldn't possibly find a timestream in which the two of you never met," said Laz, "because then there wouldn't be a Portal to the New Place. He couldn't escape from you with a simple side step, not while staying in a stream where the human race was safe."

"Do you think you're telling me anything I haven't already thought of?" asked Ivy-O.

"I'm not trying to," said Laz. "Just trying to figure out what he did. Where he went."

"Good luck with that," said Ivy-O.

"There's nothing suicidal in any of my memories," said Laz. "I doubt he's become self-destructive. He didn't kill himself."

"I never thought he was capable of that."

"But if he was still alive," said Laz, "you would have been able to find his timestreams. His past choices and his future ones. Anywhere on Earth, you could have found him, you could have kept track of him."

"What makes you think I didn't?"

"Because his disappearance is still torturing you. Which is why you started out angry with me. Because I *do* look like him, and you're so very, very angry at him."

"You're perfectly capable of making me furious without any reference to my Laz," said Ivy-O.

"Now I think we're ready to try some side stepping," said Laz.

"You mean besides your side step to put me in this chair?"

"Come on, Ivy-O," said Laz. "You know that you were already in that chair in this timestream, before I brought you here."

"Yes, I know how it works," said Ivy-O. "But you still chose a timestream where I was at a lower level than you."

Laz smiled and shook his head. "I'm sure that was how I unconsciously chose it."

"You really want to go side stepping with me?"

"It's the dance we need to do," said Laz, "and since you're grimly determined to detest me and be angry with me, let's see how it works. Help me experience your bundle of timestreams with gravity-sensing in it."

"She gives you a *bundle* of timestreams?" asked Ivy-O.

"No," said Laz. "She picks one, because she can see up and down them much better than I can."

"And how does she give you that one?" asked Ivy-O.

"It don't know," said Laz. "It just happens. I suddenly have a very sharp, clear timestream in my mind that wasn't there before. It's from her because where else would it come from. So I step into it. And there we both are."

"You don't doubt her choice?"

"I don't *understand* her choice," said Laz. "I don't know what she saw before giving it to me. I don't know anything but the moments before and after the present in that new stream."

"She puts it in your mind. She doesn't give you a set of choices."

"Did you give OrigiLaz a menu to choose from?" asked Laz.

"I didn't push anything into his mind," said Ivy-O. "I invited him into mine."

That stopped Laz cold. "Are you serious?"

"He would never have let me have so much control. So much *choice*. He had to be in control."

"Well, what a sad puppy he must have been," said Laz. "I don't know if that's part of *my* character."

"He was one of the most important people in the world before I ever met him," said Ivy-O. "He was accustomed to getting his way, always. Everyone deferred to him."

"That's not really good for anybody," said Laz.

"I mentioned that to him," said Ivy-O. "Early in our partnership."

"Early in your indentured service," said Laz.

"However you want to look at it," said Ivy-O.

"Did you *try* to select a timestream and give it to him?"

"I did, when we were first trying to work together," said Ivy-O. "But I thought I failed, because he never responded to it. Never stepped into it. Never acknowledged that he had sensed it."

"So let's try *that*, first, and find out if you really couldn't do it, or if he was just being an authoritarian buttwipe."

At once a single timestream appeared in Laz's mind and, even though it wasn't as clear or strong as Ivy's always were, he side stepped into it immediately.

Ivy-O was standing at the open front door, as if ushering him outside. "You just stepped into it," said Ivy-O. "Without judging it first."

"I've never paused long enough to judge it, or even to know what the differences would be. I mean, yes, I knew that we would still be in this house, that we'd be together. I got that much. But you by the door? It didn't stand out enough for me to notice it."

She closed the door. "You just took it on . . ."

"On faith," said Laz, completing her sentence. "Ivy never led me anywhere bad."

"But you don't know *me*."

"Somehow the Ivy I know turned into you," said Laz. "Look, stop marveling at what a naive trusting fool I am, take it for granted, and decide what you want to do with a *real* partner. One who leaves important decisions up to you instead of pretending that you don't have the skill to do what you just did."

"This is new," she said. "I don't know if being a clone instead of the original made such a—"

"Who's wasting time on pointless metaphysical speculation?

Seems to be you," said Laz. "You said that you offered him a menu of choices. You say you invited OrigiLaz into your mind. Show me how *that* works."

"Because your Ivy never gave you a choice."

"We did whatever happened when we first tried to work together. She may not know that it's possible to invite me 'in,' whatever that means. So show me, and if you can, give me some idea of how you sense gravity sources."

"Let's decide something first," said Ivy-O. "Do we want to try this with nearby timestreams, where we already exist? Or do we want to twine ourselves up and try for something remote?"

"Local at first, please," said Laz.

It didn't come into his mind the way Ivy's timestreams did. Instead, it was as if his own view of nearby timestreams suddenly expanded—side to side *and* end to end, showing him more timestreams and farther up and down all of them.

None of them was as clear as Ivy's choices had always been, so as he examined them—thought about them, of course, because he couldn't actually *see* anything—he began to get an idea of where each timestream led, and where it had come from. He could look back down the timestreams to places much closer to the points of divergence, the choices that had created them. He could look farther into the probabilities of the future, though in that direction they got more vague and started branching very quickly. He realized that he could easily get lost trying to track the future, and he could see that no matter what he chose, it wouldn't *control* the future. There would still be more choices ahead, nothing was guaranteed. But the choice of different pasts was completely solid. When he chose a timestream, he chose *that* exact past, and it couldn't be altered.

Humans really do have free will, he realized. Which is why everybody's choices can create new timestreams. Often with trivial differences, as with most of the differences between the menu of timestreams Ivy-O was showing him. There was one timestream where they were sitting at the dining room table, with cups of something in front of them. He chose that.

"So you were thirsty," said Ivy-O, sitting across from him.

"Curious about what was in the cups," said Laz. "Plus this was the timestream that most diverged physically from the one we were in."

"You missed a lot of differences in timestreams that looked more similar."

"Probably," said Laz. "I'm not used to dealing with timestreams that go so far backward and forward. Plus, I got a sense that I could have kept looking at more and more timestreams, ever farther away."

"You got impatient," said Ivy-O.

"I wanted to see how it worked," said Laz.

"My Laz was very patient. When he chose, he did so after real consideration. After looking at many streams, and examining many versions of the past."

"Good for him."

"I'm telling you that it's possible to take more time," said Ivy-O, "since you seem to have thought you had to decide quickly. You need to learn to scan up and down, take your time, study it out before deciding. I can hold the view open as long as you need. Plus, it takes less time than you think. What you just did, I bet it felt like you were wasting a lot of time. But it was actually nearly instantaneous in the real world."

"Everything you showed me was real," said Laz. "They were all real worlds."

"But real worlds that didn't have your current consciousness in them. Real worlds where you only had one set of memories instead of two."

"It never occurred to me that our processes could be so different. What Ivy and I do works pretty well."

"And it may work better than what my Laz and I did," said Ivy-O. "After all, I don't have much practice in making the choices for us both."

"Let's do a few more runs with minor changes," said Laz, "and then we can get out the twine and see where it leads."

It looked for a moment as if Ivy-O was going to disagree.

Laz cocked an eyebrow. "A real objection?" he asked. "Or just resistance to the idea because you don't want to take orders from a kid?"

"You weren't actually giving orders," said Ivy-O. "You were making a request. A suggestion."

"And it took you longer to realize that than it did for me to choose from the menu you offered."

"Yes," said Ivy-O. "Because I'm prickly about being told what to do."

"But you didn't mind when OrigiLaz made all the choices."

"He was a great man," said Ivy-O. "So I accepted it."

"Makes sense to me," said Laz.

"Come on, you're telling me you don't resent my taking the lead?" she asked.

"A little. I'm human," said Laz. "But I'm not interested in my feelings about it. I only want to learn how to do it both ways—you offering a menu, and you just making the choice. And I want to try it going into timestreams where we don't exist. Maybe then I can see the gravity streams or strings or whatever."

"Gravity is an attraction. It feels like really tiny tugging." Ivy-O looked at him. "You can set aside your resentment? That's really a thing?"

"Didn't you set aside your resentment of OrigiLaz?" asked Laz.

"I thought I did," said Ivy-O. "But now that I've experienced being trusted to make choices, I—"

"You like it," said Laz.

"I don't know how *you* could bear letting *her* make all the choices," said Ivy-O.

"I didn't. Most of the time, I used my own sense of timestreams and side stepped where I wanted, and she came along for the ride. Or *didn't*, if I didn't want her to."

"You could choose that? She got no vote?"

"We quarreled sometimes. I needed to go off by myself. I'm not sure whether I left her behind, or she chose to remain behind because she sensed that I needed solitude. It wasn't all cherubs and caramel apples for us, you know."

She smiled in spite of herself. "Cherubs and caramel apples?"

"Just what came to me. Gooey sweetness with a crisp bite, and the icky cuteness of fat babies with ridiculously small wings. I mean, if cherubs can fly, why aren't penguins all airborne?"

She laughed. "Okay," she said. "A few more practice runs, with me trying to show you gravity, if that's even possible. Maybe while I show you the timestreams, I can pick the one with—no, they'll all have the same gravity sources in the local ones."

"All right, then. Break out the twine," said Laz. "The sooner we move on into long-distance side stepping, the sooner we'll have a chance of accomplishing something."

13

Ivy's Plog of Plogs, the True Plog, the Plog to End All Plogs
I imagined that if I ever met my original, I could learn from her about
more effective ways to guide my side stepping partner between remote
timestreams. It did not cross my mind that she, having lost her own
partner for reasons unknowable, would look at mine and, in a word,
covet him.

Of course she doesn't love him or even care about him. He's a
means to an end, a way to restore her relevance and her freedom.
Because he's a trusting kid—I think because he himself is trustworthy
so he assumes everyone else is—it seems not to occur to him that a
woman who has already lost one partner might as easily lose another
she cares even less about.

Does she care about anyone? I have no way to know. Searching my
own heart doesn't help me at all, because despite sharing memories
of the same childhood, it's obvious that she has learned many things,
many ways of thinking and speaking and acting, that didn't show up in
whatever kind of brain-state recording they used to implant her memories in me.

So I don't know what she's thinking, and in all likelihood, despite the
vividness of many of my (our) memories, I may not understand anything
she ever thought. Nor can I guess how much Ron Smith and his ilk
were able to edit those memories before giving them to me. Could they

even read or see or hear those memories when they were outside of my brain and Ivy-O's? I have no idea of their technology. But my guess is that if they left something out, that is precisely the information I most need to have.

The very first day that she drafted Laz into her service, I made some useful discoveries. First, my connection with Laz did not depend on my being within sight of him. When Ron Smith drove him away, I felt bereft. But then I began to realize that I always knew exactly where Laz was. I didn't know what he was thinking or saying or even, really, doing, but I could still sense the bundle of causal threads arising from him. I could watch the menu of possibilities ahead of him coalesce with every decision that he made and become irrevocable reality behind him—speaking of time, of course, not of physical location.

This meant that while I had no idea what he would choose to do, or why, I always knew what he had just done.

Now, I was supposed to spend the time he was gone figuring out about how to sense gravity tugging on all the timestreams I could "see." But obviously I was only sensing timestreams whose gravity sources were the same ones that dominated every reality in which Earth was in the identical orbit. There were quivers and variations in it, but all the timestreams mostly overlapped, and all of them were completely dominated by the gravity of the Sun. I believed at some moments that I could sense that gravity as a powerful tug on all the timestreams, and then I realized that I had no idea what I was sensing because I had nothing to compare it to—no Sun-free timestream, because without the Sun there would be nothing for me to detect.

So instead of doing my assigned job—which was probably intended to be futile and frustrating so I wouldn't pester Ron Smith or Ivy-O—I concentrated on Laz. I began to try to understand what I was sensing when I was so constantly aware of him. I realized quite soon that I was not reaching out to him, searching for him, finding him. Instead, <u>he</u> was tugging at <u>me</u>. Not consciously, but there was some part of him always reaching for me.

But what was this "him" and "me"? Not our bodies, not the natural attraction of male and female that keeps the species going over the generations. Oh, maybe it began there, but he was not tugging on any emotion or physical desire; whatever it was, it wasn't in my body, or at least it didn't feel like that to me.

I think that whatever part of him does the stepping, the consciousness that carries his memories from one timestream into another, to add to the memories already there in the body he now inhabits, <u>that</u>, his deep self, is always looking for that same part of me—if it is the same part, if I even <u>have</u> that part. I think I do have it. It's the part of me that can sense the causal streams, select one, and push it into his mind. The part of me that can construct a menu of choices and show it to him.

That's what I learned from Ivy-O, that such a thing was possible. So easy, when I withheld myself from him a little bit and waited. Waited for him to come <u>find</u> me and see what I had laid out on the table for him.

He is always looking for me. That's the tug I've been feeling. Nothing to do with gravity, from the Sun or Shiva or any other sources. What I detect in that part of me that senses timestreams is <u>his</u> sense of the timestreams. He hungers for contact with me.

Now, is that love? Is that what he feels, and thinks that it's love? If so, then is it possible he's correct, and our connection consists of his love for and need for me?

Or does he sense me, too? Is he aware of some tugging in his mind that turns his attention always to me? Are we tugging on each other? That would be lovely and symmetrical, especially because while I like him and care about him, I don't feel anything like the mindless yearning that I'm told love is supposed to feel like. But maybe that's just biological love, just the yearning of the pistil for the pollen; maybe what we have is at a much deeper level, not the love of blossoms, but the love of root for root.

How botanical I am now.

Yet it seems right, because what consciousness do plants have of their hungers? Do they <u>think</u> of growing a root toward water, or do they simply grow roots and then respond by expanding on whatever roots are bringing water into the system? Do they "love" water or just have a root-building reflex when water is present?

I believe it may be a distinction without a difference. I can feel Laz tugging on me <u>all</u> the time, and I always know how to find him because of that.

But now that he's working with Ivy-O, will that need transfer from me to her? Will <u>she</u> feel the tugging?

Much bigger question, really: Does she still feel the tugging of OrigiLaz's deep self? Does she <u>know</u> that he still exists in the universe as a causal being, or does she know that he does <u>not</u>?

And now I have a new project, one that may not help me in finding new worlds for humanity—<u>that</u> project now belongs to the new team of Laz and Ivy-O. <u>My</u> project is to see if I can detect, in Ivy-O's consciousness or timestream awareness, any tugging on <u>her</u> from OrigiLaz. Since I can feel my Laz tugging on me, can I feel <u>her</u> Laz tugging on <u>her</u>?

And if I find that such a tug is happening, do I confront her with it? Or do I simply write it here, knowing that the spies will read everything I write? Do I trust Ron Smith and his team to make wiser decisions than I can make myself? Or do I take everything upon myself and, if I learn something important, simply refrain from writing it down or talking about it to anyone?

What good is it to know something, if you tell no one? The knowledge will then die with you, and those who might have benefited from it will never have it. That would be beyond unfortunate, that would be wicked.

But how could I know what's useful to others, when I haven't told them yet? I can imagine Ron Smith going, "Oh, that? Yes, Ivy-O told us about that years ago, we know that, it's just all kind of sad."

Or maybe even at this moment—or rather, at the moment Ron Smith reads this—he's saying to the rest of his team, "Holy banana split, laddies, look what New Ivy is saying here, do you think this brilliant thing might be true?"

And look, Ronnie, I know you never say "holy banana split" because that was so junior high back when I was in middle school. But that was the age I was the last time I actually got excited about anything, so when I think of someone being excited, I imagine them feeling and acting like that.

In case you decide to adopt "holy banana split," remember that someone else feeling the same thing should answer you, "no cherry!" or "whip that cream!" They both mean the same thing, for reasons clear only to girls in middle school.

I started this plog entry while Laz and Ivy-O were together for their first day. Now it has been four days and they've already found five timestreams that are clearly not the inhabited Earth. They've opened Portals into those five and sent in teams, and instead of waiting for astronomical results—i.e., Shiva or non-Shiva—they just keep looking for more streams. Ivy-O pretends she's trying to find timestreams without Shiva's gravitational influence, but I think that's crap. I think she's just looking for what I looked for—chlorophyll in a breathable atmosphere, and then hoping for luck.

Maybe, though, she _is_ looking for a tug. Not of gravity, but of Origi-Laz. Maybe she's hoping to find him again. Because maybe she feels about him the way I feel about my Laz.

And there it is. Finally in words, right on the paper. My Laz—I know, I've said it before. The Laz Who Loves Me. The Laz whom I hunger for every day that Ivy-O keeps him away from me.

The Laz that I can never stop finding and watching.

How could she possibly have ever lost track of <u>her</u> Laz? If she didn't feel what _I_ feel, by what right did she ever let him go into worlds where she couldn't see where he was? What did she do to lose him? Or if she hasn't lost him, why doesn't she simply push into my Laz's mind exactly what timestream OrigiLaz is on? Wouldn't everything go better if both Laz and his original were working with me and my original, try-ing new worlds at the same time, doubling the amount we accomplish every day?

She must have some reason for not telling us everything she knows about OrigiLaz. Because I know that she <u>must</u> know more than she's telling. I think I can feel him tugging on her. It's faint, not like the tug I feel from my Laz. But I think I can detect it. And it sure ain't com-ing from no Shiva.

Laz didn't like not being in charge. As a kid back in L.A., of course, he hadn't been in charge of anything—except himself. With his parents supposedly sharing custody of him, he went back and forth between houses where somebody else made all the decisions. But when it came to his own activities, nobody watched over him. Mom and Dad both knew that his school assignments were done, or if they weren't, he would either do them in time or had already decided not to do them at all, and it wouldn't interfere with his education or his grades in the slightest.

He could walk wherever he wanted, or ride his bike if the mood struck him. It rarely did, because riding the bike put him in the street with the insane people inside cars, while walking kept him on sidewalks or off to the very edge of the road, where he could dodge out of the way when a driver seemed particularly stupid or inattentive. His life was in his own hands.

On the days when there was a custody changeover, he usually *walked* from Mom's place to Dad's, or vice versa. They always offered to drive—or Doofus did—but even when it was raining, Laz declined. Only if there were lightning and high winds, with saturating rain so that the wind might blow shallow-rooted trees over on top of him, did he accept a ride.

That was one thing that did not really change when he woke up in his coffin at Vivipartum. Not for an instant did he even think of waiting around for someone to show up and tell him what to do. Nor did he worry about somebody else second-guessing his choices. Stealing food from abandoned supermarkets? What choice did he have? His conscience didn't bother him. After all, if the food in the cans on the shelves mattered to anybody, they would already have been taken away. The fact that they were there meant nobody cared.

That was the central fact of his life. Nobody cared. Oh, his parents loved him, after their fashion—he was always provided for, they seemed to enjoy his company. But they didn't object to the nearly complete independence of his life. And so in his solitary life in Greensboro, before Ivy awoke, all that was missing—apart from good food—was periodically checking in with his parents. He did not suffer from homesickness, since near complete freedom had been his life prior to waking—or, that is, the life that he remembered, since *he* had not actually lived any life at all.

When Ivy came, he responded by taking responsibility. Trying to treat her decently and allow her to be comfortable. His attempt to protect her from being seen naked backfired, since she could see far enough back in his timestream to know that he had seen *and* not-seen her nude body. It seemed to count for nothing with her that he had side stepped in order to avoid that stream. She taunted him until he was sick of hearing it.

He had once walked all the way from Van Nuys, through the Glen, and on to the UCLA campus, because he and a friend were having such a good conversation. The friend was a college student at the time, having graduated from high school the previous spring. Now Laz couldn't remember his name. But he could bear human company quite well.

Now he believed that he loved Ivy, while Ivy believed that he did not, or that his love would soon expire. Why do I love her? he asked himself. Is it because I saw her naked? Is it because she kissed me and held me, suddenly and without any kind of courtship? I had never had such experiences before—is it only my naivete that makes me think of it as love?

Laz did not believe that, but he couldn't reject the possibility. One thing Laz always tried to do was be honest with himself.

Here is the proof of my love, he told himself: Because I resent all the time I have to spend with the wrong Ivy, while the real one, the one I walked to Burlington with, is sequestered in pursuit of some asinine project that I don't even think is possible. Detecting the gravity of a remote vagabond planet from the timestreams alone? Ridiculous. Ivy-O had some other game going on.

And yet she was every bit as talented at gathering timestreams as Laz's Ivy. She had skills Ivy didn't have—though she had also learned some things from Ivy, so it's not as if Laz had been stuck with a second-rate copy.

No, what Ivy-O was missing was undefinable, for the first few days. Ivy-O was arrogant, with her certainty that Laz would do whatever she asked. She soon found that he would not, because he didn't know if he could trust her yet.

Then, for a whole day, Laz thought she was trying to fall in love with him, which was ridiculous—she was only a little younger than his mother, after all. But by the end of the day, he realized that she was trying to *act* as if she loved him, thinking it would make him more cooperative. Thank heaven she didn't try any snogging, because that would have been not only revolting, but also outrageous, since Ivy-O knew perfectly well how Laz felt about Ivy.

Now, after a week of opening several Portals a day, he began to notice other things that convinced him that whatever Ivy-O's agenda was, it had nothing to do with gravitation from Shiva and almost as little to do with her relationship with Laz or even with Ivy.

He realized this as they joined in a meeting with Ron Smith and the heads of the astrotech crews. In every case, the first news was that in each new Portal, Shiva was still coming, and on the identical path with that of the New Place. They hadn't found Shiva on a quicker path, or on the path that had been detected in the Old Place. Laz tried to interpret that as good news—at least they weren't regressing.

But then he noticed that Ivy-O's questions were quite odd, or so it seemed to him. "Are you collecting specimens?" she asked each team leader. "Are you finding plants or creatures that might have utility in the Safe Place, when and if we find it?"

After the fourth time, Laz asked her, "Is that part of our mission? To sample all the versions of Earth, all the evolutionary timestreams?"

"We found interesting life forms here in the New Place," said Ivy. "Isn't that true, Mr. Smith?"

"Interesting," he said, nodding. "Some potentially fatal, but those were microbes and easy to kill, since they had built up no resistance to our antibiotics."

"What about the kind of life Ivy-O is asking about?" asked Laz.

Ivy-O stiffened a little, because she had asked him not to use that nickname for her when Laz's Ivy wasn't present.

Ron Smith shrugged. "We send a biologist, usually a botanist, with each team. Just to look around. It's dangerous to bring anything back, in case it gets loose. A few spores from the wrong fern could wreak havoc here."

Ivy-O barked out a laugh. "You bring ten thousand species from the Old Place and that's somehow safe?"

"It's what we live on," said Ron Smith. "It's proven safe for *us*, even if they all act like invasive species in the New Place. It's terraforming. While bringing back life forms from these random Portal places might have devastating and unpredictable effects."

Ivy-O shrugged. But when the next team reported, she still asked the same questions. Plant or animal life that was not previously known. Did study of the vids of the test place reveal any patterns of life that were not known in the Old Place or the New Place?

Had they brought home any breeding pairs? Had they brought any fruiting plants?

I'm looking for a Safe Place, thought Laz, but *she's* looking for innovative species. Doesn't she care about saving the world? And if not, why not? Did *she* have some special escape plan that would exempt her from all that the rest of humanity would be going through in just a few years' time?

He wanted to leave the meeting and get back to the *real* Ivy, *his* Ivy, and tell her about this attitude of Ivy-O's and see what she thought it meant.

Of course, he knew he would have to get through Ivy's first wall of defense. "I'm not interested in anything she says or does. You're with her all day, so leave her behind and let's talk about the places you've been."

"I've regrown the little carbuncle or whatever it was on my little toe on my left foot," he had said the first day, by way of answer. "It was my first indication in the healing cave that I wasn't the original, because OrigiLaz's memory always included that little lump that was half toenail, half skin. Now it's grown. I think it comes from irritation from wearing shoes."

Now, every time he went back to the house where he and Ivy now lived, he would begin his conversation with that observation. "I've regrown that little thing on my little piggy toe." And she'd answer, "Right pig or left?" But once he was past that small ritual, he'd be able to bring it up, especially because it might reflect negatively on Ivy-O, and Ivy seemed to show special interest whenever that was the case.

After the meetings, though, Ivy-O took him aside. "I know you're trying to read something into my questions about the flora and fauna of the Portals we've opened. Don't. I'm just trying to find reasons why our failures aren't failures at all. I'm hoping that in some way we're also advancing scientific knowledge."

"Good," said Laz. "That makes sense, now."

But her expression showed that she still doubted his sincerity.

Could she see his past timestreams well enough to know about the content of his conversations with Ivy after the previous days' work? Or were his future probabilities so clear to her that she could tell from the timestreams opening up in front of him that he wasn't convinced? Both versions of Ivy knew too much that was inaccessible to him. His own sense of timestreams showed little more than an hour or two into the past and a few minutes into the future. Enough to get him out of the clutches of a bear or out of a burning building. But not enough to uncover anybody else's secrets.

"Laz," said Ivy-O. "You have to trust me."

"I side step into timestreams I couldn't see until you gave them to me, and I take your word for their safety and possible productivity," said Laz. "I obviously trust you. My life is in your hands every day."

"No, a piece of twine is in my hands, and in your hands. We're opening Portals, not stepping out into the dead cold of space."

Laz grinned at her. "So far, anyway," he said.

Ron Smith dropped her off at her place, and then drove Laz home. While Ivy-O was in the car, Laz let Ron Smith talk to her. Lots of chat, lots of references to events and people Laz didn't know about. As soon as she was out of the car, though, Laz asked Ron Smith: "We can do this job from anywhere. Why do we drive from Ivy's and my house to *her* house and then drive to that building where we do all our stepping?"

"Is there something you'd like to do differently?"

Laz's answer was immediate. "Just bring us to Ivy-O, or bring her to us, and then we set to work."

"Here's why I don't like that idea," said Ron Smith. "Right now, you and Ivy are together every night, able to talk freely because Ivy-O isn't there. During the time you and Ivy-O are working, you don't have Ivy looking over your shoulder, and you aren't constantly aware of her."

"Of course I'm constantly aware of her," said Laz, "just as she is aware of me. Ivy is always far more present to me than her original, who is, as far as I'm concerned, a complete stranger who has not yet said a truthful thing to me."

Ron Smith raised his eyebrows. "You don't know that," he said.

"I'm pretty sure," said Laz.

"Nor do you know if *your* Ivy tells you the truth, either," said Ron Smith.

"I'm pretty *damn* sure," said Laz.

"Laz," said Ron Smith, "you do understand that we regard *you* as the one with the least reliable judgment. Ever since you woke another copy of Ivy and she sucked your brains out of your head by mouth, you've been less and less reliable every day."

"Judged by what standard?" asked Laz, surprised that he wasn't even offended by this.

"Judged by how you comported yourself while alone—highly methodical and rational and stoical, in our judgment—and also how you comported yourself prior to snogging with Ivy."

"So being lonely and lost are considered more reliable than being mildly ecstatic and filled with hope."

"Filled with longing," said Ron Smith.

"A distinction without a difference," said Laz.

"All the difference in the world. Happiness doesn't distort your thinking, but longing does. Wishing is to rational thought like static is to radio communications."

Laz wondered who this guy was, why he thought the way he did.

"Remind me of your real name, Ron Smith?" asked Laz.

Ron Smith smiled. "Ron Smith is good enough," he said.

"Brazilian, so Smith is Ferreira, not Herrera."

"I'm from Campinas, in the state of São Paulo," said Ron Smith. "So we pronounce the double R as an H, like in 'hope' and 'hand.'"

"Feh-*hay*-rah," said Laz carefully. "So you see I do know how to look stuff up and learn from those things—what do you call them?—we didn't have any in Greensboro—ah, yes. Books."

"That's why we didn't leave you any. Because you knew how to look things up."

"Because ignorant, uninformed people do the best job of saving the world."

"We tried this with an intellectual giant," said Ron Smith, "and he disappeared on us."

"Both me."

"And you're not actually ignorant, anyway," said Ron Smith. "You seem to know every bit as much about side stepping as your original did. You just haven't done anything self-destructive yet."

"I want to learn what OrigiLaz knew," said Laz.

"Our library is currently bereft of any books or essays by him," said Ron Smith.

Laz shook his head. "If you wanted to help me, you could get more books in a second."

"Oh, I wager you'll have complete access to those books quite soon," said Ron Smith. "But *I* won't be bringing them to you."

They were silent for the last few minutes of the drive, until Ron Smith said, "The reason you have to go to the NAPSC—the North American Portal Science Center—is because that's where we have the astrotechs and biologists who pass through your Portals and test them. It's easier to bring you to them than them to you."

Laz nodded. "If you had said that in the first place, you could have spared us both a lot of needless conversation."

"I like conversing with you, Laz," said Ron Smith. "There's no such thing as a needless conversation between us."

They got home. Home being defined, in Laz's mind, as wherever Ivy lived.

She was reheating the stew that somebody had brought them for dinner.

"Is it vegetarian?" he asked.

"It might have started that way," said Ivy, "but several insects have flown into it in the past hour. We need better screens on the windows."

"We had a meeting about what the astrotechs found," said Laz.

"Since you don't look ecstatic, I'm assuming results weren't stunning," said Ivy.

"Shiva's in all of them, same trajectory."

"Apparently the goddess's gravity sense isn't working well."

"Come on," said Laz. "You never believed gravity would show up in the timestreams."

Ivy turned to him with a mock supercilious air. "Who are we to doubt the testimony of our betters?"

"We have no betters," said Laz. "*You* have no betters."

Ivy shook her head. "If you think flattery is going to get you into my bed . . ."

"I only want to get into your head. Can we please have a real conversation that isn't completely deformed by how much you resent her?"

Anger flashed into Ivy's expression and then faded quickly. "Fair enough," she said. "Mean, but fair."

"Not meant to be mean," said Laz. "I just can't figure out what she's actually trying to do."

Then he told her about Ivy-O's weird inquiries about new life forms in each Portal world.

Ivy laughed. "Come on, how many centuries did it take for human beings to even begin cataloguing the animals and plants they ate and raised and rode and saw and slept with every day? And how long after that before Westerners knew about the platypus or the megalodon?"

"Or Piltdown Man?" asked Laz.

"Exactly," said Ivy. "Why would they notice *anything*?"

"Why is Shiva on the exact same trajectory in all of the timestreams we visit?" asked Laz.

"Do you think that's odd? Maybe Shiva's on that trajectory in *all* of them."

"Not in the Old Place," said Laz.

"We only know what they tell us," said Ivy. "We don't even know for ourselves that Shiva even exists."

"Come on. Shiva was detected by Chinese astronomers and then observations and calculations from India, Iran, Russia, Brazil, Peru, and half of Europe and North America confirmed their data. If all those kids are playing in the same sandbox, I think we can rely on it," said Laz.

"Have they shown us any newspapers since we got here?" asked Ivy. "They hid all printed material from us back in Greensboro."

"And why would we believe things just because they're in the papers?" asked Laz.

"Universal skepticism isn't a good way to plan for the future," said Ivy. "But still we keep finding out that we're relying on information from somebody else."

"That's what literacy and the internet did for the human race. We can read what dead scientists and philosophers said."

"Like Nostradamus," said Ivy.

"Fools and seers, all their words are preserved."

"They have something to hide," said Ivy. "And whatever they're hiding is absolutely the most important thing for us to know."

"Ivy," said Laz. "Let's assume that everybody's telling the truth."

"Except Ivy-O," said Ivy.

"Exactly where I was heading with this," said Laz. "What is *she* hiding? What is she looking for?"

Laz and Ivy sat there silently eating their stew, which was very good, though Laz wondered whether the meat in it was from Old Place animals or New Place animals.

"You know I can't answer that," Ivy finally said.

Laz said nothing.

"All I have are guesses," said Ivy.

Still Laz ate in silence. If he pushed, all she'd tell him was what she thought he wanted to hear.

"I'm coming at it from a completely different angle," Ivy said. "A weird one."

"I would have expected nothing less," said Laz.

Ivy sat up a little straighter in her chair. A deliberate wriggle, like a mark of punctuation in the conversation. "Here's my angle of approach. I always know where you are."

Laz almost said, Duh, or, Me too, or some other flippant answer. But it seemed to him Ivy was going somewhere with this.

"And I suspect you always know where I am," said Ivy.

"Always," Laz affirmed.

"And what I'm doing?" she asked.

Laz waved that off. "I don't spy on you. As long as you're breathing, I concentrate on my own business."

"How is it that *she* doesn't know what happened to OrigiLaz?" asked Ivy.

Laz nodded. "*That's* a very good question."

"I think she does know," said Ivy. "And if he's alive, she knows where he is."

Laz leapt ahead. "Do you think she's trying to lead me to where he is?"

"She could have done that with the first side step," said Ivy.

"She needs it to look like an accident," said Laz. "But that would explain why we haven't strayed far from the situation of the New Place."

"I think she knows where he is, or at least what he was planning to do when he disappeared. I think he really was trying something far-fetched, because the survival of humanity was at stake, and nothing had worked so far. Don't you?"

"I'd like to think my original was a serious-minded, responsible person," said Laz.

"But he was a scientist. You have no memory of what Laz Hayerian meant to us all when I was a kid. I mean, immediately before getting my brain-state recorded. He was Newton and Einstein rolled into one. Your name had become an adjective, like, 'Wait a minute, I'm having a hayerian moment here.'"

"Armenian names lend themselves to being adjectivized," said Laz. "They all end with 'something-ian.'"

"OrigiLaz was a serious scientist and he had been working theoretically with timestreams for decades before Ivy-O came along and helped guide him to truly strange places," said Ivy.

"You're saying that the person who *really* held out on everybody was OrigiLaz. He performed an experiment without telling anybody except, maybe, Ivy-O, and it didn't work the way it was supposed to."

"Or maybe it did," said Ivy. "Maybe it worked *exactly* the way it was supposed to. Only it put him out of touch with Ivy-O for a while. She's trying to reestablish contact."

"By getting the botanists to look for a tree that has 'Ivy+Laz' carved in a heart on the trunk?" asked Laz.

"If I knew, I'd have told you already," said Ivy. "I'm just saying, whatever she's doing with you, it has to do with getting back in touch with OrigiLaz, not with finding a Shiva-free Safe Place for the human race."

"She doesn't want everybody to die," said Laz. "It can't just be about hooking up with the love of her life or whatever."

"No version of Laz is the love of any version of Ivy-O's life," said Ivy.

"Harsh," said Laz. The words really stung him. He also didn't believe they were true. Or at least he hoped that they weren't final.

"Do you really think she loves *anybody*?" asked Ivy.

"Nobody that I've seen her in the same room with, anyway," said Laz.

"Laz," said Ivy, "what if reconnecting with OrigiLaz is *exactly* the way she can find us a Safe Place that we can all get to in time? What if all the random opening of Portals is a hopeless endeavor, but whatever OrigiLaz did, if she can find him again, the random search is over?"

"What if," said Laz. "Should we ask her?"

"If she wanted us to know . . . ," said Ivy.

Laz recognized her point, that asking Ivy-O anything would only lead to more evasion. "This was good stew," said Laz.

"I'm going to read through all of OrigiLaz's scientific papers," said Ivy.

Only then did Laz understand the stacks of journals and books on a couple of the unused dining table chairs. So this is what Ron Smith meant when he said Laz would have access to them. Ivy had asked for them and here they were now. "You haven't graduated from high school yet," said Laz.

"I'm very, very smart. And after all, they were written by a version of *you*, so how hard can they be?"

Laz gave her the chuckle she was asking for. "If he had written anything pertinent to this, don't you think Ron Smith and his team would have found it?"

"They've never side stepped," said Ivy. "They've never gathered up timestreams. Would they know a hint if they saw it?"

"Would we?"

"I'm trying to prepare myself to do just that," said Ivy.

"So should I," said Laz.

"No," said Ivy. "Your work is to obey Ivy-O for a while longer, and keep watching to see if you learn something from what she says and does. And maybe you'll find the Safe Place completely by accident."

Laz knew that she was right. Ivy was the one with freedom of action.

Laz *hated* not being able to make his own decisions.

"I will obey like a good . . . servant," he said.

"You don't get it, do you?" said Ivy. "You're not a servant *or* a slave, which was what you almost said before you corrected it to servant."

"What am I, then?" asked Laz.

"You're the genie," said Ivy. "From the bottle."

14

The New Place Plog of Lazarus Hayerian #1

I'm no longer isolated, writing on scraps of paper in order to keep my sanity and hold thoughts clearly in my brain. Now I have two versions of Ivy, both nasty to me whenever they want, and both absolutely essential to anything I need to accomplish. I have Ron Smith. I can't pretend to be alone.

So why am I lonelier than ever?

I suspect that this is the true tragedy of the human condition. The more closely we're involved with other people, the more isolated and misunderstood we feel. Because nobody can possibly know us, and we can't possibly know anybody, not even ourselves. Dad used to say that in a half-joking kind of way, I think because he hoped it would console me.

Here's how I imagine his reasoning: Laz, my son, you feel completely apart from even your friends, and it makes you sad. But everybody feels alone almost all the time, and it only gets worse. So you're not <u>alone</u> in your loneliness. Does that make you feel better?

No, Dad. It made me feel hopeless. So I didn't think about it much. I just walked somewhere and thought different thoughts. I also had friends who were able to take my mind off my isolation by proving that I wasn't actually isolated.

How would someone who could side step take himself out of reach of the Ivys. Ivies? How could he <u>hide</u> among the timestreams?

Is there someplace where timestreams don't exist? Or where they're concealed from view? Assuming that anything Ivy-O said is true, that's what OrigiLaz did.

Here's where I am, in thinking about this problem. What I do, what Ivy and Ivy-O do, all takes place in the instant of Now. When I side step into another timestream, different things have just been happening, and the future will be different, but the actual moment of transfer is exactly the same distance in time from whatever the First Moment was. In the Big Bang or the Mind of God, the first tick of the infinite clock. Count forward, and it's the exact same duration from Tick One to the moment of my side step.

So nothing I do can hold back time, or move me through time any faster than the normal one-second-per-second rate of time travel that everybody uses.

And that's all that Ivy and Ivy-O can see. They can give me a timestream or show me a menu of timestreams but the only spot in each timestream that I can move to is Now.

But I'm not a theoretical physicist. OrigiLaz was. What if the impossibility of time travel was something he wasn't altogether sure of?

Not me, now—I've never seen what I'm about to describe. I'm only <u>imagining</u> that maybe OrigiLaz could see it. What if he looked at individual timestreams and instead of picking one and side stepping into Now in that stream, what if he looked at the immediate past or the immediate future and stepped <u>there</u>?

Wouldn't he then become invisible to Ivy-O?

What if he kept stepping slightly back and slightly back in one timestream, and just kept doing that for a while, how far back could he go?

I imagine him going back, because the past is fixed. Ivy and Ivy-O can see farther up and down the timestreams, but they see much farther into the past because the streams narrow down, and because they're set in stone. What already happened in a timestream is irrevocable. I can pick a different timestream where it didn't happen that way, but once I side step into a timestream, I'm stuck with that timestream's past. I can't change it in any way.

But if OrigiLaz started moving back into those fixed timestreams, would they <u>stay</u> set in concrete? Or would each moment he moved to be his new Now? A new fulcrum in time where he could make changes?

If he went back far enough, would all the old rules of time travel kick in? Try not to run over your grandpa with a brand-new '58 Chevy before he's fathered your mom! Don't meet yourself in the past or—

All nonsense. It can't happen. It's too contrary to the laws of physics. Despite all the crazy thought experiments, we've never found any credible evidence that holds up upon examination that causality ever moves any direction but forward. To travel back in time is to move a causer to a point earlier than his own causation. Just not possible.

But it would explain everything.

Ah, but any explanation that explains everything probably explains nothing.

That idea runs through my mind over and over. I can't remember who said it, but it's so obvious that maybe nobody ever thought it needed saying. Anything that explains everything is obviously not connected with reality. Because everything has more than one cause, and more than one effect. So to say <u>one</u> thing explains everything is ridiculous. Because no <u>one</u> thing ever explains <u>anything</u>.

My brain isn't just convoluted, it's positively tied in knots.

I can't talk about this with Ivy-O because she doesn't pay attention to anything I say, anyway. I'm there to take her into whatever timestreams she wants to sample, and that's it. I can't talk about it with Ivy because she's really sensible and she'd talk me out of this in about five minutes of rational discussion.

Can't talk about it with Ron Smith because I don't know if they'd go overboard believing it, or put me in a straitjacket. "Laz, can you still side step while wearing this straitjacket?" "Why yes, Ron Smith, I believe I can." "Then we'll just leave this on you until you stop talking crazy, is that okay?" "I understand perfectly, Reinaldo Ferreira, and I agree with your decision to take away my ability to scratch or blow or pick my nose at will."

Laz finished writing the first episode of his New Place Plog and went into the kitchen, where Ivy was reading a printed journal, seemingly enthralled with it. On impulse, Laz walked up behind her, put his hands on her shoulders, leaned down, and kissed her on the cheek.

As he expected, she didn't tear her eyes away from the page. But she did say, "That's nice," as Laz walked away, and it didn't even sound sarcastic. At least he chose to hear it as not-sarcastic. As if she really did think it was nice for him to give her a peck on the cheek before he took off for a day of work with a woman who looked exactly like her except older and meaner.

Laz didn't have much to say to Ron Smith on the way to Ivy-O's place to pick her up. Either Ron had already found a way to read the plog that Laz had just finished writing, or he hadn't. Maybe he had an ear implant and somebody was reading it to him straight into his head while they were riding in the car. Didn't matter. Because what Laz had *not* written down was what he planned to do about things.

Ivy-O came bounding out to the car as if she were excited to see Laz. Or Ron Smith. Or just excited to be out of the house with important work to do. She looked happy. Laz assumed it was an act, and she was probably planning something devious.

Well, today I'm planning something, too, Ivy-O. And it won't be devious, either. It'll be right out in the open.

They got to the mostly underground NAPSC building and instead of going on in with Cheerful Ivy-O, Laz sat down on the exquisitely comfortable lawn in front of the entryway, lay back in the grass, and closed his eyes.

"Nossa," said Reinaldo Ferreira, lapsing into a mild Brazilian curse. "He's on strike."

"If by 'he' you mean me," said Laz in a perfectly normal voice, "then you're mistaken. I am not on strike. I just figure that we're going to do all our work out here in this fine weather, so why go inside and sit around in chairs until the teams are ready? When they're ready, this is a good place to work."

"Why are you doing this?" asked Reinaldo "Ron" Ferreira "Smith."

"Because the grass is comfortable, the sun is shining, the air is cool, there's a slight breeze, and if you had actual human DNA you'd be lying on this lawn, too."

Ron Smith lay down beside Laz. Not close, but not far, either. "You're right," he said.

"Ah, but I already knew I was right, so your saying so is actually an attempt to manipulate me into doing something you want me to do."

"I want you to get up and go inside so we can do a little planning."

"There's nothing to plan," said Laz. "Not for me. Ivy-O will push a timestream into my mind, or, if she's feeling generous, she'll give me a menu of choices, which will mean nothing to me because I have no way of seeing far enough up or down the stream to know what I'm choosing. Meet with her. She's the boss of this outfit."

Ron Smith replied with silence. Such a long silence that Laz might have dozed off; certainly it felt as if he was suddenly startled awake when Ron Smith said, "I see your point."

Laz knew that he could not possibly see his point, but why argue?

"I don't know how to make it different," said Ron Smith.

"There *is* no way," said Laz. "I wasn't complaining, just choosing one of the few things I can actually choose—like where to put my body while all the decisions are being made."

"Ain't life a bummer," said Ron Smith.

"I'm alive, and for most clones, that's doing pretty well," said Laz. "I'm already at the head of my class."

"Cloning is just another way of starting a human baby," said Ron Smith. "And the speed-growing processes that were once so uncertain and frightening are now a known science. You aren't going to develop weird cancers or organ breakdown; there are no traces of those chemicals left, and all your bodily structures are normal. So despite the fact that all your DNA came from one individual, you're still a living, breathing human being."

"With full rights?" asked Laz. "Can I vote? Own property?"

"We're working on that," said Ron Smith.

"So . . . not a perfectly regular human being."

"Society and government can sometimes move slowly. But since you're the only living side stepper, Laz, and the inheritor of an admired and beloved name, if *you* want to vote, some government here will pass special legislation to allow it. Or at least they'll introduce such legislation, and then you can simply step into a timestream where the legislation passes. You know how it's done."

"I do indeed," said Laz. "But in the meantime, thank you for allowing me to rest here on this grass. Greensboro didn't have any good grass."

"Fescue doesn't thrive in that fungus-prone climate," said Ron Smith.

"Now couldn't you have left me a note explaining that? 'All the grass here is crap, Laz, because the climate in this place promotes mold that kills the fescue.'"

"We decided no messages."

"We."

"Mine was the slightest of all the votes," said Ron Smith, "since I was only the head of the team that carried out the decisions. But I voted to keep all reading material out of the way. Except signs. Clever of you to find the name of the town on the water meter."

"Ron Smith," said Laz. "I'm going to be interested to find out how

Ivy-O responds to what I'm going to be doing today. She may throw a tantrum—though my Ivy never has. She may go to you to manipulate you into trying to manipulate me into doing things the way she wants. But let me assure you that the thing I'm going to insist on is perfectly reasonable. It will create some balance in our relationship."

"You *hope* it will create balance."

"Oh, it *will* create balance. Either she'll compromise with me and we'll keep right on working, or she'll refuse, and at that point, she and I will cease to be partners, I'll go back to the partner that I think of as the *real* Ivy, and Ivy and I will keep making Portals with, in my opinion, a much better chance of success than Portals I make with Ivy-O."

"So you won't be on strike," said Ron Smith. "You'll just fire Ivy-O."

"If she won't work with me in a balanced way, then yes, she's out of a job—or I'm out of a job. But since Ivy is at least as capable as Ivy-O, and has the added advantage of never having misplaced a partner in space-time, I think it will be very much like getting a promotion."

"I agree," said Ron Smith. "Is that what you'd like me to go in and tell Ivy-O in our meeting? That she needs to cooperate or you're no longer working with her?"

"That's too theoretical. I don't want her to have time to figure out a way to fool me into thinking she's compromising with me. I want to simply confront her with it and see how she responds. It might reveal something about her true agenda."

"Which is *not* saving the world from Shiva?"

"Not directly," said Laz. "Don't pretend you haven't listened in on Ivy's and my conversations. You know what we're thinking."

"I have some idea, yes," said Ron Smith. "Don't think of us as spies, though, Laz. We're more like chaperones."

"Keeping us safe from each other."

"Yes. Lone male, lone female, same house . . . just begging for trouble."

"We know we're always being watched," said Laz.

"As I said," answered Ron Smith. "Chaperones."

Laz smiled a little, because he realized that it was pretty much true. Not that Ivy and Laz *needed* a chaperone. "Go on in and have your meeting," said Laz. "I won't wander away."

"You have never broken your word to me," said Ron Smith. "And you gave me fair warning just now. I trust you, Laz. So I will go to that meeting, and I won't tip my hand—or your hand—to Ivy-O."

Ron Smith didn't wait for a reply. He got up—bounded up, actually, is what it sounded like, though Laz didn't open his eyes to see—and walked briskly along the lawn to the entrance.

Laz really did sleep then, because thinking wasn't going to do him any good, and he was sleepy because he had spent most of last night thinking about what he was going to write in his plog, and what he was going to do with Ivy-O. Now that all was set, he could use the sleep.

He woke up because somebody kicked his foot. It was rather a hard kick, but he had the vague idea that it might not have been the first kick. He might have been sleeping very soundly.

It was Ivy-O who had kicked him, of course. "Did you know that you snore?"

"All my mistresses complain about it," said Laz. "But when they do, I side step them out of my life."

Ivy-O didn't even laugh—though Ron Smith chuckled a bit.

"Get up, Laz," said Ivy-O. "You have to hold your end of the twine, and we don't want to create a Portal right here, blocking the entrance to the Science Center."

"And by 'we' you mean everybody who is not me," said Laz.

Laz still hadn't opened his eyes, but he knew she was rolling *her* eyes.

"Shiva's getting closer by the minute," said Ivy-O.

"And by the year, and by the nanosecond," said Laz. "That's how Newton's laws of motion work. Have you noticed that we're working entirely in a Newtonian universe, in this project? Gravity, inertia, even linear causality."

"They taught metaphysics in high school?" asked Ivy-O.

"I was a self-motivated learner," said Laz.

"Then kindly motivate your butt over to the area where they want the Portal to be, if we find a useful Portal," said Ivy-O.

Laz, eyes still closed, rose to his feet and extended his arms like a cliché of sleepwalking. "Lead me, fair Ivy-O," he said.

"Call me that again, and I'll only give you timestreams that put you neck deep in hog poo."

"Ron Smith, you heard her threaten me, didn't you?" said Laz.

"I don't have a sense for hog poo in the timestreams," said Ivy-O.

"Or for gravity," said Laz.

No answer from Ivy-O.

Laz opened his eyes. She had already walked away, her steps more or less silent on the grass. Laz looked at Ron Smith, who seemed to have taken everything in stride.

"You see what I did there?" said Laz softly.

"You called bullshit," said Ron Smith, "and she had no answer except to walk away."

"Glad you're here to watch this," said Laz.

"Me too," said Ron Smith.

Laz and Ron Smith walked over to where Ivy-O was already giving orders to the astrotechs, who listened placidly and obeyed her every time she ordered them to do things exactly the way they always did them.

Ivy-O saw him and held out a string. She didn't step toward him at all, obviously intending him to close the distance between them. But Laz didn't. He stopped about three steps away and held out his hand for the string.

"So we're playing the petulant child today, is that it?" asked Ivy-O.

Laz said nothing. Just waited for the string. She took the three steps, and put it into his hands. She closed his fingers around it.

"Please tie it to my wrist, Ivy-O," said Laz. "It's hard to do that one-handed."

Of course Ivy-O could see that there was something in the wind, and decided not to play his game. So instead of getting mad at him, she simply tied the string around his wrist. At first she drew it so tight that it would have cut off his circulation, but when she actually tied the knot, it wasn't that tight after all. "Square knot," she said. "Not a bow. I don't want it to come off accidentally."

"And another string," said Laz, "tied to some permanent feature of this landscape."

"Is a tree permanent enough for you?" asked Ivy-O.

"More permanent than any human," said Laz. "It'll do."

Some of the astrotechs did the work of attaching twine to a couple of trees, and then tying the other end to Laz's ankles and wrists. Ivy-O watched with a display of boredom. "Why are you suddenly so uptight about attachment?" she asked.

"Don't you think I should be safe?" asked Laz.

"You're safe," she said with some impatience.

"And you know this because . . ."

"Because I've got you," she said. And then she realized that this left her open to an obvious remark, and so she said, "I had nothing to do with your original getting lost. He cut the twine himself. Are you planning to do that? No? Then you're safe."

At last it was time. Ivy-O sat down on a canvas chair that the astrotechs had brought out of the building with them.

Laz looked at the guy who had carried and set up the chair. "You've got a PhD, right?" Laz asked him.

"Two," he answered.

"Did you ever think you'd be setting up chairs and tying strings to people?" asked Laz.

"It's part of the job," said the double PhD. "You should see the nasty work that the guys in zoology have to do."

"She's about to tell my fortune now," said Laz.

"And maybe everybody's fortune," said Double Doc.

The guy had a point. If he was part of saving the world, who cared if part of his work was setting up a chair for a timestream diva?

But Ivy would have set up her own chair. Or sat on the lawn.

To be fair, Laz's Ivy was younger and more spry. Don't be mean, Laz told himself. This isn't about punishing Ivy-O, it's about figuring out what's going on.

A timestream came into Laz's mind.

It was almost a reflex by now, to side step immediately into the stream.

But Laz held off.

Usually Laz and Ivy-O didn't talk at this stage of the process. Presumably Ivy-O's full concentration was on the timestreams, and Laz didn't want to distract her.

But now he did.

She was still holding the timestream in his mind, while Laz examined it. He'd never done this exact thing before, so it took a little while for him to feel his way into it without actually side stepping. It wasn't seeing, it wasn't probing. He just allowed himself to become aware of the timestream.

It wasn't like the timestreams he sensed when he was doing his easy local jumps. In those, he already understood the context and concentrated on the differences from the current stream.

This one, though, was not like the current timestream at all. Nor was there any person for him to focus on. Usually, of course, the person was himself, and in reading his own attitude within the timestream he could sense when it was a safe jump or a dangerous one. In this case, though, no people at all. As he peered forward and then back, the only changes were in the light—morning, noon, evening, night.

He tried to sense his surroundings, or what his surroundings would be if he side stepped into it. No pig poo—Ivy-O really had been joking.

"What are you waiting for?" asked Ivy-O.

"I'm not waiting," said Laz. "I'm looking."

"I already looked," said Ivy-O.

"Thank you, seeing-eye dog," said Laz. "I may not see as well as you and Ivy do, but I see something, don't I? And if I don't take the time to look at what you present to me, how will I learn to see any better?"

Ivy-O sighed, but it wasn't a full-blown adolescent sigh. More of a mere exhalation of a pent-up breath. "I don't know if you can learn anything from just one timestream," she said.

At once there was a selection of timestreams in his mind, what they were referring to as a menu. "What am I seeing here?" asked Laz.

"Multiple timestreams," said Ivy-O. "You've seen them before."

"These very ones?" asked Laz.

"No. What would be the point of that?" asked Ivy-O. "You've seen a group of timestreams before."

"This is the kind of thing you showed OrigiLaz?"

"You know it is," said Ivy-O.

"So how did he pick?"

"I don't know. He was in charge, remember? I assembled some timestreams, and then he stepped into one."

"Did you hold on to the ones he didn't side step into?" asked Laz.

"I remembered where they were, at first. In case he asked me to go back to one."

"Did he ever?"

"No."

"And he never said how he chose?" asked Laz.

"Asked and answered," said Ivy-O.

"Answered but not understood," said Laz.

"Understood but not believed," said Ivy-O. "Are you trying to learn, or just catch me doing something weird?"

"We both do weird things," said Laz. "That's why we're here, to save the world weirdly. But if OrigiLaz saw enough in these arrays of timestreams to make a choice, he must have known how to interpret what's there. Because it's not seeing at all, it's just . . . knowing. And I don't know."

"Yes you do," said Ivy-O, "because you've been working with timestreams most of your life. You don't *ever* see anything."

"But I always had a context," said Laz.

"When you and your Ivy tried some long-distance steps, what did you see then?"

"She just gave me a timestream and I stepped. We were still just experimenting. You can tell me, though. You can sense which timestream I'm examining, right?"

He felt her somehow touch or flex or point at the one he was concentrating on. None of those words was exactly right. There *were* no words for the senses they were using.

"You sense the direction of flow, yes?" asked Ivy-O.

Yes, of course! That was so obvious to him that he hadn't realized he was sensing it. He examined the timestream in the direction of flow. And as soon as he knew he was doing that, he was able to spot the exact Now of that particular timestream. The Now was moving forward, of course, at the rate of one second per second, but as he watched, Laz began to understand what was being caused, and what was causing it. Air was moving in this timestream; not just moving, but blowing. There was a brisk wind. Not a gale, nothing that would tip over a sailboat. But enough to flutter leaves on the . . .

"There are leaves," said Laz.

"Yes," said Ivy-O. "Not fronds, leaves."

"So there are deciduous trees in this timestream," said Laz.

"Or something like deciduous," said Ivy-O. "Might be evergreen. Might be palmate or pinnate or whatever. But not pine needles, not ferns with fronds, not palms with really big fronds. Leaves on trees."

And now Laz could sense that yes, the movement of leaves in the wind was both high and low—not just bushes, not even a hedgerow or an orchard, where the trees were pruned to keep them low enough for picking. Wild trees, very tall ones.

"Did you pick this one because of the leaves?" asked Laz.

Ivy-O chuckled. "Leaves are kind of the minimum," she said, "if people are going to live there. It suggests seasons, and blossoms, and pollinators. Insects and the creatures that eat them. I don't know what you can actually sense, but there is water nearby, with a rippling surface . . ."

Laz could tell right where it was. How had he missed it before?

"And now and then a splash," said Ivy-O. "Might be a fish coming to the surface to get an insect or a berry that dropped into the water. Might be a frog diving. Nothing as big as an alligator—I really do try to avoid large predators, just for convenience and to avoid panicked running."

"When you sense these things," said Laz, "you don't have to search for them."

"I've been doing this a long time," she said. "I take a lot in at first glance. Things that you have to search for. So it's quick and easy for me to find green vegetation, woody plants with leaves, blossoms, insects, insectivores, the basic lie of the land."

Laz moved his attention to another timestream.

"I'm with you," she said, and he could tell that she was.

"How is this one different from the other?" asked Laz.

"As I said, the leaves and such, that's basic, that's first glance. I picked these because beyond the minimal habitability, or at least breathability of the place, I'm checking for air quality. Don't want a lot of volcanic ash—that's a bad sign. I've run into earthquakes now and then—no point in going to a place that's tectonically unstable. But that's more just chance. Volcanos, though—those are climate wreckers, or can be."

"But what are you looking *for*?" asked Laz.

"I'm trying *not* to detect the gravity of Shiva," said Ivy-O. "I know you've given up on that idea, because your Ivy has given up, but here in the New Place, after they told me she was still coming, and pointed out the place in the sky, I was eventually able to sense *something* in the timestreams of the New Place. And so I look for those same things in each timestream I examine."

"How can it be clear?" asked Laz.

"It isn't," said Ivy-O. "If it were easy, we'd succeed more often. As in, ever."

"So you can sense gravity sources," said Laz.

"The Sun is overwhelming. Like the horn of a big semi truck. Or a train whistle. Then the Moon, because it's so close. I can sense the pull on the tides. I think all humans can sense the gravity of the Sun and Moon, but because we all live in one timestream—so far as we know, anyway—they're just background noise, we tune it out. But it's there. Sun, Moon, and then Jupiter, Saturn, Neptune, Uranus. Venus. Mars. Mercury is too close to the Sun, always—can't find its gravity at all. And Mars is like the faintest whisper, constantly slipping in and out of my awareness."

"Shiva would have to be fainter still," said Laz.

"But not undetectable," said Ivy-O, "or astronomers would never have known it was there. Well, they *would*, because the asteroid-finding satellites would have bounced signals off it. But by that time, it would have been way too late—even if we had found the New Place, there wouldn't have been time to transport a significant fraction of the human species, and certainly no time to establish an industrial system, a transportation system, medical manufacturing and health care—it's a good thing the gravity scopes in the Old Place were so sensitive."

"As sensitive as you?" asked Laz.

"Far more sensitive!" cried Ivy-O. "Remember they had to point out what direction it was coming from? I'm not good at *discovering* things, particularly when all I've got is the timestream instead of the real place, with the real sky."

"You won't be surprised to know that I can't feel any of the gravity at all."

"Don't be silly," said Ivy-O—and when she said it, she sounded like Laz's Ivy. Same voice. Same teasing sound. It was unnerving. "You're feeling one huge source of gravity and you know it."

"Well, of course, I'm standing on Earth, so I—"

"Yes, but you also feel it in the timestreams." And somehow, Laz could sense that she was showing him. How everything was falling inward onto the Earth, except when something stopped it. Leaves hanging to trees strong enough to rise upward against gravity.

"And now look for the Sun," said Ivy-O . . . and she showed him. "Moon," she said. "It's on the other side of Earth in *this* timestream, but it's overhead in *this* one."

Laz could follow what she demonstrated. But he was quite sure that this was like explaining the working of a car engine to a three-year-old. "Thank you," said Laz. "Thank you for showing me."

"There's no point in it," said Ivy-O, "because you'll never be good at it."

"Why are you so sure of that?" asked Laz.

And then came the obvious answer. "Because *my* Laz spent a lot of time trying to do it. To sense timestreams like I do. He got better at it, but he never came close to really experiencing them as I do. As your Ivy does. You're not blind to it. Let's just say you have metaphorical cataracts. Or myopia. Interference, blurring. And you don't hold a map of timestreams in your mind. Nothing wrong with you, I'm not criticizing. Because I can't side step, and believe me, I've tried. Before I even met Laz—the first one—"

Laz was pretty sure she had almost said "the real one."

"Once I heard about what he could do, I tried to do it, of course. And later, when he had side stepped with me and brought me along, local trips into bodies we already had, and then the longer trips, with strings to help us open up Portals—I could sense what he was doing, but I couldn't find anything inside me that could do that thing. No switch. No step."

"So we need each other," said Laz.

"We already knew that," said Ivy-O.

"No, *you* already knew it," said Laz.

"O ye of little faith," said Ivy-O.

"Exactly," said Laz. "Are you saying that you can't detect Shiva's gravity in these timestreams you assembled, but you *can* feel Shiva's gravity in other timestreams that you rejected?"

No answer.

Ron Smith piped up then. "I think that's a really lovely question, Ivy, and I hope you can answer it, if not right now, then as soon as you start to feel the urgency of this project."

"I already feel the urgency," she said, testy now.

"Ivy-O," said Laz. "Are any of these timestreams even possible for us? Is there really any chance that they *won't* have Shiva heading for our solar system?"

Long silence. "When we start the day's work," Ivy-O finally

answered, "we have these astrotechs waiting. Very, very smart people, and we have them doing menial tasks, and I feel urgency to give them a task that will cause them to . . ."

"We don't need make-work tasks," said Double Doc. "If you took longer searching for timestreams, could you improve the odds of finding timestreams that have a chance of being a Safe Place?"

"See?" said Ron Smith. "You aren't doing day care here. If they cool their heels for three hours or three days, while you search for something with real possibilities, they won't mind. Or they won't mind any more than archaeologists mind using tiny brushes to dust their way down through a dig."

Laz then piped up. "But Ivy-O, do you know for sure that all these timestreams *do* have Shiva?"

"No," said Ivy-O. "I have no idea at all."

"Will you ever have an idea, before we open a Portal, whether it will be a Safe Place?" asked Laz.

"Probably not," said Ivy-O.

"When you and OrigiLaz found the New Place, did you sense *before* opening the Portal that it had potential? That Shiva was not on the same course here in the New Place?"

Long pause. Then Ivy-O said, "No idea at all. It was random chance. After we found the New Place, and opened a whole bunch of Portals so that people from every continent could travel to a fairly nearby place—that took weeks, as you can imagine—after that, my Laz and I worked very hard to figure out what made this timestream special, what might have made it recognizable."

"Did you ever make any progress?" asked Laz.

"Sometimes we thought so."

"But?"

"Sometimes we thought not. Same amount of evidence in both cases. None at all."

"So making random stabs into distant timestreams is really the only method that has ever worked," said Ron Smith.

"Yes," said Ivy-O. "But it isn't the only method that *might* work. Every side step with Laz here, I keep thinking, is this one different? Could I be detecting something in this timestream?"

"So this array of timestreams in my mind," said Laz. "Is there any of them that seems particularly promising to you?"

"No," said Ivy-O. "When I first gathered them, I hoped. By the time I got them spread out for your examination, I was pretty sure there was nothing to them. But what if I was wrong? What if one of them is perfect and then I discard it because I can't tell from the timestream alone? What if my blindness keeps making me reject one Safe Place after another? You astrotechs, I'm not giving you busy work, I'm not treating this labor like day care. I'm hoping that what I've done might be good enough, and you're the only ones who can tell me."

Laz couldn't help but notice that for Ivy-O, opening Portals was *her* task, her accomplishment. "What I've done might be good enough," she had said. Not "what we've done." And that was fair, kind of. She was the one identifying timestreams. All he did was actually open the timestream and make the connection—just trivial execution of *her* plan.

Another long silence while Laz tamped down his resentment of Ivy-O.

Laz finally decided to take responsibility for how things were turning out. After all, *he* was the one who slowed things down and started examining the timestreams. He was the one who called this all into question. "Ivy," he said, leaving off the offensive "-O" even though he hated calling this woman Ivy. "Do you have a favorite among this bundle of timestreams?"

"The one I first handed to you," she said. "Though I have no rational or evidentiary basis for my preference."

"We're all strung up like a fishing net mating with a harp," said Laz. "What do you say you give me that one again, since I can't really tell them apart anyway, and let's go side stepping."

It was noon before the astrotechs had their equipment set up in the new Portal. Meanwhile, Laz and Ivy-O remained strung to each other and to their anchors back in the New Place. Sometimes Laz came back to their starting point while Ivy-O crossed through, holding on to twine. The longer they stayed and the firmer their own mental connection with this new Portal became, the more sure they were that they wouldn't lose it.

The astrotechs probably had no idea that it was even *possible* for them to lose a new timestream. But what did they think the strings were for?

It didn't matter. They'd have data about Shiva in this timestream by tomorrow. Not final data, but a good first indication. The hardest thing to confirm would be Shiva's absence; her presence, of course, meant failure, and that was the easiest thing to detect.

Meanwhile, Ivy-O spent time wandering around in the new Portal area, going to the limits of her twine connection to the Science Center grounds. Laz was with her often enough to take note of what she was looking at. She mostly followed the botanist around. She plucked a few leaves.

"Should you be doing that?" asked an astrotech.

"Because of these missing leaves," said Ivy-O, "a caterpillar will not be fat enough to survive the winter, so it will never emerge from its cocoon, so the butterfly will never mate, and blossoms will go unpollinated. Eventually, the small mammal that would have become the first primate will fail to thrive because a certain nutrient will be missing from its diet, and so primates will never evolve."

The astrotech grinned at her. "Yes, ma'am," he said. "Collect all the leaves you want. This world will be much better off without primates."

"If it turns out Shiva isn't coming in this timestream," said another astrotech, "we're all set to completely wreck natural evolution on this planet."

"And that's fine," said Laz, "because there'll always be other timestreams very close to this one, in which we don't come, and we don't bring a billion or two friends along, and we don't bring our destructive herbivores and introduce the savage carnivores of the Old Place. So we can step over now and then to check on how those butterflies are doing, or those proto-primates."

"Until you die," said Double Doc.

"Oh, I'm sure they've got other clones of me hibernating in other places," said Laz. "*I* will die, but the side stepping wunderkind Lazarus Hayerian will always exist, somewhere."

"Until the Earth falls into the Sun," said Double Doc.

"But that's always been true," said Laz. "Of the whole human race. We will always exist. Until we don't."

Meanwhile, Laz saw Ivy-O putting other leaves into her pockets. Not very scientific. Real chance of contamination. She can't possibly learn much from studying these leaves. Or from the holobiome surrounding the trees. "Try not to get an intestinal parasite," said Laz.

"I'm not chewing on them," said Ivy-O.

"I know, you're going to stitch them into a rug or a wall hanging," said Laz. "But none of us are following any serious protocols against contamination."

"Those would add hours and days to each test of a new Portal," said Double Doc. "And every hour and every day brings us closer to the end of the human race. So if we have to fight off an ugly intestinal parasite, but Earth is still around in five hundred years, I think that's a good trade. You?"

"Couldn't agree more," said Laz. "Go ahead and chew the leaves, Ivy." Once again, he left off the "-O"; once again, he felt guilty about it.

By the time their workday was over, they had opened a total of three Portals, and three teams had crossed through and set up monitoring equipment. All the Portals led to uninhabited timestreams, though tomorrow a set of drones would be launched from each to do some mapping and detect signs of sentient life.

Meanwhile, as Ron Smith drove them home, first to Ivy-O's place, he explained how things would work now. "We've got no duplicate for Laz," he said, "so Laz works every day. But our brilliant, wonderful Ivys will alternate days with Laz. Between times, you can each work on whatever project you think shows most promise. Laz's Ivy is working on reading everything OrigiLaz ever wrote. What will you do?"

Ivy-O regarded Ron Smith steadily. "So I'm half-fired."

"You're getting days off to recuperate," said Ron Smith. "Working with Laz is hazardous duty."

"You were hoping to get me fired today, weren't you, Laz?" she asked him. She sounded cheerful about it.

Laz shrugged. "I was hoping to get a lot of chips flying, and then let the chips fall where they may."

"You want to work with Ivy," said Ivy-O. "Your Ivy."

"Bring back your Laz," said Laz, "and then you can work with *him*."

They were at her house. The car had almost stopped moving when she opened the door and swung her legs out and strode to her door.

"Just when I think I've got things working smoothly," said Ron Smith, "you have to say something deeply offensive."

"She asked if I wanted her fired," said Laz. "She already knew the answer. There was no point in lying."

"There's always a point in lying," said Ron Smith. "Saying nice things that aren't true is the glue that holds civilization together. Candor is a killer."

"I'll keep that in mind," said Laz.

"No you won't," said Ron Smith. "You're a self-righteous idiot and you always have been."

"Oh, back to smoothing things over, I see," said Laz.

"Those are some of your best features," said Ron Smith. "You always think you're right—how could you function if you *didn't* have that level of self-regard?"

"It wasn't the self-righteous part that bothered me," said Laz.

"Oh, you know you're not an idiot. I was using it as a term of endearment."

"Glad to hear that," said Laz. "Are you going to come in and tell Ivy yourself?"

"Tell her what?" asked Ron Smith.

"That she and I are teaming on alternate days."

Ron Smith shook his head. "Of course not. You're working

together every day now. Only when Ivy-O thinks she might have found a real humdinger of a timestream will she get access to your side-stepping skills."

"So you lied to her," said Laz.

"I mollified her," said Ron Smith. "I smoothed things over. She's used to me by now. She knew enough to go along with what I said, because she knows that if she does what I suggest, things will go more smoothly for everyone, her included."

"What have you lied to me about?" asked Laz.

"Nothing important," said Ron Smith. "Is your bed comfortable? Is the food good? Is your house warm when you want it warm, and cool when you want it cool? Do you have privacy when you want it, and company when you want that?"

"But I still don't know what you have planned for me," said Laz.

"I don't have *anything* planned for you. You're the one who's going to change everything. By finding a Safe Place. Till then, nothing changes."

"Are you mad at me?" asked Laz.

"Never," said Ron Smith. "But why would you imagine that I might be?"

"Because I upset the status quo," said Laz. "With what I did today. My . . . demonstration?"

"Tantrum," said Ron Smith. "But you had been very patient till now."

"Why didn't you stop me?" asked Laz.

"Because you would simply have stepped into a timestream where I decided to see what you were going to push Ivy-O to do."

"So you outguessed me, and you let me throw my tantrum in *all* the timestreams."

"What if I got stuck in one of the timestreams where you didn't do it, and I would never see what you did?" said Ron Smith.

"Everyone is always trapped in all the timestreams," said Laz. "Even if we find a Portal to a Safe Place, all the people in timestreams where we didn't find it will die a hideous death as the world ends. We can't save all the worlds, doing what we do. We can only provide one escape hatch for one version of reality."

"I've thought about this a lot, Laz, as you can imagine," said Ron Smith. "About the fact that there are people in every timestream, who think they're living in some kind of definite reality."

"We can't bring them all to the Safe Place," said Laz. "There wouldn't be room, and there wouldn't be time."

"The number of people on timestreams that fail is infinite," said Ron Smith. "But the only version of me that will live on into the next decade is whichever version happens to be in the same timestream as you when you find the Safe Place. And one of me is all I need, as long as I'm that one."

Laz laughed. "So you're content with what I did today."

"I admit it. I really believed that Ivy-O could sense more than it turns out that she can," said Ron Smith. "I was happier when I was deluded, of course."

"Everyone is," said Laz. "You folks saw to that when you edited my memory, so I woke up thinking I was seventeen. Much happier than if I had known the world was ending and it was my job to fix it."

Ron Smith looked out the window for a minute.

"What did I say wrong?" asked Laz.

"I just don't know why you have the idea that we edited your memory," said Ron Smith.

"Because I don't remember anything after high school," said Laz.

Again, Ron Smith did not respond. Until he finally did. "Laz, when we're going to clone somebody, we record their brain state. It's an analog process, not a digital one. There is no way to take that recording and probe it and find anything at all. We have no idea how to read it. We can't play it like a movie on a screen. All we can do is pour it into your head, and we have to do it pretty slowly, so your brain can make or find useful neural pathways. It used to be a very lossy process. Only a complete loon would think we could *alter* that recording and have it make any sense at all to the person whose memory it became."

"Well, I never knew that," said Laz. "Memory transfer was still at the science article phase of development, last I remember, and I didn't pay attention because I knew it would never apply to me."

"How wrong you were," said Ron Smith.

"So Ivy wasn't edited either," said Laz.

"Can't be done," said Ron Smith.

"Look, her memories when she woke up didn't include ever meeting Laz Hayerian. So her brain state must have been recorded before anybody knew she was going to be important. Or something got chopped off at the end."

"Nothing was chopped."

"So she was recorded before she proved her usefulness to Origi-Laz," said Laz.

"Good reasoning," said Ron Smith.

"Thank you for the pat on the head. My question is, if it's true, why was she recorded at that stage of her life?"

"I'll have to look that up."

"In other words, you don't want to tell me," said Laz.

"Oh, I want to tell you, or at least I want to be *able* to tell you, if I should decide that telling you was a good idea," said Ron Smith.

"*Not* telling me is a bad idea," said Laz. "Does that help tip the balance?"

"It might, when I find out the answer."

"And the same question applies to me. I was a precocious kid, and I was side stepping since I was about ten. My parents didn't *know* that I was doing it—nobody ever does, except Ivy—but they knew that I always got perfect scores on tests, I never got injured, I never got sick, and even though I walked all over Southern California, I never got lost, I never got hit by a car, and I never got picked up by cops for vagrancy. But there was nothing about me that would make me worth recording. Why was my brain state recorded at age seventeen?"

"A superior question. One of the best," said Ron Smith.

"This time you *do* know the answer."

"I truly do not," said Ron Smith. "We talked about it among ourselves. Putting together your existence was a project that began only after we were in the New Place and OrigiLaz disappeared and we found out that Shiva was still coming even here, so we needed you. Kind of desperately."

"If I was gone, how did you get—"

"Nobody had ever successfully cloned somebody from old DNA, especially from partial DNA like you find on hairs. We had a lot of your hair. Getting DNA intact enough for cloning was going to be such a mess. In all likelihood, your clone would have looked like a surrealist painting. Or cubist. And then the people on that team found that the little carbuncle or whatever it was on your little toe had been frozen, the last time you had it removed, and nobody had ever purged the inventory, so it was still there."

"I was grown from that ridiculous warty growth?" asked Laz. He acted offended, because to do so was funny; actually, though, he was horrified, because that seemed to him like cloning him from a tumor. A thing that wasn't supposed to be there could be used to assemble a body that consisted only of parts that *should* be present?

"It took a few tries before a healthy, normal embryo could be started from that source. But all of this would have been moot—it wouldn't even have been done—if we hadn't had a recording to play into your head. We didn't have time to hatch you as a baby and raise you to adulthood or whatever stage you're at right now. We had to have you spring out of the box fully loaded."

"So why didn't you use a later brain state?" asked Laz. "One where I already knew what I knew."

Ron Smith said, "One of the team found something OrigiLaz had written. In a journal or something like a diary. Speculation that he was already too old to do the work, and if only he could be young and naive again—"

"I bet he wrote 'stupid,' not 'naive'—"

"He may have. Probably did," said Ron Smith. "He thought that he might be able to see things better, more clearly, if he had a young brain that wasn't already cluttered with so much unhelpful knowledge, with so many dead ends clearly marked off so he never went back to them."

"And you didn't have any of his later brain states," said Laz, guessing.

"Two of them had been taken, both of them after we all migrated here, to the New Place. But we found that they had been destroyed."

"How?" asked Laz.

"Sabotage," said Ron Smith. "Not everybody thinks that world-hopping is either green enough or godly enough. Then we became reasonably sure that the saboteur was OrigiLaz."

"Come on, why would I do that?"

"OrigiLaz might already have been planning to leave. Maybe he wanted to force our hand, to *make* us revive him as a clone. And if we did, he didn't want him—you—to be limited by all the things he had already learned."

"So you only had a copy of my brain state from while I was still in high school."

"It wasn't in any place we would have expected. We found it by chance, really. Because you're right, it was recorded long before you were important. OrigiLaz, I mean."

"Again I ask. Why was it done?"

"I have no idea. It was in a group of experimental brain state recordings from the earliest days of getting recordings good enough to be useful."

"I was an experiment?"

"Think back," said Ron Smith. "Did you volunteer for anything in high school? They would have called it a nondestructive transient brain state, NTBS."

"No," said Laz. "No memory of any such thing under any title."

"Your father signed to authorize it. He also signed up to pay for preserving it. So it was there to be found."

"So I was a matter of 'just in case,'" said Laz.

"Your dad's decision to get an early brain state recording might yet save the world."

"Or not," said Laz. "But it brought me into existence as the lovely specimen of redundant humanity that I am right now."

"You were cloned as a replacement for someone who was already gone," said Ron Smith. "Not redundant at any moment of your existence."

"Until now," said Laz.

"There's only one of you that we know of," said Ron Smith.

"I'm redundant like a worker about to be laid off. The job I can do isn't the job we need."

"Well, you're still closer to doing it than any other living person," said Ron Smith.

"I just make trouble. I just make Ivy-O a little crazier."

"I'm quite glad you brought her deceptions into the open. I needed to know the truth about her supposed gravity sense, because I have to report to my superiors."

"And who are they?"

"The people who run this world, as long as it exists," said Ron Smith.

"Will I ever meet any of them?"

"At the celebration when you are given every medal and award that the human race can offer, because you found us a Safe Place."

"I won't ever *find* anything," said Laz. "*They* find things. Ivy and Ivy-O. I merely side step into whatever they found."

"People already know the name Hayerian. Trust me, the glory will go to you."

"That seems unfair."

"Does either Ivy seem to hunger for publicity and honors?" asked Ron Smith.

"Let's see when the time comes," said Laz. "I know *I* don't."

"But OrigiLaz came to like it. To look for it, depend on it." Ron Smith shook his head.

"Then let's hope Ivy-O finds OrigiLaz and brings him back.

Then *he* can have the glory and honors. He's used to them."

"But I may be wrong about all the fame going to you. Because they're both way prettier than you. Much more photogenic."

When they got to the house, Ron Smith came inside and told Ivy about re-partnering her with Laz. She shook her head. "I finally get him out from underfoot, and now you're putting him back?"

"It's your burden," said Ron Smith. "Deal with it."

As soon as Ron Smith was out of the house, Ivy glided—no, nearly flew—across the room and into Laz's arms. She covered his face with kisses, something he had seen only in movies—and only in the kind of movie Mom watched alone, except when he watched with her. He had never understood just how great it felt yet also how completely out of control. It was way better than a dog licking your face, that was for sure. But she didn't slow down for him to give *back* any kisses. And how could he, when *her* face and lips were always a moving target.

Finally she settled in for one long, very fine kiss, then pulled away and said, "I certainly do overexpress my enthusiasm, don't I?"

"I think you showed admirable self-restraint," said Laz.

"I'm going to show even more self-restraint now," Ivy answered. "I'm going to put dinner into serving bowls and we're going to dine together."

"Like every other night since we've been here," said Laz.

"Want to see if we've got any twenty-year-old canned tuna and canned ravioli and mandarin oranges from a jar?" asked Ivy.

"I have pretty nice memories of providing you with fine victuals from the shelves of Harris Teeter."

"And I was grateful," said Ivy. "Well, eventually I was grateful. When I got hungry enough."

He reached out a hand and gently rested it against her cheek. "Ivy," he said, "I'm so glad that when you got all enthusiastic just now, you came to me."

"Well, I certainly wasn't going to go ape like that over Ron Smith," said Ivy.

"It might have brightened his day," said Laz. "But it would have ruined mine."

"Are you telling me you get jealous if I shower affection on other guys?"

"I get jealous of your pillow, and jealous of your pajamas."

She burst out laughing.

So did he.

"We really shouldn't do that," she said, "when our mouths are full of food."

15

Lazarus Hayerian's famous unknown plog:
I'm back and forth on this issue. Is it _failure_ to cycle through hundreds of timestreams, finding out every time that they're right in the bullseye for destruction by Shiva?

Or is it success, because now we know hundreds of timestreams that are _not_ the Safe Place?

It might be the latter case, except that eliminating two hundred and twenty timestreams doesn't seem like much of an accomplishment, compared to the infinite number remaining to explore. Infinity minus two hundred and twenty means we only have _an infinite number_ remaining.

In terms of our odds of success, every day might as well be the very first day. We have very little chance, and the next day we still have the exact same infinitesimal chance. Nothing changes.

Except that when I _do_ pass a day with Ivy-O, she continues to add to her collection of botanically trivial leaves and other plant parts. I have no idea what that means. I don't even know what she does with them. Make salads? Feed them to caterpillars? I've even asked her a couple of times, working my way around to the question very carefully, in completely natural ways. She always catches on partway through my buildup and answers me the same way. "Why do you care? If you want to know anything about me, go ask your Ivy. She should understand me, probably better than I understand myself."

She's not my Ivy. We both woke up at Vivipartum, but neither of us has any proprietary claim on the other. We try to get along, and sometimes we seem to be getting on very well, but then we quarrel or come to our senses after an hour of snogging or get excited about some idea because nice as it is for our bodies to find some kind of pleasurable connection—Ivy's phrase, not mine—it's much more exciting, much nicer, if you will, to connect mind to mind.

Ivy-O is convinced that Ivy's and my connection comes entirely from the fact that she's the first girl who was ever willing to let me kiss her. Ivy-O's phrasing, of course, because Ivy didn't "let" me kiss her, she demanded it. Not that I wasn't willing, mind you. But I didn't propose it or offer it or wheedle for it. If she saw desire in my attitude or something, it was unconsciously displayed on my part.

But Ivy-O always has to make sure I know that she would never have permitted high-school-age Laz to lay a hand on her. She held out for Nobel Prize—winning Laz. Though of course she didn't hold out for anything, she was just born long after he was, and as far as I know, they never even held hands, let alone kissed.

Why does Ivy-O want to hurt me? It's not very hard to do it. I've learned over these past months that I'm sort of a fragile person. I brood over everything. It bothers me if anyone doesn't like me, which is borderline insane, because nobody is actually liked by everyone. But am I <u>really</u> liked by anyone?

So, because nobody will <u>ever</u> read this plog except, of course, Ron Smith and his entire team, I'm going to put down the question that I brood about in my weariest, most unguarded moments: If we find a Safe Place, will Ivy and I ever make children and raise them together? Or, having achieved our mission, will we go our separate ways, she to find someone she likes better, and me to live a life of lonely brooding about whatever it was about me that kept her from loving me?

Such are the sad dreams of the somewhat depressive high school senior who finds himself having to do, not a man's job, but a god's job. That's right, you heard me. Gods are supposed to have infinite knowledge, or at least they should know which questions to google. Gods would know which timestreams contain a Safe Place, or if there's no such place, they'd know <u>that</u>.

So Human Resources in this corporation that I think of as Find a Safe Place, Ltd., really did a bad job when they hired <u>me</u>. I'm so out of my depth. I'm the wrong hire. The only thing that keeps me in this ridiculous position, on such a high salary— i.e., everything I ask for and everything I need except Ivy's ~~love devotion passion~~ half-hearted attention—the only thing that keeps me in this impossible job is the fact that all my bosses are even more incompetent than I am. That's as good a reason to keep at it as any other.

"I've been thinking," said Laz.

Ivy smiled and sat down across from him. The food was quite warm and it was their job to eat dinner before it got cold. But that never stopped them from talking—sometimes so long that the food *did* get cold.

"I'm glad to hear it," she said.

"About our age difference," said Laz.

"We don't have one," said Ivy.

"But we used to. OrigiLaz was born more than twenty years before Ivy-O, right?"

"We have access to calendars now," said Ivy. "We could look it up and work it out."

"Two-and-a-half decades, give or take. How old was OrigiLaz when he became famous?"

"He was a post-doc in Seattle when his work first hit the national media," said Ivy. "So I—well, Ivy-O—was just in the process of being born. I have no memories of Life Before Lazarus Hayerian Was Famous."

"I'm not sure how long the process of speed-growing a clone takes," said Laz. "They did a great job with you. Perfect, in my opinion. But why did they record your brain state before you ever met OrigiLaz?"

Ivy frowned. "I thought you said they edited our brain states."

"I did say that, but I didn't *know* it. Ron Smith told me a few months ago that brain states cannot be nondestructively edited. It's been bothering me ever since."

"Well, that's interesting," said Ivy. "Maybe my parents really loved me and were afraid they might lose me."

"I have no doubt that they loved you," said Laz, "because what's not to love? Still, recording brain states is rare because it's hugely expensive and there has to be a reason for taking up the vast amount of storage space that brain states require."

"They loved me a *lot*."

"Look, the obvious answer to this," said Laz, "is that we only exist to be having this conversation because we're the end product of the only timestreams that put both of us back into the world as clones of roughly the same age."

"But that's always true of everything that ever happened. We only know about it because we're in the timestream where it happened. All the timestreams where they didn't record our brain states don't include *us*."

"OrigiLaz did have his brain state recorded twice as an adult," said Laz. "But he destroyed them both before he disappeared."

"Why?" asked Ivy.

"My real quandary," said Laz, "is whether he knew beforehand that the youthful recording of his brain state even existed. Did he think he was making it *impossible* to produce a workable clone? Or did he believe that the only clone worth growing was one in which I didn't have any preconceptions?"

"Guessing motives is a waste of time," said Ivy.

"I know."

"I was quoting you, so I know you know."

"Ivy," said Laz, "something is really screwed up about all this. There was no reason for *either* of us to have our brain states recorded at the ages where it happened. When they took mine—I mean the one they dumped into my head—brain state recording was still in its infancy. I may have the earliest recording that actually worked. Why would they do that when OrigiLaz was only still in high school? And you, why record you before you ever met him?"

Ivy gave it some thought. "I've wondered about the same things," she finally said. "But what I finally concluded was that way back when, probably before they found the New Place, OrigiLaz and Ivy-O realized that they were doing dangerous stuff and one or both of them might die. We talked about that before, right? So they shopped around in the most improbable local timestreams, and chose the one in which for some reason your family got your brain state recorded. Maybe they volunteered you as a test subject. Maybe you volunteered yourself."

"I don't remember doing that," said Laz.

"And I don't remember asking for my brain state to be recorded. It was certainly something we couldn't possibly afford. But the timestreams existed, and OrigiLaz and Ivy-O chose to enter first one, then the other. So we were waiting there as clones to—"

"No," said Laz. "The recording happened *long* before they created our clones. And like I said, OrigiLaz destroyed a couple of later recordings of his brain state. Ron Smith has elaborate reasoning about why he would do that, but we have no evidence."

"For all we know," Ivy agreed.

"But Ron Smith's team found that recording, and with that in hand, knowing that the New Place was a failure, too, they installed us in coffins at Vivipartum quite recently. We were speed-grown, we knew that. But OrigiLaz couldn't have had anything to do with the decision to wake us up at the same time."

"Well, that's right," said Ivy. "We live in a world where improbable things happen. We're responsible for a lot of them, because we sometimes pick oddball timestreams. But all of this coming together . . ."

"Now, maybe this is all part of God's plan for us," said Laz.

"If God actually had plans, would he let idiots like us screw around with causality?" asked Ivy.

"He would if we were part of his plan."

"This is why scientists try to keep supernatural powers out of the discussion," said Ivy. "Science has to do with finding testable, discoverable causes and results. If God's just randomly flipping switches, then nothing means anything."

"Ivy, OrigiLaz *was* a scientist. Not a loon. He wasn't God, but he *did* have plans, rational ones."

"That's a lot to take on faith," said Ivy. "Plenty of scientists have also been loons."

"As a hobby," said Laz. "But science was their job."

"You're saying this because you know I've read everything OrigiLaz ever wrote, and most of what was written about him, at least by people who actually knew him."

"You have had your nose buried in his work for months and months," said Laz.

"If I've read anything that held a clue to what he was doing, I missed the significance."

"What are you reading right now?" asked Laz.

"You mean that you expect that, quite coincidentally, I happen to be reading exactly what will open a window into OrigiLaz's mind?"

"I mean that maybe you're in the process of reading something helpful."

"I'm not," said Ivy. "I'm reading a memoir by OrigiLaz's doctoral committee chairman, who clearly was out of his depth trying to deal with OrigiLaz's mind."

"You're right, that can't possibly be of any use. What else have you read lately?"

"What I just got was a stack of photocopies of the closest thing to a journal that OrigiLaz ever kept," said Ivy. "But it's not very close. It's his working notes on time theory."

"There is no time," said Laz. "There is no time theory."

"Well, that was the debate, wasn't it?" asked Ivy. "Is time just a word for the chain of causality? That's all *we* sense, in the timestreams. They're really causal streams. But you've resolved the question?"

"Did OrigiLaz?" asked Laz.

Within a few minutes, dinner was cleared away and they were both reading photocopied pages of OrigiLaz's working notes. The pages weren't numbered or dated. They had been arranged in what some curator from Ron Smith's team thought was the order of writing. But there was internal evidence that the order was wrong. Notes that seemed to refer back to things he hadn't yet written.

"You're kind of a messy thinker," said Ivy.

"I know that," said Laz. "I just hoped OrigiLaz, being so famous for smartness and all, would be more organized."

"Listen to this," said Ivy.

She says she doesn't actually see anything, she just knows, she perceives. It doesn't enter the brain through her senses, any more than I detect streams through my eyes or ears or any other sense. It all happens in the brain. But since that's the case, why doesn't our brain do what it does when we read fiction, or dream? Why doesn't it show up in our brain as full visualizations? Then we might be able to find more clarity.

"So he didn't know any more than we do," said Laz.

"He was *reaching* for something and it kind of makes sense," said

Ivy. "Why *don't* we visualize? And why do I have as much clarity as I do *without* some kind of visualization? At least a map, right?"

"Wishing won't make it so," said Laz.

"Laz, think a minute. This isn't *wishing*. What goes on in our minds when we detect the timestreams, that's a mental construct. So why isn't it more complete? Why doesn't our brain turn these causal chains into stories, the way that we do with dreams?"

"Because we're sane?" asked Laz.

"Because we don't think of them the right way yet," said Ivy.

"I hardly think of them at all. I see a few nearby timestreams and I decide almost by instinct which one to side step into."

"Not by instinct," said Ivy. "Please try to be rigorous with this. You make your decision based on little information. You haven't really tracked very far forward with the timestreams so you hardly know what you're getting into, right?"

"If I choose wrong, I can always choose again."

"Your nickname should be Lazy," said Ivy. "How many times have you ever stuttered in your side stepping? How many times did you guess wrong and have to side step again immediately?"

Laz shrugged. "I don't remember *ever* doing it, but why would I—"

"Without *knowing* the timestreams in any detail, you always choose right. Or at least well enough."

Laz smiled. "What, you think I have some natural talent?"

"I think that your unconscious mind is making the decisions. You are unconsciously processing a lot more information than ever shows up in your conscious mind. Because you need to decide immediately, don't you? You have to decide before there's enough time for conscious decision-making."

"Yes, probably. But that's not how *you* work," said Laz.

"Because I don't decide anything," said Ivy.

"You decide everything. Till Ivy-O taught you how to show me menus of timestreams, you selected one and put it in my mind and then I stepped. Right?"

"You were very trusting," said Ivy.

"You were never wrong," said Laz. "Did *you* have time to examine all the alternatives?"

Ivy thought, and then said, "No. I'm not as quick as you, but no, I don't look down a whole lot of timestreams. There's one that seems more desirable than the others. I check it just a little and then push it into your mind. Unless I'm trying to give you a menu of choices."

"The only point that matters here is that it's an unconscious process. It's not a reflex, because every choice is different so reflexes wouldn't work. But it's never a fully informed choice, either, because we decide much more quickly than that."

"So we just leap to conclusions," said Ivy.

"Our failure rate would be way higher. No, our unconscious mind is able to apprehend far more information about the timestreams available to us than we are ever actually aware of. Our unconscious mind is like a chess master looking at an array of pieces on the board. If the men are arranged as their positions emerged in a real game, then the chess master immediately knows how the game is going and where it's likely to end. He doesn't think it through, he's just seen so much that he *knows*."

"He assumes," said Ivy.

"His unconscious mind perceives what must be perceived in an instant, and provides him the solution. It's the same for both of us. We don't visualize because our unconscious reaches a decision *before* it has time to visualize or process anything. It's done before our conscious mind even engages."

"You sound so smart, Laz. Maybe you really *are* the identical twin of the greatest scientist of the age."

"This isn't science, Ivy," said Laz. "This is philosophy. Figuring out what can't be ascertained from the evidence."

"No, that's religious faith you're describing," said Ivy.

"The boundary between faith and philosophy has never been as clear as the philosophers like to pretend," said Laz.

"I have one other quote from OrigiLaz that you need to hear," said Ivy.

"Don't read it aloud, show me," said Laz.

She slid the paper across the table to him.

Now I see.

"Ivy," said Laz, "this is like something you write down when you half wake up from a dream. It means nothing without context."

"Here's the context that I think it has. This paper was buried in the middle of the stack because the top half clearly belongs in the context of—well, let's say it was correctly placed. But now look at that last sentence. The page was only half used, and then this got added in."

Laz studied the page, noticing things. "The handwriting is bigger than the writing on the rest of the page."

"And more hurried," said Ivy.

"And the line has a slant to it, it isn't parallel with the other writing."

Ivy smiled. "Your handwriting is the same way. Always in neat lines. You always space the lines evenly, even when you're hurrying.

So what does it tell you about that one sentence."

"It wasn't written at the same time as the rest of the page," said Laz.

"Here's what I think. I think that all of these writings were in separate stacks because he had five or six sets of notes going at a time—like you, a little scatterbrained, but you know where everything is, right?"

Laz could only agree.

"But he has a powerful insight, or he discovers something. And so he writes it down, not in the correct stack of notes because there *is* no correct stack. He writes it down because it's the most important note he has ever written."

"Come on, Ivy," said Laz.

"'Now I see,'" Ivy repeated. "Ordinarily, that would just mean, 'Okay, I get it now.'"

"But that's not a big deal," said Laz.

"He wouldn't write it bigger, and with more excitement. He wouldn't write it down at all! When would you ever *write* in your own notes, which only you will ever read, a statement like, 'Okay, I get it now'?"

"So he wasn't using 'see' metaphorically," said Laz.

"He meant exactly what we were speculating about. After years of side stepping without even the slightest visualization of anything, now he's visualizing. Now he sees."

Ivy's hands were trembling, so the paper shook.

"What does that really mean, though?" asked Laz.

"No!" Ivy was almost shouting. "I forbid you to talk yourself out of this. After all his years of side stepping, after being pushed here and there by Ivy-O even though he resented this younger woman leading him around, suddenly OrigiLaz breaks

340

through and instead of side stepping without knowing anything, *now he sees*."

"It feels like you're just making up a story now."

"Of course I am," said Ivy. "That's what science *is*. And history, and philosophy, and everything else. Making up stories to explain the evidence, and then testing the story against the evidence, and against *new* evidence, to see if it fits."

"But we don't have any evidence to test this against," said Laz.

Ivy just looked at him as if he were the stupidest person in the world.

"Ivy," he said defensively, "I don't *see* anything!"

"Neither did he, until right before he jotted that note out of nowhere."

"What difference does it make?" asked Laz. "Sounds like it would just slow me down."

"Maybe slowing down, seeing the timestreams, maybe *that's* how we determine whether a particular timestream has a better chance of being the Safe Place," said Ivy.

"But just because *he* figured out a way to slow down the process and visualize, doesn't mean that *I* can do it," said Laz.

"Laz, of course it means that you can. You *are* him."

"I am *not* him. I'm a half-assed copy, with mental abilities derived from a primitive version of brain-state recording."

"You're a younger, more flexible, less hide-bound, more open-minded version of him. That was the plan when they brought you back so young. That was *his* plan."

"It couldn't have been his plan. He probably didn't even remember that his brain state had been recorded while he was in high school. I certainly didn't."

"Laz, if he could *see*, if he could take time and study origins and outcomes, maybe he chose it all. Maybe he side stepped into the timestream where we both had younger brain states, and where we were going to be revived together. Maybe he could really *see*."

Laz shook his head. "I have no reason to disbelieve your story," he said, "but I also have no evidence to compel belief."

"Of course not. How could you have evidence?"

"When you invent a story to explain all the known facts, then of course the known facts will fit the story," said Laz. "It's a reciprocal arrangement."

She stood up, leaned across the table, and kissed his forehead, like a mother kissing her child good night. "That's what I love about you, Laz. You're so smart you're dumb."

"I'm glad to hear that's an endearing trait," said Laz.

"Laz," said Ivy, sitting back down. "This is completely far-fetched. Off the wall. But don't write it off. Think about it. Try to work on it."

"I'm sure I can talk myself into some kind of hallucination that I can call visualization of the timestreams—"

"No, I'm sure you can't. You have too much integrity for that, Laz. Let's tell Ron Smith that we need some time off. To recuperate. To *think* before we keep on making random stabs into distant timestreams."

"He won't like it."

"But he'll let us do it," said Ivy. "Does he have a choice? Will he get better results by forcing us to keep doing something that hasn't worked yet?"

"It worked to find the New Place."

"The New Place isn't a Safe Place," said Ivy. "So it hasn't worked yet."

"Let me think about it tonight."

"It's tonight right now. Think think think." Then she laughed. "Me ordering you to think is also worthless. But I know you, Laz. You *will* think about it, even if you think it's ridiculous."

I'll think about it, thought Laz, because you asked me to. But what he said was, "I'll take some time off from thinking about how you look in the morning, and see if I can work up some thoughts about visualizing timestreams."

"How I look in the morning," echoed Ivy. She made a grotesque face. "This should keep you awake at night."

Laz did not say: Your face keeps me awake most nights. She didn't like him to replace serious talk with sentimental twaddle. Never mind that his sentimental twaddle was far closer to his heart than any of the intellectual stuff they talked about.

"Of course they were listening in on this whole conversation," said Ivy.

"They always are," said Laz.

"So now they're discussing how to respond to our request for a couple of days off."

"They can stay up all night arguing about it," said Laz. "In the end, we'll get our way." He spoke louder, so as to be heard by all the bugs in the house. "So, guys on Ron Smith's team, you might as well go to bed and get a good night's sleep."

16

Lazarus Hayerian's unencrypted memoir
Since I was ten, I could correct almost any mistake I noticed.
I could correct my very best friend out of my life, because we
were bad for each other. But here's the problem: I was never
able to correct mistakes that I didn't know about. If something
went wrong in my life, I had to know it at once in order to fix
it, because my ability to sense what came before and was coming
after in nearby timestreams was quite limited.

Like when I side stepped Stever out of my life, I didn't go
back to the day we met because I couldn't travel in time. I
also couldn't _see_ back that far to find points of divergence. All
I could do was find nearby timestreams in which I hadn't done
my most recent outrage with Stever, and then step into that
timestream to find out why. I had to go to three timestreams
like that. In the first two, Stever was dead. Car accident in one,
a beating that caused fatal brain damage in another. It was on
the third try that I found out that Steven Weaver's family had
never moved to Southern California.

That was the most effective way to get Stever out of my
life (and vice versa) without his being dead. I couldn't choose his
death! I still loved him and cared about him. (In fact I still do.)
But I googled his family and found them in Wisconsin or some

other state that I don't care anything about. He was alive and doing fine. But he and I had never gotten in trouble by pranking people, and my grades were outstanding. Different life, different me—in everyone else's life.

I could not sense far enough backward or forward to know much about what I was doing when I side stepped. I was never stepping blind, but I wasn't all that well informed, either. No map of the past or the future. Nothing like what Ivy describes.

What if I could actually <u>see</u>? What if I had time to examine the past and the future and see what was actually going on in a particular timestream?

If that happened then yes, I would write "Now I see" in big sloppy letters right here on this paper, regardless of what else was written on it. I would write it in purple ink, that's how excited I'd be.

But I can't see. And I'm very skeptical about Ivy's idea that wishing might make it so. I've never had good results from wishing. People who can side step don't spend much time wishing for anything. We just go to different timestreams until we find outcomes we can live with.

And then one day our full-time job is to save the human race and, with luck, the planet we live on, regardless of how the continents might be reconfigured. My job. And all I can do is <u>wish</u> that my tool set were capable of accomplishing that.

"Go to bed and dream of powers you'd like to have," said Ivy.

"Good idea. Sweet timestreams to you, too," said Laz.

Laz didn't know when they had reached an agreement about good-night rituals, but about a week ago she started kissing his cheek good night. And tonight she kissed him on the lips—a ridiculously, ostentatiously sisterly kiss, but still. It made him just the tiniest bit crazy. She was going to have to stop rewarding him for good behavior by bestowing kisses like dog biscuits.

When he thought of dog biscuits, he thought of StarKist and the Pack of Four. He hadn't thought of them in months.

After it became clear that Laz couldn't possibly supervise the Pack of Four and still do anything else, and after several incidents of the Pack of Four attacking other dogs and making menacing moves at children in a park several kilometers away from the Science Center, Ron Smith informed them that the dogs would have to go to an obedience school for the time being, so Laz and Ivy wouldn't be distracted by them.

"Or you could put up a fence," said Laz. "A tall one, with concrete foundations, so that if they turn out to be diggers, we won't have a problem."

"I take it they aren't housebroken," said Ron Smith.

"We never let them in the house except once, and then they broke pretty much everything they could reach," said Ivy.

So within a few days of arrival, the dogs were off being taken care of by somebody else. Now, thinking of Ivy giving him kisses like dog treats, it occurred to Laz that he wasn't a very good pet friend. Once Ron Smith had removed them, he barely thought of them at all.

When he went to bed, instead of allowing himself to think of the feeling of Ivy's lips on his, and how much nicer a different sort of kiss would have been, he thought about the Pack of Four. The way they menaced him at first—their formation at the entrance to that first Harris Teeter, and how they waited outside the door of the employee break room for him to come out. They were always smarter than dogs should be, but starvation could concentrate the mind of beasts other than humans.

He fell asleep thinking about the way they surrounded him on the way to Vivipartum, and how he hurled a decent-sized stone at StarKist and then broke something in another dog, and while they were trying to recuperate, he shared food with them. It occurred to Laz that in that sequence of events, he had made himself the alpha of that small pack of dogs. So StarKist, the erstwhile alpha, now obeyed Laz and followed him, while the others still followed StarKist. Dogs were still wolves in the back of their minds.

They never built us a fence, thought Laz. They do everything I ask for, but they never built us that fence with a concrete foundation to keep the dogs from digging. We could have had the dogs here all along, if they had built the fence. They certainly have chain link here, they must have fence posts, they must have concrete. Why don't we have a fence?

So he fell asleep thinking of the dogs, worrying about the dogs, wondering why his request for a fence wasn't honored, wondering what kind of person he was to have forgotten all about the dogs, thinking, At least Ivy's as big a jerk as I am. She never mentioned the dogs either. Except, well, now and then. She's not as big a jerk as I am, because at least she remembered them.

When you fall asleep thinking about your missing pack of dogs, obviously that's not at all what you dream of. Instead, your randomly firing synapses start making completely unrelated stories. Dreams of kissing the woman you love but not at *all* in a brother-sister way. And dreams of . . . well, no, once you start dreaming about the kissing, your mind isn't going anywhere else.

But when Laz woke up in the predawn light, so he could barely make out anything in the bedroom, he realized that he *had* been dreaming about the dogs.

And not just dreaming, because right now he had a very clear vision of talking to Ron Smith in some future moment, asking him about the dogs. And Ron Smith shook his head. Laz could only hear fragments: "Obedience school. Waste of time. Danger to others. Not letting them near *you* and *Ivy*. Too unpredictable. Violent. Distraction."

They had put the dogs down. Not a week after Ron Smith took them into his custody, they had been euthanized.

Laz was weeping quietly to himself when the door to his room opened. Ivy stepped in.

"I might have been naked," said Laz.

"You weren't," said Ivy. "You were grieving for the dogs."

Laz nodded.

Then he wondered how she knew.

"It was just a dream," he said. "It probably isn't true."

She looked at him strangely. "Just a dream? I don't see your dreams."

"What, then?"

"That was a timestream, stupid human male," she said. "It still is. Look. You're still holding on to that timestream."

"It's nothing like a timestream," said Laz, even as he realized that it was in fact a timestream.

"We plant the suggestion that OrigiLaz could actually visualize timestreams," said Ivy, "and then that very night your unconscious mind makes that jump and you wake up with visible timestreams in your head?"

"Not time*streams*," said Laz.

"Look at the timestream. You're still holding it, look at it."

Laz realized that yes, he could move up and down the timestream, and see things very clearly. "I could actually hear him say stuff," said Laz. "Not clearly, but . . . enough words to know."

"Whatever you saw on this timestream, I also saw," said Ivy. "As if you were pushing it into *my* mind."

"Maybe I was," said Laz. "But I have no idea how I did it."

"You didn't," said Ivy. "Not consciously. Maybe your unconscious mind is finally showing your wide-awake brain what your unconscious has been seeing all along."

"So this isn't new," said Laz, "it's what I was always doing, but now I can finally see it while I'm awake."

"Here's what I think," said Ivy. "This is a huge breakthrough, but maybe it only happens when you just wake up from what you *think* is a dream. So maybe right now is the very best time to find a timestream where StarKist and the Pack of Four are not dead."

"You think they really are dead?" asked Laz.

"It's simple enough," said Ivy. "Just find a timestream where they built the damn fence you asked them for. I bet the dogs are alive inside that fence."

Laz was very reluctant to let go of the clearly envisioned timestream, because what if he never saw any timestream that clearly again? But the next stream he looked at was just as clear. All he did was look, not into the future, but at the present moment in other timestreams until he found one with a chain-link fence, concrete foundations, and dog poo everywhere.

"That's it," said Ivy.

"Not till I know it's *our* dogs and not some replacement animals they tried to placate us with," said Laz.

It didn't take long, moving down that timestream, to see the dogs come bounding up for dinner at the back door of the house. They could see Ivy herself taking out the dog dishes.

"Wouldn't you know it," said Ivy. "I knew I'd end up taking care of them."

"We'll trade off feeding them, morning and evening," said Laz.

"What if you're off gallivanting around with my evil twin?

"We must share the responsibility," said Laz.

"We obviously have some kind of arrangement in this timestream we're both studying. As soon as you side step us into this timestream, then we'll have all the memories of the versions of us that are already in it."

Laz side stepped into that timestream. Instantly, they were fully dressed, ready to leave for their day's work, and Ivy was at the back door with the dogs, setting down two of their food bowls. "Come on, Ivy," he said, "I can't take my turn if you've already done it while I get dressed."

"Wear fewer clothes," said Ivy, "or feed them in your pajamas."

Laz walked up behind her and handed her the other two bowls of food. She set them down.

The memories of the self that had lived with these dogs all along were kicking in. That self had never missed the dogs; indeed, he had often felt burdened by their care.

StarKist, as usual, was the first to begin eating. Laz now remembered paying attention for about a week to see if there was one bowl each dog always ate from. But no. StarKist chose whichever bowl he wanted, and then woe betide the other dog that dared to eat from the chosen bowl.

StarKist was the Guy-in-Charge, thought Laz. He's also My

Dog, and there are timestreams in which I let him die.

Laz walked away from the door, lest he become ridiculously emotional. There were timestreams in which he tried to hug StarKist while he was eating—always a stupid move. This was the best choice. And he wouldn't smell like dog all day.

Ivy closed the kitchen door while the dogs munched at the food in their bowls. She started to come toward him and then stopped cold in the middle of the kitchen. "Do I kiss you good morning in this timestream?" she asked.

"Yes you do," said Laz. "You never did it in the timestream we just left. The one where the dogs were—"

"There's no such timestream," said Ivy. "And in this timestream, we didn't have our conversation about that one sentence in Origi-Laz's working notes."

Laz smiled. "I like the morning kiss policy here."

"I like the fact that Ron Smith and his team of voyeurs don't know what we've been thinking about," said Ivy.

Laz walked to her and took her by the shoulders. "I think I'm expecting a kiss about now."

"Don't you have an off switch?" she said.

"You constantly flip it on," said Laz.

"But I didn't," said Ivy. "I can't help your expectations."

He let go of her shoulders. "What an unfriendly welcome for a side stepper with only the kindest of feelings toward you."

"Laz," said Ivy. "You need to sit down somewhere and start looking at things in faraway timestreams."

"Shouldn't we go where the astrotech teams are?" asked Laz.

"If you can look without stepping," said Ivy, "then you can do your looking *here*."

"I don't know how this makes any difference," said Laz. "I don't know what I'm looking *for*. Shiva is invisible to the naked eye. It'll still come down to the astrotech teams ascertaining what we have or haven't found."

Ivy leaned up and kissed him on the lips. A nice kiss. Not passionate, but not sisterly either. "Now that I have your attention, will you please sit down? Or lie down. The couch is big enough."

Now that she had given him the doggy treat, he wanted to say something snotty, like, "If you want me to roll over and play dead, I'll do it." But instead he realized that she *could* have slapped his face to get his attention, so maybe some part of her preferred the kiss, and she had more experience with searching among timestreams, so he should listen to her. "What am I doing here on this comfy divan?" he asked.

"Whenever we find a faraway timestream that we think *might* be promising—though we never know what we're sensing anyway—what do we do?"

Laz was thinking now. She sat beside him. "We go to the Science Center," he said, "and a team of astrotechs helps us set up a Portal and then they set up their equipment and check the sky—"

"Good. So if you can sense much farther down timestreams than before, what are you likely to find on any such timestream?"

"Astrotech teams . . . but they don't tell us the results. It takes at least a week for them to report their data."

Ivy shook her head. "Within a couple of days they have enough data to know that Shiva is almost certainly still there. So their body language shows that they're now just going through the motions—still doing their jobs, collecting data, but without hope. Without enthusiasm."

"I never noticed that," said Laz.

"I did," said Ivy. "So here's what I suggest. Take a few minutes, move down the faraway timestream till you see the astrotechs."

"They won't go there till we tell them to, so—"

"In your clear vision of the timestream, you'll see the causal paths that *might* happen. Because once you're holding on to a faraway timestream, there are at least some timestreams in which we actually side step—*you* side step—and we make a Portal and the team sets up."

Laz closed his eyes. He started casting for faraway timestreams.

"No," said Ivy. "Go farther."

"There's no *distance* in timestreams," said Laz. "We *say* 'faraway' but the streams don't have any location in space or time."

"They didn't before," said Ivy. "Look at what you're *seeing*. Look at how your brain is visualizing the timestreams you haven't actually started examining yet."

Laz let go of that first timestream and started ranging farther, reaching farther. Before this morning, he had no idea how Ivy and Ivy-O knew how to distinguish far timestreams from near ones, but now he could actually see the amount of variation among timestreams. It was as if they were hanging from an invisible ceiling, like twines and strings. Only they didn't hang straight. They were bundled together, twisted into ropes and cables. Many timestreams were very close together, while nearby bundles were also intertwined, but there were gaps between bundles.

Here's near and far, thought Laz.

"Yes," whispered Ivy. "Don't talk about it, just look."

She didn't want their exploration to be overheard, Laz realized. They had already said too much, probably. Though maybe no one was watching them this morning. It was possible.

He kept ranging farther and farther among the dangling strands, parting them like curtains.

Till he came to a region that didn't show very much intertwining at all. Just single strands, isolated, hanging down.

"Look at one of these," said Ivy. "*Don't* side step. Because I think these are lifeless timestreams."

"Why?"

"Timestreams branch off into multiple paths because people and animals have made choices that might have gone different ways," said Ivy. "But in lifeless versions of Earth, nobody's choosing anything. Rocks fall. Earthquakes happen. But they all have mechanical causes. If a rock is going to break when the stresses become too great, then it will always break at exactly that moment. No choices, and therefore no variations, no timestreams."

"If there are no choices," said Laz, "then why are there so many of these isolated strands?"

"There aren't all that many," said Ivy. "Look how far apart they are. Maybe back in the chaos of planetary formation, there *were* variables of the Schrödinger's Cat variety, things that could go either way, so in that case, we get a couple of timestreams. Both still dead, but different. I think there are more causal strands in any of those major bundles back in the living worlds than all of these dead-world strands put together."

"So you already know what you're seeing?" asked Laz.

"I'm seeing it for the first time, just like you," said Ivy.

"How do you know, then?"

"Educated guesses. If you doubt me, though, take a peek at some of the isolated strands."

Ivy was right. Bare rock, with no green, no soil, no insects or birds, absolutely nothing moving except when the wind moved dust.

"Lunar," said Laz.

"Not really," said Ivy. "And no, I've never been to the Moon. But it has no atmosphere. Earth has wind."

"The atmosphere," said Laz.

"I didn't see a need to check, but in school I learned about the original reducing atmosphere. Methane. No free oxygen. Nothing we can use. Our breathable atmosphere was created by bacteria in the ocean. And it took a few weeks or centuries or millions of years to get an atmosphere that could support oxygen breathers like us."

"My feeling is, this has been an interesting excursion," said Laz. "Now let's get to work."

"Remember, we aren't stepping anywhere," said Ivy. "Not without strings or twine or whatever. I don't want to be the second Ivy to lose her Laz."

"How sweet of you," said Laz, "to think of me as yours."

"They're going to be here to pick us up soon," said Ivy.

"I'm going to go into my room," said Laz, "and think my beautifully visualized thoughts, which you can also see wherever you are. But you stay where you can intercept them at the door and tell them I'm coming out when I come out."

"If we just don't answer, won't they know?" asked Ivy.

"If we just don't answer," said Laz, "they'll break down the door to see if something's wrong."

"They don't have to break down the door, silly," said Ivy. "They have more keys than we do."

Back in his room, he thought of sitting up on a chair, so there was no risk of his falling asleep. But then he remembered that it had been in a state of hypnagogia when his unconscious mind started delivering visualized timestreams. Or maybe it was hypnapompic, as he was waking up. But it was one of the transitions between wakefulness and sleep, so maybe dozing off wouldn't be fatal to the process.

Besides, if he went to sleep, Ivy would come in and wake him up.

Or not. Because there was a good chance that she resented the fact that he could now see timestreams better than she could.

Not for long, he thought. Now that we know it's possible, now that she's experienced it coming through *my* brain, she's going to learn to do it herself.

There's also no way to prevent Ivy-O from doing the same. Or maybe she can already do that. Or maybe she can see into my head so this morning she found out everything we're going to find out.

Keeping secrets is hard, thought Laz. It's also pointless. Everybody finds out, so why conceal it?

Now that he could find the boundaries of life on Earth, he started searching the remote edges of the crowded, twisting, life-filled timestreams. Whenever he looked at those timestream bundles, he found life—green, chlorophyllic, photosynthesizing life. A few of them had no animal life, but he knew that was probably deceptive. In those timestreams, evolution might not have put insects in the air yet, but there were certainly microbes. Still, it was interesting that without a lot of animals, there were so many timestreams. But when a plant grows, it might twist left, it might twist right; a passing wind might bend the twig or break it; life brought complication and variation even without animals hunting each other through the vegetation.

There was no possible correlation between life on Earth and the approach of Shiva, of course. Shiva could just as easily approach dead Earths as vibrant versions of the planet. Even so, Laz wondered if out near the edges of the living threads, he might have a better shot at finding timestreams without Shiva, if only because they had already looked into so many nearer timestreams.

Before this morning, in order to eliminate a timestream, or a cluster of closely related timestreams, they had to assemble a team and go through the whole process. Now, though, Laz only had to raise the possibility of calling in an astrotech team, and then look at the timestreams where they did their probing of the sky. Then he'd watch a few days of the techs working—it only took a minute or so to scan ahead—and then, sure enough, just as Ivy had told him, the body language of the techs told him that they had found evidence of Shiva, still on a fatal course toward the solar system.

He couldn't sense Ivy watching with him, but he knew she would be—and if he discarded a timestream and she thought he shouldn't have, he knew she'd come charging into the room and set him straight.

He still needed her. He couldn't do this without her. She didn't have to fear that the team would dissolve.

Of course she did. Because they weren't in charge of this.

Maybe she could learn to see the way he did—the way Origi-Laz had almost certainly seen—and then she might be better able to experiment with side stepping herself.

A thought began to play in the back of his mind. Ivy-O with her plant-gathering on every timestream she visited with him. What was she doing? He could *almost* understand it.

But no, his problem right now wasn't figuring out Ivy-O. It was finding a timestream where the astrotechs didn't get discouraged, but instead got—

Excited.

It was three in the afternoon when it happened. Laz had dozed off twice. One time, Ivy had come right in and wakened him. The next time, she didn't. He woke up having lost an hour. Maybe she let him sleep because she realized that he needed it. Maybe she had drifted off herself.

But he was awake now, and he looked at the clock in his room because he wanted to be able to tell Ron Smith when it was that he found the place.

The astrotech team was not dejected. Day two, day three, and finally as they were packing up their equipment on day four, they had a spring in their step, they were jabbering happily to each other. The body language was clear.

He kept a firm hold on that timestream.

He got off the bed and walked out into the living room. Ivy wasn't there.

She was in the back yard, throwing things for her favorite dog to fetch. StarKist mostly ignored her—she was *not* his alpha—but the dog that Laz had injured back at the beginning of their relationship, *he* responded to Ivy's attention and her gentle speaking-to-dogs voice. He still had a limping, twisted gait, because his pelvis had healed, but in the wrong shape. She officially named the dog John Wick, which she assured Laz was ironic; but in fact she called the dog Wicky or Wicked or Wick. Laz made it a point to never use his old name for the dog, Hip, because it was her dog now. He didn't distract it by calling to it.

Wicky fetched when Ivy threw things. None of the other dogs did. Maybe that had to do with their original breeds. Laz had no idea, he had never studied traits of dog breeds. But he knew that Ivy was *not* concentrating on what he found, or she would surely have abandoned her doggy games and come inside to be excited with him.

"No," she told him softly when he joined her outside. "I'm not showing any excitement because I don't want them to know that we already know something even without actually side stepping there."

Secrets again. "They'll know soon enough," said Laz.

"But what if we're wrong?" said Ivy. "It looked clear enough to me, so I'm sure we're right, but what *if* we're wrong? Then we raise hopes for nothing. The boy who cried wolf and all that."

Laz pointed at StarKist, who was either chasing his tail or dodging an insect. Laz wondered briefly if it was an insect from the Old Place or maybe a New Place insect. He wondered if it was a stinging insect or a biting one.

And he realized he had lost track of the timestream in which the astrotechs seemed to be happy.

"Don't worry," said Ivy. "I have it. They're not substantial. We can both gather them and hold on to them without interfering with each other."

"I can't believe I lost it," said Laz.

"You didn't," said Ivy. "You still had it. In half a second you would have realized it. But I spoke up to reassure you before you found it, because I'm so nice that I didn't want you to be worried for even a half second longer than necessary."

"You're all heart," said Laz.

"An anatomically grotesque idea," said Ivy. "Shall we go out and see if the car is still waiting out front?"

"Of course it is," said Laz. "I'm sure they overheard enough of this morning's conversation to know that *something's* up."

"What you accomplished all in one day," said Ivy.

"What *we* accomplished," said Laz. "We're still a team, and I need you as much as—"

"Baloney," said Ivy, "but I don't mind."

"Of course not," said Laz.

"If the world gets saved . . . ," Ivy began.

"Let's go test it out and find out just how saved it might be," said Laz. "For all we know, further testing will reveal that if we move to *this* new Portal, we'll only delay Shiva's arrival by another twenty years."

"Possible," said Ivy. "The best outcome would be to find Shiva, only she's on a safer trajectory. If we don't find her, then we have no idea if she'll pop up later, the way she did in the New Place."

"But now that we have a methodology," said Laz, "we can search more and more."

"I think we should find more Safe Places than one," said Ivy. "Spread out the risk, divide the populations so that no one timestream has to support the entire population of Earth. Say we find nine other timestreams that have no Shiva problem, that means that each timestream only has to take on a tenth of the world's population."

She saw the big picture better than Laz did. He needed her as much as ever. The world needed her.

There was nobody in the car, but when they got in, the car announced it was going directly to the Science Center. That implied no stopping to pick up Ivy-O, and Laz was fine with that.

Even without Ron Smith in the car, Laz figured they were still listening in on whatever they said to each other. So they kept it innocuous. Ivy got Laz talking about how she thought Wicky was getting horny, and they ought to think about finding mates for the dogs.

"I think they have pictures of the Pack of Four under the definition of 'mongrel' or 'mutt' in the dictionary," said Laz.

"I think it's illegal to inbreed to keep a particular strain pure," said Ivy. "It only magnifies whatever defect the subspecies has. So mongrels are actually kind of valuable."

"That brings hope to an Armenian American like me," said Laz.

"Why, were you hoping to mate with a collie or a poodle? No poodle would have you, Laz. I hope you aren't offended."

Then Laz's earlier speculation came back to him with more clarity. "I think I know what Ivy-O might be doing with her plant-gathering," he said.

"Let's hear your hypothesis," said Ivy. They always tried to call their mad speculations "hypotheses" to remind themselves that they were only guesses until they had been put through the wringer of serious analysis and comparison with the data.

"Maybe she's blazing a trail," said Laz.

When Ivy didn't answer, he went on. "Pioneers going into virgin forest would use hatchets to chip a blaze in the trunk of a tree. The white wood showing through was easy to spot, even at twilight, so—"

"I know what blazing a trail is," said Ivy. "But I don't know why she'd need to."

"So she would know if she's already been to a timestream before."

"Laz," said Ivy, "I never lose track of a timestream, especially not one we've explored. If I never forget, neither does she. She's not cutting off sample leaves and bringing them home because she's afraid she'll accidentally explore the same timestream twice."

"Oh," said Laz. "I didn't know you two have such perfect memories. Mine isn't that good."

"Yes it is," said Ivy. "You just don't trust it enough, that's all."

Or you trust yours too much, Laz did *not* say in reply. But of course she could probably read his skepticism in his face, because she rolled her eyes and looked away.

"Okay, you always know," said Laz. "But how? It's not like we have a grid like on a map. 'Today we're working F-5. We finished with F-4 yesterday.'"

"Wouldn't that be nice," said Ivy. "Trust me on this, Laz. Even without your map grid, Ivy-O and I always remember where we've been."

Within a couple of hours the twines were set and the techs started dragging through the heavier chains that couldn't easily be broken—the foundation of a full-fledged Portal, if one should turn out to be necessary.

Then the astrotechs came through. Both Laz and Ivy were already there waiting for them. Laz watched them set up. He even helped carry things for them, because it was work he could do, while freeing the experts to do the jobs he hadn't the skills for.

It only got weird for the astrotechs when they had things set up and they noticed Laz and Ivy were still there. "Don't you have more timestreams to explore?" Double Doc asked Laz.

"Maybe not," said Laz. "Maybe this is the one."

Double Doc smiled. Then his eyes squinted a little. "Do you know something I don't know?"

"You're the one with two doctorates," said Laz. "I don't think there's *anything* that I know and you don't."

To avoid more questions, Laz went over to where Ivy seemed to be studying the vegetation. He saw part of a big folded-over leaf showing from the pocket of her jacket. "So you're trying Ivy-O's trailblazing technique?" asked Laz.

"Your talk about trailblazing made me wonder," said Ivy.

"What if Ivy-O is still working on learning to side step herself? She said she was trying to do that when she lost OrigiLaz. The blaze idea made me think, what if she's using the broken-off leaves and twigs as hotel key cards, so she can side step to these locations herself?"

"We're only doing faraways now," said Laz. "That would be scary dangerous, to side step to a remote location where there's no Portal in place."

"But if she has a big leaf from home *and* from the place she's already visited, maybe there's no worry at all."

"Because nobody ever had a leaf blow out of their hand in a strong gust of wind," said Laz.

"If Ivy-O learns to side step, then I'm not going to be left behind," said Ivy.

"I'm not sure that competitive streak is as charming as you think," said Laz.

"If I'm competitive," said Ivy, "then so is she. We're identical, you know."

"We don't *know* if she can side step, and whether she can or not, we have no idea whether she uses the plants she's collecting to accomplish it."

"What if I turn out to be better at it than she is? Because I'm coming to it so much younger?"

"What if you turn out to be better at side stepping than I am?" asked Laz.

"Then we'll both have to deal with crippling cases of envy," said Ivy.

"No matter how our skills do or do not improve," said Laz, "can't we please keep exploring together? Can't we kind of keep pace with each other?"

"Oh, you mean that you'll slow down to stay back with me on this vision thing?" asked Ivy.

"You're keeping up just fine," said Laz.

"No, I'm not keeping up at all," said Ivy. "I can see what you're seeing, but only because you're seeing it. I'm along for the ride, I can't see anything on my own."

"Yet," said Laz.

"Yet," Ivy agreed.

To avoid making the astrotechs suspicious again, Laz and Ivy forced themselves to leave that timestream and return back through the new Portal.

Laz and Ivy spent four days going through the motions of opening up eight more Portals. They chose timestreams that were near to the one that led to happy astrotechs, though they didn't dare to disappoint themselves by exploring too far down these other streams. With nine teams of astrotechs in place, they were out of personnel for a while. So they went back and visited with all the tech teams, reaching the first one just as things were finishing up.

While they watched the body language of the techs—who weren't actually *saying* anything about their findings because that would be unscientific and premature and potentially humiliating if they were wrong—Ivy said, very softly, "One thing bothers me."

"Yes?" asked Laz.

"We didn't see ourselves along that timestream. Yet here we are."

Laz thought about it. "It wasn't a local. We weren't side stepping into ourselves. We found this place a different way."

"If it was true vision," said Ivy, "shouldn't we have seen ourselves?"

"No," said Laz. "Because the timestream we happened to look at that closely was an amalgam, the way future timestreams always are. A bunch of possibilities, and we see the ones that are most common. Maybe the most common ones don't have us, and now we happen to be in one of the rare realities where we *are* here."

"Good save," said Ivy.

"Or I'm wrong and we've screwed this up completely by being here," said Laz.

"You're right," said Ivy. "Let's get out of here."

"As you wish," said Laz. "But I'm staying to help them carry equipment back to the Science Center."

"Aren't you nice," said Ivy.

"About time you noticed that," said Laz.

The astrotechs were practically dancing as they carried the equipment through the Portal of twine and chains that led them back to the electric golf carts that would transport it all into the Science Center.

Ivy sidled up to Double Doc, who was red-faced from carrying a particularly heavy and awkward stability stand. The actual instruments were all in protective cases, but the platforms and such weren't as conveniently designed. "Double Doc," she said, "this is a really heavy, awkward piece of equipment."

"Yes," he said.

"Everybody says it's the heaviest, most awkward one to carry."

"So they say," said Double Doc.

"Yet you practically trotted through the Portal."

"Did I? Just eager to get home to a nice hot bath," he said.

"No preliminary results?" she asked.

"I can't answer that till we've run a lot of tests to make sure we're not getting false results."

"If they turn out to be false," said Ivy, "would that mean that Shiva is *not* coming, or that she is?"

"Ivy," said Double Doc, "I could lose my job or at least the respect of my peers, but if anybody deserves to have an answer to that only slightly oblique question, it's you."

"I do deserve it," said Ivy.

"Will you promise not to tell Laz?" asked Double Doc.

"Absolutely not," said Ivy. "I can't keep secrets from him anyway."

"That's what I thought," said Double Doc.

"So you won't tell me, because I won't lie to Laz?"

"No, I'm telling you right now. Because if the results were bad, I wouldn't hesitate to say, Shiva's right there."

"So you're saying she's not."

"I'm saying that we may have found Shiva or a similar wandering planet above the plane of the ecliptic, but heading in quite a different direction—heading farther from our solar system, and unlikely to have any deleterious effects on Earth."

"Or Jupiter," said Ivy. "Really, I care very much about what happens to Jupiter."

"The old scoundrel has always had a way with women," said Double Doc.

"Speak more politely of the gods, please," said Ivy.

"Ivy, if our data is backed up by later teams conducting different tests with different equipment, you and Laz just took us to a genuinely Safe Place."

At that point, they were among other techs loading things onto the carts. Ivy helped Double Doc load on the stability stand. One of the guys said to Double Doc, "So you told her?"

"She guessed from the way we were all walking happy," said Double Doc.

"I'm fine with telling her. She's not a civilian. She and Laz *are* the team."

"Damn straight," said Ivy. With a grin.

That opened the floodgates on the team's good cheer. They were slapping each other on the back, singing, making rude jokes, and many other signs of glee all the way back to the Science Center.

A week later, Ron Smith came to Laz's and Ivy's house about noon. It was their day off, so he found Ivy running around the yard with Wicky happily trotting at her heels, while Laz was in the kitchen trying to make a complicated dish he remembered seeing on a cooking channel when he was in middle school. It smelled good, but when Ron Smith said, "Time to talk," Laz just took things off the heat and followed Ron Smith and Ivy into the parlor.

"We don't have time to run the full gamut of tests before we start terraforming in the Portal you just opened," said Ron Smith. "We've got the agriculture guys in there already, running soil tests and selecting crops to try. The geneticists are seeing how digestible the plant life is likely to be. And we have drones scanning for any kind of animal life. Insects we have. We're hoping to find no higher life forms than amphibians."

"Because it's okay to destroy the habitat of amphibians," said Ivy.

"That's how we see it," said Ron Smith. "Unless we find tiny buildings and vehicles constructed by clever-fingered toads."

"So we're done?" asked Laz.

"Not a chance. First of all, our preliminaries from the other

Portals you've opened recently are also showing Shiva on a route that poses no threat. There's a chance that she's disturbing something in the Oort Cloud or the Kuiper Belt, and in ten thousand years a comet that never came close before will aim right at us. But by then, we'll probably have the technology to bust up or reroute inconvenient comets. Not our problem, anyway."

"So we have multiple Safe Places," said Laz.

"Yes, probably," said Ron Smith. "And we need to open Portals to each of them from every part of the New Place that had Portals from Earth. So we can get the maximum number of people through before Shiva arrives in *this* timestream."

"Oh, yeah," said Ivy. "I guess that's part of the job. Lots of doors."

"Right now the governments are dealing with some sticky questions. For instance, here in the North and South American area, do we send people from every nation and language through every Portal, so that every place has a mix of everybody, the way we did with the New Place? Or do we separate worlds by languages, so that Portuguese speakers go to one of these Safe Places, and speakers of Mexican Spanish and Cuban Spanish and Chilean Spanish and, of course, English and Canadian French and all the surviving Native American languages each get their own entire continent?"

"Do they all have people with the technological knowledge?"

"They all think they do," said Ron Smith. "So the third question is, if we give them separate continents—and I'm reasonably sure that the two of you can side step often enough to get as many separate timestreams as we need—do we connect all these Safe Places with a central world? A hub? So we can trade with each other or bail each other out from famines or whatever through Portals, even after *this* world is gone?"

"We can do everything you've said," Ivy answered, "but it takes time to lay out a Portal and then get a reliable structure built."

"We're not going to wait to build a nice permanent gate the way we built between the Old Place and the New Place in Kentucky," said Ron Smith. "We only did that after the fact. Most of the migration took place with only chains and then chain-link fences funneling people from one timestream to the other."

"With that powerful wrenching sensation midway through," said Ivy. "I wonder why *we* don't feel that when we first step through."

"That gut-wrenching feeling is a symptom of the growing disparity between the Old Place and the New Place," said Ron Smith. "It came as the first glimmer of Shiva in that timestream. When we first went through, there weren't any gut wrenches or headaches or dizziness or seizures."

"So our job now is to set up Portals leading from and to different places in the timestreams," said Laz. "And to create Portals *between* the new Safe Places, if we can."

"Here's the thing that's still puzzling me," said Ron Smith. "For all those weeks and months, you never found anything that didn't have Shiva in it. Then a couple of weeks ago, you don't come out of the house till nearly noon—"

"It was three in the afternoon," said Ivy.

"And you didn't say a word during the whole trip to the Science Center," said Ron Smith. "But from then on, *every* timestream you portalized had no danger from Shiva in it. Every one of them."

"Lucky streak?" asked Laz.

"Give me credit for at least some small fraction of your brain power," said Ron Smith. "One of you had a breakthrough that morning."

"Did we?" said Laz.

"Are you going to tell me what happened?" asked Ron Smith.

"If we tell you," said Laz, "that information will certainly get to Ivy-O."

"Yes," said Ron Smith. "Why wouldn't it?"

"We don't want it to," said Ivy.

"Why not?"

"Because she's been doing weird stuff and has never given us an honest answer about *what* she's doing and why," said Laz.

"So you're going to be just as deceptive back? That's not getting even," said Ron Smith. "That's just making things worse."

"At some point, she'll break the logjam," said Ivy. "Till then, what we learned remains locked within a very small group."

"So you're going to treat Ivy-O as if she weren't part of the team, as if this success wasn't at least partly the result of her work," said Ron Smith.

"It wasn't," said Ivy. "It was in spite of her deceptiveness that we learned what we learned."

"So you did learn something," said Ron Smith.

"Obviously," said Ivy. "There are nine Safe Places already. There's a chance to get everybody through the new Portals into the nine worlds we've found so far—if they all pan out."

Ron Smith sat there nodding, saying nothing for a while. Then he straightened up and looked cheerful again. "Oh, by the way, congratulations on finding nine needles in the haystack."

"Thank you," said Ivy.

"Good job of smoothing things over," said Laz. "You really have mastered that."

"It's going to be harder to smooth things over with Ivy-O," said Ron Smith.

"You'll tell her what you tell her," said Laz, "and she'll react however she decides to react, and meanwhile millions of people are going to be passing through all the Portals."

"Are the teams ready to start hardening the new Portals we make? Are the other countries—well, how do we get there?" asked Ivy. "Are there airports?"

"Heliports," said Ron Smith. "And a few airports for flights across oceans."

"So our main delay is going to be transportation within this world," said Ivy.

"Probably," said Ron Smith.

"Wouldn't it be ironic," said Ivy, "if the plane carrying us should happen to be struck by lightning in transit, and blown to smithereens."

Ron Smith stiffened but still kept smiling. "Wouldn't you just side step to a reality in which that didn't happen?"

"If the plane were simply going down, heading for a hard landing, sure," said Laz. "But if the plane blows to smithereens, we'd be in smithereens too."

"Can't side step after being smithered," said Ivy. "But we'll try not to think about that when we board the plane."

17

Plog of Lazarus Hayerian, Side Stepper Emeritus

I believe we've worked our way out of a job. Wherever there was already a Portal between the Old Place and the New Place, there are new Portals open between the New Place and each of the Safe Places. That still left us with the New Place as the only vector connecting all the Safe Places, and when the New Place blows, that would cut us all off from each other. So we made one of the Safe Places a vector for all the other Safe Places.

Now it's up to all the governments to work out who goes where. We make Portals, not decisions.

As it stands right now, there are certain groups that demanded to have places that were not only safe from Shiva, but safe from groups that have been trying to destroy or oppress them for generations or centuries or millennia. What surprised me—but not Ivy—was that the persecutors howled in protest when their victims seemed to be headed for freedom and safety.

Of course, by putting all these havens in the same Safe Place, Ivy says that it's only a matter of time until these victims of persecution start persecuting each other. But for right now, there's plenty of space between them. Armenians get to rebuild Armenia without any Turks around; Jews get an area roughly analogous with Israel, with nobody wanting to drive them into the sea.

Millions of Dalits, or Untouchables, were able to choose a version of the Indian subcontinent without anybody lording it over them, and several Native American tribes or language groups got exclusive rights to something like their original homeland.

There are enough timestreams and Portals that nobody has to put up with persecution from any other group. And Ivy and I stand ready to open up new Portals into timestreams where still more groups can develop in splendid isolation. There's talk of an Irish homeland where English is banned and only Irish can be spoken, and the Ainu, the Australian Aboriginals, the Lapps, and many others have organized groups agitating for homelands.

I'm glad that so far, the Portal Authority is refusing to grant an autonomous homeland to any group with fewer than five million would-be migrants, unless their history of exclusion and persecution is so severe that it would be unjust to refuse them even if there are only ten thousand. And below that, it makes no economic or genetic sense to isolate anybody.

Somebody's going to have to name these timestreams or the confusion will become permanent. Or else everybody will eventually seal off their access to the vector world, and gradually they'll forget those other Safe timestreams exist.

Humans get to decide what they'll do. That's one of the nice things about being human.

Meanwhile, StarKist and the Pack of Four are still living in our yard in the New Place, and we have to decide where we're going. I personally hope Ivy and I can stay together, but she has already said that she doesn't see the point, since I can find timestreams perfectly well without her. I can't quite bring myself to say that I can't find a reason for living without her, because that's too melodramatic and she might think I'm making some childish threat of suicide if I don't get my way. So I keep my words and thoughts to myself, as we tour the Safe Places to see how things are working out before either of us picks one.

I can't tell or guess whether this migration through Portals is going better than the previous ones. Ron Smith told us that the first time, they had time to get every living human through the Portals, but while I think he's being honest, I don't believe the claim. I think there are always people who don't believe what they're told, especially by the government, and other people who want to stay hidden. I think the Old Place probably has dozens or hundreds of people scavenging from grocery stores the way Ivy and I did in Greensboro. They'll eventually die of malnutrition or they'll start gardening. And then Shiva will come.

And it's already too late for them to change their minds. Once we had all the new Portals between worlds, Ron Smith authorized teams to dismantle every Portal between the New Place and the Old Place. Now nobody can go back there or get here from there.

Except us. Ivy and I are tempted sometimes to make one last trip for old times' sake. What stops us is that before the Portals were closed, there was already a lot of interference, like static in the timestreams. We're not sure we can get there, and if we get there and stay a bit too long, we're afraid we won't be able to get back.

Wherever OrigiLaz is, I hope he's not in the Old Place. He's not me, exactly, but he's close enough to me that I wish him well. I want him to be alive and to stay alive.

This is a kind of benediction to my plogs. I'm pretty sure Ron Smith and his team have saved copies—probably digital—of all my plogs, and Ivy's, too, so that when somebody writes a history of how the human race side stepped its way out of Shiva's path, they'll be able to reconstruct our entire character from the idiotic things we wrote. Well, I wrote idiotic things. Lovesick mooncalf, I think the technical term is.

After all our time together, I can't imagine why Ivy isn't sick of me. I'm not sick of her, but I also don't want to impose my company where it isn't welcome. So the outcome of that set of causes and effects remains unknown. Neither Ivy nor I has looked down that path, because each of us would know if the other looked, and we want to be able to make up our minds as we go along instead of looking for a future we like and stepping into it.

I always thought that people who refused to find out if they were having a boy or a girl were somewhere between stupid and insane. "We want to be surprised." Why? What possible advantage could there be in not knowing what gender list of names they should be considering, and all that?

But that was only true because the sex had already been decided by nature, and they were simply blinding themselves to a fact that they could not change if they wanted to.

What happens to Ivy and me, that's entirely a matter of our

choices. Nothing is set in stone. There is no <u>fact</u> already decided. There's just us. And so for us not to look down our timestreams to see what happens based on future choices we make, that's a way of preserving our freedom. And no matter what our hopes and fears might be, we value the ability to make free choices more than pretty much anything.

Laz and Ivy stood at the front gate of their chain-link-fenced yard. The dogs were already gone, packed up in nice animal shipping cages and trucked away toward the Portals. Of course they complained bitterly through the whole process, but Laz was able to choose a timestream in which nobody packing them up got bitten. Ivy agreed that nobody should be bitten because Ivy and Laz had sentimental feelings about half-wild dogs.

They hadn't yet decided where they were going or if they were going to stay together. The issue of staying together was off limits; they barely referred to it, and always talked as if they were making joint decisions, even though Laz knew perfectly well that they had no formal commitment to each other. By contrast, through the whole time they were making Portals and then touring all the Safe Places, they had gone back and forth on the question of which Portal, and where in that timestream, they'd choose for their permanent home. What about here? What about there?

One big problem was that too much publicity had gone out during the Second Migration, as people were calling it—or the Great Division, as it was called by those who were insane enough to demand that all the billions of humans ought to go to the same world.

There was no human community that did not know the faces and names of Lazarus Davit Hayerian and Ivy Maisie Downey—or

Ivy Lopez, as Hispanic people usually called her. They could not go anywhere and live anonymously.

"All I want to be known as is 'the woman whose dog has such a weird walk,'" Ivy said one time.

"We could have plastic surgery and go around with different faces," suggested Laz.

"Then you wouldn't love me anymore," said Ivy.

"All the more reason for you to do it—to get rid of me," said Laz. They were both laughing as if it were a joke, instead of its being Laz's greatest dread. They knew that they wouldn't go into seclusion, partly because a lot of people were scared that the Second Migration would be no more a permanent solution than the first one had been. If not Shiva, there'd be something else. And people needed to know that the Side Step team was still available, if needed.

So as they stood at the front gate, looking down into the yard that had been their home for all these years, Laz had a lot of bittersweet memories. Living together had been hard for him, on an emotional level, but he also dreaded the thought of living without her. He had been happy here, or at least hopeful of happiness.

They had made the breakthroughs that saved the human species and a lot of other Earth-origin species as well. There had been talk among Ron Smith's team of dismantling the house and chain-link fence and transporting it to one of the Safe Places as a kind of living monument. Ivy had killed the idea with laughter. "Oh, I can imagine the guided tour," she said. "'Here is the toilet where Laz Hayerian pooped and peed. Ivy's toilet is in another room, but out of respect for her privacy, we won't be showing you that.' And then some kid asks, 'Did they, like, make the beast with two backs?'"

Laz howled at that—not laughter, just howling, like a dog in pain. "Shakespeare?" he asked. "You think there's some future kid who'll ask if we were 'doing it' by quoting Shakespeare?"

Anyway, once Ron Smith knew that they seriously didn't want any kind of preservation of this house, the whole idea was dropped. "But we want to build you a house somewhere. Or houses. Whatever you want."

"I just don't want to be in the same timestream as Ivy-O," said Ivy.

Laz felt the same way, but he was content to let it be Ivy's demand.

"She agrees with that desire," said Ron Smith, "so you definitely won't be sent into the same Safe Place."

And now it was the day when they were going to leave the house behind, and go to temporary quarters near the Portals until they chose which one to go to. The Old Place was sealed off already, and soon the New Place would be, too. Choices had to be made. A house or houses had to be built.

"An apartment will do just fine," Ivy had said.

To which Ron Smith had replied, "It will not do at all, because your neighbors would hate the security precautions and the steady stream of tourists and fans and worshipers that are bound to pester you."

"Can't you just shoot them on sight?" asked Laz.

"You're all about saving lives," said Ron Smith.

"He was joking," Ivy said.

"He only meant it about twenty-five percent," said Ron Smith.

Which Laz figured was a pretty good estimate.

Now the car was coming up the road. Laz and Ivy had only a suitcase each—the clothes they'd need over the next few days, plus some toiletries and writing materials. Everything else had been packed up and would be delivered wherever they decided to go.

Ron Smith got out of the car to invite them in.

"The dogs are okay, right?" Ivy asked.

"I don't know why you're so worried that somebody will put them down," said Ron Smith.

"You know why," said Laz.

"But we're not in that timestream now," said Ron Smith.

"Same dogs. Same trouble."

"No," said Ron Smith. "They're much tamer. Far less feral, far less dangerous than when you first arrived."

"I'm not sure if I'm happy about that," said Ivy. "Why should they give up being who they are?"

Ron Smith laughed. "For the same reason that we train children not to poo and pee wherever they happen to be when the urge strikes them," he said. "We have to live together. Dogs evolved because they were accommodating themselves to humans. It's the only reason they're not still wolves. You'll find he's the same Chicken of the Sea that he always was."

Laz narrowed his eyes. "Don't try to fool a side stepper into thinking that he's ended up in a weird timestream where the alpha of the Pack of Four was not named StarKist."

"StarKist? Was that a brand name or something?" asked Ivy.

"Not funny, and not fun," said Laz. "It's the thing that bothers me the most about all this. The people, the places, the pets, the monuments, the everything that gets left behind in the timestreams we didn't choose. There are infinite timestreams in which no Portals were ever opened, and billions of people will die or are already dying."

"Since you don't travel in time," said Ron Smith, "you can't side step and save them. It's already too late."

"And there's an infinite number of timestreams like that, so even if we had a thousand years it wouldn't be enough time," said Ivy.

"I still imagine I can see them dying," said Laz, "hear them screaming as the atmosphere bursts into flame."

"And then silence," said Ivy. "Billions of people have already died on Earth. We all know from childhood on that it's the fate awaiting us all. What we did was to save the species, the cultures, the languages. Not the individuals. People died during the migrations, there were traffic accidents, industrial accidents, diseases, just like always."

"Doesn't change how I feel about it," said Laz, "because if it's in your power to save somebody, then it's your responsibility to do it."

Ivy just shook her head.

"I think we're just rehashing discussions you two have already had," said Ron Smith.

"Ad infinitum," said Ivy.

"I bore her, I'm afraid," said Laz.

She put her hand on his. "I love that you're the kind of man who feels responsible for the whole world."

"But I don't," said Laz. "I only feel responsible for each and every individual in each and every timestream that I couldn't save."

"So, you collectively saved the world," said Ron Smith, "but you individually let most of them die."

"That's about it," said Laz.

"You're a loon," said Ivy. "You're going to let your conscience force you into a major lifelong depression."

"Here's the deal, kids," said Ron Smith. "We don't know what's coming in the future. It won't be Shiva—we know where *she* is and where she's going. But it'll be something. Maybe next year, maybe a thousand years from now. If it's next year, we'll call you out of retirement. But in a thousand years?"

"No timestream has us living that long," said Laz.

"Not that we've checked," said Ivy. "Neither of us wants to see our own death."

Or each other's death, for that matter, Laz thought but refrained from saying.

"That's why," said Ron Smith, "I want your first stop in Portal City to be a recording facility."

It took a moment for Laz to understand. "A brain state recording facility."

"And we want you to give us good samples of DNA, so we can have a record of your genome as well as frozen samples ready to clone," said Ron Smith.

Ivy smiled simperingly—an expression that Laz always dreaded, because it meant she was going to say something supremely hurtful. "Ron Smith, really. Why would you want our brain states now, when we had so much success with having us wake up at high school age so we had to work it out from scratch?"

Ron Smith nodded. "You're mocking the idea," he said, "but there were people advocating for that. Your previous brain state recordings are being duplicated and preserved, in case they're needed. But we want to be able to restore you—"

"Clone us," corrected Ivy.

"With all the knowledge and skill you currently have," Ron Smith finished.

"So in effect you want us to potentially live forever," said Ivy.

"So many old myths and legends end with a promise that though the hero is gone, when his people need him, he'll return," said Ron.

"But we won't return," said Laz. "Somebody else will return with our memories."

"More to the point, they'll return *thinking* that they're us, *remembering* that they're us," said Ivy. "But they won't *be* us."

"Exactly," said Ron Smith. "The legal decisions have already been made—DNA donors have no proprietary rights over their clones. Clones are full-fledged people from the moment they're conceived. No more starting up clone farms and then killing off the surplus. If you grow the body—or speed-grow it—once those cells are dividing and shaping themselves into human life, they're alive."

"Why weren't we told about that?" asked Ivy.

"Your minds were on something else," said Ron Smith. "We didn't want to have this conversation then."

Neither Laz nor Ivy said anything more. In Laz's case, it was partly because he didn't want to commit to anything without knowing what Ivy thought, and mostly because he had no idea what he thought.

"While you're thinking about this, and later when you're discussing it, there are a few things you should know. First, all surveillance of you was discontinued when you opened the last Portal. We watch over you still to protect you, but we have no tactical need to listen in on your private conversations."

"Well, *now* we can start being candid with each other," said Laz.

"Exactly right, you obnoxious twerp," said Ivy. Then she grinned. But since it was exactly what Laz feared might be her real feeling, it didn't strike him as funny. She must have seen that in his face, because once again she laid her hand on his.

"Second," said Ron Smith, "I want you to decide whether you

think your life, since waking up, has been a long round of uninterrupted suffering because you were cloned and woke up with somebody else's memories. Or has it been a pretty cool life so far, full of meaning and even some happiness. And four dogs that you kind of love. What if somebody a thousand years from now woke up with a fresh new healthy strong adult body, and with your memories up to today. Do you think they'd hate being you, or they'd feel good about being alive, about being *you*, even if that's just an implanted memory?"

It wasn't a bad way to frame the question.

"We'll think about it," said Ivy.

"No, you won't," said Ron Smith. "I'm not going to pretend you have a free choice in this. We're going to record your brain state, even if we have to tie you down or drug you. We're going to get DNA samples. And we're going to leave them as our most treasured gift to the future of the human race."

"And here I was starting to relish my new freedom," said Laz.

"Oh, you're going to be free. Once we're done getting the next round of cloning prepared for, then you're free, and a grateful world will make sure you never need to work for a living as long as you're alive."

"You won't have to drug us," said Ivy. "Or tie us down. Of course we'll allow our brain state to be recorded. Of course you can have the samples. We didn't go to all this trouble saving so many people because we thought it was a *bad* idea for us to have been brought to life again."

Laz breathed a sigh of relief. Now he knew what Ivy thought, and because of what she said, he knew what *he* thought. "Goes for me, too," he said.

"Third," said Ron Smith.

"There's *another* thing?" asked Ivy.

"My team has a pool going on whether you two will get married, get married and have babies, have babies and get married, have babies and never get married, or walk away from each other and that's it."

Ivy gave a hoot of laughter. "Cheater! Trying to get a jump on all the other bettors."

"I've already posted my bet," said Ron Smith. "I won't change it. But I also won't tell you what it is."

"He covered all the possibilities," said Laz.

"Not allowed," said Ron Smith. "I'm not asking what you're going to decide, because I doubt that you know. I also think that neither of you finished high school, and neither of you seems to know what you want to do with your lives. University? A profession? A trade? A lazy retirement? Sorry that it'll be a while before we have luxury beach resorts, so there's no life of wealth and fabulousness possible yet. But you're young. We'll have those things eventually. There are a lot of possible futures. I don't want you to commit to any of them right now. I'm just telling you, there's a team of people who care about you, who know you about as well as any human being can know another, and they want you to be happy."

"That's very kind of them," said Laz.

"It's also a pail of hogwash," said Ivy. "Here's what the pool is really about. When do they sleep together? Will they make babies? And here's the clincher: If they make babies, will the babies have some mix or combination of their abilities?"

Laz laughed, but Ron Smith didn't. "That's a different pool," said Ron Smith. "I was on the brain state recording team, the one that didn't want to bet on your genes getting mixed into a new generation and seeing if there's a hereditary component to what you can do."

"I was joking," said Ivy.

"No you weren't," said Ron Smith. "And *that* pool has more subscribers than the one I described. However, for what it's worth the talented-babies pool was mostly astrotechs, and the will-they-marry pool is mostly my people. We know you better, we care about you more. While the astrotechs merely saw you working together and had all kinds of discussions about who was in love with who, and who loved the other person more."

"Well, that's just stupid," said Laz. "I love her way more than she loves me, if she loves me at all. Romantically, I mean, as opposed to in a sisterly way."

"Then you might be amused to know that the astrotechs, after observing you closely through many rounds of Portal-building, reached quite a different conclusion."

"Oh, be serious," said Laz.

"Why are we even having this discussion?" asked Ivy.

"Because I've been keeping my mouth shut about your personal lives for years," said Ron Smith, "and this is *my* retirement from the discipline of my work with you."

"So, finish it," said Laz.

"They overwhelmingly thought that Ivy was crazy in love with you, while your very calm behavior, Laz, convinced them that you were probably indifferent to her, romantically. A few thought you might be gay, a few thought your heart still belonged to a high school sweetheart that you remembered fondly even though she'd be in her seventies now, maybe. But only a few thought you loved Ivy as much as she loved you."

Laz laughed again. "They're loons," he said. "You're making this up."

"Am I?" asked Ron Smith. "Am I messing with you? Manipulating you? No, kids, I'm not. I'm no longer getting paid to do that. I'm just giving you information about how you appear to others."

What Laz was noticing was that Ivy was looking out the car window, saying nothing, expressing nothing.

"And I thought," said Ron Smith, "that even though *my* team has heard Laz profess his love many times, and Ivy far more rarely and subtly, when they heard about the astrotechs' pool, they agreed with them."

Ivy turned her head to look coolly at Ron Smith. "You've had your say," she told him. "This subject will never come up again."

Ron Smith nodded. "Agreed."

"I hope that someday it might come up between *us*," said Laz.

"It won't be nonsense about betting pools and who a bunch of total strangers think loves the other person more."

"Oh," said Laz. "That's right, we won't discuss *that*."

"Fourth," said Ivy. "Because you're not the only one with lists of information."

"Okay," said Ron Smith. "We're almost at the recording facility, so perhaps a little haste?"

"It's a very short question, really. Would you be so kind as to record the brain states of the Pack of Four, and take their DNA, too?"

Ron Smith laughed.

Laz didn't. "I can't believe I didn't think of that," he said to Ivy.

"It's why you still need me around now and then," she said.

"Why?" asked Ron Smith.

"If you wake up our clones with all our memories," said Ivy, "they'll remember StarKist and Wicky in the Pack of Four, and they'll miss them. Why make their lives any harder than they have to be?"

Ron Smith shook his head. Then he changed it into nodding. "We can't record the brain states of other species at the facility we're taking you to, but there *are* people working on canids, both brain state and cloning, and we can take your animal companions to that facility before we return them to you."

"I suggest you sedate them during the procedure," said Laz.

"Oh, we always sedate animals," said Ron Smith, "or we end up with poor quality recordings. They don't like being compelled to hold still."

The car stopped in front of a building—or rather, the surface entrance to a building that was almost entirely underground, with nothing but a flat smooth lawn and a few vents and pipes and air conditioning units on the surface. "And this lovely and informative car trip has come to an end," said Ron Smith.

"I have more questions," said Ivy. "But they can wait."

"I have one more," said Ron Smith, "and it can't wait. It happens that all of your parents are still alive. Laz, yours are very old. But they're alive and lucid."

Ivy shook her head. "They're not *our* parents. They don't know *us*. And if we show up looking all young and everything, it'll just break their hearts. Take Ivy-O to meet her mom and dad. That's the child they raised."

"My parents wouldn't even know me," said Laz. "And I bet that all the publicity about us, all the pictures—I bet that has caused them a lot of grief."

"Just wanted you to have the option," said Ron Smith. "Especially if you wanted your clones to remember meeting with them."

"No," said Laz. "They aren't our parents. They didn't actually raise us."

"But if they ask you," said Ivy. "If it ever comes up, I'd like you to tell my parents that I appreciate all that they did for Ivy-O. They were good parents."

"Ditto for mine," said Laz. "I still have good memories of them. They matter to me. And if OrigiLaz is still around, he'd agree with me."

Ron Smith nodded. "That'll do. That's kind of you both. If they ask, that's what we'll say."

Ivy took Laz's hand after they got out of the car, and held his hand as they went inside. Ron Smith led them, they took an elevator down three floors, and as they waited on a sofa outside the recording room, Laz said, "What are your 'more questions'? Since they obviously weren't about your parents or an old high school boyfriend."

"Just speculation, really," said Ivy. "What would it be like if we had to raise a baby like me, or a baby like you?"

"Raising you would be hellish," said Laz, "because you'd always know what the result would be of anything you said or did—including how badly your parents would punish you for misdeeds."

"Agreed," said Ivy. "But raising you would have to be worse."

"Au contraire, ma fille," said Laz, knowing that it was weird to call her his daughter, but he didn't know enough French to choose a better word. "I was the easiest baby in the world to raise."

"Oh, right," said Ivy.

"I was side stepping from birth," said Laz. "I didn't realize it, but I was. So lying there in my crib, if I needed my diaper changed, I didn't have to cry and cry like any normal child, while my poor ignorant parents tried to figure out why I was crying and what they should do about it. No, when I gave out one single cry, there was always at least one nearby timestream in which my folks rushed to me and immediately did exactly what I wanted—because I left any timestream where they couldn't figure it out."

"How nice for you," said Ivy.

"My parents thought they were geniuses. 'Whatever he needs always turns out to be the first thing we tried. He's the easiest baby in the world,' which was an oblique way of pointing out that they were absolutely perfect parents."

"Because," said Ivy, "you eliminated any timestream where they didn't do exactly what you wanted."

"Basically, yes."

"So you manipulated and controlled your parents."

"As did you. The difference is that mine couldn't see what I was doing. They just believed I was the perfect baby, born to perfect parents. But that wasn't your only question, was it?"

"I still have a few simple ones, really," said Ivy. "I want to find out where OrigiLaz went. I want to find out if there's any chance he's somewhere that Shiva won't destroy. If I find him in time, I'd like to rescue him, if he needs rescuing."

"That's really kind of you," said Laz.

"Not really," said Ivy. "Because while Ivy-O met him as a famous adult, I met him as a seventeen-year-old kid who always tried to treat me with kindness and decency. It's that seventeen-year-old that I want to locate and save, even if he's grizzled and curmudgeonly now."

"That's the most romantic thing I've ever heard you say," said Laz. But he said it as if it were halfway toward being a joke.

"And there's something that I want to make sure is in your

memory when they record your brain state today." With that, Ivy put her arms around him and kissed him long and hard. "And don't you forget it. You always acted as if I did this to manipulate you. But I meant it every time, from the deepest places in my heart. I think I'm better qualified than anyone to say this. You're a good man, Lazarus Hayerian."

His only answer was to resume the kiss. It was still going on, with only a few interruptions for breathing, when the door opened and Laz walked in to set his memories in stone, so they would last a thousand years.

ABOUT THE AUTHOR

ORSON SCOTT CARD is the author of award-winning novels *Ender's Game* and *Speaker for the Dead*. Though these novels were never intended for a young audience, they have been widely used in schools. More recently, Card has written for young adult readers as well as adults: the Pathfinder trilogy (*Pathfinder*, *Ruins*, *Visitors*) and now the beginning of the Side Step series: *Wakers*.

In addition to science fiction, Card writes contemporary fantasy novels (*Enchantment*, *Magic Street*, *Lost Boys*, *The Lost Gate*) and his Micropowers series (*Lost and Found*, *Duplex*). He still writes and directs plays, including his freshened scripts for Shakespeare's *Romeo and Juliet*, *The Taming of the Shrew*, and *The Merchant of Venice*.

Card was born in Richland, Washington, and grew up in California, Arizona, and Utah. He served as a missionary for the Church of Jesus Christ of Latter-day Saints in Brazil in the early 1970s. Recently he has joined the faculty of Southern Virginia University as a professor of writing and literature.

Card currently lives in Greensboro, North Carolina, with his wife, Kristine Allen Card.